CW01221029

Spirit: The Kingdom

By Jay Wilkinson

The balance between good and evil has always remained fairly even. Without one side, the other would have full and total power over all that was, all that is and all that is yet to be. Perhaps this is why it happened, no-one can say for sure.

All that we can be certain of is the side which we stand on and the sacrifices that we must face along the way. Homes, once filled with laughter and warmth, now lie in ashes. Our loved ones, the echoes of their voices still linger in the air, have been ripped from our embrace. We stand amidst the ruins, the remnants of our shattered lives scattered at our feet. But you know what they say about a man who fights with nothing left to lose. We will just take a moment's silence now to remember those who gave their lives today, so that we can stand and fight tomorrow.

Chapter 1

Silence filled the night, staring across the moonlit ocean Jaw sat there, perched on the edge of a cliff gazing upwards and out to sea. He was reminiscing about his childhood, as he often found himself doing at this time of night. It was not one of his more enjoyable pass-times.

Had circumstances been better, then perhaps Jaw would have been able to look back on his life more fondly, but the fact remains that his past had not been all that kind to him. He had friends and was generally liked by most, but that all changed in one night.

As he sat there, lost in thought, a delicate creature fluttered into view. A moth, drawn to the muted luminescence of the night, it circled around Jaw before gracefully landing on the back of his outstretched hand. Its wings, fragile and intricate, bore a pattern that seemed to shimmer in the subdued moonlight.

Jaw observed the moth with a sense of detachment, its presence a fleeting distraction from the weight of his memories. The insect, indifferent to the burdens that occupied his mind, stood still on his hand. In that moment, a sense of connection formed—a silent communion between a lone hermit and a creature of the night. The moth, as if only resting for a moment, a respite in its otherwise mysterious journey, took flight from Jaw's hand. It danced in the air for a brief moment before disappearing into the obscurity of the night.

Jaw gazed after the departing creature, a wistful smile playing on his lips. If only it were as simple for him to lift off into the vast expanse of the night sky, leaving behind the complexities and sorrows that tethered him to the earth.

He sighed as he sat daydreaming, head tilted back staring, transfixed on the stars above, flames lapped through his mind and then suddenly a single droplet of cold water spattered against his cheek, dragging him back into reality. As he stood up, the moonlight painted him in an ethereal glow, revealing a man weathered by time in his late twenties. His brown, messy hair tousled by the night breeze, and a hint of stubble adorned his jaw, giving him a rugged appearance. His eyes, blue like the ocean below, reflected the soft moonlight, telling stories of a past etched in hardship. Cloaked in crude and worn clothes reminiscent of a bygone era, Jaw's silhouette against the night sky carried the weight of his history. The tattered garments whispered tales of struggles, loss, and resilience.

The cliffs around him echoed with the distant sounds of the ocean, creating a poignant moment of solitude and reflection. The scars and lines on his face, illuminated by the moon, became visible markers of a journey filled with both sorrow and strength. The rain clouds gathered, obscuring the stars and casting a shadow over the ocean. Feeling the subtle shift in the weather, Jaw turned away from the cliff's edge, his memories lingering like the encroaching murmurs of distant thunder. As the first few raindrops spattered against the ground, he began walking purposefully into the woods behind him.

The forest enveloped him in a tapestry of sound—rustling leaves, creaking branches, and the distant growl of the chasing rain. Jaw navigated the well-trodden trail that wound its way through the ancient trees. Each step resonated with the soft crunch of dampened leaves beneath his boots. The path led him deeper into the heart of the woods, the trees standing as silent sentinels guarding the secrets held within. Occasional glimmers of moonlight filtered through the dense canopy, revealing the visage of Jaw as he pressed forward, his figure a shadowy presence in the dim-lit woods. As Jaw ventured deeper into the woods, the atmosphere grew more charged with each step. About twenty minutes into the journey the pitter-patter of rain on leaves intensified, creating a rhythmic symphony that echoed through the forest.

The trees creaked and shook in response to the shower, their leaves rustling with the weight of the downpour. The trail beneath Jaw's boots transformed into a slick, muddy path, challenging each step. The rain painted a darker hue on his clothes, emphasising the wear and tear of his journey. Despite the increasing discomfort, Jaw pressed on, the forest around him illuminated by the occasional flashes of lightning that danced across the sky. The once familiar trail became a blurred path, softened by the rain's veil. Each footfall now carried the weight of determination, a resilience against the elements. As he continued, soaked to the bone and resolute, the destination he sought lay ahead, a sanctuary from the storm's embrace.

He emerged from the woods, and in the clearing loomed three large silhouettes—buildings that stood like stone barriers against the storm. Approaching the closest structure, Jaw fumbled through the soaked darkness to find the door. The patter of raindrops on the building's roof and walls acted as a form of disorientation as he sought the familiar handle. His fingers grazed the sodden surface, tracing the edges until they found the cold metal of the door handle.

Jaw shut the door with a firm push, the faint drumming of the storm persisting outside. Swiftly navigating the darkness, he found his way to an old stone fireplace. Crouching down, he retrieved an aged metal tinderbox from the mantlepiece, its worn surface cold beneath his touch.

Clacking the flint together in the firebox, Jaw persisted until a spark danced to life, setting the kindling ablaze. The flames grew, casting a warm glow that unveiled the dark corners of the room. Standing back up, he wasted no time shedding his soaked clothing, leaving them on the back of a nearby chair, which he dragged closer to the fire. Boots overturned, he placed them by the hearth, the heat already beginning to chase away the chill.

In the flickering light, Jaw surveyed the now-illuminated room. It may not have been grand, but it was home. A small wooden table, now supporting only one chair, stood against one wall, bearing an open book, a quill, and an inkwell. On the opposite side of the room, a wardrobe stuffed with a chaotic array of clothes and oddities strained against its capacity, one door refusing to close properly.

Against the remaining wall, a scruffy, unmade wooden bed beckoned. A crudely fashioned cloth pillow, filled with various feathers, rested atop a mattress made from a large burlap sack of straw and wool. The cloth cover, a patchwork of mismatched old clothing, added a touch of makeshift comfort.

Jaw stood by the fire, clad in naught but a loincloth, the heat from the flames kissing his scarred, battleworn skin. Retrieving the fire poker from a pile of old logs near the fireplace, he returned the tinderbox to its place on the mantle. Hanging the hooked head of the poker off the inside door handle, he crossed the room toward the bed.

The moment he laid down, the sound of the tempest and the crackling fire created a soothing lullaby, and Jaw succumbed to the embrace of sleep, seeking refuge from the storm in the familiarity of his humble abode. As he slept, Jaw's dreams wove an all-too-familiar tapestry...

In the dream, Jaw found himself seated in the rustic embrace of the old barn, accompanied by a friend from his childhood—Fenn Sage. Fenn, a boy slightly older than Jaw, shared the stone floor with him in the warm glow of a brass candle lantern that flickered with each breath. It had been quite some time since Jaw had seen or heard from Fenn.

Fenn's features emerged in the dancing light—the beginnings of small whiskers and stubble covered his lower jaw and upper lip. His fair skin, sprinkled with freckles, framed tawny orange hair in a scruffy, curled mop. Despite his young age, Fenn's appearance and demeanour held a maturity that hinted at experiences beyond his years.

Fenn's father, a village Elder with a deep-seated aversion to magic, held a contrasting perspective to his son's innate talent in the arcane arts. Despite this tension, driven by a promise to his late wife, Fenn's father had taken measures to nurture the boy's magical abilities. The culmination of this effort led to Fenn's imminent departure to Astius, the great port city housing the mages tower—an academy for the most exceptional wizards, witches, and mages.

In the dream, the two boys sat on the barn's stone floor, a temporary haven when not in use for grain harvest. Jaw's parents, the farming family of the village, ensured its utilisation went largely unnoticed. The barn served as a clandestine refuge for the village youth. Between them, rested the brass candle lantern, its flame dancing to the rhythm of their hushed conversation. As the dream unfolded, the significance of the impending departure hovered, unknown to both boys at the time. Little did they realise, this moment in the barn was a prelude to a significant juncture in Fenn's life—the day before he would embark on a journey to Astius and the mages tower. Fenn's voice carried the authority of someone well-versed in the arcane. "First things first, spend some time studying fire's nature. If you rush in blind, you won't control the spell's form," he stated matter-of-factly.

Perplexed, Jaw responded, "I don't get it." The intricacies of spellcasting seemed to elude him.

"You need to observe the aspects of fire and understand what defines it," Fenn repeated, mistaking Jaw's confusion for a lack of detail.

Growing more bewildered, Jaw admitted, "Honestly, I don't understand half of what you're saying." The complexity of magical theory left him feeling utterly lost.

Fenn sighed, trying to simplify his explanation. "Look at the fire. Fire is hot... yes?"

"Yes, fire is hot," Jaw replied, a sense of embarrassment creeping in.

"Right, so why is the fire hot?" Fenn asked, prompting contemplation.

A long pause drowning them in silence. Jaw's gaze remained fixed on the candle flame, and Fenn watched him intently. The realisation that this was a dream had already dawned on Jaw, but attempts to alter the course of events proved futile—a prisoner to the memory he was forced to relive.

Fenn broke the silence, saying, "Once you've studied fire enough and know its properties, you'll be able to do something like this." He extended his hand, palm facing up, and curled his fingers as if cradling an apple. "Fire ball." he said with conviction and intent. A ball of fire materialised between them, hovering just above Fenn's palm, its dance illuminated the barn.

Jaw stared, transfixed by the mesmerising display. Fenn then closed his hand, forming a point with his fingers and thumb. The flames, confined within the small gap, shot upward before being extinguished.

"No point in staring in wonder at that one," Fenn said. "You won't learn anything from it because it's not natural in origin. A cast spell does not have to abide by the same rules as the natural element it is mimicking."

"A ball of flame conjured by a mage, for example..." Fenn continued, opening his hand once more, and the fireball immediately returned with a whoosh and a faint crackle. "Can be as hot..." The ball grew in intensity and deepened in colour. "Or as cold..." The ball reduced in size and turned a pale shade of blue. "As the mage who controls it wills it to be." Fenn concluded, closing his hand once more, dispelling the ball, and gesturing back towards the candle.

Jaw's attention snapped back to the candle's flame, which now seemed dull in comparison.

After a few minutes of uncomfortable silence, with Jaw simply staring at the fire and Fenn watching eagerly, Fenn stood up and brushed himself down. Jaw, aware of what was to happen next, tried to speak or move, but he was powerless, forced to watch Fenn prepare to leave.

"Well, I have other things to do today, another busy week ahead," Fenn monologued. Jaw fought the memory, desperately wanting to say "don't go," but he was unable to change the course of events.

"...And on Ixesday, I'm helping the alchemist gather herbs," Fenn concluded, unknowingly sealing his fate. Whether this was for the best, Jaw never learned.

"No problem," Jaw said with a smile. "I will stay here and keep practising!"

"Ok, good plan! I will come back and check on you in a few hours," Fenn replied in delight as he turned and walked to the door of the barn.

He reached out and placed a hand on it before pausing and glancing back. "Don't do anything I wouldn't do!" he said with a chuckle as he pushed against the door and left.

As time passed, Jaw simply sat there for what felt like hours, at first complying with the course of the memory and studying the fire.

However, the monotony of studying the fire soon grew tiresome for Jaw. Instead of fixating on this seemingly pointless task, he let his mind wander towards other memories from that period of his past.

This recurring dream, a relentless loop, had become an unwelcome companion. Each time it presented itself as a haunting replay of that particular day. Despite his efforts, Jaw found himself incapable of altering any aspect of this torment. The dream, like an unyielding spectre, unfolded predictably, and the consequences of its destination loomed ahead.

In his attempts to make sense of this haunting experience, Jaw had taken to documenting these nightmares in his journal upon waking. He couldn't escape the familiarity of the scenes, yet he hoped that by dissecting the details, he might uncover some hidden meaning.

Suddenly, breaking from his passive observation of the fire, Jaw reached forward, opening the lantern and placing his hand inside. The heat of the flame gradually warmed his skin as he brushed his fingers through it, the tips turning black from the smoke. As he inspected his hand, he recalled the original event, foolishly thinking, "How hard could it be?" The irony of his past naivety still weighed on him, even after all these years.

Upturning his hand like he was holding an apple, Jaw waited for something to happen, but nothing did. In his mind, he knew precisely what was about to transpire. He shook his hand, attempting to loosen joints and muscles, flexing his fingers repeatedly while concentrating on the heat and sensation of the fire. Again, nothing happened.

Jaw slumped backward, laying on the cold stone floor. A deep sigh escaped him as he raised his hand into the air, palm flat, fingers outstretched, pointed upwards and away from him.

"Fire," he mumbled under his breath, almost without intent. The word hung in the air, devoid of reason or purpose, an afterthought that slipped from his lips at the moment of defeat.

Suddenly, flames erupted from Jaw's outstretched hand, wild and explosive, dancing in all possible directions. Before he could comprehend the unfolding chaos and close his hand, it was already too late. Every perceivable surface in the barn was set ablaze, and thick black smoke billowed in the upper reaches.

Jaw had no choice but to react swiftly. Rolling onto his stomach, he clambered to his feet, sprinting towards the barn doors as fast as his young legs could carry him. Racing outside, he dashed through adjacent fields. Unbeknownst to him at the time, he was spotted fleeing the barn by someone, just as this same person had apparently witnessed Fenn leaving some time before.

Reaching the river, Jaw threw himself into the cool water, thinking it a clever move to wash away the smell of smoke from himself and his clothes. He knew the Elders would undoubtedly launch an investigation into the barn's destruction.

After ensuring he was clean, Jaw lay in the grass on the riverbank, drying out in the sun. Satisfied with this part of his plan, he decided to take the long way home, and to meander through the sprawling fields that unfolded before him as he walked all the way around the village. The sun hung lazily in the sky, casting a warm golden hue over the landscape. A gentle breeze rustled through the tall grass, carrying with it the fragrances of wildflowers and freshly tilled earth.

The fields stretched out in undulating waves, a patchwork quilt of green and gold as far as the eye could see. Each step carried him through a sea of grass that swayed in rhythm with the whispering wind. Butterflies flitted from flower to flower, their delicate wings a kaleidoscope of colours that added a vibrant touch to the serene scene.

In the distance, a copse of trees beckoned, their branches providing a cool respite from the sun's gentle warmth. As Jaw approached, he noticed a small stream weaving through the shade, its clear waters reflecting the dappled sunlight filtering through the leaves.

Birdsong filled the air, a chorus of chirps and trills that harmonised with the rustling leaves. The meadow seemed to hum with life, a peaceful symphony that drowned out the distant echoes of the barn's fiery demise.

The journey took him through a beautiful blossoming meadow, where shades of purple, yellow, and white painted a picturesque canvas against the green backdrop. The air was sweet with the scent of blooming flowers, and he couldn't resist plucking a few.

As he continued his leisurely stroll, the sun began its descent, casting long shadows that stretched across the landscape. The changing sky became a masterpiece of warm tones of orange and pink that gradually deepened into the rich purples of twilight.

The path eventually led Jaw back to the familiar surroundings of his village. Along the way, he encountered fellow villagers going about their evening chores, the warm glow of hearth fires beginning to glow in the windows. The scent of freshly baked bread wafted through the air, a comforting aroma that hinted at the evening meals being prepared.

Finally, after several hours of walking, Jaw arrived at the outskirts of his village, he noticed lavender growing along the roadside and decided to mix it in with the assortment of flowers he had been carrying. He took a moment to savour the peaceful beauty of the countryside before making his way toward the familiar silhouette of his home on the horizon.

Before entering the house, he stole a glance at himself in the reflection provided by the water in a bucket on the front porch, ensuring his expression betrayed no hint of guilt.

Upon entering, his mother immediately inquired, her tone devoid of judgement or accusation, as if merely curious. She didn't even turn to look at him as he entered.

"Where have you been?" she asked.

"The meadow," Jaw replied coolly. "I brought these back for you. I know you like them." He offered up the flowers as his mother turned around.

"Oh! Thank you!" she exclaimed, taking the flowers and giving them a sniff. Turning back towards the sink, she began putting them into water, and the tension of the moment seemed to dissipate in the familiar warmth of their home.

His mother stood as a figure of quiet strength and grace. A tall brunette woman, she had a slim frame that towered above most in the village. Her physical presence exuded a sense of resilience, a quality mirrored in the way she carried herself through life's challenges.

On that particular day, a red cloth ribbon hung delicately from her hair, tying it back into a ponytail that cascaded halfway down her back. The ribbon seemed to catch the sunlight, casting a warm glow on her rich, chestnut hair. Strands of hair escaped the ponytail, framing her face with a natural and effortless beauty.

Her eyes, a deep shade of brown, held a mixture of warmth and wisdom, reflecting the experiences of a life filled with both joys and tribulations. Lines of laughter and careworn creases etched the corners of her eyes, testament to the stories she hid within.

She wore a simple but well-worn dress, the fabric whispering of years gone by and memories made. The garment spoke of a life dedicated to nurturing a family and weathering the storms of existence with unwavering determination. Despite the simplicity, there was an elegance in the way she wore it, proof of the timeless grace that defined her.

"Where's dad?" Jaw inquired, his eyes scanning the familiar corners of their home.

"He had to go out. Someone set the grain barn on fire. Should be back soon, though. Do you want to help me lay the table for dinner?" his mother responded sweetly. She turned away briefly, placing the pot of lavender and flowers in the middle of the table, the fragrant scent filling the air.

The setting sunlight poured through the window, glistening in her eyes and illuminating her face, her skin was mostly smooth, yet it bore the character of time, a single scar on her right cheek telling a story that Jaw had always known. Despite this mark, her features retained a gentle and soft quality.

Jaw agreed, and the mother and son duo began the task of setting the table for their evening meal. The alluring smell of the mutton stew, lovingly prepared throughout the day, wafted through the air. Fresh bread from the Bakers awaited, a delightful addition to the hearty feast that Jaw knew all too well he would not be sampling.

Just as they finished arranging the spoons and plates, the door creaked open, and his father strode in. His very appearance commanded a hush in the room, his fathers authoritative presence caused a cold chill to run down Jaw's spine. The fear of being caught out in his lie, suddenly became far more likely.

"Hey, son," his father greeted, exhaustion evident in his voice as he settled into a chair. "Trouble at the grain barn, had to sort it out."

"Is everyone okay?" his mother inquired, her concern etched on her face.

"Yeah, everyone's fine. Just a mess to clean up," his father replied, running a hand through his hair, sweeping it out of the way of his face.

With that, the family sat down to dinner, the air filled with a mixture of familial warmth and the unspoken complexities that marked their relationship.

Jaw's father, a man of intelligence and wisdom, was often not given the credit he deserved. Having witnessed more years than his wife, the passage of time left its mark on his appearance. He bore an aged and lean countenance, not quite a man in his twilight years, but the prevalence of grey hair hinted at the experience and hassle of everyday life. Looking back on it now, Jaw had done nothing to alleviate the greying, and in some ways could be held mostly responsible for this rapid appearance of ageing.

From a young age, Jaw's father took it upon himself to educate the boy, instilling knowledge and life lessons. Yet, their relationship was marked by a divergence in interests. His father, well-versed in agriculture, botany, and history, sought to pass on the practicalities and traditions of their village. However, Jaw's passions lay elsewhere – in the realm of beasts, magic, combat, and the allure of adventure.

The clash of their interests often led to heated debates around the dining table. Jaw's father, with his wealth of knowledge, tried to guide him towards a more conventional path. Still, the young man's heart yearned for the mysteries beyond their village, and no amount of education on crops or historical anecdotes could sway his fascination with the fantastical and the unknown.

"Dinner smells nearly as lovely as you," His father playfully remarked, aiming the compliment his wifes way, a cheeky smile accompanying his words.

"Well, we had better eat it while it's still hot, then!" she chirped, diverting the attention to the imminent feast.

Seated around the table, the trio prepared to indulge in the delicious mutton stew. Bowls were filled generously with a hearty mixture of potatoes, leeks, parsnips, and the occasional chunk of mutton. The tantalising aroma rose from the bowls as they were passed around.

"The lavender is a nice touch, Lily!" Jaw's father expressed his gratitude, accepting his bowl with appreciation.

"Thank you! Jaw picked them from the meadow," Lily replied, shifting her husband's attention towards their son. His father's curious gaze focused on Jaw just as he reached for a piece of bread.

"Been at the meadow all day, then, boy?" he asked, a tone of curiosity in his voice. Normally, the idea of Jaw spending an entire day at the meadow would have sparked an argument, but Jaw felt that a simple "Yes Sir" would be the lesser evil this time. Before he could respond, a loud knock at the door interrupted the moment.

Strangely, no one moved to answer it. A sense of unease crept over Jaw as another, louder knock followed, accompanied by the clanging of metal on stone and the sudden onslaught of rain. The dream unravelled, and Jaw jolted awake, the echoes of the mysterious knocking lingering in his mind as he sat bolt upright in his bed.

Chapter 2

Without delay or hesitation, Jaw rushed across the now dark room, his hands grabbing his shirt and trousers on the way. He hurriedly, yet quietly, dressed himself, his movements purposeful. Simultaneously, he retrieved the fire poker from the floor with his other hand. The cold touch of metal against his fingers heightened his awareness as he prepared for what lay beyond the door.

Placing his hand on the door handle, he waited in the darkness, the only audible sounds being the rain beating down outside and the muffled breathing of his uninvited guest. He listened carefully to the distinct sound of raindrops pattering against fabric on the other side of the door.

Abruptly, another round of banging echoed, accompanied by a male voice shouting, "IS THERE ANYBODY THERE?!" Jaw pulled the door open with all his might, catching the intruder off balance mid-knock. Seizing the opportunity, Jaw thumped the man roughly in the stomach with the hand still holding the poker, causing the stranger to collapse onto the floor.

"What's your business? Who are you?!" Jaw aggressively interrogated the man on the floor, pointing the poker down at him. Despite the cloak, drenched through by the rain, Jaw could clearly see the outline of a sheath on the man's left hip.

"Reach for your weapon, and I'll strike you so hard with mine that you won't get up again!" Jaw threatened coldly.

"Alright! Alright!" the man said, a hint of panic in his voice. Clearly, this was not the reception he anticipated. He raised his hands toward his head, ensuring they were visible. "My name is Micharas Ranger. I'm from the nearby town of Celleos," he explained hurriedly.

"Right…and what? You trying to rob me in the rain? Is that the plan?" Jaw asked, maintaining his guard, his eyes locked onto the stranger.

"No, it's not like that at all!" The man protested his innocence. "I came out here looking for help. You see, I'm one of the hunters from our settlement, and I heard from another that he had discovered a hermit living in the woods recently," Micharas continued to explain.

"And what is it that you think I can help with, Micharas Ranger?" Jaw asked snidely.

"Our town has been attacked, and the survivors have been laid siege in our town hall. Merrymill, our closest neighbouring settlement, is four days' travel west of us, so I thought I would try here first," Micharas concluded.

Jaw reached down towards his hostage's hand, his intentions unclear. Micharas closed his eyes.

"Bloody idiot! Skulking around in the dark, lucky I didn't kill you. Get up!" he said. Micharas opened his eyes, finding a hand offered to him. He chose to accept it and was pulled to his feet. He groaned as he held his stomach. "Well, as you can see, it's just me living out here," Jaw said matter-of-factly.

"But what about the other two buildings?" Micharas had clearly tried knocking on the other doors before this one.

"My workshop and stables…and you had better not have upset my horse!" Jaw pointed the poker at him threateningly for a moment before pushing the door shut with his free hand, instantly dulling the sound of the rain. He crossed the room to the fireplace and threw a dry log and several wood chips into the remains of the fire before poking at them. He held out his hand to confirm that there was still enough warmth coming from the embers buried beneath the soot, and it wasn't long before the kindling started to catch alight.

Meanwhile, Micharas stood in the doorway, looking around the room, uneasy with the situation he had now found himself in.

"You're dripping on my floor," Jaw said jokingly as he walked past him again towards the cupboard, opened the door, and grabbed out a candle lantern. Unintentionally leading his guest back across the room, Jaw lit the wick at the fire before mounting it into its holder and placing it in the middle of the table. He dragged the other chair across with his spare hand and sat down on one side of the table, packing away the book, quill and inkwell to one side in a neat stack.

"Sorry," Micharas replied, removing his cloak and following him. It was at this point that Jaw's speculation was confirmed, it had been an empty scabbard on the man's waist, just as he thought. The fire crackled playfully in the hearth, casting shadows across the room as Micharas, a worn and tired man in his early thirties, stood before Jaw. His clothes, a patchwork of mud, blood, and rain, clung to his thin yet toned form. Short brown hair framed his face, slightly tousled from the relentless rain outside. Green eyes, weary yet resilient, scanned the room, taking in the rustic details of Jaw's dwelling.

In the dim light of the fire, Micharas's clean-shaven face revealed a stoic expression. His larger-than-average nose added character to his countenance, though it didn't draw undue attention. Micharas seated himself across from Jaw, who observed the newcomer with a mix of curiosity and concern.

"So, Celleos was attacked?" Jaw's inquiry carried a softened tone, an attempt to ease the tension that lingered in the room.

"Yeah, yesterday night, just before dawn. Only a few people would have been up, and it would have been just before the guard changeover too,"

Micharas explained, his voice betraying the weight of recent events.

Jaw's curiosity pressed on, a barrage of questions forming in his mind. "So you weren't there when it fell? What about the Elders? Surely they would have been enough to defend it?" His words were measured, though the urgency in his tone was palpable.

"No, I wasn't. And how do you know so much about our town? Have you been watching us?" Micharas, grappling with his own set of questions, sought answers from the enigmatic recluse.

"No, I have no interest in your town, but you didn't answer my question." Jaw's response held a hint of impatience, a sudden crackle from the fire punctuated the room with a burst of sound.

"Oh yeah, sorry, the Elders... well, I'm not sure how old your information is, but most of them are dead. It's just Elder Sage left now, and he isn't even a shadow of his former self anymore." Micharas's words hung in the air, the weight of loss echoing through the room. Silence surrounded them, broken only by the occasional snap and pop of the flames.

Jaw's gaze fixed on the flickering candle, memories and emotions intertwining in the dance of darkness. The storm outside mirrored the turmoil within him. Finally, he looked up, his eyes a canvas of conflicting emotions. "How?" he asked, the word heavy with unspoken history.

"Old age mostly," Micharas responded, a simple explanation for a complex reality. The answer, however, brought little solace to Jaw, for whom the news seemed more like the fading of memories than the loss of significant figures. Yet, Micharas remained unaware of the intricacies of Jaw's connection to Celleos.

Jaw's eyes narrowed, absorbing Micharas's harrowing account. The flickering flames cast an eerie glow across the room as the recluse processed the grim tale. "You were not there when the attack happened," Jaw observed, seeking clarity.

Micharas shook his head solemnly. "No, I was out hunting. Came back to smoke rising from the town. Dropped my kill and ran."

The hermit maintained his intense gaze, curiosity driving him to unravel the events that led to the besieged town. "But what happened before the attack? Any signs, any warnings?"

Micharas leaned back, tracing the genesis of the nightmare. "Ok, it all started about four months back. One of the guards was found dead on the outskirts of town. We thought it was some dispute, someone caught doing something they shouldn't have been. But there were no stab wounds, no broken bones. It was like he just dropped dead."

Jaw considered the information, his mind sifting through possibilities. "Magic, perhaps? Some dark sorcery?"

Micharas shook his head, dispelling the notion. "No, even a spell would have left a mark. Or at least that's what Elder Sage said. So, the town went on, uneasy but carrying on with life. Then, a guard claimed to see two people carrying weapons on the outskirts. No tracks, no sign of them. Guard was given leave, blamed on stress. But then in the late hours of last night, they struck. It was calculated, as though they knew exactly where and when to do so…"

Micharas took a deep breath, reliving the nightmare. Burning buildings. Bodies, dismembered and littering the ground. Creatures, humanoid but pure evil. Their pale skin and black eyes, like endless, starless voids staring straight into his soul. The recent memories were clearly painful to recount, an icy cold shiver ran down his spine.

"Anyway, as I was saying... I was on the outskirts of Thorne Woods, returning from a successful hunt with a wild boar slung over my horse. Smoke on the horizon caught my eye, and I knew something was amiss. Hastily, I released the boar and galloped toward the town," Micharas narrated, his words drawing vivid images in the mind of his curious host.

Approaching the town, the familiar stone walls stood tall, their imposing presence seemingly unchanged. "The gate was intact, the walls undisturbed. It was as if they emerged from the shadows within the town itself," Micharas continued, a sense of urgency in his voice.

Jaw leaned forward, his focus unwavering. Micharas's tale took a perilous turn as he described encountering archers on the east side. "Arrows rained around me. One found its mark, felling my horse," Micharas explained, a tinge of regret in his voice.

As the chaos unfolded, Micharas deftly manoeuvred, diving off the steed and into a very dexterous forwards roll, leaving behind his quiver and bow which had been fastened to the saddle of his mount. The urgency of his escape was paramount, he reached the supply hatch of the Sleeping Dragon Inn, on the outside of the town wall. "I drew my sword, swift and decisive, cut the lock, and dove inside, sealing it behind me with a piece of wood," he concluded, the tension lingering in the air.

"I travelled through the narrow tunnel until it opened up into the cellar of the tavern. A ladder at the end of the room took me up through a trapdoor and into the bar area. I cautiously ascended through the trapdoor" He emerged into the once lively interior of the Sleeping Dragon Inn, now reduced to a scene of destruction. The view that met his eyes told a story of complete devastation.

The bar, once a welcoming hub of camaraderie, now lay in ruins. Splintered wood and shattered glass covered the floor. The counter, where patrons once enjoyed their drinks, was now a broken, charred remnant of its former self. The air was thick with the acrid scent of burnt wood and lingering smoke, evidence of the recent violence that had unfolded within the inn.

As Micharas carefully surveyed the wreckage, his gaze fell upon a broken window. Through the shattered glass, he glimpsed a chilling sight—a patrol of the invaders, their humanoid forms moving with an unsettling purpose. The flickering flames from the roof above cast an eerie dim light on the ruined interior, creating a macabre dance of light and darkness.

The roof, ablaze with fire, posed a time-related dilemma for Micharas. The crackling flames threatened the stability of the structure overhead, adding urgency to his decision. Should he stay and risk the ceiling collapsing upon him, or venture out into the perilous unknown, potentially facing the enemy patrol outside?

He felt the weight of the moment pressing upon him, each passing second heightening the tension. The decision loomed like a shadow in the flickering light, and Micharas knew that whatever choice he made would shape the course of this momentous journey through the ravaged town.

"I decided to hold tight for a moment and let them pass, as I sat quiet though the beams above me began to creak, the weight of the structure that they supported now becoming too much. As soon as they were out of sight of the window I made a dash across the street and down the adjacent alleyway. My goal was clear to me, I had to find any survivors." He continued.

As Micharas pressed forward through the darkening alley, the setting sun cast a deep red hue upon the bleakness that surrounded him. The emotions evoked by the atmosphere were suffocating, enough to bring a weaker man to his knees. The mutilated bodies that littered the path bore witness to the brutality that had unfolded, and the stench of blood hung thick in the air, interwoven with the smell of smoke.

The brutal silence that enveloped the town was periodically shattered by blood-curdling screams, a grim symphony of executions echoing through the desolation. Each cry sent shivers down Micharas's spine, a haunting reminder of the peril that lurked in every shadow. As much as the impulse to intervene and save a fellow survivor tugged at his heart, he sternly reminded himself of the greater mission at hand.

"No," he thought resolutely, suppressing the urge to deviate from his path. Every moment spent chasing a single victim risked the unravelling of his larger objective—the Town Hall. In times of crisis, it had always been the rallying point for the townsfolk. The guards would likely be defending it, a beacon of hope amidst the chaos.

However, the closer Micharas drew to the Town Hall, the more conspicuous the absence of combat noise became. The unsettling quietude heightened his senses, each footfall echoing in the desolate streets. Doubt gnawed at the edges of his determination as he braved the ominous stillness, unsure of what awaited him at the heart of the town's gathering place. The journey to the Town Hall had become not just a physical challenge but a psychological test.

Finally, he turned a corner, and there, bathed in the eerie glow of the flames, stood the Hall—a lone sanctuary in the midst of such bedlam. Micharas, a mixture of relief and dread washing over him, examined the untouched surroundings. The unburnt hedges stood as witnesses, and the undisturbed flowers hinted at an unnatural boundary the creatures dared not breach.

The air itself seemed to hold its breath as Micharas approached the white stone stairs leading up to the Hall. The building stood proud, yet the absence of guards heightened the disquiet within him. Questions swirled in his mind, adding to the weight of uncertainty that pressed upon him.

With mounting unease, he ascended the steps, the tapping of his footfall accentuating the silence that cascaded through the area. "No guards?" he whispered to the wind, the words hanging in the stillness like an unanswered riddle. Compelled by a need for answers, he banged forcefully on the doors, the sound reverberating through the quiet surroundings. A moment of suspense lingered before muffled yells from within signalled the presence of those who had sought refuge in the Hall. The journey was far from over, and the mysteries of the night clung to the air like a veil of foreboding.

The resonant sound of approaching steel clanked through the Hall as someone inside moved toward the doors. A gruff voice, authoritative and familiar, cut through the air. "Who is it?" inquired Sir Erik, the commanding presence of the Captain of the Town Guards was unmistakable.

Micharas, relieved at the prospect of finding familiar faces, declared his identity. "It's Micharas Ranger. I am seeking survivors. How many of you are there?"

Sir Erik's response carried both weariness and urgency. "Enough that we might rebuild should we make it through this, but never mind that right now, Micharas. How many of you are there? Are the streets clear?"

Micharas, his mind already formulating a plan, began to speak, "No, I scarcely think I could clear them alone either. Perhaps if you could spare a few guards, we could—"

His words barely left his lips before being interrupted by Erik. "There are no more guards. We were ambushed as myself and my men gathered the townsfolk to bring them here. They stayed behind as those fiends attacked..." The captain's words trailed off, for in that moment, a sudden shiver ran down Micharas's spine, an ominous feeling of being observed by a malevolent force.

Turning slowly, Micharas's widened eyes surveyed the area. As the muffled conversation continued from behind the door, he realised the chilling truth. At the point where the street met the grounds of the Town Hall, a small army of grotesque figures stood, their cruel gaze fixed upon him. The revelation struck like a bolt of lightning, and Micharas found himself facing an unforeseen threat, alone and exposed. Leading this evil force was a towering figure, standing at a menacing height of nearly eight feet. Clad from head to toe in thick black metal, he exuded an air of dark authority. A deep purple cloak, tattered and damaged at the bottom, hung from his shoulders and flowed down his back as he moved through his forces, each step that he drew closer caused Micharas's heart to beat a little faster. In his hand, he clutched a maul of gigantic proportions, a weapon so massive that it would typically require two ordinary men to lift. Yet, this formidable figure carried it effortlessly in one hand, the head of the maul flattened and now resembling that of a sinister spade.

His exposed muscles, not shielded by armour, bulged with scars and wear from countless battles. A visorless helmet revealed his pale, white face, framed by a gruff beard that added to the treacherous atmosphere surrounding him. The black, soulless eyes within were so deep and devoid of light that they seemed to absorb the surrounding flames and embers, casting a chaotic shaded veil over his haunting visage. In the presence of this colossal leader, the very air seemed to thicken with a sense of foreboding, underscoring the imminent danger that Micharas now faced.

Micharas's ears suddenly tuned back in to the one-sided conversation that Sir Erik was having on the other side of the door. "...If we are going to make it out of this, we will need more help." The words replayed in his mind, and without another word spoken, he took off. Charging down the stairs, he skipped over them several at a time, vaulting over a hedgerow and through a patch of flowers, he plunged into the night-shrouded alleys, the sounds of his footsteps the only companions in the desolate darkness. His breaths, now ragged and uneven, reflected off the dilapidated buildings that loomed over him, a threatening reminder of what his pursuers were capable of.

As he traversed the twisting alleys, the oppressive darkness seemed to consume him, every step a gamble with the unseen. The flickering flames from distant fires cast grotesque shadows on the cobblestone streets, creating distorted shapes that played tricks on his senses. The distant cries of evil creatures echoed "I think he went this way!" "Find him!", they mingled with the unsettling creaks and groans of the abandoned structures around him.

The night became a labyrinth of uncertainty, and he felt the weight of imminent danger pressing on him from all sides. A distant howl from behind him pierced the silence, sending a shiver down his spine. He quickened his pace, the adrenaline-fueled urgency propelling him forward.

Amid the turmoil, he stumbled upon the lifeless remnants of the once-vibrant town. Bodies lay strewn across his path, their vacant stares and twisted, mutilated forms haunting his every step. The dim glow of a flickering lantern illuminated a macabre scene—a discarded cart, overturned barrels, and an unsettling silhouette painted on the wall by the feeble light.

The eerie atmosphere intensified as Micharas sprinted through the alley, each step echoing like his own thunderous heartbeat. The ghastly bodies served as now grizzly reminders of the horror that had unfolded. Fear gripped him as he navigated treacherous twists and turns, a wrong step potentially sealing his fate.

Despite the danger, he pressed on, his determination fueled by the urgent need for help. The distant sight of The Sleeping Dragon Inn became a beacon of hope, promising safety and a chance to console his own mind. Yet, with each passing moment, the creatures closed the gap, their ominous presence pushing Micharas to the brink.

Finally, as he neared the inn and much to his surprise, he discovered it was still standing but for how much longer only the Gods could know. He devised a plan to lose his pursuers. Darting into a concealed alley, he hid behind a stack of crates, holding his breath and praying that the creatures would pass by without detecting him. The night hung heavy with tension as he waited, hoping that this brief respite would be enough to ensure his survival and the crucial aid he sought for the besieged town.

As Micharas cautiously emerged from his hiding spot, the cold night air clung to his sweat-soaked skin, creating an unsettling chill. The lapping flames from distant fires cast long, dancing shadows that distorted the figures of the three humanoid creatures now staring directly at him. Their pale skin seemed to absorb what little light remained in the desolate alley.

Two of them brandished gleaming, blood soaked swords, the steel reflecting a malicious glint. The third, a towering figure, hefted a massive battle-axe with considerable weight. Micharas felt a knot tighten in his stomach as he eyed his adversaries. With an agile grace, he unsheathed his sword, its blade catching the light. Without pause for their own safety they rushed towards him.

The first two lunged forward, their movements swift but predictable. Micharas danced between their strikes with practised precision. The clash of steel echoed through the alley as he deftly parried the first blade before cutting the jugular of his attacker, he then swiftly countered the advances of the second sword with calculated strikes of his own, placing the tip of his sword into the soft armpit of the second foe. He forced the weapon up and past the creature's armour before unleashing it outwards and spraying the ground with its blood. His movements were a symphony of deadly grace, each swing executed with the fluidity of a seasoned hunter. His years of training teaching him not to waste energy, making each and every movement count.

As the first two creatures crumpled to the ground, their dark eyes lifeless, Micharas turned his attention to the imposing figure wielding the battle-axe. The creature swung the weapon with brutish power, forcing Micharas to evade with acrobatic finesse. The alley became an arena of clashing steel and grunts of exertion.

In a moment of miscalculation, Micharas found himself momentarily off balance, the battle-axe descending with alarming speed. The impact of the blow sent shockwaves through his arms, and for a brief, heart-stopping moment, it seemed the tide might turn against him as he just barely managed to place his weapon in the way of the strike.

Grim determination flashed in Micharas's eyes as he swiftly adapted to the situation. With a deft twist of his body, he dodged a follow-up strike and, in a move that seemed almost supernatural, spun on his heel. His blade sliced through the air in a seamless thrust, finding its mark, it bore forwards and into the left eye of his prey. The creature let out one final blood-chilling cry as its brain finally found peace. A dark liquid oozed from the fatal wound, and the creature collapsed to the ground with a thunderous crash, the battle-axe slipping from its grasp.

Micharas stood amidst the fallen foes, chest heaving, the now distant sounds created in fierce combat lingered in the silence that followed. As he observed the aftermath, a strange and disgusting spectacle unfolded before him. The corpses of the humanoid creatures began to undergo a grotesque transformation.

At first, it started as an unsettling quiver, a distortion in the fabric of their dark forms. Then, like a nightmarish illusion, their bodies began to warp and contort. The once-solid flesh seemed to liquefy, dripping down in rivulets of black, sticky liquid. The swords and battle-axe clattered to the ground, their metallic clang resonating in harmony with the hideous display.

Micharas recoiled in visceral horror, the sight triggering a profound sense of revulsion within him. The stench of burning, putrid flesh filled the air as the creatures disintegrated before his eyes. The black liquid pooled around them, leaving behind only lifeless skeletons, stark reminders of the evil force that had wrought havoc upon Celleos.

For a moment, Micharas stood frozen, his mind grappling with the reality unfolding in the alley. The revulsion he felt surpassed even his deepest-seated hatred for their kind. It was an unsettling reminder of the unnatural, otherworldly nature of these creatures. The act of melting, like a dance of decay, shattered any preconceived notions he had harboured about them.

In that harrowing moment, Micharas confronted the true depth of the abomination that had befallen his town. The repulsive scene etched itself into his memory, leaving an indelible mark of horror that would linger long after the last echoes of battle had faded.

Micharas, soaked his soul in the moments respite before hearing the unmistakable sound of footsteps approaching, he sprinted towards the looming silhouette of The Sleeping Dragon Inn.

As he reached the entrance, the once-welcoming tavern now stood as a fortress battered by flames. Micharas, fueled by a desperate need for refuge, approached the heavy wooden door. In haste, he grasped the handle and pushed with all his might, throwing his shoulder into the door. But it would not budge, blocked from the inside by fallen timbers. Panic surged within him as his pursuers closed in.

Frantically searching for an alternative, Micharas recalled seeing a broken window to the side. Without hesitation, he lunged towards it, shards of glass crunching beneath his boots. The adrenaline-fueled urgency propelled him through the shattered frame, narrowly escaping the grasp of the encroaching creatures. In the process, his sword slipped from its sheath, clattering to the ground outside.

For a moment, he briefly considered retrieving his weapon. The cold steel, now lying vulnerable on the wet ground, beckoned to him. However, the demonic visage of the approaching creatures urged him to prioritise escape over armament. With a reluctant glance at the abandoned sword, he made a split-second decision, leaving it behind.

Inside the inn, he had landed in the darkened interior, surrounded by overturned, charred furniture and shattered glass. Micharas, now weaponless, moved towards the bar, his senses sharp and focused even through the haze of smoke. He approached the trapdoor leading to the cellar—a potential escape route that would carry him to freedom.

The creak of the wooden door behind him signalled the creatures drawing near. Micharas lifted the trapdoor and descended back into the dimly lit cellar that he had travelled through less than an hour before.

However, his momentary relief was shattered when he heard the unmistakable sound of the creatures forcing their way through the door above. The supporting beam of the roof, weakened by the relentless assault, gave way with a splintering crack. Micharas, frozen in the cellar, watched in horror as the collapse reverberated through the inn, as the building above him crumbled.

Dust and soot rattled free from the floorboards. The once-sturdy roof now lay in ruins, a testament to the unyielding pursuit of these malevolent entities. The creatures, now hopefully crushed, would pursue him no longer, however with this relief came a realisation that his safest route back into the town was no longer an option.

As Micharas contemplated his next move in the dimly lit cellar, the gravity of the situation weighed heavily on him as he pressed on through the tunnel.

"After I escaped the town I just had to sneak out of the line of sight of the archers on the walls and I made my way here." Micharas concluded, the end of his harrowing journey resonating in his voice. As Micharas recounted the horrors, Jaw's expression had shifted from curiosity to concern. The world outside the cottage seemed to crumble under the weight of the unfolding tragedy.

Jaw sat across from Micharas, the flickering candle lantern casting shadows on their faces. Taking in the harrowing events he had just detailed, Jaw leaned forward and asked, "I just have one final question, the man you mentioned, Sir Erik was it? I assume he now leads your town?"

Micharas, snapping back to the present, responded, "No, Sir Erik is the Captain of the Guards. Our leader is Sir Shane. He was appointed to the position by the King of The Eastland Castle himself, some years ago."

Jaw absorbed this information, nodding thoughtfully. "Sir Shane, appointed by the King. I see." After a moment of contemplation, he met Micharas's eyes and declared, "I'll help you reclaim your town. We can't let such darkness go unchallenged."

Micharas, a nervous chuckle escaping him, quickly realised the way that it may have come across and apologised, embarrassment etched on his face. "Sorry, it's just... there are so many of those creatures in the town. I hardly think the two of us could handle them all."

Jaw, unfazed by the remark, gave Micharas a sturdy look. "I understand the challenge," he responded. "But consider the alternative—a four-day journey to

Merrymill. Gnomes aren't known for meddling in Human affairs. We might be your best chance at reclaiming your town."

The weight of the decision hung in the air as Micharas contemplated the options laid before him.

Micharas, sensing the urgency, started to stand, but Jaw, still seated, watched him intently, as Micharas clearly struggled to drag himself to his feet again. "It will be dawn soon," Jaw remarked matter of factly. "You need to dry your clothes and shut your eyes, even if it is just for a couple of hours." His tone of voice was calm and yet commanding at the same time.

Micharas protested, his determination evident. "Every moment counts. I can't afford to rest while the town is in danger. We need to get back there as soon as possible."

Jaw remained resolute, his expression unchanged. "I have agreed to help you, not do everything for you. If you rush back out in the rain now, you will have no energy by the time we reach the town. What use would you be to anyone then? Rest. We will let the storm die down a little, and leave at dawn."

With that, Jaw rose from his chair, picked up the candle lantern, and stepped out into the calming rainstorm. As he stood in the open doorway, wind fighting to extinguish the candle, he turned his head slightly to the side so that Micharas could see the corner of his smile silhouetted between the light of the cabin and the darkness beyond. "My name is Jaw, by the way." And with that, he left. Micharas felt conflicted from this brief interaction with his host and newly met ally, and yet he knew that he was right.

He began to peel away his soaked clothing and plaster them to the back of the chair before drawing it over to stand in front of the fire. He then paused for a moment, fighting against his desire to dress and leave. Finally defeating his doubts, he lay in Jaw's bed and drifted almost instantly off to sleep.

Chapter 3

Micharas awoke to the subtle scent of burning wood, a fragrance that momentarily transported him back to the harrowing scenes of Celleos. Panic surged through him, but as the fog of sleep lifted, he quickly discerned reality from the haunting memories. The reassuring realisation settled his racing heart.

Swiftly dressing and pulling on his boots, Micharas ventured outside. The light drizzle that replaced the torrential rain created a misty ambiance around him. Guided by the rhythmic clang of metal striking metal, he followed the sound to one of the other two buildings nearby. The noise grew more distinct with each step, promising a glimpse into the activities transpiring in this temporary refuge.

Micharas followed the enticing scent of bacon as he approached the building, the clanging of the forge growing louder with each step. As he rounded the corner he encountered a large wooden door that had been propped open with a fire iron, the warmth of the forge quickly captured him in its embrace. The interior was dimly lit by the glow of molten metal and the dull fire of the forge.

In the centre of the room stood Jaw, hunched over an anvil, hammer in hand, skillfully shaping a blade. The orange glow of the metal reflected off his weathered face as beads of sweat glistened on his forehead. The rhythmic dance of the hammer and the resonant clang of metal filled the space, creating a symphony of craftsmanship.

The air was thick with the distinct aroma of hot metal and the savoury fragrance of bacon. Micharas's eyes were drawn to the anvil, where the partially formed blade lay, its edges still glowing with the heat of the forge. Jaw's experienced hands moved with precision, shaping the weapon with a practised grace.

As Micharas watched the blacksmith at work, Jaw momentarily paused, wiping his brow with the back of his hand. He looked up and noticed Micharas standing at the entrance. With a nod towards a nearby plate, he spoke, "Your breakfast is ready." On the plate sat a generous serving of sizzling bacon and some freshly baked bread, a welcome sight after the events of the night.

Jaw returned his attention to the blade, explaining, "This here is a crucial step. The balance of the blade is key for effective use. You want it to feel like an extension of yourself, not just a weight in your hand." He resumed his work, the hammer striking the metal with a controlled force that spoke of years of expertise. The bacon's enticing scent mingled with the metallic tang of the forge, creating an oddly comforting atmosphere within the structure.

Micharas's gaze wandered around the forge as he ate his breakfast, taking in the various tools, metal scraps, and unfinished projects scattered across the workbenches. Among Jaw's recent creations, Micharas noticed a gleaming longsword with an intricately detailed hilt, showcasing Jaw's skill in both functionality and aesthetics. Beside it, a sturdy-looking battle axe leaned against the wall, its blade showing signs of recent use. The craftsmanship was evident in the careful balance and sharpness of the weapons.

As Micharas looked around, Jaw glanced at the weapons he had made, a sense of pride evident in his eyes. "Those are my recent works," he commented, gesturing towards the longsword and battle axe. "Blacksmithing is more than just putting metal to the forge; it's about understanding the requirements of each piece, forming it the way that feels right for each unique weapon."

Micharas's attention was then drawn to an array of weapons hanging on the central beam that rose from the floor, splitting off in either direction to support the roof. These weapons seemed to differ in craftsmanship from the one Jaw was currently forging. They had piqued Micharas's curiosity. They seemed to tell a different story, displaying a range of designs and qualities. The dim light of the forge flickered over the assortment, creating a sense of allure that hinted at the tales each weapon held.

Micharas, still captivated by the weapons on the beam, spoke with a hint of nostalgia in his voice. "I have a brother who's a blacksmith. Andarius. When we left the Capital to move to Celleos he stayed behind, studying under a master weaponsmith there."

Jaw looked up from his work, intrigued. "You have siblings?"

Nodding, Micharas continued, "Two brothers. Andarius, the blacksmith, is the eldest. Then there's Antonious, my younger brother. He was a hunter like me, but about eight years ago, he went missing. It's presumed he had an accident while out on a hunt, but they never found his body."

There was a melancholic pause before Micharas added, "I prefer to think he ran away, started a new life somewhere. A life where he's happy and healthy." The memory of his missing brother lingered in his eyes, a mix of sadness and hope.

"What about you," Micharas asked, "any family?"

Jaw's response was blunt and cold, "No." The abruptness of his reply cast a sudden chill over the conversation, creating an oddly unsettling silence. Micharas sensed that delving into Jaw's personal past wasn't a welcome avenue.

Deciding to change the topic, Micharas pointed towards the weapons on the beam. "Impressive work here. Are these your creations as well?" He hoped to steer the conversation toward a safer, more neutral ground, away from the sensitive territory of Jaw's past.

As Micharas scanned the weapons hanging from the beam, he marvelled at the variety before him, each telling its own story.

His eyes first fell on a broad, double-edged sword with a well-worn leather-wrapped hilt. Detailed and possibly magical runes adorned the crossguard, suggesting a touch of mystique. The detailing was impeccable, the blade gleaming in the soft light of the forge. This was a warrior's tool, a validation of battles fought and victories won.

Hanging gracefully next to the sword was an elven longbow. Crafted from dark, polished wood, it exuded elegance. Intricate carvings depicted scenes from elven mythology, including great beasts of legends, showcasing the finesse of its artisan. The silver thread of the string added an ethereal touch to the functional design, a blend of art and war.

Micharas then turned his gaze to a massive dwarven warhammer hanging towards the pinnacle of the beam, its iron head elaborately engraved with dwarven symbols. The sturdy oak handle, embellished with silver inlays, spoke of both functionality and power. It was a weapon fit for a dwarf, a testimony to their kind.

A smaller, yet equally impressive, rogue's dagger caught his attention next. The slender, razor-sharp blade was designed for quick, silent strikes. Wrapped in black leather, with a dark blue gemstone pommel that glimmered in the dim light, it was a dagger that spoke of stealth, and precision, the kind that an assassin would carry.

Finally, his eyes settled on a nautical sabre, a true masterpiece. The blade, with its gentle curve and layered steel, resembled rolling ocean waves. The ship's wheel-shaped guard added a maritime flair, while the braided leather-wrapped handle evoked the image of ship rigging. Hanging next to it was a carved wooden sheath depicting a ship navigating turbulent waters. It was a unique and ornate piece, a treasure among the weapons collected.

"No, I didn't," Jaw replied. Micharas caught him looking at the weapons fondly out of the corner of his eye. The blacksmith's gaze lingered on each one, memories etched into the steel and wood.

With purpose, Jaw took the blade that he was making by the tang and plunged it into a bath of water. The hiss of steam billowed around the blade, creating an ephemeral dance in the air. As the steam subsided, Jaw removed his gloves, revealing calloused hands that bore the marks of countless battles and years spent working the forge. He approached Micharas, standing before the pillar of weapons.

"Each of them, I acquired through my adventures," Jaw explained, his eyes glinting with the fire of past exploits. He began recounting tales in his mind of duels won, alliances forged, and hidden islands discovered. The weapons, once mere tools, had become symbols of Jaw's journey through the tapestry of life, each thread woven with danger, triumph, and the indomitable spirit of a seasoned adventurer.

Micharas couldn't help but be captivated by the complex design of the sabre. Its ornate style and the meticulously carved sheath depicting a ship navigating the vast ocean left him in awe. He gestured towards it, a look of admiration in his eyes.

"This one is incredible," Micharas remarked, his vision fixed on the nautical masterpiece.

Jaw, his expression tinged with a mix of pride and gratitude, began to recount the story behind the sabre. "Ah, that one belonged to an extraordinary captain I once knew—Captain Rufus. A towering figure, tall and muscular, with a shaved head and a scruffy beard. A man of the sea, and a man I owe a great debt to."

As Jaw spoke, his eyes seemed to travel back to the memories held within the weapon. "Captain Rufus taught me more than just how to swing a blade. He shared his wisdom about the world, about the currents of life, and the storms that test a sailor's mettle. This sabre was his companion through many adventures, and now it stands as a testament to the lessons he imparted to me."

Micharas listened intently, a newfound respect for Jaw's connection to the weapons growing with each word. The sabre, once wielded by Captain Rufus, now hung among the other relics, carrying the weight of shared experiences and the debt of gratitude that Jaw held for the sea-faring mentor.

Jaw's hand reached up to the sabre, unhooking it from the beam with a familiar grace. He then turned to Micharas, the sabre held out as an offering. "Here," Jaw said, a rare warmth in his usually stoic demeanour. "You take it."

Micharas, taken aback by the unexpected generosity, hesitated at first. "I can't possibly accept this," he began, realising the significance the sabre held for Jaw. It was more than just a weapon; it was a tangible connection to an important part of his past.

Jaw, however, insisted, a look of certainty in his eyes. "I'd be happy to part with it if it means the weapon will be used for its purpose once more, instead of gathering dust in here. The blade has been yearning to travel again, and it wouldn't be right to keep it on display. It's not what Rufus would have wanted."

There was a hint of loss and remorse in Jaw's voice, revealing that Captain Rufus was no longer among the living. The sabre, now offered to Micharas, carried not only the weight of its own history but also the unspoken memories of an adventurer's journey and the bonds forged on the high seas.

Micharas hurriedly placed his plate on a nearby worktop, brushing off his hands on his trousers to clean them before graciously accepting the gift. "I will make sure it sees adventure then," he said with a grateful smile.

Jaw, with a playful grin, added, "Also, you won't be much use today if you don't have a weapon." This statement snapped Micharas back to the reality of the present, a sudden eagerness to leave striking his face. The weight of his mission and the dangers that awaited in the town ahead loomed in his mind, and the sabre now held a dual purpose—to honour its past and to carve a new path in the present.

Jaw nodded, his gaze shifting towards the blade in the bath. "I will finish my weapon," he declared, gesturing towards the work in progress. "And then we will leave."

In the meantime, Jaw instructed Micharas on where to find some necessary equipment. "You will find a shield in that box over there, a bow on the wall, and several arrows in a quiver hanging up near it. Grab those, and I will get to work."

Micharas rushed to the designated locations, gathering the items as instructed. Meanwhile, Jaw resumed his work on the blade, moving with a practised efficiency. He attached the guard, carefully securing it to the tang, ensuring a firm grip for its wielder. The hilt followed, a carefully crafted and shaped piece that added both form and function to the weapon. Next came the pommel, a finishing touch that balanced the blade and completed its aesthetic.

Once satisfied with the assembly, Jaw turned his attention to the sharpening process. He secured the blade in place and began the rhythmic motion of drawing it across the whetstone. The sound of metal meeting stone echoed in the forge, a cadence of preparation for the impending journey. Each pass honed the blade to a keen edge, ready to meet the challenges that awaited in the town.

Micharas stood by, the gathered equipment in his arms as he observed Jaw working on the blade. With each pass bringing the weapon closer to perfection. As the blade reached its optimal sharpness, Jaw turned his attention to cleaning it, running a piece of leather across the steel with a practised motion.

"So, if you are an adventurer, what are you doing out here in the woods?" Micharas inquired, his curiosity had become too much and he could not help but attempt to pry.

Jaw paused for a moment, his focus lifting from the blade to meet Micharas's eyes. "It's a long story," he replied, a hint of complexity in his tone. "I no longer consider myself an adventurer, but we can discuss it further if you like while we walk."

With that, he took the sheath for the newly crafted blade, appearing as if it had been waiting patiently on a nearby workbench. Whether repurposed or freshly made, Micharas didn't dwell on it, his attention following Jaw's preparations.

Jaw grabbed several long strips of leather, tying them around the hilt to provide a secure grip during their journey. The round wooden shield, once in Micharas's possession, found its place on Jaw's upper back, securely fastened for easy access. The sheath, now attached to Jaw's belt, completed the ensemble.

He then turned back towards Micharas. "Let's go," he said, the determination in his eyes matching the readiness of their equipment. As they stepped out of the forge, Micharas couldn't help but feel a sense of anticipation for the journey ahead, surrounded by the echoes of stories etched into the weapons in Jaw's collection and the unspoken tales awaiting them in the besieged town.

The large wooden door swung closed with a resonant thud. In the stillness of the forest, the two men set off, their footsteps muffled by the damp ground beneath them. Micharas slung the bow across his chest, the quiver snugly secured to his belt on the opposite side of the sabre.

As they ventured into the woods, the air carried the invigorating scent of rain-soaked earth, mingling with the ever-present fragrance of pine. Mud clung to their boots with each step, the tranquillity of the forest was interrupted only by the distant chirping of birds, their melodies weaving through the trees like the sound of a gentle river.

The two men walked in harmony with nature, their shared purpose evident in their silent strides. The vibrant green canopy overhead provided a natural ceiling for their journey, the occasional rays of sunlight filtering through the leaves, creating patterns on the forest floor.

"So," began Micharas, breaking the silence. "Why would an ex-adventurer be living out in the woods as a hermit? Practising blacksmithing of all things." He asked, a hint of joviality in his voice.

"After the death of my parents," Jaw began, his voice carrying the weight of memories, "I roamed the world for quite a number of years. I traversed lands, crossed seas, and faced challenges that tested me to my limit."

A glint of nostalgia flickered in his eyes, though it was quickly replaced by a serene determination. "In those years, I felt the pulse of life, witnessed the grandeur of landscapes, and encountered the diversity of civilizations. It was an odyssey that shaped me in ways I could never have foreseen."

Jaw continued walking, his sights fixed on the path ahead, roots and fallen leaves crunching beneath their boots. "But after a while, the wanderlust began to wane. The world, vast and vibrant as it is, no longer called me to explore its every corner. Instead, I yearned for something else—a connection with nature, a simpler existence."

He gestured to the towering trees around them. "So, I found solace here, amidst the trees and the silence. This isolation was a deliberate choice, a chance to pursue a goal different from the adventures of my youth. I sought something that I had read about several years before, that during my travels I discovered to have more merit than the legends gave it credit for."

Jaws words gave a sense of mystery to his tale. Choosing not to linger on the tragedies in his past, he pursued new goals and even still to this day it seemed that he was in pursuit of something extraordinary.

Micharas, now intrigued by Jaw's enigmatic story, couldn't help but question further. "What's that then?" he inquired.

Jaw, without hesitation, posed a question of his own. "Tell me, are you familiar with the Gods?" he inquired, his vision flickering over to his travelling companion as he spoke.

"You might need to be a little more specific." Micharas chuckled. The conversation took on an ethereal quality, as if the ancient trees themselves seemed to eavesdrop.

"The Grandmasters specifically. Do you know how they became Gods?" Jaw questioned, his words carrying a weight of ages, as if he were unravelling a secret woven into the fabric of existence.

"Oh them, no," Micharas replied, with humility in his voice. "I only know that they earned it somehow."

Jaw nodded knowingly. "Well, you aren't wrong," he confirmed, the resonance of his voice blending with the rustle of leaves overhead.

Jaw's revelation unfolded like ancient parchment being unfurled, revealing secrets long hidden in the annals of time. Micharas, walking alongside him in the deep woods, listened intently as the hermit blacksmith shared the lore he had discovered.

"You see," Jaw began, his voice carrying a sense of reverence, "the three Grandmasters were originally Dwarves. I discovered this when I happened to be in the Xanthian Halls, the capital of the Dwarves. They seem to have quite the collection of lore regarding their ascension to Godhood. They look upon the Grandmasters somewhat differently from the rest of the mortal races."

As they traversed the forest, Jaw continued to weave his tale. "I then went on to discover that the very title 'Grandmaster' is of Dwarven origin. The Dwarves view the martial world of combat from a class perspective, separating it into Melee, Magic, and Ranged."

"That's not unusual; lots of civilizations and orders do the same," Micharas interjected, his interest evident in his voice.

"True," Jaw acknowledged the man's wisdom, trying not to be too condescending in his explanation. The two men navigated over a fallen tree in the woods, Micharas keeping pace with Jaw. "But the Dwarves take it one step further by giving rankings to each of the combat classes. Level one signifies basic knowledge or a novice, level two indicates a more adept knowledge, level three denotes advanced knowledge or expertise in the matter. And then, level four represents the true mastery of that combat class. The rank of 'Grandmaster' is reserved for any individual who has reached level four in all three of the combat classes. As such, only the three Dwarves; Ixes, Harreros and Balus have ever achieved it."

Micharas, intrigued yet sceptical, voiced his concern, probing the tale for consistency. "How does that make them Gods?" he asked, as though scrutinising a theory that seemed too fantastical to be true.

Jaw, continuing the narrative with a dedicated tone, explained, "It would seem that not only does each stage of the ranking system have a measurement for prowess, but they also seem to offer those that achieve each rank a trait, almost naturally gained as someone reaches the next rung on the ladder. I did not take note to identify and memorise them all, but the rank of Grandmaster also has one such boon."

"Godhood?" Micharas ventured, his voice laced with innocent curiosity, trying to anticipate the answer.

"In a way," Jaw elucidated. "Apparently, when a being reaches Grandmaster status, they become immortal. Not invulnerable, however. It's more of a continuation of life in the event of death. They simply get back up and carry on as though nothing happened. It seems to include some sort of natural healing process." The revelation hung in the air, making it evident to Micharas that Jaw himself was not fully aware of how this feat was achieved.

"Incredible!" Micharas exclaimed. "No wonder only three people have ever achieved it then. You hear all the time about great heroes who are warriors, archers, or mages, sometimes even battlemages, but rarely do you hear about people striving for complete mastery of combat."

"Exactly," Jaw concluded.

"So I assume that you are out here studying this theory then?" Micharas asked, with a sense of uncertainty.

"Not quite," Jaw replied. "I'm trying to become a Grandmaster."

Micharas contemplated this for the briefest of moments before letting out a snorted laugh. "I mean no disrespect, but from what I know of magic alone, you would need to study somewhere like Astius. That's without considering the swordmasters and master hunters or archers of the world that could teach you more from their lifetimes' experience than you could learn in the isolation of the woods in many lifetimes."

Jaw let out a sigh. "Perhaps. Perhaps if the opportunity to travel again arises, I will take it," he said with a smile, acknowledging the limitations of his current secluded pursuit. The two men continued their journey, surrounded by the symphony of nature and the secrets that lingered in the woods.

As they pushed forward, the splash of puddles and squelch of mud beneath their boots accompanied their conversation. Micharas, eager to fill the air with casual dialogue, recounted bits of his life in Celleos, the memories of his family, and his role as a hunter before the recent chaos.

The conversation transitioned seamlessly from their personal histories to more trivial matters, such as favourite foods and tales of past adventures. Micharas spoke of the thrill of hunting, and Jaw shared anecdotes from his travels.

Soon, the edge of the woods came into view. The transition from the sheltered embrace of the trees to the vast openness of the countryside was abrupt. The air changed, carrying the scent of the fields and smoke in the distance. The dense tree cover began to thin, allowing glimpses of the open fields beyond.

Celleos sat at the heart of the landscape, a collection of destroyed buildings and winding streets, surrounded by its high walls. Smoke curled upwards from the ruins. Micharas and Jaw paused at the threshold of the woods. "We ought to make a plan." Micharas suggested wisely.

The two men crouched at the edge of the woods, the midday sun burning high above them. The once-secret entrance to the town, now compromised, left them with limited options. They huddled together, their voices hushed as they discussed their plan of entry.

"So, the secret entrance is out of the question," Micharas pointed out, a furrow forming on his brow as he surveyed the ruined town in the distance.

Jaw nodded solemnly. "Indeed. We need another way in. Scaling the gates seems like the only viable option."

Micharas glanced towards the town's imposing gates, a sense of unease settling in. "Scaling the gates won't be easy, especially with those archers on the walls. We'll be exposed."

Jaw, his eyes narrowing in contemplation, agreed. "It's a risk we'll have to take. The longer we stay out here, the more time those Alts have to wreak havoc and potentially the more of the town and its inhabitants are lost." He pressed coldly, in an attempt to coerce action from his companion.

Micharas raised an eyebrow, as he processed what Jaw had said. "You called them Alts? Is that what they're called? How could you possibly know that?" A sense of alarm and accusation carried in his voice, suspicion evident in his gaze.

Jaw met Micharas's eyes with a steely resolve. "I've encountered them before, in my travels. They're dangerous and unpredictable. Knowledge is power, Micharas. We need every advantage we can get."

Micharas's expression shifted from suspicion to a reluctant acceptance of the explanation.

"Though, the creatures that you mentioned are slightly different from the ones that I have encountered. They seem to be missing their primitive troup. A strain that hovers closer to the ground they usually travel on all fours. I am not complaining by any means as I personally hated having to deal with that unit class but we should keep our guard up that they may be present. The large individual that you mentioned last night with the shovel for a weapon sounds familiar too, though I highly doubt it's the same being that I encountered several years back." Jaw continued, he clearly has had a lot more experience with these creatures then he was originally willing to let on. Micharas, ever practical, broke the silence that followed Jaws revelation of information.

As they strategized, Micharas couldn't shake the feeling of being watched. He scanned the town, his instincts on high alert. "We need to time it right. Wait for a moment of distraction, maybe when the archers shift positions."

Jaw nodded in agreement. "Patience will be our ally. We strike when the time is right."

"We still have a fair distance to travel in the open, even when they are changing shifts. How do you propose we get close enough to the gate?" Micharas asked, his voice a low murmur.

Jaw, his eyes narrowing slightly as he considered the question, finally spoke with a sly grin playing on his lips. "I have an idea, though it will not be without risk." The hint of mischief in his expression teased at a plan that walked the fine line between audacity and danger.

Micharas studied Jaw's face, searching for any signs of hesitation or doubt. The sly grin remained, revealing a confidence that piqued Micharas's curiosity. "Risk, we can handle. What's the plan?" he inquired, his tone a blend of caution and determination.

Chapter 4

"When you said risk, this is not what I imagined," Micharas muttered, his voice a low grumble. Squatting behind Jaw, he followed cautiously as Jaw stood in front, shield raised in defence. The two men had edged closer to the town, strategically waiting on the hedge line for the archers to change positions.

The wait wasn't long, fortunately. As soon as the archers started to move, Jaw took action. They moved in a formation, slowly advancing toward the town. Micharas with his bow drawn in one hand, an arrow knocked against the string in the other. While blocking arrows with a shield was at least plausible, it was not what Micharas would have called a good plan.

Nevertheless, Micharas found himself positioned at the back of their formation, a perspective that offered a clear view of the archers and the potential threats they faced. As they inched closer to the town, uncertainty lingered in the air, a tense anticipation of what awaited them atop the shadowed walls.

"This seems like a terrible idea." Micharas protested quietly.

"I know, if it works though, you owe me a drink." Jaw chuckled his voice no more than a murmur as they drew closer.

"If this works, the whole town owes you a drink!" Micharas joked back. No sooner had they spoken that an enemy archer on the wall spotted them. With lightning reflexes honed through years of practice Micharas drew and released his arrow. It flew up onto the wall and caught the target square between the eyes. He watched in relief as the body dropped back and out of view.

As soon as the body fell backward, the two men broke into a sudden dash toward the gates. Adrenaline pumping, they reached the solid wooden barrier that was the gate, its surface covered in metal studs and began the challenging climb. The wet surface offered little grip, and the studs boasted barely any purchase, the ascent was far from easy.

Jaw's experience as an adventurer and the strength in his arms helped him navigate the treacherous climb, but even he struggled. At one point, his foot slipped, and he dangled momentarily from his fingertips, but with a determined effort, he regained his footing.

Micharas, agile and accustomed to traversing challenging terrain, made swift progress. He maintained focus, each movement calculated to avoid the damp patches on the wood that could prove slippery. The sounds of the town, a chaotic symphony, echoed within as they ascended.

The top of the gate seemed like an elusive goal, but they persisted. Micharas led the way, setting the pace. Finally, Jaw reached the summit, Micharas offered him a hand and pulled him up the final bout of the climb, the two emerging onto the wall that overlooked the beleaguered town.

The absence of a gatehouse worked in their favour, allowing them to scale onto the wall without obstruction. They crouched, catching their breath as they surveyed the town from this elevated vantage point. The danger was far from over, however, as they could clearly see more archers further along the wall in either direction.

Suddenly, movement caught Micharas's keen eye – another archer, positioned on the opposite side of the wall, just across the top of the gate had spotted them.

Instantly, the archer reached for a horn hanging by its side, an ominous sign that danger was about to escalate. Acting on pure instinct, Micharas didn't hesitate. His hand moved to the quiver at his hip, fingers closing around an arrow. With fluid precision, he drew against the bow string raising it in the same movement and released, the projectile sailed effortlessly through the air and found its mark.

The creature crumpled, the ominous impending blast of the horn silenced before it could echo through the town. Micharas's eyes remained sharp, scanning for any signs of further threats.

Jaw pointing towards the isolated building nestled in the back of the town, surrounded by a garden. "I presume that's the town hall," Jaw remarked. Even from this distance the doors to the hall did not appear to have been breached. Perhaps the invaders had been waiting for something, or maybe a protection spell was in place, keeping them at bay.

"That's it," Micharas affirmed with a nod, he appeared relieved at the promising state of the hall. All was not lost, at least not just yet. "Let's get down there then," Jaw instructed.

The two men carefully made their way along the wall towards the guardhouse, the only building providing direct access to the top of the wall. From here, they could make their descent to street level, a realm likely patrolled by groups of Alts.

While traversing the rooftops presented a safer route, offering concealment from ground-level threats, it introduced a different kind of danger. The elevation would raise them into the direct line of sight of archers stationed on various parts of the wall. The constant threat from arrows loomed, prompting Micharas and Jaw to need to move with caution and utilise whatever little cover the damaged buildings could provide.

Adding to the complexity of this option, the structural integrity of the rooftops became a concern. Some buildings had suffered significant damage, and the risk of collapse weighed in on their decision. The aftermath of the storm the previous night added an additional challenge, leaving the sloped roof tiles wet and slippery. Each step would need to be deliberate, a dance with danger as they navigated the precarious terrain.

And this is why they had decided the smarter option would be to brave the streets. As they approached the guardhouse, the urgency of their mission intensified.

Micharas and Jaw reached the door leading down into the upper-floor of the building, their ears catching the muffled sounds of voices emanating from within. The low, guttural tones suggested a fairly large group of Alts rested inside, their discussion suggesting an ominous threat to the town. The two men exchanged wary glances before pressing their ears against the door to better discern the conversation within.

Inside, the gruff and uneducated voices of the Alts carried a sense of malevolence and anticipation.

"Waitin' on orders, we are. Gotta smash the Town Hall, boss says. Big fight!" one Alt grunted, the words rough and coarse.

"Town Hall smash! Town Hall smash!" another joined in, the chorus echoing through the chamber.

A third Alt, with a deeper voice, seemed to be giving some form of direction. "No smash 'til boss says. Waitin', waitin'."

The crude articulation and simple vocabulary painted a vivid picture of the Alts' brutish nature and their eagerness to wreak havoc upon the town. Micharas and Jaw exchanged a silent acknowledgment of the imminent danger.

Jaw's movements were deliberate and silent as he drew his sword, ensuring that no telltale sound would betray their presence. Micharas, equally stealthy, extracted an arrow from his quiver and pulled it tight against the bowstring. The gruff voices on the other side of the door seemed clustered as they continued their discussion, only three in number. Jaw gestured with a free hand, indicating the concentration of the voices.

With a quick, decisive kick, Jaw sent the door flying inwards on its hinges. The element of surprise was theirs. Micharas loosed his arrow with swift precision, the projectile tore through the air with a shrill whistle and a crunch embedding itself in the back of the skull of one of the Alts. Simultaneously, Jaw surged forward, his sword flashing in the dim light. A controlled strike brought down a second Alt as he slid the blade straight across its throat, while Jaw, propelled by the force of his charge, barreled over a table and collided with the final adversary.

The Alt, caught off guard, toppled backward with the chair it was sitting in, crashing to the ground. Jaw, undeterred by the shifting battlefield, plunged his blade into the creature's chest, finishing it off with a bone breaking twist, silencing its crude utterances as he rode atop of it backwards to the floor. The clash of steel and the thud of bodies hummed briefly in the confined space as they subdued the last of their unprepared adversaries. The room fell into an uneasy silence, broken only by the final gurgles of the Alt who had been left to bleed out.

Jaw, rising from the chaotic encounter, wiped his blade clean on a discarded piece of clothing. The dim light cast dancing shadows on the walls, and the air hung heavy with the scent of metallic blood.

Micharas, bow still in hand, surveyed the scene with a mix of relief and wariness. The three Alts lay motionless, their crude features contorted in death. However, a bizarre transformation was underway. As their life force ebbed away, an otherworldly phenomenon began to unfold.

The Alts' flesh started to melt away, as if subjected to an unseen force. The grotesque process consumed not only their bodies but also their equipment, leaving behind a dark, visceral sludge. It oozed from the disintegrating remains, forming a pool of inky blackness on the cold floor. Their skeletal structures, once hidden beneath layers of grotesque anatomy, were now exposed, stark against the unnatural residue.

Jaw and Micharas exchanged glances, witnessing a sight that defied the laws of nature. The room, once echoing with the clash of steel and the thud of bodies, now bore witness to an eerie transformation. The air seemed charged with an unsettling energy as the last remnants of the Alts dissolved.

"Disgusting," Micharas exclaimed, his face contorting in a mixture of horror and repulsion as he retrieved his arrow from the pile of bones on the floor. He wiped it clean with a cloth and returned it to his quiver, shaking off the remnants of the otherworldly sludge.

Jaw nodded in agreement, though his demeanour remained strangely unfazed by the grotesque transformation, as if he had witnessed such horrors many times before. The two men continued their exploration of the building, descending through its lower floors. It became evident that the invaders had made use of the structure as it was originally intended, as a barracks, a use that hinted at a level of understanding and organisation within their forces. The barracks showed signs of crude personal belongings scattered about, and markings on the walls that suggested a rudimentary hierarchy among the Alts.

As they moved through the building, Micharas couldn't shake the realisation that the Alts were not the mindless brutes they first appeared to be. There was a method to their madness, a structure underlying the chaos.

Finally, the pair stepped out of the building into the desolate street. The town bore the scars of the relentless onslaught. Debris littered the cobbled pathway, remnants of buildings crumbled under the weight of the attack. The air hung heavy with the acrid scent of smoke, the silence and complete absence of human life echoed through the narrow alleys.

Corpses of humans lay scattered along the street, a haunting reminder of the brutality that had unfolded. The town, once a bustling hub of life, now stood in stark contrast, a shadow of its former self.

The journey through the barracks had offered a glimpse into the invaders' calculated approach, and now, as they traversed the battlefield itself, the juxtaposition of strategy and beastlike aggression became painfully clear.

The two men moved further down the streets, before them lay a crucial decision point: a fork in the road that presented two diverging paths—one through the derelict buildings and back alleys, the other down the high street. Both options, at this point, seemed devoid of immediate threats.

Jaw spoke first. "We need to consider our options carefully. The derelict buildings and back alleys offer cover, making it easier to remain unseen. However, they might also harbour surprises—hidden threats or ambush points. On the other hand, the high street provides a more direct route, but it's exposed, leaving us vulnerable if there are any archers or patrols waiting."

Micharas nodded, his gaze scanning both routes. "Time is a factor, too. The longer we take, the greater the risk of encountering more Alts or facing complications."

After a moment of contemplation, Micharas made the final decision. "We'll take the high street. Speed is our priority right now."

Jaw nodded in agreement, and they continued moving at a jog. At first, the high street appeared devoid of danger. The shop fronts, once lively with commerce, now stood in ruin. Broken windows, shattered displays, and remnants of fire painted a grim picture.

As they jogged along, tension built with each step. The stillness of the street amplified the sounds of their running. Micharas couldn't help but glance at the shop names, the once-familiar places now reduced to rubble. "The Curiosity Emporium... The Prancing Unicorn Inn... all gone," he muttered under his breath.

Suddenly, Micharas caught a glimpse of movement in the reflection of a shattered storefront window. He halted, his hand signalling Jaw to stop. A cold chill ran down his spine as he realised they had walked straight into an ambush.

"There," Micharas whispered, pointing subtly to a rooftop where the top limb of a bow betrayed the presence of an archer. The trap was set, and the realisation tightened the knot of tension in the air. The street, once seemingly empty, now began to fill with Alts from every available entrance. They lurched forth from the darkness, seemingly waiting for this moment. There must have been twenty of them, if not more. How could they have been this reckless?

"My, my, what do we have here," a female voice, cold and sinister in tone, came crying from an alleyway. She stepped forward, revealing herself. The female Alt was a chilling sight—black hair cascading like a waterfall of shadows, pitch black eyes devoid of any emotion, and pale skin that seemed almost as white as ice. A wicked smile played on her lips, she wore black robes adorned with gory trinkets. A necklace of severed fingers hung around her neck, each digit a grotesque trophy. Several interesting-looking potions dangled from her belt line, some glowed with malevolent intent, and in her hand, she wielded her weapon—a staff made from a severed demon's arm. The fingers clenched around an eyeball, a truly unsettling sight.

She surveyed Micharas and Jaw with a predatory gaze, her eyes gleaming with an otherworldly wickedness. The Alts surrounding them shifted restlessly, their grotesque forms creating a nightmarish tableau on the desolate street. The ambush had been orchestrated, and now they were at the mercy of this sinister Alt leader and her horde of twisted followers.

The Alt leader's command echoed through the streets, "Kill them," she said in a tone that seemed like the embodiment of steel. It was cold and stern, a sharpness that cut through the crowd. Despite speaking at a normal volume, her words easily pierced through the grunts of her peons. Minions surged forward with a relentless determination to snuff out the lives of Micharas and Jaw. The air itself turned against them, ears filled with the sounds of scrambled footing and war cries, silhouetted by the escalated beating of their hearts, creating an almost metronome-like drumbeat in their ears. The Alts closed in, outnumbering and surrounding the would-be heroes.

As the first wave reached striking range, Micharas and Jaw readied their weapons. The glint of steel in their hands contrasted with the grayscaling of their foes' features. The Alts wore black, stone-like armour, cobbled together from a mixture of leathers and cloths. A variety of weapons, from huge blades to crude axes and makeshift clubs, were clenched in their evil, bloodthirsty hands. Each weapon bore witness to the savagery of their kind.

The clash began, a frenzied dance of steel and gore. Micharas and Jaw, fighting back-to-back, faced the onslaught with a combination of skill and desperation. Their swords cleaved through their adversaries, but the sheer number of Alts threatened to overwhelm them.

The first Alt charged towards Micharas, a huge club peppered with spikes and nails raised above its head in preparation to strike. Micharas quickly lowered his stance and manoeuvred under the dropping arm of his attacker. With a swift upwards slash, his sabre flicked across the Alt's exposed neck as another one lunged towards him, sword extended forward.

Meanwhile, Jaw faced off against an Alt with two large axes. The beast sent a strike cleaving towards Jaw's midriff. In a desperate attempt to evade, he backed up into another enemy engaged in combat with Micharas. The axe narrowly missed his stomach, and with its passing, he rotated his body in a clockwise turn and rolling forwards towards the danger. As he rolled, he slashed with his blade at the back of the knees of the Alt he had just backed up into, spotting the weak spot as he moved, thinking that any help felling Micharas's side of the horde would likely be appreciated.

Micharas watched as one of his combatants disappeared backward into the raging crowd. As he glanced past the lunge of his attacker, with a deft strike, he sucker-punched the sword-wielding Alt in the nose with his free hand, flung his sword-wielding hand to the side, and cut down another foe approaching within his peripheral. He watched briefly as Jaw rose from the crowd ahead of him, jumping forwards with a lunged stab and dispatching yet another Alt. Micharas wasted no time observing the chaos, leaning backward, narrowly avoiding a thrusting blade that pierced towards his face.

Jaw landed on the floor, the dead now building up around them, their disgusting, slimy residue creating a slick pool beneath their feet. His confidence burst like a flame discovering a deposit of air inside a lump of wood. A smile crept across his face. Another axe tore down towards him; with a practised parry, he knocked the weapon's head to the side using the fuller of his blade. Despite his foe striking with two hands on its weapon, Jaw used just one. He backhanded his attacker, kicked it sharply in the groin, and decapitated it as it dropped to a knee before him.

Micharas, too, was feeling the thrill of battle. A great monster of a sword tore through the air with precision and power towards his abdomen. He timed his movements and chose the riskiest path he could to approach his foe, rolling over the true edge of the weapon as it bore towards him. He rose from the far side, seeing a spark of fear in his enemy's eyes as he stood before him in a perfectly safe condition. The creature had no way to return the mighty size of its weapon back in that direction in time and let out a war cry, its shout abruptly cut short as Micharas threaded his sabre into the open gullet of the overly armoured Alt and straight up into its brain.

As one Alt fell, two more seemed to take its place, the dark forces multiplying like a nightmarish hydra. Micharas and Jaw, though skilled in combat, found themselves beset on all sides, surrounded by a legion of devilish warriors. The rhythm of combat suddenly quickened, forcing the pair back towards each other.

A new wave of Alts surged forward from the alleyways, their armour clattering as they closed in. In the midst of the chaos, Micharas and Jaw moved with an almost desperate precision. Their movements were a dance of survival, a delicate balance between attack and evasion.

Micharas, in the midst of a fluid series of strikes, suddenly found himself disarmed as an Alt's weapon clashed against his sword, sending it flying out of reach. Without hesitation, he swiftly drew his bow, a sense of urgency replacing the fluidity of his movements. He rapidly notched one of the few remaining arrows in his quiver, eyes scanning the approaching horde. An Alt bumped him as Jaw delivered a killing blow to another before kicking it backward into the crowd. Micharas accidentally let go of his arrow but with all the potential targets around them, it was no surprise that it found a home in the eye of an Alt.

The carnage continued to unfold as Micharas swiftly adapted to the situation. With his sword out of reach, he embraced the rhythm of his bow, seamlessly transitioning from melee to ranged combat. His eyes, sharp and focused, scanned the approaching horde. He released a quick volley of arrows, each finding its mark with deadly accuracy. Two Alts crumpled to the ground, their grotesque forms leaving a trail of black sludge as they fell.

Jaw, not to be outdone, danced through the throng with his sword, cutting down two more Alts with a lethal grace. The first fell victim to a precise strike, the blade severing its neck, while the second met a brutal end as Jaw's sword plunged into its heart. The street echoed with the wet thud of collapsing bodies and the grotesque symphony of their otherworldly transformation.

Micharas reached for his quiver to draw another arrow but discovered it to now be completely empty. A surge of adrenaline fueled his movements as he retrieved his fallen sword. With a swift motion, he seamlessly transitioned back into the melee, his blade dancing through the air as he dispatched another Alt with a well-timed slash. The creature crumpled to the ground, its armour stained with the foul remnants of its demise.

Jaw, in his relentless assault, faced an Alt wielding a massive warhammer. With a quick sidestep and a calculated strike, he disarmed the creature, sending the warhammer crashing to the ground. Before the Alt could react, Jaw's sword found its mark, ending the creature's malevolent existence.

Exhaustion clung to Micharas and Jaw like a suffocating cloak as they pressed on through the relentless onslaught. The battle had taken its toll, leaving them panting and their movements slower. Each strike and parry felt like a herculean effort, and the weight of the ongoing conflict bore down on them.

In a moment of dire need, three arrows descended from the heavens, finding their targets with deadly accuracy. Three Alts crumpled to the ground, their bodies joining the grotesque massacre that filled the streets. Micharas, in the midst of a power struggle with an Alt, spared a moment to glance around, his eyes searching for the unseen archer.

As another arrow embedded itself into the temple of the very Alt that he had his blade locked with, Micharas's mind raced. He recalled a fleeting moment when he had spotted an archer on a rooftop, dismissing it as an Alt. Now, however, doubt crept in. Was it possible that there was another force at play, a potential ally hidden in the shadows?

Jaw, catching his breath, spared a nod of gratitude towards Micharas, assuming the assistance to be from him. The tide of battle had momentarily shifted, but the relentless horde showed no signs of slowing. The mystery of the rooftop archer lingered in the air, adding an additional layer of uncertainty to the already tumultuous battlefield.

"ENOUGH OF THIS!" The female Alt's sudden outburst shattered the tension that had settled over the chaotic battlefield. Her once icy demeanour morphed into a seething annoyance, as she raised her hand, with thin white skin, it glowed eerily as it captured the late afternoon sun. The atmosphere crackled with an impending sense of dread as the purple energy coalesced around the eyeball of her grotesque staff.

"DIE!" she cried, the word a venomous command. The crowd of Alts before her reacted with swift terror, scattering in all directions like leaves caught in a sudden gust of wind. A clear path emerged, creating a direct line between the female Alt and her intended target: Micharas.

Jaw, recognizing the imminent danger, sprang into action. With a quick manoeuvre, he positioned himself between Micharas and the oncoming onslaught. Drawing the wooden shield from his back, he held it firmly in front of him, a makeshift barricade against the impending magical attack.

The air around the female Alt crackled with volatile energy, and the anticipation of impending doom hung heavy in the air. The purple energy on her staff intensified, creating an ominous glow that cast eerie shadows on the grimy street.

The sudden rush of air past Micharas's ear was the only warning before an unseen force tore past him at breakneck speed. The wind seemed to make way for whatever it was that hurtled towards Jaw and the menacing Alt. Jaw's shield emitted a clunking noise as it was forcefully pulled forward and away from his grasp. However, he tightened his grip, refusing to let go as the street filled with an ear-piercing, blood-chilling scream.

Jaw lowered his barrier to witness a shocking scene. The female Alt's finger falling towards the ground before her, severed cleanly from her hand. An arrow, now coated in her dark, blood, protruded from the door frame beside her. The scream echoed in the aftermath, creating an unsettling resonance in the air. The sudden intervention had halted the impending magical onslaught, leaving an eerie silence in its wake.

"You will pay for this insolence!" she screamed, whirling her staff overhead. A loud crash from the side signalled the arrival of the giant Alt that Micharas had described earlier. The monstrous creature burst through a solid brick wall, seemingly in response to the screams of the woman. Its arrival was chaotic, the debris and rubble it threw into the alley adding to the mayhem.

As the towering figure emerged, the witch commanded, "Ethor! Deal with them!" With a nod, he turned to the party. An aura enforcing fear exuded from him. "Yes, my Lady," he said in his gravelly tone, acknowledging her command with a sinister compliance.

"Good," the witch said with a wicked grin, a shade of pride in her underling. "I will await your report of the battle." She concluded, stamping the butt of the staff onto the ground and shouting loudly, "Recall!" Suddenly, a thick fog of purple and sanguine cascaded forth, rushing outwards in all directions. It swept through the streets, buildings and corpses in mere moments. Static energy seemed to afflict each of the Alts as the fog reached them. And in an instant, it was gone, vacuumed back towards the epicentre. With it, so was the evil sorceress.

The two men were left standing in the presence of the mighty Alt. His armour now bore more scratches than Micharas remembered, possibly a result of his rush through the buildings to answer his master's call. "This is going to be fun," he said in a deep, booming, condemning voice. The air around him hummed with demonic energy as he crunched his neck from left to right, the sound resembling mighty oaks falling in the woods. The pair realised that they no longer stood alone on this battlefield as the sound of footsteps rattled down the alleyway behind them.

Micharas turned to see a small boy approaching, no older than eighteen. He had short, scruffy brown hair and a devilish grin on his face. His attire, leather armour befitting a hunter, spoke of experience and agility. He wore a cloak that seemed to blend seamlessly with the shadows, a quiver full of arrows hung at his side and a bow in hand hinted that he was their archer on the rooftops. "You didn't think I would let you have all the fun, did you?" he joked boisterously as he approached them.

Micharas narrowed his eyes as the boy approached, a glint of scepticism and wariness in his gaze. He glanced back at Jaw, whose attention remained steadfast on the formidable Alt warrior looming before them. The confusion etched on Micharas's face upon seeing this boy was mirrored by a scowl of understanding and outrage from the massive foe as he too observed the archer.

"Well," the Alt warrior grumbled as the newcomer seamlessly joined their group. "This explains a few things. Looks like we are getting closer at last." With those words, he dropped into a sprinting position, clutching his gigantic spade in one hand.

"Guys, can this wait until later?" Jaw pleaded with his companions, a sense of urgency in his tone. While his eyes remained locked on the Alt, he felt a burning energy building up behind him as the boy walked alongside them.

"Sure thing," the boy chirped up almost arrogantly. His hands moved with grace and purpose as he rapidly drew an arrow from its spot in his quiver, readied it at breakneck speed, and loosed it towards their foe. The Alt, despite being less than ten metres away, still seemed to have time to react to the incoming projectile of death, a sly smile playing on his lips.

With a swift turn of his cheek, the Alt managed to rotate his helmet to the perfect angle, deflecting the incoming arrow effortlessly. The projectile harmlessly bounced off his armour, leaving him untouched and unfazed. A low grunt escaped him as he burst into a sprint, closing the distance with alarming speed.

Micharas, anticipating the clash, dove to the left with his sword in hand, ready to flank and engage in combat. However, the Alt's focus shifted abruptly toward the boy, his weapon arm extended to the side, ready to strike on impact. The young man seemed to freeze in the face of imminent danger.

Jaw, acting with rapid counter-movement, stepped in to intercept the charging Alt. His blade slashed across the brute's exposed forearm as he collided with the unstoppable force. In the midst of the clash, the boy snapped to his senses, quickly readying another arrow.

Despite the cut, the Alt disposed of Jaw with brutal efficiency, converting his momentum into a devastating sideways kick to the outside of Jaws knee. This was enough to send Jaw crashing to the ground with a loud thump. The Alt, far from finished, grabbed Jaw by the shoulders and rotated, dragging his body across the archer's line of fire, preventing him from taking the shot. With a forceful continuation of his rotation, he discarded Jaw toward Micharas, catching him completely off guard as they collided and bounced backward through the cobbled street.

The Alt, having neutralised his immediate threats, turned his attention back toward the archer, who now stood only a few metres away at most, poised for the next deadly encounter.

He swiftly released the arrow, and a moment of horror gripped him as the Alt stood unyielding. No flinch, no movement—just a stoic acceptance of the penetrating hit. The arrow found its mark, puncturing straight through the creature's jaw, lodging itself into bone, blood dripping down his face and forearm. Unfazed, the Alt charged the archer with aggressive swings, determined to close the distance.

The boy had no option but to retreat, dropping to the floor in a backward evasive roll to narrowly avoid the impending blow. However, in the heat of the battle, all of his remaining arrows spilled from his quiver, scattering across the cobbled street. Doubling down on his attack, the Alt continued to spin with the momentum, launching into a second cleaving effort as the boy regained his feet.

Forced to act on survival instinct, the young hunter threw himself back in a rapid backstep manoeuvre, passing the corner of the nearest building. A smile lifted his cheeks, hopeful that the obstruction would delay the relentless warrior, if nothing else.

The bladed head of the maul collided with the building's corner, sending solid lumps of rock and debris raining toward the boy. He grabbed his thick cloak, swiftly releasing it and casting it toward the incoming debris. Luck was on his side as the material wrapped around the stones, dropping them to the floor as the momentum of the two objects cancelled each other out.

The Titan had orchestrated this encounter as a mere distraction, aiming to dispatch the much smaller opponent swiftly. As he collided forcefully with the boy, sending him sprawling to the ground, Micharas emerged seemingly from thin air, striking the side of the Alt's armour with his sword. Yet, the Alt perceived it as nothing more than an inconvenience—a brief interruption diverting his attention from the archer. He turned swiftly, the mighty maul swinging for Micharas, who, in the close proximity to the fiend, had little time to react. Just in time, he deflected the sharp edge of the spade away from his body with the edge of his own sword. Despite the successful deflection, the spade collided with Micharas's chest, sending him tumbling across the street. This time, Micharas felt considerably more pain from the encounter, lying there winded for a moment. In his staggered daze, he placed his hand on a familiar object.

Meanwhile, the colossal foe returned his full attention to the small archer lying defenceless on the ground. The Alt's blood-soaked hand grabbed the boy by the throat, lifting him into the air with unnerving strength. Despite the earlier injury to his muscle, the Alt displayed formidable power as he performed this horrific act. As he pulled the boy closer to his face, the archer, gasping for air, was powerless to resist. Even in the grip of suffocation, he clung tightly to his bow.

Suddenly, Jaw materialised out of the shadows. With a swift and calculated strike, his sword embedded deep into the brute's arm, a burst of sparks emanating from the strike as it deflected off of an adjacent piece of armour plating. Micharas, fueled by the opening, deftly drew his bow, a relic slung across his back, and armed it with the scavenged arrow.

As the creature's grip on the boy's throat loosened from Jaws' strike, the young archer dangled, holding onto its forearm. With an almost gravity-defying move, he pulled himself up, suspended in the air for a heartbeat. His bow clenched in one hand, he shot a deliberate glance to Micharas, who stood poised, waiting for the opportune moment.

The mighty Alt, sensing a threat, turned its head toward Micharas. In that split second, the young archer exploited the creature's blind spot. Placing his feet on its broad, heavily armoured chest, and kicked backward with all his might, breaking free from its grasp. Seizing the window of opportunity, Micharas released his arrow. It sliced through the air, akin to a pebble skipping across a still lake.

Yet, the brute anticipated the move, lowering its head to expose the frontal portion of its skullcap helmet. The arrow collided, meeting resistance against the formidable defence. As the boy soared backward, he spotted the repetition in their foe's defences. Launching into a mid-air backflip, he readied his bow.

In a breathtaking sequence, the entire skirmish unfolded with an exhilarating intensity, each movement a symphony of calculated strikes and desperate evasions. The culmination, a fleeting moment, left the battlefield transformed, the echoes of the encounter lingering like a whispered legend.

Jaw's eyes widened as the arrow, deflected by the Alt's helmet, arced toward the boy mid-flip. The hunter, displaying astonishing reflexes, caught the projectile, swiftly re-knocking it against the string of his own bow. In a seamless motion, just as his back was on the verge of meeting the blood-soaked floor, he released his attack, sending it diagonally upwards like a streak of vengeance. The arrow lodged itself straight between the eyes of the mighty beast with such force that it knocked his head backwards as it found its mark.

The battleground now silent, the combat had reached its gory conclusion. Micharas, Jaw and their new companion surveyed the scene, witnessing the Alt's demise. Its colossal form began to dissolve, mirroring the fate of its fallen counterparts. As if consumed by a demonic force, the creature's body melted away, leaving behind a stark skeleton and a pool of visceral black slime. Within moments, what was once a formidable foe now existed only as remnants, a haunting reminder of the ferocity that had unfolded in that blood-soaked streets of Celleos.

A sense of unease settled upon the trio as they observed the aftermath of this encounter. In contrast to their previous victories, an eerie difference unfolded before them. The bones of the fallen Alt, usually left behind as lifeless remnants, now radiated an otherworldly green glow. The luminosity intensified gradually, casting an ethereal hue across the scene. Then, with a mysterious grace, the bones themselves vanished from the slurry of remains, leaving the onlookers with a profound sense of uncertainty.

"Well, that's new," Jaw voiced with a hint of bewilderment as they witnessed the vanishing bones. He turned to find his two companions, Micharas and the hunter, locked in a spontaneous embrace. Jaw, perplexed, confronted the sudden shift in dynamics.

"Now I'm confused. A few minutes ago, it felt like there was a deep-seated rivalry between the two of you, and now this? Who exactly are you?" Jaw demanded, his tone reflecting the perplexity that hung in the air.

Chapter 5

Micharas, still holding the boy, "I am so happy you are safe. Where have you been?" he asked with a mixture of relief and curiosity.

"I haven't been gone that long, have I?" the boy remarked, an earnest honesty in his words, suggesting a genuine belief in the brevity of his absence. Micharas released him from the embrace but retained a tight hold on his vambraces. He stared at him for a moment, then his eyes widened. A look of shock and confusion swept over him as he turned to Jaw.

Jaw shrugged. "I still don't know who this is," he replied, as though waiting to be enlightened.

"Sorry," said the young archer, pulling free from Micharas's stunned grasp. Micharas watched as he extended a hand toward Jaw for a shake. "My name is Antonius. I'm Micharas's younger brother," he said, accompanied by a friendly smile.

"Ah, the brother that went missing," Jaw acknowledged, gratefully shaking Antonius's hand. "I am Jaw..." he began to introduce himself.

"Never mind that," Micharas interrupted, a sense of urgency in his voice. "Look at him. He has not aged a day since he disappeared!" Jaw, looking at the boy with a mix of concern and confusion, tried to grasp the significance.

"I can see that he is quite young, true, but this is my first time meeting him. I have nothing to compare his appearance to," Jaw joked, attempting to lighten the mood. However, Micharas didn't seem to find it amusing.

"Where have you been?" Micharas demanded, his tone now serious.

"What do you mean, not aged a day? How long do you think I have been gone?" Antonius asked, genuine concern evident in his voice as the mystery of his lost time unfolded.

"While I am sure this story will be very interesting," Jaw chimed in, "Are there not people still held up in the Town Hall? Perhaps they should take priority?"

"You are right," Antonius replied, turning his attention to Jaw. "So what happened here?" he asked as the two of them began to walk towards the Hall.

Micharas, grappling with the lingering shock, blinked heavily in an attempt to drag himself back to reality. The stress of the day had clearly taken its toll on him. He gripped at the air a few times before shooting off after the other two down the alley. "Wait for me!" he shouted, urgency cutting through his voice as he chased after them.

As the three men ran through the streets, they quickly filled in Antonius on the events that had led them to this conclusion. Micharas, still processing the newfound information about his brother's unchanged appearance, recounted the battles they had faced and the mysterious occurrences that unfolded in Celleos.

Antonius listened with a mix of astonishment and concern, occasionally glancing at Micharas as if trying to gauge his reaction. Jaw, in his typical straightforward manner, provided additional details and clarified certain points. The tale unfolded with the rhythm of their hurried footsteps echoing through the empty streets.

As they approached the grounds of the town hall, the imposing structure loomed before them. The air crackled with tension, not only from the recent battles but also from the unknown challenges that awaited them inside. The steps leading to the entrance seemed to stretch out, inviting yet foreboding.

Antonius, absorbing the gravity of the situation, finally spoke, "This is a lot to take in, but we need to focus on the task at hand. Let's check on the survivors and see what we're dealing with."

Micharas nodded, his mind still wrestling with the revelations about his brother. Jaw, ever pragmatic, added, "Once we ensure everyone's safety, we can figure out the rest. Let's go."

The trio ascended the steps of the town hall, their collective determination pushing them forward.

The resounding thuds broke the silence of the quiet dusk of the day as Micharas forcefully knocked on the imposing doors of the town hall. The heavy silence that followed was broken by the distinct sound of metal clashing against the ground, indicating the swift approach of Sir Erik, the town's formidable defender.

"Who is it? Micharas, is that you?" Sir Erik's voice, tinged with a mix of concern and anticipation, reverberated through the sturdy wooden door.

With a joyful tone that betrayed his relief, Micharas confirmed, "It is, Sir Erik!" His voice carried the weight of a man who had faced uncertainties and emerged victorious.

A sense of trepidation coloured Sir Erik's next question. "Do you have an army? Is the town safe once more?" The situation weighed heavily on his words.

With a deep breath, Micharas responded, his relief palpable in his words, "I don't have an army, but I brought back help. The town is ours again. It's finally over." There was a quiver in his voice, as if the emotional toll of the recent events threatened to overwhelm him.

As they stood there, absorbing the gravity of the moment, another set of urgent footsteps approached the doors. A stern and yet slightly piggy sounding voice cut through the air, commanding, "Get out of my way." The trio listened as Sir Erik stepped back, and the strained grunts of a man working to remove an obstruction reached their ears.

A sigh accompanied the new voice, "Remove this barricade at once," he ordered, the weight of authority evident in his voice.

"Of course, Sir," came the prompt and respectful reply from Sir Erik, a man dedicated to maintaining order and safeguarding the town. The door creaked open, revealing a short, stout man in his mid-forties. His figure was engulfed by a long, flowing white gown that almost touched the ground. A chainmail hood rested back across his shoulders, contrasting with a full set of steel-plated armour proudly adorned with the Celleos insignia – a blue dragon coiled around a grove of trees on the breastplate.

Upon noticing the trio, the man's gaze flicked up, but he quickly averted his eyes, seemingly uninterested. In a shrill and ungrateful tone, he began to push past them, all the while loudly airing his grievances about the state of his town. His remarks were crafted to make it sound like the trio was responsible for the town's current condition.

"I can't believe the audacity! Look at the state of Celleos! What have you been doing all this time?" he exclaimed, casting accusing glances at Micharas, Jaw, and Antonius. "It's a disgrace! Do you think this is how a town should be maintained? Oh, no, not at all! Unbelievable!"

He continued his tirade, making sure to emphasise each word as though the trio bore the sole responsibility for the town's apparent decay.

Micharas, choosing to ignore the incessant complaints of the short man, turned his attention back to the doorway where a tall and proud figure stood. The man was almost six foot five inches tall, dressed head to toe in silver-plated armour. Despite its clear expense, the armour had no unnecessary trimmings or embellishments, reflecting a modest yet imposing appearance. A long white cloak hung from his shoulders, proudly displaying the mark of the Celleos Guard. His sword, a large claymore, was secured on his back.

This imposing figure was none other than Sir Erik, Captain of the Guard. As Micharas approached him, relief and gratitude etched across his face, he gestured towards his companions.

"Sir Erik, allow me to introduce Jaw, a steadfast warrior and ally who helped us reclaim the town," Micharas said, indicating the sturdy man beside him. "And this is Antonius, my younger brother, who has returned after being missing for some time."

Sir Erik's green eyes widened in a mix of surprise and acknowledgment. "A warrior, a brother returned. It seems today brings both challenges and blessings," he remarked, extending a hand to Jaw and then to Antonius. "Thank you for your assistance. The town owes you a debt of gratitude." He grasped their hands in his tight grip as he greeted them.

Jaw and Antonius both nodded in acknowledgment, expressing their readiness to assist further if needed.

As Jaw, and Antonius were engrossed in their introductions to Sir Erik, the persistent short man interrupted, reclaiming the attention with his whiny voice as he ascended the stairs toward them.

"What about this town?" he complained, his tone demanding immediate attention. Micharas sighed, offering a begrudging introduction, "And this is our leader, Sir Shane."

Jaw extended a hand in a gesture of greeting, but Sir Shane merely looked at it with disdain before pushing past, displaying a clear lack of respect. Standing at roughly 4 feet 6 inches tall and equally as wide, Sir Shane's glistening face reflected the light of the setting sun, hinting at a mixture of animal fats or perhaps sweat from his climb up the stairs. His shoulder-length brown hair and perfectly trimmed goatee added a peculiar touch to his round demeanour.

"I appreciate your help, gentlemen, but I will take it from here," he declared, implying that he had been actively involved in the efforts thus far. With a dismissive "Right," he turned towards Sir Erik, a scowl of rage gradually spreading across his round little face.

Sir Erik, realising the error of his impertinence, promptly took a knee. "Better," Sir Shane remarked, observing as his subordinate knelt before him. "Go and release the peasants from the function room. They need to start making this all..." He gestured broadly at the town with loathing in his tone. Lacking words to describe his disgust at the state of it, he bellowed, "Better!"

Sir Erik rose to his feet with practised efficiency, acknowledging Sir Shane's command. He promptly left to carry out the instructions, leaving the trio of Micharas, Jaw, and Antonius standing before Sir Shane.

"You are free to go," Sir Shane declared dismissively, as though casting them aside. Jaw and Antonius exchanged puzzled glances, clearly taken aback by the abruptness.

"Hold on a damn..." Antonius began, his anger evident in his voice. However, his protest was swiftly interrupted as Micharas seized him and dragged him away by the scruff of his neck. Jaw, sensing the need to follow, trailed behind the brothers as they exited the gardens of the hall.

Before long the streets outside were now filled with the bustle of people leaving the hall, but the energy was far from the usual liveliness of the town. Despite the multitude of lives saved, the atmosphere remained heavy with grief. Many had lost their lives, and the destruction was unparalleled. The once well-kept and loved homes now lay in ruins, belongings destroyed by the rain or the fire. The streets, which had recently stood in solemn silence, now echoed with the wails of sorrow and despair. The return to their homes brought little solace to the town's inhabitants, faced with the heartbreaking reality of their losses.

As the last remnants of daylight faded, the trio found themselves standing by the gate, contemplating their next move.

Antonius, with a sense of curiosity and eagerness, broke the silence. "What now?"

Jaw, considering the events of the day, spoke up, "Well, I guess I'll return in a few days to talk with Sir Shane."

Micharas, however, had a different plan in mind. "Nonsense," he insisted, looking at Jaw. "You must be shattered after the day we've had. The least I can do is return the favour and offer you a bed for the night."

Jaw hesitated for a moment, appreciating the offer but not wanting to impose. "That's very kind, but I wouldn't want to intrude. I'm sure the two of you have a lot to catch up on."

Micharas was persistent. "I insist. I can cook something for us to eat while I catch up with my brother. Plus, I would love to hear what you plan to do next. I assume you want to move into the town?"

"Something like that," Jaw replied with a smile, recognizing the practicality of Micharas's suggestion.

"Very well. Lead the way," Jaw agreed, allowing Micharas to guide them towards a night that promised more than just rest. The journey back to Micharas's place became an opportunity for the three men to share their thoughts, plans, and reflections on the day's events.

As they walked through the darkened streets, Micharas spoke, "You know, Jaw, Antonius here has been missing for quite some time. I've been trying to find him for years. The fact that he hasn't aged a day since he disappeared is... bewildering, to say the least."

Antonius, chiming in, added with a touch of humour, "I haven't been gone that long, have I?"

The brothers exchanged glances, their connection evident in the unspoken understanding between them. Micharas, however, couldn't shake the shock of seeing his brother again after so long, unchanged by the passage of time.

Jaw, sensing the weight of the moment, asked, "How did this happen? And where have you been all this time, Antonius?"

Antonius, now the centre of attention, began recounting his journey, unveiling a tale that was both mysterious and captivating. As the conversation unfolded, the trio weaved through the dimly lit streets, the night air carrying the echoes of a story that seemed to transcend the boundaries of time itself.

"I was out hunting in the morning, no more than just a few days ago..." Antonius began to explain.

The morning sun still lazily rising, casting a warm golden glow across the landscape. The stream nearby whispered tales of serenity as its crystal-clear waters meandered through the heart of the forest.

Antonius was on the hunt, moving with the quiet grace that comes with familiarity with the terrain. The forest was alive with the hum of nature awakening. Birds greeted the day with melodic symphonies, and a gentle breeze rustled the leaves overhead. The air was crisp, carrying the earthy fragrance of moss and pine.

"As I crouched by the stream, my senses heightened. I could hear the babbling water, the rustle of leaves, and the distant calls of woodland creatures. Ahead of me, a deer grazed peacefully, oblivious to my presence." The morning painted a scene of tranquillity, a canvas of nature untouched by the unseen danger that awaited him.

Antonius drew his bow, the wood creaking ever so softly, and an arrow, finely crafted and feathered, nestled against the bowstring. With each heartbeat, he synchronised his breathing with the rhythm of the forest. The world narrowed to the target before him, and he marvelled at the beauty of the moment.

"With a deliberate exhale, I released the arrow." Its flight an extension of Antonius's intention. For a brief instant, time seemed to pause as the projectile soared gracefully, cutting through the morning air. The world held its breath, and in that suspended moment, the forest embraced the elegant dance between predator and prey.

Yet, the tranquillity was shattered, not by the echo of his arrow finding its mark, nor the cry of an animal defeated. But by an unexpected force. Something struck the back of Antonius's head, jolting him out of the hunter's trance. Antonius watched as the forest fell away beneath him, leaving him in nothing but darkness.

As the three weary men approached Micharas's home, the silhouette of the modest structure stood resilient against the dimming twilight. The outer walls bore scars of time, but it seemed to have escaped the rampant destruction that marred the rest of the town.

The door, though slightly ajar, swung open with a creak as Micharas pushed it gently. They entered the main room as the scene unfolded in the faint moonlight filtering through the windows. The furniture, normally arranged with a semblance of order, now lay scattered. Chairs were haphazardly placed, and one lay broken on the floor. The air inside carried the cool scent of pine mixed with a subtle hint of ash.

Micharas led the way, acknowledging the disarray. "Looks like the Alts paid a visit," he remarked, eyeing the broken chair. "Surprisingly, they didn't make as much of a mess as I expected."

The fireplace, standing against one wall, seemed untouched. Micharas knelt down, assessing the situation. He picked up the broken chair, a casualty of the recent turmoil, and placed it carefully in the hearth. "This should make for good kindling," he said, taking a tinderbox and striking two pieces of flint together to ignite the fire.

As the flames embraced the makeshift fuel, the room gradually filled with a warm, flickering glow. Shadows danced on the walls, revealing the scars and trophies of Micharas's life as a hunter. The broken chair, now consumed by fire, symbolised resilience amid chaos—a theme that resonated throughout the town.

"Make yourselves comfortable," Micharas invited, picking up the other chairs and righting the table. "I'll get a stew going, and we can talk more."

The fire's warmth began to dispel the evening chill as Micharas busied himself, making some food. The other two men, Jaw and Antonius, found seats amid the rearranged chairs.

The walls of the room, bathed in the flickering light, displayed a hunter's legacy. Mounted antlers filled the spaces above the fireplace, each pair a trophy to a victorious pursuit. A collection of handcrafted bows, carefully strung and maintained, hung from hooks. Between them, a modest assortment of knives and daggers gleamed in the firelight.

A pheasant, its feathers resplendent, hung from a peg near the door. It seemed to have been a recent catch, still awaiting Micharas's skilled hands for preparation. The floor, beneath their feet, bore the weight of a sturdy pelt rug—a testament to the harshness of the wild and the resilience of those who navigated it.

As Micharas worked on the stew, the room transformed into a tableau of the hunt, a fusion of rustic charm and practical necessity. Two other doors remained closed, their mysteries hidden for now. One could only wonder what lay beyond —perhaps more trophies, tools of the trade, or the quiet solitude of Micharas's personal space.

Antonius settled in his chair as he continued to recount his harrowing tale. "I woke up, some time later. I was no longer in the forest, that much was certain. Instead, I found myself chained to a wall in a dungeon."

The flickering flames seemed to emphasise the horror of his words, the warmth of the fire, a contrast to the cold reality of Antonius's captivity. Jaw leaned forward, his eyes intent on the narrative unfolding in the dimly lit room.

"The air was damp, and the stench of decay lingered. The only sound, the occasional drip of water echoing in the cold, stone confines. I strained against the chains, but it was futile. I couldn't recall how I ended up there or who had captured me."

Antonius continued his narrative, the firelight casting shadows on the walls as he unveiled the darker chapters of his captivity. "Before me, there was a table covered in tools, clearly designed for torture. I scanned the room, but there was no light, no windows. As I peered through the darkness, I could only make out the vague shapes of objects around me."

The room seemed to close in, the trophies on the walls now silent witnesses to a more sinister tale. Jaw's expression mirrored the growing unease in the room.

"As I hung there, all I could think about was how much my head was throbbing with pain and wondering what was going to happen next. I was left there in the dark for what seemed an eternity, but in reality, it was probably no more than a few hours."

A chilling sensation swept through the room as Antonius described the oppressive darkness that had enveloped him. Then finally a reprieve came in the form of a sliver of light, teasing him from under and around the door at the end of the dungeon. His senses heightened as he listened intently, the sound of footsteps down the corridor signalling an ominous turn in his captivity.

The door creaked open, revealing a grubby little Alt male. He shuffled into the room, his hunched figure casting a shadow against the dimly lit chamber. The sputtering candle holder he carried barely illuminated his twisted features. His black eyes, narrow and malicious, glinted in the feeble light. His white ghost-like skin reflected the flame. He wore brown dirty clothes that hung from him as though designed for a specimen of more suitable stature.

Taking a moment to look up at Antonius, the Alt placed the candle holder on the table furnished with torture devices. The metallic instruments gleamed threateningly, reflecting the grim purpose they served. The darkness seemed to encroach further as the Alt turned his attention to Antonius.

The Alt's voice slithered through the stale air, his words a guttural murmur that seemed to originate from the depths of malevolence. "You'll tell us what we want to know, one way or another," he hissed, his tone dripping with sadistic delight. The shadows played on his contorted face, emphasising the sinister angles of his features.

Antonius, still disoriented from the blow to his head, strained to comprehend the Alt's threat. The Alt leaned in closer, his breath carrying the acrid scent of dampness and decay. "Your secrets will spill like blood, staining the pages of our victory," he continued, each word a venomous whisper.

He turned and began to select an object from the table before him. The Alt's hand closed around one such instrument, its surface coated in a rusty patina that hinted of agony and suffering. The dim candlelight revealed its twisted contours, casting elongated shadows that danced along its cruel silhouette. Grotesque shapes and jagged edges stuck out in all directions, hinting at a purpose most unforgiving. As the Alt examined it with a malevolent fascination, the very essence of the instrument seemed to exude an aura of dread, as if it held the secrets of torment within its corroded frame.

More footsteps taunted in the corridor, heralding the arrival of multiple figures. The grubby Alt, his evil intentions momentarily set aside, hurriedly returned the sinister tool to its place and assumed an unsettlingly upright posture.

Two distinct figures emerged into the dimly lit dungeon. The first was the large Alt, whose towering and imposing frame filled the doorway. His grotesque appearance was reminiscent of the one that they had encountered in the streets, yet there was an eerie sense of alteration in the creature's features. His armour was different, less of it and yet it was undoubtedly the same brute.

Beside the large Alt stood the witch, her silhouette draped in a tattered robe that seemed to dance with evil intent. The air seemed to thicken as she entered, her presence exuding an unnatural aura. Though Antonius recognized her from their earlier confrontation, there lingered an intangible transformation between this one and the one that they fought. Again her attire was less grand, her presence less threatening and yet the two of them still exuded the same level of unease as they had in the street.

As the duo cast their unsettling gazes upon Antonius, the dim candle light flickered, casting harrowing shadows that accentuated the disquieting ambiance of the dungeon.

"This is the poacher that you picked up from Thorn Woods?" she inquired, her voice carrying a chilling elegance. The monstrous Alt, standing beside her, responded in a gravelly voice, "It is, my Lady."

The witch shifted her attention to the torturer, her eyes penetrating as she sought information. "And what have we found out from him so far?" The Alt began to explain that he had only recently arrived before them, but his words were abruptly silenced by the witch's raised hand, halting his explanation. "Come and find me when you have something then," she commanded, her presence leaving the room as she continued down the corridor.

As she departed, the witch left a lingering air of uncertainty. The smaller of the Alts, standing before Antonius, grumbled in an attempt to convey respect, though his twisted form betrayed any semblance of true deference. "Is there anything in particular you wish to know from this one?" he asked. The witch's response was succinct and ominous: "Everything." With that, she turned and left, leaving the Alt to decipher his orders.

The creature snarled after her inquiry about the body, seeking clarification. "Do with it as you see fit. Once he is dead, I have no further use for him," the witch replied without a backward glance. The Alt, visibly more at ease in his twisted posture, cast a smile upwards toward Antonius, anticipation and malice glinting in his eyes. The huge Alt, having taken a final glance at the captive, closed the dungeon door with a resounding thud.

Antonius, recounting the chilling event, found himself back in the present as his older brother, Micharas, began distributing bowls of food. The echoes of fading footsteps down the hall marked the diminishing chance for survival and freedom.

"So what happened next?" Jaw asked inquisitively. "Did you die?" he joked with a cheeky grin. While Antonius had been talking, Jaw had already been thinking about this joke, checking his companion's face for visible signs of scarring or torture. In the lack of any evidence to suggest that he had come to harm, Jaw came to the conclusion that while it might not be in the best taste, at least it should not cause major offence.

Micharas looked at him in disgust, but before he could begin berating him for such an unempathetic question, he was interrupted by Antonius.

Antonius, his expression a mix of weariness and a hint of a bitter smile, responded to Jaw's question. "Well, I'm standing here, aren't I? So, no, I didn't die," he said, his tone slightly lifted from the forced humour. Jaw's attempt at humour earned a disapproving look from Micharas, who seemed ready to reprimand him.

As the men continued to eat, Antonius's gaze drifted into a distant stare, his eyes fixed on his food but clearly lost in the haunting corridors of memory. Both Jaw and Micharas exchanged concerned glances, silently acknowledging the weight of the past that Antonius carried.

Suddenly, Micharas, seeing his brother lost in thought, gently nudged him. "What happened next?" he asked, bringing Antonius back to the present.

In the dungeon, as the Alt reached for a torture device once more, a wicked grin played on his lips. "This is going to be fun," he mumbled sinisterly. Antonius, anticipating the impending pain, closed his eyes and looked away, bracing himself. The room was filled with a bright flash of light, and as Antonius cautiously opened his eyes, he saw another figure standing there. It seemed like an angel, a saviour amidst the darkness.

The angel swiftly waved his hand towards the Alt and shouted the words, "Convert Gas!" His tone was devoid of remorse as the Alt crumbled to its knees. Seemingly gasping for breath, the spell had stripped its lungs of air, leaving it suffocating on the ground. The room, once filled with the Alt's destructive presence, now echoed with the sound of its desperate struggle for air. The sudden shift in the atmosphere left Antonius both relieved and awe-stricken by the angel's powerful intervention.

The figure then quickly stepped over the dying Alt, waved his hands at the shackles that bound Antonius, and calmly instructed them to "Release." With a clank, the locks that bound him let go, and he fell to the floor, his arms strained from his time hanging from the wall. Antonius reached up to grab the outstretched hand of the figure bathed in light.

"The moment our hands touched, he was gone, and I was in Celleos, standing on one of the walls, watching the two of you entering the Guard House. I had my bow and my quiver on me. Oh, and this," Antonius concluded, suddenly remembering a small token that he had completely neglected until now.

He reached inside his quiver and from out of the lining retrieved a small piece of parchment, it had been folded in half and for some reason was addressed to "The Celleos Heroes".

"Well, I guess that's us," Micharas said, as Antonius handed the note to his brother. Micharas studied it, and the two brothers exchanged puzzled glances.

"What do you make of this?" Jaw asked, leaning forward to get a better look.

Antonius furrowed his brow. "It seems like a list of places, but why are the first four crossed off?"

"Maybe those are places where something already happened, and we're somehow involved?" Jaw suggested.

Micharas nodded in agreement. "Could be a list of locations affected by recent events, and we're being called to action."

Antonius traced his finger over the names on the parchment. "The Xanthian Halls, Dampwell Village, Dedbell Village, Celleos, The Eastland Castle, Astius and Darkmist Village." "What could connect these places?"

Jaw pondered for a moment. "Are they in any particular order? Could it be a journey or a sequence?"

Micharas shook his head. "Doesn't seem to be in any logical order. They could be following the road from the West, but the Xanthian Halls are to the far North so that doesn't seem right, and if it's coming from the West then there are a lot of places missing between them. Maybe it's random, or maybe the order doesn't matter."

Micharas got up from the table and began making the group a cup of warm mead that he had sitting in a pitcher not too far from the fire. He returned and distributed them among the others.

Antonius took a thoughtful sip of his drink. "Could it be places where something is yet to happen? And the first four are already resolved?"

"That's an interesting thought," Jaw mused. "Like a checklist, and the first four are ticked off."

Micharas stood up, collecting the empty bowls. "Whatever the case, it seems we have a new mission ahead."

Jaw looked at the other two. "So how do we proceed from here?" he asked.

Micharas pondered for a moment before suggesting, "I think our first step should be to visit Sir Erik tomorrow. He might have some insights or information that could help us make sense of this note."

Antonius nodded in agreement, his weariness evident in his eyes. "Sounds like a plan. I'm curious to see what he makes of all this."

As the trio continued discussing their next steps, Antonius slowly looked up, he was suddenly aware that someone had been watching them. His gaze fixed on the window. A hooded figure stood there, shrouded in darkness. Antonius let out a small cough, unassuming but obviously an attempt to grab the other two's attention.

The party swiftly grabbed their weapons, Micharas with his trusty bow, Jaw with his formidable sword, and Antonius with his own bow. They rushed outside, adrenaline pumping, ready for a confrontation. However, to their surprise, there was nothing there. The figure had vanished.

Micharas squinted into the darkness. "Must be exhaustion playing tricks on us," he concluded. "Let's get some sleep. We can't make sense of anything in this state."

Reluctantly, they headed back inside, their weapons still in hand. Micharas sighed, "It's been a long day. We need rest." He clapped Jaw on the shoulder as he passed him. Before closing the door, Jaw tilted his head back, gazing at the starry night sky.

The heavens seemed to stretch infinitely, each star telling a tale of distant worlds. The crisp night air whispered through the streets, and for a moment, the weight of their quest felt distant, replaced by the vastness of the cosmos. He listened intently to the world around him and noticed a faint dripping sound, like rain droplets sliding from the rooftop into a bucket of water. With a smile to himself and a sideways glance down the street, he went back into the house.

Micharas led the way, showing Jaw to his room, the door creaking open to reveal a space that exuded a rustic charm. The flickering glow of a bedside candle revealed a comfortable bed with a simple yet well-made quilt, and a small wooden nightstand stood sentinel. The walls, adorned with various trophies from Micharas's hunting expeditions, painted a story of a life intertwined with the wild.

"Make yourself at home, Jaw," Micharas offered with a small smile, the room resonating with the earthy scent of seasoned wood. A small window, complete with a thin curtain that swayed gently in the night breeze, offered a view of the moonlit woods.

As Micharas headed toward the spare room, Antonius observed his surroundings. The spare room, though not as decorated, had its own quaint charm. A pair of twin beds stood against opposite walls, covered with neatly folded blankets. A simple wooden dresser and a modest wardrobe provided the essentials for the night.

"Cosy enough," Antonius remarked, looking at the beds, which seemed to invite a peaceful night's rest. The spare room lacked the personalised touch of Micharas's own, but it emanated a sense of warmth nonetheless.

The three companions settled in for the night, the flickering light of the fire casting dancing shadows across the main room. The note rested on the table, a silent reminder of the mysteries that awaited them. As sleep claimed them one by one, the night held its secrets, and the world outside awaited the dawn of a new day.

Chapter 6

In the early hours of the morning, before the first rays of sunlight painted the sky, Jaw quietly rose from his slumber. The others still slept, and as dawn beckoned him, he chose to embrace the quiet solitude of the waking town. Dressed and ready, he ventured into the streets of Celleos for a morning walk.

The cobblestone streets welcomed Jaw with a hushed serenity. The town, illuminated in the gentle hues of pre-dawn, was a canvas of subdued colours awaiting the touch of sunlight. The few early risers moved about, each engaged in their own small efforts to mend the wounds inflicted upon their beloved town.

As Jaw strolled through the awakening streets, he witnessed a quiet symphony of resilience. The rising sun painted the buildings with warm tones, casting long shadows that told stories of yesterday's challenges and today's determination. The air, still kissed by the chill of dawn, gradually warmed with the sun's ascent, creating an atmosphere of both hope and renewal.

The townsfolk, like silent artists, engaged in the delicate dance of restoration. A baker swept the front steps of his shop, sorrow carved on his face as he prepared for a new day. Children, armed with makeshift brooms, joined the collective effort to clear debris from the streets.

Damaged facades stood as a reminder to the trials faced by the town, but amid the remnants of destruction, a spirit of unity prevailed. Residents, sleeves rolled up and hearts aligned, worked together to rebuild what had been lost.

Jaw, a silent observer in the early morning stillness, absorbed the hum of conversation and the rhythmic sounds of repair work. Laughter, though tinged with fatigue, resonated with a newfound camaraderie. The town, bruised but undefeated, was determined to rise from the ashes.

The morning sun, now fully embracing Celleos, became a beacon of hope. As Jaw continued his walk, the warmth inspired him and those around him to envision a brighter future.

The early morning light cast a warm glow on the somewhat familiar street that Jaw traversed. Though many of these houses seemed new in their construction, despite the damage that they had sustained from battle there were a few of them that told tales of an earlier era, with stories etched into their timeworn walls. A time before this town was surrounded by walls, when most of these homes were just farmland.

Jaw halted before an old dilapidated building, its exterior bearing the marks of a mystery unsolved. Vines climbed the cracked walls, attempting to reclaim what was once abandoned. The roof, now missing a few tiles, exposed timbers worn by the passage of time. Faint echoes of a forgotten past lingered in the air, telling stories of lives lived within these walls.

The building, though untouched by the recent flames of warfare, carried a darkness that seemed to transcend the physical damage. Jaw approached an old gate, rusted by years of neglect, and with a creak, he pushed it open. The path beyond was overgrown, reclaiming its territory from the hands of civilization. Weeds and wildflowers stood tall, as if nature itself sought to blanket the scars of human history.

Jaw proceeded up the path, each step resonating with a sense of intrusion into the forgotten. The air around the old building held a mysterious energy, and as Jaw ventured closer, he felt an unspoken connection to the tales concealed within its crumbling walls.

Jaw threw his shoulder into the stubborn door, its rusty hinges protesting with a haunting screech before relenting to the force. The smell of charred wood and lingering ashes greeted him as he stepped over the threshold. The interior, once the heart of a bustling farmhouse, now lay in ruins, evidence to the unforgiving power of fire. The earthy aroma of damp soil, intertwined with the delicate fragrance of wildflowers and the faint whisper of a passing breeze, permeated the air.

The atmosphere inside, once weighed down by the tragedy of a long-extinguished fire, now felt more like an ancient conversation between the building and the encroaching wilderness.

Broken furniture lay scattered, some overtaken by vines that coiled around the once defined edges of their design, while others bore the scars of a blaze that had danced through the rooms in a forgotten ballet.

As he explored, Jaw traced through the imprints of destruction etched into the remains. A skeletal fireplace stood as a sombre witness to the warmth that once filled the space, now reduced to a silent relic. The old dwelling seemed to breathe with a history seeking preservation, not in the midst of decay but rather in the gentle embrace of nature's tendrils.

Moving through what once might have been a kitchen, he encountered a cracked bowl, an artefact from a time when the heartbeat of family life emanated from within these walls. The muted echoes of laughter and the aromas of long-lost meals lingered in the air. He closed his eyes for a moment and inhaled briefly, fooling himself into smelling the food cooking.

The exploration of the farmhouse unfolded like a journey through time, with each room revealing a silent narrative of resilience against the ravages of the fiery tempest of its past. The home, now embraced by nature, exuded a quiet beauty—a testament to the cyclical dance between decay and renewal.

Jaw carefully crouched down among the remnants of what was once a bedroom. The furniture, now reduced to chunks of charred wood, bore the brunt of the fire's wrath. This room had been the epicentre of the destructive flames that had consumed the farmhouse.

As he explored the room, the sun streamed through the holes in the roof, casting perfect beams of light through the dust that had lain settled for more than a decade. He noticed a peculiar stone slab near the window. With a deliberate movement, Jaw dislodged the stone, revealing the outside world to the insects that scurried away from the sudden intrusion of light.

Beneath the stone, coated in cobwebs and dust, lay a small wooden box. Jaw delicately lifted it, cradling it in his hands as though it held a precious part of his life. The box seemed to emanate a silent energy. The room, now silent except for the rustle of leaves and the distant bustling streets.

Jaw carefully opened the small wooden box, revealing its precious contents. Nestled within the weathered interior was a single coin. Crafted from platinum, the coin bore the symbol of a crown on one face, regal and commanding. The other side showcased an intricate design, each detail a testament to the artistry of its creation.

As Jaw delicately lifted the coin from its resting place, he marvelled at the weight of history held within its polished surface. He rolled it over the back of his fingers, feeling the cool metal against his skin. Running it between his thumb and index finger, he traced the contours of the crown and the delicate patterns that were engraved onto the opposite side.

Lost in his contemplation, a sudden movement above startled him. A crow, perched on a rafter, took flight, its wings slicing through the air with a sharp rustle. The unexpected departure of the bird brought him back to the present.

Clutching the coin tightly in his hand he made his way back across town to

Micharas's house.

As he approached the house he noticed smoke coming out of the chimney. He pushed the door open and entered Micharas's home, the morning sun casting a warm glow across the room. And the inviting aroma of breakfast filled the air. Micharas was already busy in the kitchen, and greeted him with a smile.

"Good morning," Micharas said, glancing up from the stove. "Up for an early stroll, I see. Take a seat; breakfast will be ready in a moment."

Jaw nodded appreciatively and settled into a chair at the table. The room was filled with the comforting sounds of sizzling food and the promise of a satisfying meal. As Micharas continued to prepare breakfast, the two engaged in casual conversation about the upcoming day.

"So, anything interesting happening in the town?" Micharas asked, flipping some sausages in the pan.

Jaw leaned back in his chair, considering the question. "Not as far as I could tell. people are just trying to proceed with their lives, pick up the pieces and move on, you know?"

Micharas nodded thoughtfully. "That's all that they can really do now."

Micharas skillfully worked in the kitchen, the enticing aroma of sausages and scrambled eggs filling the room. The small talk between Jaw and Micharas continued until Antonius, rubbing sleep from his eyes, joined them.

"Just in time for breakfast," Micharas exclaimed with a grin, dishing out generous portions onto three plates. Antonius, still shaking off the last remnants of sleep, yawned and scratched his head. "What are you two talking about?" he inquired as he entered the room.

"Nothing important, eat up, and we can go to see Sir Erik about the note," Micharas informed him, placing a plate in front of Antonius and then Jaw. The room now filled with the savoury scent of breakfast, the trio settled down to enjoy the meal.

"I still don't understand," Micharas voiced his confusion as the trio walked down the street towards the Guard House. "How exactly did you go missing eight years ago to me, but only a few days ago to you and then return to this time at the same age that you left?" he continued, his perplexity evident in his furrowed brow.

Antonius shrugged, his expression mirroring his lack of comprehension. "How should I know?"

"Some sort of magic, if I had to guess," Jaw added to the conversation, attempting to find a reasonable explanation that didn't require much more thought on the subject.

Jaw, always one for breaking the tension with a bit of humour, decided to lighten the mood. He looked up at the sky, squinting in the sunlight, and then turned to his companions with a grin.

"Beautiful day we have here, isn't it?" he said, gesturing towards the clear blue sky.

Antonius glanced up, acknowledging the weather. "Indeed, it's a welcome change from the recent chaos."

Micharas chuckled, appreciating the attempt to shift the conversation. "True enough. At least the weather seems to be on our side today."

"Maybe the Gods decided we've had enough drama for now and threw in some sunshine for good measure," Jaw joked, his eyes twinkling with mischief.

Antonius couldn't help but smile. "Well, I'm not one to question the gods. If they want to brighten our day, who am I to argue?"

As the trio approached the tattered Guard House, their playful banter echoed against its dilapidated walls. The once-proud structure bore the scars of battle, it remained standing yet was nothing more than a hollow, desanctified, husk of its former self.

Within sight of the Guard House, Sir Erik's efforts to bolster the town's defences were evident. New recruits, drawn from the dwindling pool of able-bodied residents, gathered under his watchful eye, undergoing training to protect what remained of their home. The atmosphere hummed with a mix of determination and uncertainty.

Two guards stationed at the entrance engaged in lighthearted banter as the trio approached. "Halt, who goes there?" one of the guards bellowed in a jestful tone, a spark of camaraderie in his eyes. Their faces lit up with recognition, and one of them, a burly man with a thick beard, called out in a jovial tone, "Well, well, if it ain't Micharas! You bringing some trouble to our doorstep, or just here to share some of those legendary sausages of yours?"

The other guard, a younger fellow with a mischievous glint in his eye, chimed in, "I heard those sausages can conquer even the fiercest hunger. Any chance you brought some for us, Micharas?"

Micharas laughed heartily, his friendship with the guards evident in the easy camaraderie. "Ah, you know me too well! Unfortunately, no sausages today we're actually here to see Sir Erik about something important. Business, you could say."

The younger guard added, "Business? Sounds serious. Should we be on our best behaviour, then?"

Antonius, joining the banter, replied with a smirk, "Best behaviour would be appreciated. We're here to discuss a matter of some delicacy with Sir Erik."

The burly guard, now wearing a more serious expression, nodded understandingly. "Got it. Well, you know where to find him. Good luck with your business, and maybe next time bring some of those sausages."

As the party entered the ground of the Guard House, they observed the training grounds filled with new recruits practising swordplay under the watchful eye of Sir Erik. However, their attention was quickly drawn to a hooded, cloaked figure engaged in conversation with the captain. Antonius nudged his brother, pointing out the stranger.

"That's the person that was outside the house last night," Antonius asserted, his tone carrying an accusatory edge. Though uncertainty lingered, Micharas decided to address the situation diplomatically.

Approaching Sir Erik and the hooded figure, Micharas greeted them with a nod. "Good day, Sir Erik. It seems we've arrived at an interesting moment. May we join your conversation?"

Sir Erik turned toward the newcomers, recognizing them. "Ah, Micharas, good to see you. Of course, join us. I was just discussing matters of importance with our mysterious friend here."

The hooded figure remained silent, their attention focused on the captain and the approaching group. Sir Erik gestured to the newcomers. "This is Micharas, a long-standing friend and ally. And these are his companions."

Micharas exchanged pleasantries, though his gaze lingered on the hooded figure. Antonius extended his hand in a gesture of amicable introduction, offering a handshake to the mysterious stranger. However, the figure, clad in a dark set of luxurious purple robes, did not reciprocate the gesture. Instead, they watched the group with an air of uncertainty. The robes, crafted with intricate details, flowed down the figure's body in a regal manner, hinting at a certain opulence.

The face of the stranger remained entirely obscured by a veil of magical darkness emanating from their hood. This enchanted shroud concealed their features, leaving an air of mystery in their wake. The robes hung loosely from their shoulders, carefully designed to conceal the shape of their frame and all other clothing underneath. A matching cloak, complete with the same level of craftsmanship, cascaded down, adding to the air of mystique surrounding them.

Long, wide sleeves gracefully dangled from their arms, adding a touch of elegance to their attire. Matching gloves completed the ensemble, seamlessly blending with the overall dark and enigmatic theme. The stranger stood like a spectre, a silent presence veiled in purple, their gaze piercing through the magical darkness that shrouded their face.

Jaw, taken aback by the stranger's cold reception and apparent reluctance to reciprocate the customary gesture of a handshake, felt a surge of frustration and suspicion. The recent encounters with the Alt mage had left a lingering distrust in his mind, and the perceived rudeness of the hooded figure only added fuel to the fire.

Without a moment's hesitation, Jaw drew his sword, the metallic blade gleaming in the sunlight. His companions, Micharas and Antonius, exchanged surprised glances, not expecting such a swift and drastic reaction. The tension in the air escalated as the blade was unsheathed, the steel reflecting the uncertainty that now hung between the two parties.

"Enough of this cloak-and-dagger act!" Jaw exclaimed, his frustration evident in his voice. "If you're here to talk, then talk. But we won't tolerate disrespect."

The figure remained silent, the magical darkness still shrouding their face, and a palpable unease settled over the group. The guard recruits practising in the yard paused their training, eyeing the unfolding scene with wary curiosity. The Guard House grounds became a stage for a confrontation fueled by mistrust and an urgent need for answers.

The hooded figure's hands rose in a gesture of peace, prompting a cautious relaxation from Micharas and Antonius, who had poised to draw their weapons the moment she had begun to raise her arms. As the stranger reached for the edges of the hood, a shattering sound echoed through the air, like a glass hitting the stone floor in an empty temple. And with it the magical darkness dissipated. In its wake emerged a woman.

She stood before them, a vision unveiled, her appearance transcending the mundane. Pale in complexion, her eyes bore the deep, mesmerising hue of ethereal waters, drawing one into their depths. Long brown tresses cascaded down her shoulders like a flowing river, an earthly contrast to the enchanting pools within her gaze.

Her allure wasn't readily apparent; it lingered beneath the surface, a subtle grace that whispered of something extraordinary. The simplicity of her presence belied a profound beauty, leaving the beholder to uncover the layers of elegance that unfolded with every glance.

The mysterious woman extended her hands in a calming gesture as she spoke, her voice carrying a soft yet authoritative resonance that sought to soothe

the tension in the air.

"I understand your caution, especially in times like these," she began, her eyes reflecting a sincere intent. "But I am not your enemy. My purpose here is not to bring harm but to offer assistance. The threads of destiny have woven us together, and I am here to guide you through the intricacies that lie ahead."

Jaw, his grip still firm on his sword, eyed her with scepticism. "Destiny is not my friend. It is a path walked by others who are incapable of carving one for themselves."

The woman's gaze held a depth of understanding, as if she carried the weight of the world's uncertainties. "I do not expect blind trust. My actions will speak louder than my words."

At that moment, Sir Erik cut into the conversation in a hope of disarming the situation "Jaw, Antonius, Micharas, I can vouch for Lady Katherine here," he said with a nod towards the woman. "When we were besieged by the Alt, she cast a powerful spell over the town hall, concealing it from their prying eyes. Her magic shielded us while we awaited Micharas's return."

Jaw's stern expression softened slightly as he regarded Sir Erik's words. Antonius and Micharas exchanged glances, the realisation dawning that this mysterious woman had played a crucial role in protecting their town during a moment of peril.

Sir Erik continued, "Lady Katherine is a powerful mage, and her motives thus far have aligned with ours. She actually sought me out this morning to speak with me regarding her plan going forwards."

The woman, now known as Lady Katherine, maintained a composed demeanour, allowing the weight of Sir Erik's endorsement to settle in the air.

The unease within the trio gradually settled down as they considered the newfound information.

"So what are your motives exactly?" Jaw asked, sword still in hand. While the others had immediately dropped their guard at hearing Sir Eriks testimony, he had not gotten as far as he had in life simply by blindly following the crowd.

Lady Katherine met Jaw's gaze, understanding the emotions and reservations in his eyes. With a calm manner, she began to unravel the purpose behind her presence.

"My motives are rooted in the preservation of life," she explained, her words resonated with sincerity. "The Alts are advancing, targeting not only Celleos but other settlements—Deadbell Village, Dampwell Village, and likely more. My goal is to anticipate their next move, to discern where they will strike next, and to provide a warning to those in harm's way."

Jaw's grip on his sword remained steady, but a flicker of consideration crossed his features. Lady Katherine continued, "We need to unite against this common threat. I believe your destiny is entwined with the fate of these lands, and together, we can stand against the encroaching darkness."

It was at this point that Jaw, sensing a connection between Lady Katherine's mission and the note Antonius possessed, glanced at Antonius and subtly beckoned for the note. As the weight of Lady Katherine's words settled, Jaw lowered his weapon, returning it to his side.

"It's funny you should say that," Jaw took the note from Antonius and handed it to Erik. "This came into our possession recently." He explained as the two of them looked over the note.

Sir Erik took the note from Jaw, his eyes scanning the list of places with a furrowed brow. "The Xanthian Halls, Dampwell Village, Deadbell Village, Celleos...," he mumbled, tracing his finger over the names. "And the first four crossed off."

Antonius interjected, "We thought it might be a checklist, places where something has already happened."

Micharas nodded, adding, "We speculated it could be a call to action, to protect these places from potential threats."

Lady Katherine, her gaze fixed on the note, spoke thoughtfully, "The pattern matches the Alt's recent attacks. They've been systematically targeting settlements. Based on the list we can assume that their next target will be The Eastland Castle."

Jaw leaned against a nearby weapon rack, crossing his arms. "So, what's the plan then?"

Lady Katherine, her eyes reflecting a quiet confidence, responded, "The plan is woven in the threads of fate. Destiny has brought us together for a purpose, to stand against the encroaching darkness. The Alt's campaign is methodical, but so must be our defence."

Sir Erik, having listened intently, spoke up, "Then I recommend that you start with The Eastland Castle."

"Are you not coming with us?" Micharas asked inquisitively, the disappointment evident in his voice.

"My duty is to protect this town and to serve Sir Shane." Erik replied with a sense of duty in his voice. "I must ensure that even in my absence, Celleos remains fortified."

Micharas nodded, understanding the weight of Sir Erik's responsibilities. "Your commitment to Celleos is commendable. Look after it." He said, extending a hand toward the Captain of the Guard.

As they exited the Guard House, the late morning sun hung high in the sky, casting a warm glow over Celleos. The town, still in the process of recovery, hummed with activity. Residents went about their tasks, rebuilding what had been lost. The four of them, Lady Katherine, Micharas, Jaw, and Antonius, stopped just outside of the Guard House boundary, contemplating the challenges that awaited them.

Micharas, a man of practicality, spoke first. "We don't have coin to spend, so we'll have to rely on the generosity of the townsfolk. Let's start by asking around, see if anyone can spare food, water, or any other supplies for our journey. Let's meet at the front gate at midday. We'll set out from there."

Jaw, always direct and to the point, nodded in agreement. "Right. We'll need to travel light. Only take what's essential. Weapons, basic gear, do not bother to gather much food however. If I am travelling with two hunters, I expect a fresh meal each day," he joked with a smile.

Antonius, note in hand, chimed in, "I'll check with Elder Sage, see if he has any spare maps that could be useful. Knowing the terrain is key to a smooth journey."

With a plan in mind, the trio set off in different directions. Lady Katherine opted to go her own separate way into the town to prepare for the long travel ahead. They approached the townsfolk with humility, explaining their mission and the urgency of the situation. The response was mixed, but the resilient spirit of Celleos prevailed. Some donated dried goods, others offered water skins, and a few even contributed basic supplies.

Jaw, visiting the blacksmith, managed to procure a few spare arrows for Antonius and a sturdy leather vest from salvaged materials. The blacksmith, recognizing the urgency of their quest, offered what little he could spare.

Antonius, in his interaction with the remaining town Elder, was met with a mixture of sympathy and understanding. The old man, a seasoned individual who had seen his fair share of turmoil, handed Antonius a detailed map of the surrounding regions.

As the trio reconvened near the town gates, their makeshift supplies gathered, they found themselves joined by Lady Katherine. She stood by the gates, her presence a silent acknowledgment of the shared journey that lay ahead.

Micharas, his travel pack laden with provisions, looked towards his companions. "Any clue on how far away the capital is?"

Antonius folded the map carefully, securing it within his armour. "Elder Sage said it's about thirty days' travel on foot."

Jaw, adjusting the strap of his newly acquired leather vest, nodded. "About that," he confirmed. "It is a shame we don't have horses."

Micharas looked over towards the town's stables, now utterly destroyed. When the Alts attacked, it was the first place to fall.

Antonius, glancing around at their meagre supplies, voiced a concern. "Thirty days is a long journey. We'll need to be resourceful and make every day count."

Jaw, with a reassuring grin, slapped Antonius on the back. "Don't worry, my friend. We'll manage just fine."

Lady Katherine, who had quietly observed the exchange, chimed in with a warm smile. "You three make quite the team. I'm genuinely looking forward to our travels together." Her words held a sincere tone, despite a subtle hint of awkwardness and unnecessary formality in her voice.

As the midday sun hung high in the sky, casting a warm embrace over the road just beyond Celleos' gates, the makeshift band of adventurers prepared to embark on their journey. The air was filled with a gentle breeze, carrying the scent of rejuvenation from the rebuilding town.

Lady Katherine stood with them, her presence a harmonious addition to the group. The crunch of the gravel under their feet mixed with the clinking of gear and the soft rustle of fabric as the trio—Micharas, Jaw, and Antonius—adjusted their travel packs. The weight of the upcoming journey settled on their shoulders, mingling with the anticipation of the unknown.

Jaw, his sword secured at his side, and shield on his back, glanced back toward the town. A sense of nostalgia and duty lingered in the air. Micharas, a stalwart figure, had exchanged a few last-minute words with some of the townsfolk who had gathered to bid them farewell, before he hurried to catch up with the others.

Antonius, holding the detailed map provided by Elder Sage, traced his fingers over the winding paths that awaited them. The parchment crinkled softly under his touch, a tangible representation of the challenges and discoveries that lay ahead.

Lady Katherine, her eyes reflecting a mix of determination and hope, spoke to the trio, "May our journey be guided by the threads of fate, weaving a path through the unknown. Together, we shall face whatever challenges arise." Jaw rolled his eyes as he turned to walk away. She did not notice.

As they set off along the path, a feeling of liberation swept over them. The sunlit road stretched ahead, inviting them to venture into the mysteries of the realm. Birds chirped in the distance, adding a melodic backdrop to the scene. The weather, serene and clear, seemed to symbolise the possibilities that awaited the group on their journey.

Micharas led the way, Antonius by his side, Jaw bringing up the rear. The townsfolk, standing by with a mixture of gratitude and well-wishing, offered a final wave from the gate, while high above on the wall Sir Erik watched them leave. Lady Katherine joined the trio, her presence seamlessly blending into the newfound fellowship.

The gates closed behind them, marking the end of one chapter and the beginning of another. The landscape unfolded like an open book, its pages waiting to be written with the tales of their travels.

And so, with the sun high in the sky and the promise of a new horizon beckoning, the trio—now a quartet—set forth on their quest, ready to face whatever awaited them on the road ahead.

Chapter 7

The afternoon sun burned high above the winding path as the quartet embarked on their journey. Lady Katherine, Micharas, Jaw, and Antonius walked in a loose formation, the rhythmic sound of their footsteps marking the beginning of their quest.

The road stretched ahead, flanked by tall trees that whispered with the gentle breeze. Micharas, at the forefront, led the way with focused determination. He occasionally glanced at the map clutched in Antonius's hand, ensuring they stayed on course.

As they traversed the wooded path, Antonius seized the opportunity to initiate conversation. "So, Lady Katherine, what kind of magic can you do?"

Lady Katherine adjusted the strap of her bag and smiled, choosing her words carefully. "All kinds," she replied with a smile. "I have practised it for most of my life, so I moved through the elements and various forms of application as I studied."

Micharas looked astonished. "That is very impressive! I have not met many mages in my life, but those that I have tend to practise just a single subject or a refined collection of spells." He seemed genuinely impressed by her claim.

"But do you specialise in anything in particular?" Antonius pushed further, attempting not to pry too much into their arcane companion's business.

Lady Katherine paused for a moment, contemplating the question or perhaps her answer. "Well, if I had to pick one that I am specifically better at, then I guess it would be Animus magic," she concluded with a cheery smile.

As the conversation unfolded, Lady Katherine shared tales of her magical endeavours, recounting instances where her mastery of magic had proven invaluable. The group listened with genuine interest, discovering the depth of her abilities and the versatility she brought to their ensemble.

The afternoon sun cast dappled shadows on the forest floor as the quartet continued their journey. After sharing tales of her magical exploits, Lady Katherine turned her inquisitive gaze toward Antonius. "So what about you?" she asked curiously. "I am to understand that you are Micharas's younger brother; however, you seem much younger than the rest of us."

Antonius smiled at the inquiry. "Yes, that's correct. I am Micharas's younger brother, though the age difference has been influenced by certain... circumstances."

Lady Katherine's eyes sparkled with curiosity. "Circumstances? Do tell. I find these sorts of things quite intriguing."

Antonius hesitated for a moment, his gaze briefly flickering to Micharas and Jaw, who walked ahead, seemingly absorbed in their own conversation. "Well, until recently, I was missing. By recently, I mean until yesterday. Without going into it too much, I was kidnapped by the Alts, and the rest is a bit of an unknown. Apparently, I have been gone for eight years, but to me, it feels like I was only gone a few days at the very most."

Lady Katherine's expression shifted, a mix of fascination and confusion. "The Alts can manipulate time? That's extraordinary." She then immediately changed the subject, as though the matter bored her or perhaps it had touched a sore spot in her knowledge, and she no longer wanted to discuss it further. "So you are the archer of the group then?"

Antonius nodded, a hint of pride in his eyes. "Indeed. Though my older brother is also an archer, I'm just better," he said smugly.

"What are you two talking about?" Micharas inquired as he and Jaw dropped back to become more involved in the conversation.

"We were just discussing your younger brother's superior prowess with a bow," she joked playfully.

"Well, Lady Katherine, while Antonius here excels in archery, I'm no slouch myself. I served as the town hunter in Celleos for quite some time," he began, not to be outshone by his brother.

Lady Katherine's interest piqued. "Town hunter? That sounds like a significant responsibility. Tell me more."

"It was a responsibility, but I took pride in it. The town relied on the hunters for fresh game, and it was my duty to provide. There's a certain connection to the land when you're out there, tracking and stalking your prey. It's not just about the skill with the bow; it's about understanding the woods, knowing the habits of the creatures you pursue," Micharas explained with a distant glint in his eye.

As they walked, Micharas recounted tales of his time as the town hunter, describing the delicate balance of maintaining the local wildlife while ensuring the safety of the townsfolk. He spoke of tracking elusive creatures through the dense forests and providing the town with fresh game.

Antonius chimed in, "It's not just about hunting either. Micharas is an expert tracker. He could find the same stag week after week out in the wilderness; it's just a shame he couldn't hit it!" he joked, immediately starting to dash away from his brother's grasp.

"Cheeky little sod!" Micharas shouted after him, choosing not to give chase.

Lady Katherine observed the bow slung across Micharas's back and the sabre at his side. "Impressive weapons you have there. The bow is expected, but what about the sabre?"

Micharas chuckled, running his fingers over the hilt of the sabre. "Beautiful, isn't it?" He pulled it out of its sheath as they walked to demonstrate the full splendour of the blade. "It has served me well. Jaw here has a knack for finding quality weapons."

Lady Katherine's gaze shifted to Micharas's hip, and then across his back, the two places where a quiver would typically be. "I couldn't help but notice, Micharas, you carry a bow, but I didn't see any arrows. Do you not use them?"

Micharas's expression shifted slightly, a mix of nostalgia and a hint of sadness. "I used to carry arrows, but I lost them during the attack. It's been challenging to replace them, given the state of the town. But I'll manage. I always do."

"Wait," Antonius stopped the conversation in its tracks as he returned to the group. "How exactly do you not use arrows?" His question posed to Lady Katherine. He was not sure if she was being naive or if she knew some sort of arcane solution to the need for ammunition.

"Well, for starters, there are magical bows. There are enchanted bows that don't require physical arrows. They can either conjure arrows on the spot or draw upon magical energy, eliminating the need for ammunition," Lady Katherine began to explain, her knowledge and wisdom evident in how quickly and easily she produced such information.

Micharas's eyes widened with interest. "Magical bows, you say? I've never come across such a thing. How do they work?"

Lady Katherine gestured with her hands, conjuring a faint magical glow. "Well, some of them can create arrows out of magical energy as you draw the string back. It's like the bow itself forms the arrow, so you never run out. Others can summon arrows from the surrounding area, using the environment as a source. And there are even bows that have a continuous supply spell, ensuring an arrow is ready in your hand as long as the bow is drawn."

Antonius looked fascinated, his curiosity evident. "That sounds incredible. Do you own one of these magical bows?"

Lady Katherine chuckled, shaking her head. "Unfortunately, no. They're quite rare and often associated with skilled mages or legendary archers. But I've read about them in books and heard tales from other magical scholars."

Jaw, who had been listening quietly, finally spoke up. "Seems like magic can solve a lot of problems, even the lack of arrows. What other tricks do you have up your sleeves?"

Lady Katherine grinned mischievously. "Oh, there is a bag full of tricks. Aside from arrow-summoning-related magic, there are spells to enhance the arrow's speed or make them explode on impact. Some mages can even imbue arrows with elemental effects like fire or ice. It all depends on the mage's specialisation and creativity."

As the day unfolded and the encroaching night hinted at its arrival, the party discovered a suitable spot to rest and replenish their energy. Lady Katherine, despite initial hesitance, revealed her resourcefulness by foraging edible plants, showcasing an adaptability that surprised even her companions.

As the evening settled in, a crackling campfire cast its warm glow over the group. In the flickering light, stories flowed like a meandering river. Micharas regaled them with tales of mythical creatures encountered in the woods, confessing that, despite numerous attempts, he had never managed to bring one down. Antonius, in turn, delved into the vast knowledge Lady Katherine possessed, recognizing the potential for honing his archery skills under her guidance.

Sensing an opportune moment to unveil a glimpse of her magical prowess, Lady Katherine gracefully rose from her seat. A subtle wave of her hand conjured a ball of ethereal blue light, bathing the campsite in its gentle glow. "While I may not wield a blade or a bow with finesse, I possess this ability. I will do my utmost to stand by your sides, offering magical support should the need arise," she said with conviction in her voice.

With practised grace, she manipulated the light, creating spectacular illusions that danced in the air. The display captivated the attention of her companions, with the exception of Jaw, who observed with a look of concern and incertitude.

"I have no doubt you will," Micharas responded, transfixed by the magical spectacle.

Lady Katherine continued, her tone sincere yet unnecessarily formal, "I share this not to burden you with my protection but to assure you that I am here as a companion, not a charge. In times of conflict, you owe me no obligation for defence. We journey together as equals."

As the first day of their adventure drew to a close, they all drifted off to sleep under a blanket of stars and a canopy of trees. All except for Jaw, who stayed resolute and vigilant through the night. His eyes pierced the darkness, a sentinel against the unseen perils that might lurk in the shadows. Wary and watchful, he sat on guard throughout the night, back against a tree, a silent protector as they ventured into the unknown.

As the next few days unfolded, the adventurer's journey pressed on, leaving the familiarity of the dense forest behind. The winding path led them through expansive fields bustling with wildflowers, their vibrant hues creating a picturesque contrast to the lush greenery. Micharas, ever vigilant at the front, ensured they navigated the terrain at an unfaltering pace.

Conversations continued, threading through the fabric of their journey. Lady Katherine shared glimpses of her past, though the focus remained on the present landscape and the road ahead. Micharas exchanged tales of his and his brother's childhood, as well as bringing Antonius up to date on the events that he had missed. The group's anecdotes weaving seamlessly into the tapestry of their shared experiences.

The weather danced to its own rhythm, transforming the canvas of the sky. The sun, a benevolent guide, bathed the landscape in golden warmth during the day. Gentle breezes whispered through the grassy fields, a melody accompanying their footsteps. As the journey unfolded, the sky transitioned from vast blue expanses to the fiery hues of sunset, painting the horizon in hues of orange and pink.

The terrain shifted beneath their feet as they ascended hills that rolled like waves frozen in time. Each step brought them closer to the edge of a sprawling swamp. The air hung heavy with moisture, and the scent of earth and decay permeated the surroundings. Tall grasses and twisted trees stood tall, marking the boundary between the hills and the murky expanse that lay ahead.

Clouds gathered overhead, casting shadows that danced on the swamp's surface. The weather took a capricious turn, as the sun bowed to the encroaching rain. Drops cascaded from the heavens, painting the landscape in a glistening sheen. The quartet adjusted their pace, trudging through the muddy terrain with a shared determination.

As the swamp's edge drew near, the quartet paused for a moment, surveying the murky waters and tangled vegetation that lay ahead. "Wonderful," Micharas was the first one to speak, demonstrating his sarcastic opinion of the obstacle that now lay before them.

Micharas clenched the map in his hands, frustration evident in his furrowed brow. The party stood at the swamp's edge, uncertainty looming like the thick fog that clung to the murky waters. Antonius' jest hung in the air, briefly breaking the tension. "Perhaps it sunk?" he quipped, earning a glance from Micharas.

The warrior's frustration spilled out, "There is meant to be a path through this!" He turned the map this way and that, as though hoping a different angle would reveal the elusive trail they sought. The dirt road they had followed so far had led them to this unexpected obstacle.

Antonius, seeking humour in adversity, added with a smirk, "Do we have any other choice?"

Lady Katherine, recognizing the delicate nature of the situation, spoke cautiously, "Perhaps it would be wise to explore other options before venturing into unknown terrain. Going around might take longer, but safety should be a priority."

Micharas considered the suggestion, still studying the map. "Going around could add up to ten days to our travel time," he mused, contemplating the implications.

Jaw, seemingly unfazed by the swamp's foreboding appearance, chimed in, "How long would we be in this swamp then?"

Micharas responded, "Not long, a few days at most. But we don't even know if it's safe to walk through." He emphasised the uncertainty, his eyes scanning the swamp's edge.

As the debate unfolded, Jaw, embodying his impulsive nature, allowing for a moment his intrusive thoughts to get the better of him and took a step into the swamp, producing a loud squelch. "Seems safe," he declared with a grin, proudly showcasing the barely dampened tops of his boots.

Micharas, alarmed by Jaw's rash move, immediately began berating him. "That part might be safe, but we don't know if there are deeper sections. If we get stuck or, Gods forbid, attacked in it, then our journey ends!" The weight of the potential consequences hung in the air, urging caution.

Antonius, trying a more practical approach, suggested, "Can you use magic to help?" His eyes turned to Lady Katherine, a glint of curiosity in them. He was eager to witness the mage's abilities in action, hoping for a solution that would bypass the swamp's risks.

Lady Katherine, deep in thought, contemplated the suggestion of using magic to navigate the swamp. "Well," she mumbled to herself, considering the potential drain on her magical energy. Meanwhile, the background symphony continued with Micharas shouting at Jaw, who was receiving a helping hand to extricate himself from the swamp's grasp.

Antonius couldn't contain his anticipation, his mind conjuring fantastical scenarios of Lady Katherine transforming the swamp into a field or conjuring a bridge across its murky waters. Perhaps she might even make them all levitate, floating gracefully across the surface.

After a brief moment of introspection, Lady Katherine looked up, meeting

Antonius's expectant gaze. "I suppose there is a spell that could help and not be too tiring to constantly use all day," she concluded, a hint of determination in her voice. "Okay, stand back," she instructed with a delicate and commanding tone.

The party obediently shifted away, giving her the space she needed. Jaw, still in the process of shaking off the clinging mud, dragged his boots backward across the grass. Antonius followed behind Lady Katherine, eager to witness the arcane solution she had in mind.

To everyone's surprise, her solution mirrored Jaw's, with an extra magical step. As Lady Katherine's foot dropped off the grassy lip, she uttered the incantation, "Ascent Repartus." The barely audible words caused the ground beneath the swamp to rise, creating a small stone plinth that met her foot. With each subsequent step, she repeated the process, though it would seem she no longer needed to say anything to achieve the effect, and the ground lifting to support her weight.

"They won't stick about forever, so we will need to move quickly," she warned, her eyes focused on the magical plinths. "That said, if you are standing on one, then it should not rescind into the swamp." The "should not" in her speech did not sound all that convincing, at least not as far as Jaw was concerned.

The party, now intrigued and relieved, followed Lady Katherine's magical path across the swamp. Antonius marvelled at the simplicity and elegance of her solution, appreciating the practicality of her magical prowess. Micharas, having successfully rescued Jaw from the swamp's clutches, watched with a mix of gratitude and curiosity as the group traversed the otherwise impassable terrain.

As the party moved forward, guided by Lady Katherine's magical stepping stones, the swamp reluctantly yielded passage. The air hummed with the sound of insects, as well as the croaks of frogs and toads alike, as the group ventured deeper into the heart of the murky expanse.

Several hours passed, and the sun began its descent, though it was barely visible through the clouds at this point. Despite the challenges, it was yet another successful day on their journey towards The Eastland Castle.

"We should find somewhere safe to stop for the night," Micharas shouted from the back of the line. Overhead, the clouds had gathered in an aggressive barrier, a building storm they had been monitoring for the past few hours. The ominous mass threatened to unleash its fury, potentially raising the water level in the already drowned swamp around them. In hindsight, none of them had the forethought to bring any form of cover in the event of a storm.

The party, alert to Micharas's concern, scanned the surroundings for a suitable spot to weather the impending storm. Lady Katherine, with a quick glance at the darkening sky, took charge of the situation. "There," she pointed to a slightly elevated mound of land, seemingly untouched by the swamp waters. "It's our best bet for a dry place to rest."

Following her guidance, the party hurried toward the elevated ground. With each step, the air grew heavier, a prelude to the impending tempest. The distant rumble of thunder sounded through the swamp, underscoring the urgency of finding shelter.

As they reached the elevated mound, Lady Katherine's eyes scanned the area. "We need to create a barrier to shield us from the rain," she declared, her mind already formulating a plan. "I can use magic to manipulate the water and divert it away from our campsite."

They all watched with anticipation as she gracefully gestured with her hands. A shimmering barrier formed in the air, creating an invisible dome that extended over their chosen resting spot. Lady Katherine's control over the magical elements was evident as the raindrops diverted around the protected area.

The party settled within the enchanted barrier, the sound of rain drumming on the invisible shield. Lady Katherine, satisfied with her makeshift shelter, joined the others as they unpacked their belongings. Despite the storm raging outside their magical haven, the party found themselves in a surprisingly tranquil pocket, shielded from the elements.

"What now?" Antonius asked, his voice cutting through the heavy air.

They surveyed the swamp, its murky waters stretching into the gloom, surrounded by twisted trees and tangled vegetation. There was little they could do but wait out the storm. "How long will this hold?" Micharas inquired, gesturing toward the shield that now protected them from the relentless rain.

"I should be able to sustain it through the night at least. Though if it looks like it stops raining, I will let it down earlier so as not to strain myself too much," Lady Katherine reassured them, a gentle smile gracing her lips.

Jaw, however, remained watchful. His gaze never strayed far from Lady Katherine. It wasn't a look of admiration or jealousy; it was something deeper. He had seen magic before, plenty of it, but this was different. The spells she cast, he noticed that half the time she did not speak. Some of the words he heard her use weren't even from the common language. It was a kind of magic rarely documented, a dangerous magic that stirred distant memories in Jaw. She cast a spell and then didn't need to repeat the incantation or remain in place to sustain it. He wasn't threatened, but cautious.

As the party settled into their impromptu shelter, gathering wood for a fire from around the ground as well as that which Antonius had stored in his travel pack, the distant sound of thunder rumbled ominously. The clouds overhead had amassed into an aggressive front, threatening to unleash further fury at any moment. The rain continued its relentless assault on Lady Katherine's magical shield, the droplets creating a rhythmic drumming that underscored the tension in the air.

The elevated piece of land they had chosen for refuge provided a slightly drier haven within the swamp. The ground beneath them was a mix of soft earth and twisted roots, creating a natural platform that, while not entirely comfortable, offered a reprieve from the swamp's murky depths.

As the party went about their tasks, Antonius and Jaw gathering wood, Micharas inspecting the map once more, the storm's distant growls became more pronounced. A moth, delicate and small, briefly sought shelter on a nearby chunk of wood before fluttering out and through the invisible barrier. Jaw watched its escape with a thoughtful expression, then grabbed another log and passed it over to Antonius with a smile. "Here's another one," he said, chucking it his way.

As the night deepened, the crackling flames of their campfire cast its warmth on the party gathered around it. The rain outside continued its relentless downpour with no signs of stopping, but within the magical shield, they found a pocket of safety and relative comfort. The conversation flowed, through plans for the future, dreams of the sun rising on a clear day, and the anticipation of reaching the capital.

Jaw, as he had throughout the journey, remained a silent spectator, playing the role of a witness to the lively discussion. Micharas, increasingly aware of his friend's reticence, saw an opportunity to draw him into the camaraderie of the group. "Jaw, why don't you tell us about your adventures for a change?" he gently encouraged, his eyes conveying a genuine desire to know more about the hermit's past.

"Yeah, tell us about this Captain Rufus man," Antonius chimed in, his eyes sparkling with excitement. Micharas had previously spoken about the legend of the sword he carried, but the details were solely from Jaw's accounts.

Jaw, with a subtle smile, obliged. He held his hands out to the fire, the flames casting a warm glow on his weathered features. As he began to speak, the rain outside seemed to fade away, replaced by the distant echoes of his adventures in far-off lands. He regaled the group with tales of quests that made their current journey seem like a gentle stroll across the countryside. Foes aplenty and dangers incomparable to the rain they currently sheltered from or the foes that they now sought to overcome.

Micharas, with an encouraging nod, listened intently. The stories unfolded like ancient scrolls, revealing a world of mythical creatures, hidden realms, and the trials faced by Jaw and his companions. The firelight danced in Jaw's eyes as he recounted battles against formidable adversaries and the challenges of navigating treacherous landscapes.

As the night pressed on, Jaw delved into the tale of a once-beloved king who had turned tyrant, plunging the kingdom into darkness. He spoke of a perilous quest to overthrow the tyrant, a journey fraught with betrayal, cunning plots, and battles that tested the limits of their courage.

The party, huddled around the fire within the protective bubble of Lady Katherine's magic, listened with rapt attention. Micharas, in particular, marvelled at the depth of Jaw's experiences and the resilience with which he faced the trials of his past. It was a moment of shared storytelling, a bond forming among the companions as they glimpsed the rich tapestry of Jaw's adventures, illuminated by the flames that danced with the rhythm of his tales.

As the night wore on, the relentless rain began to ease, its steady drumbeat gradually fading into a sporadic patter. One by one, the members of the party succumbed to the weariness of their journey, finding solace in the embrace of sleep. Around the dwindling campfire, the enchanted shield still holding firm, Lady Katherine and Antonius gradually drifted off into the realm of dreams.

Only Micharas and Jaw remained, their silhouettes outlined by the flickering flames. Micharas, still playing the vigilant leader, turned to his companion with a question that hinted at both curiosity and concern. "Are you planning to keep watch again tonight?" he inquired, his gaze steady.

Jaw glanced around the swampy surroundings, the rain now reduced to a gentle drizzle. "I don't see a real need to, to be honest," he admitted, his eyes surveying the desolate landscape. "We are in the middle of nowhere. I feel like if anyone was going to attempt to sneak up on us out here, we would most definitely hear them coming, even with the rain."

Micharas nodded, considering the wisdom in Jaw's perspective. The tranquillity of their secluded spot seemed to affirm the hermit's rationale. With an unspoken agreement, the two men decided to embrace the respite of sleep, trusting the night to guard them as they journeyed through the realm of dreams. The fire, its embers glowing softly, continued to cast a warm glow over their makeshift campsite, a small bastion of calm amid the untamed wilderness.

The next morning, as the sun rose, so too did the adventurers. They slept peacefully through the night, undisturbed by the rain and the perils of the swamp, refreshed and ready for a new day. No sooner had they all risen from their places of rest than they were once again off, following Lady Katherine across the swamp.

Chapter 8

The party trudged through the murky swamp, hopping along behind Lady Katherine as she generated the magical stepping stones. The air hung heavy with the damp scent of decay, and the twisted trees loomed like spectral sentinels in the fading light. As the sun dipped below the horizon, a collective weariness settled over the group.

The desire for solid ground grew with every step, the promise of relief echoing in their minds. The encroaching darkness added an element of urgency to their pace, each member silently yearning for the elusive edge of the marsh.

Finally, after what felt like an eternity of navigating over the mire, the far edge of the bog emerged from the shadows. A collective sigh of relief rippled through the party. The sight of firm, dry land beckoned to them like a sanctuary after the gruelling journey through the inhospitable landscape and with pure determination they pushed forwards for a few more hours until they finally freed themselves of the marsh that now lay behind them.

"We made it," Micharas muttered, a weariness evident in his voice. "Solid ground at last."

Antonius chimed in with a half-hearted chuckle, "I never thought I'd be so glad to see normal land again. No offence to the swamp, but I've had my fill."

Jaw nodded in agreement, a subtle smile playing on his lips. Lady Katherine, though fatigued, mustered a reassuring smile, acknowledging the shared sentiment among the weary adventurers.

The party, surrounded by the unsettling darkness, paused on the solid ground that marked their escape from the swamp. The absence of celestial bodies created a disorienting void, leaving them suspended in an inky abyss. As they considered finding a place to rest for the night, a strange and ominous noise disrupted the silence, echoing through the night.

"We should find a place to rest for the night," Micharas suggested, his voice weighted with the exhaustion of the day's journey. "Somewhere dry and away from this cursed quagmire."

Antonius, stifling a yawn, nodded vigorously. "Agreed. My legs feel like they're about to stage a rebellion."

Lady Katherine, however, interjected, her voice carrying an undertone of concern. She listened intently to the night, her gaze fixed on the hill ahead. "Can anyone else hear that?" she asked, her expression shifting from weariness to alertness. The group, now attuned to the ambient noise, realised that a strange backdrop of sound emanated from somewhere beyond the hill.

Jaw voiced the collective unease that lingered in the air. "It sounds like drums."

The revelation hung in the air, a palpable tension settling over the party. The distant rhythmic beats painted an ominous picture against the night. The party exchanged wary glances, a silent acknowledgment of the shared apprehension that loomed in the darkness.

Micharas, his instincts sharpened by years of navigating unknown terrains, spoke with a measured tone. "We should approach cautiously. The marsh might be behind us, but it seems we've stumbled upon another problem."

As they moved toward the crest of the hill, the rhythmic drumming grew louder, its cadence weaving a foreboding tapestry in the night.

The party, peering over the hill, could clearly discern a large gathering of people in the darkness below. A bonfire burned in the middle of their camp, casting eerie shadows on the figures surrounding it. Despite the distance and the shroud of darkness over the hills, the party recognized the unmistakable signs of an Alt war band.

Antonius swore loudly as his brother yanked him backward, away from the edge of the hill. "What do we do?" Antonius asked, his concern evident in his voice.

"We attack," Micharas replied without hesitation, his gaze fixed on the distant war band. He didn't pause to consider the consequences. "If we stay here, they'll attack us as soon as they realise we're here. If we try to sneak past, we risk being caught, and they might catch up to us further down the road while we rest."

Jaw nodded in agreement. "So we need a plan."

"I'm not following one of your plans again, Jaw. No offence, but the last one, while it may have worked, was ballsy to say the least. There are more of us this time, so we can focus on splitting their mass and dispatching them into more manageable groups," Micharas continued.

"So we divide and conquer?" Antonius asked, his excitement evident. "I like it, plus we have a nice bit of high ground around them to take advantage of."

"That brings me to my next point. There are hills surrounding them. I have no doubt they'll have scouts or archers lining those hills. Antonius and I will try to clear them without raising the alarm," Micharas explained, his strategic mind at work.

Jaw listened intently, acknowledging Micharas's proficiency in devising plans on the fly. "And what about Lady Katherine and me?" he asked.

"Jaw and Lady Katherine, I want the two of you to trace the hills as we clear them. Stay out of sight but get closer to the camp. If things go bad, we need you there and ready to lend your aid," Micharas instructed, pointing at them as he spoke.

"What do we do once the hills are clear?" Antonius inquired.

"I'll make my way down to the camp too and join Jaw, relieving Lady Katherine so that she can fall back and join you on the hillside. Then you two can kick things off by laying down some ranged chaos, and we will sweep through the camp, taking care of any that are left," Micharas concluded. "Any questions?"

The silence that followed suggested to him that everyone knew their part to play in this skirmish. And with that Micharas and Antonius started moving down the hill as quickly as they could to get into position.

Jaw and Lady Katherine found themselves alone for the first time since they had met. Jaw suggested, "We should get moving too," his eyes scanning the surroundings.

As they moved down the hill, sticking closely to the shadows, in a hushed darkness, Lady Katherine hesitated for a moment before breaking the silence. "Jaw," she began tentatively, "I couldn't help but notice you watching me. I hope I haven't said or done anything to offend you." her voice, just a mere whisper.

Jaw, focused on their imminent task, glanced at her briefly. "This isn't the best time," he replied in a low voice. "Let's focus on the task at hand, and we can talk about it later." Despite the urgency in his tone, there was a subtle reassurance that they would address her concerns when the situation allowed.

With the precision of seasoned assassins, Micharas and Antonius stealthily cleared the hilltops surrounding the Alt war band's camp. After the covert operation, Micharas slid down the hill towards the other two, positioned just outside the camp. They had managed to infiltrate so close to the unsuspecting Alts that they now crouched behind a tent within the band's perimeter. The Alts remained blissfully unaware of the imminent danger lurking in the dark.

Micharas gestured with his thumb for Lady Katherine to leave, and she moved with feline grace, low to the ground, making her way up the hill, staying enveloped in darkness. In hushed tones, Micharas briefed Jaw on their visible foes. "Antonius did a quick count, looks like about a hundred of them, if not more."

He anticipated some reaction from Jaw, perhaps a hint of panic, but the man simply nodded, signalling his understanding of the scale of the impending skirmish. Jaw readied his sword, his stoic response unsettling yet strangely reassuring to Micharas. Placing a hand on Jaw's shoulder, Micharas gripped his own sword, and the two men waited in tense anticipation for the signal to attack.

The wait was short-lived as a humming sound suddenly drowned out the Alts' chatter and drumming. The ground beneath them began to shudder. Micharas and Jaw peered around the tent, witnessing the unfolding spectacle of Lady Katherine's spell. It began as a small speck of darkness, a stark contrast against the bonfire's glow, before rapidly unfurling into an event horizon of destruction. A black hole manifested in the centre of the Alt camp, dragging many of them to a grim demise. Frantically, the Alts sought anything to anchor themselves, their blood-curdling screams echoing in the night. Some succeeded in affixing themselves to the camp surroundings, only to be stretched and warped by the galactic force wreaking havoc.

The chaos unleashed by Lady Katherine's spell left Micharas and Jaw momentarily captivated, the surreal scene unfolding before them. The duo then snapped back to the task at hand, surging forward from behind the tent to take advantage of the confusion within the Alt camp.

The black hole, having wrought its destruction, folded in on itself, vanishing as swiftly as it appeared, taking with it all the Alts it had ensnared. Micharas, caught in the ebb and flow of battle, clashed blades with an Alt wielding a glaive. A swift kick to the outer thigh sent the Alt sprawling to the ground, providing Micharas the opening he needed. His blade descended with lethal precision across the Alt's throat, a quick, efficient end.

Meanwhile, arrows hailed down upon the battlefield as Antonius unleashed his deadly volley from the shadows. Each arrow found its mark with deadly accuracy, punctuating the chaos with the Alts' cries as they fell to his ranged onslaught.

Micharas, having dispatched his initial foe with a lethal grace, pivoted seamlessly to engage another Alt. The battle was a dynamic dance of steel and fury, and with each calculated move, he cut through the Alt warriors. His sword sliced through the air, meeting its mark with deadly precision. A well-timed parry and counterattack left another Alt sprawled on the ground.

Simultaneously, Jaw, the hulking presence on the battlefield, swung his sword with devastating force. His attacks were broad and sweeping, creating a perimeter of danger around him. As an Alt approached, he met the challenge head-on, deflecting the thrust of its spear with the fuller of his weapon and following it along. With a rapid rising strike away from the handle of his foes weapon he cut it down, slicing up its chest, throat and face in one long arcing slash.

Amidst the melee, Antonius continued his deadly rain from the shadows.

Arrows soared through the night, finding their targets with unerring accuracy. His vantage point allowed him to pick off Alts attempting to flank their position, his arrows a silent but lethal force on the battlefield. He watched as two Alts approached Jaw from his blind side while he engaged with another two in front of him. Antonius quickly readied an arrow and loosed it towards the closest one to him, it struck hard against the beast's temple and folded it to the ground. A second arrow left his bow almost acting as an instantaneous succession to the first as it toppled the second. He then switched his attention to the foot of the hill where several Alts had broken from the pack and focused them instead.

Antonius watched as the foot of the hill suddenly became a deadly slope of ice as Lady Katherine dropped to her knees and placed her hand on the ground "Retheram" she howled as she did. Her voice cruel with intent as the Alts glided backwards down the hill, unable to find traction they slid straight into a rising barrier of ice spikes that jutted menacingly in their direction from the ground as they approached at speed. They were no match at all for the powerful magic that ended their sorry existences.

The duo's coordination on the battlefield became evident as Micharas and Jaw, though engaged in separate skirmishes, maintained a silent communication. A glance here, a nod there – an unspoken understanding that allowed them to complement each other's movements. Antonius, aware of the flow of combat below, adjusted his shots to cover the gaps in their defence.

The battlefield, once chaotic, began to take shape under their calculated assault. Alts fell one by one, the trio's combined efforts whittling down their numbers. Arrows from Antonius thinned the ranks, while Micharas and Jaw pressed forward, creating a deadly pincer movement.

Lady Katherine observed the unfolding spectacle. Sensing a critical moment, an opportunity to disseminate the dwindling enemy forces, she held out her hands as though pushing against a wall. "Negative Lightning" she said as a single unholy bolt of arcane energy streaked across the sky, lighting it up for a mere instant, it found its mark amid the battle and arced across the battlefield, finding vulnerable Alts and decimating them in an instant in the wake of the spells destructive force.

Micharas, his blade gleaming in the brief light, faced off against a burly Alt wielding a massive war axe. The Alt swung with brutish strength, but Micharas stepped out of the way nimbly, avoiding the heavy blow. With a quick step to the side, he ducked beneath a sweeping arc of another Alt with a greatsword and countered with a swift slash to the Alt's exposed side. The Alt stumbled, and Micharas switched his attention back to the Alt with the axe. He placed his foot on the head of the axe as it struck the ground and lunged forward threading his sabre through an opening in the Alts helmet and ending its life. He withdrew his sword and without looking delivered a backward slash, spraying the blood off of the end of his weapon while simultaneously opening the throat of the attacker to the rear of him. As he did an arrow struck it hard in the temple, throwing it to the ground at force.

Micharas turned toward the dark hillside and raised his arms in the air as if to question the archers timing, "I had that one!" He shouted jokingly.

Meanwhile, Jaw grappled with two Alts armed with dual short swords. The Alts attacked in a flurry of strikes, their movements quick and aggressive. Jaw, though slower, compensated with a solid defence. He drew his shield from his back and struck the first Alt as it came towards him, blades ready to shred through him. His strike was devastating to say the least as the Alt was not only knocked off balance by the offensive defence of its opponent but the shield actually struck the pommel of one of its weapons forcing its own sword up and through its skull. Jaw bowed under the defeated foe, tossing it over him on his shield and using its flailing legs to knock back the second target. No sooner had the body passed over his head, he quickly and ruthlessly lunged forwards with his sword, the Alt readied itself in preparation to block but there was no blocking Jaws swing.

Not even the former leader of the Alts Ethor could have prevented the force that Jaw struck with, his blade connected hard with the Alts sword which it had crossed together for optimal defence. But Jaw just cleaved through them, his sword unhindered, undeterred by the kinetic blockade of steel cut through the Alt like paper.

In a single moment the battle was over as the final Alt, a large heavily armoured individual wielding a halberd was dropped to its knees by an arrow. As Antonius released a second arrow towards it Lady Katherine pointed to the projectile mid flight and muttered something under her breath, the spell knocked it ever so slightly off of its original course as it made contact but seemed to empower the shot. It struck the plated body of the Alt and as it did so the spell triggered. It was as though the arrow had gained a second wind of momentum and launched itself straight through the target's armour and out of the other side.

Despite the overwhelming odds and the exhaustion from the day's travel across the swamp they had not only taken on the Alt war band but eviscerated their foe, leaving no survivors. The excitement and relief was evident in their expressions and body language as they reconvened at the foot of the hill.

As the adrenaline of battle began to subside, the four of them gathered in a small circle at the foot of the hill. The darkness and silence now encapsulated them, separating them from the grizzly scene of the camp.

"That was quite the display, Lady Katherine," Antonius remarked, breaking the silence. "I've never witnessed anything like that."

Lady Katherine smiled, a mix of exhaustion and satisfaction evident in her eyes. "It's a spell I've been perfecting over the years. Negative Lightning. Effective, isn't it?"

Micharas nodded in agreement. ""Effective" is an understatement. You saved us a lot of trouble with that one, especially considering their numbers."

Jaw, who had been mostly silent since the battle's end, grunted in approval. "Good spell. Very good. I especially liked the black hole."

Antonius shifted the conversation slightly, "And what about you, Jaw? That move with the shield was... impressive. I didn't know you could fight like that."

Jaw shrugged, a rare hint of a grin playing on his lips. "Fighting's fighting, no matter the setting."

Micharas clapped Jaw on the shoulder. "Well, your skills came in handy today. We wouldn't have held the line without you."

Jaw smiled at him, "Thanks, but you dont give yourself enough credit, I swear you were fighting against the odds more than I was. Perhaps my reckless battle tactic is rubbing off on you more than you would like to admit?"

Micharas chuckled to himself, "Yeah maybe. Let's hope not though hey?"

Lady Katherine spoke up, addressing Micharas, "Your plan worked well. Divide and conquer seems to be our winning strategy."

Micharas inclined his head in acknowledgment. "It's about leveraging each of our strengths. We complement each other."

Antonius chimed in, "Now, what's our next move? We've attracted attention, no doubt. The Alts won't take this defeat lightly."

Micharas's eyes scanned the darkness thoughtfully, its depths like an inky black void of nothingness. "We need to keep moving, put more distance between us and this war band. They'll regroup, but we'll be ready."

Lady Katherine, looking towards the dark expanse of the swamp they had left behind, spoke with a touch of concern, "What if they send more after us? We can't keep fighting every war band in these lands."

"We'll cross that bridge when we come to it," Micharas replied. "For now, let's focus on putting this swamp behind us and making some headway towards the capital."

With a shared nod, the group began to move. Antonius was the last to follow them, "Can we scout the camp first?" he asked innocently.

"Couldn't hurt." Jaw said to Micharas as the two of them led the group.

"Only, I am running low on arrows." Antonius continued, jokingly.

As they approached the aftermath of the battle, the Alts lay scattered and broken, their flesh and equipment reduced to a disconcerting black sludge. Bones were the only remnants left untouched.

Antonius crouched beside one of the fallen Alts, a look of grim disgust on his face as he removed the arrow from its skull. "We should gather what we can and move quickly. This place gives me the creeps."

Micharas agreed, "Antonius, how many arrows do you have left?" he stole a glance at his brother's quiver as he asked.

Antonius checked his quiver, frowning. "Only a handful. Enough for another skirmish, but we need to find a way to replenish our supplies."

Lady Katherine, glancing around, noticed a tent that seemed untouched by the magical destruction. In fact, it seemed to radiate an unnatural darkness that stood out from the surrounding chaos, and this was in contrast to the natural darkness that coated the rest of the scene.

"Over here," she called out, drawing the attention of the group. She pushed through the thick leather opening of the tent and entered. Inside the tent, she was greeted by an unusual mirror, its frame made of stone. Unlike any mirror she had encountered before, it didn't reflect the scene around her. Instead, it displayed an abyss of darkness.

"What kind of mirror is this?" Antonius asked, perplexed as he joined her. In the brief moment that she had been in the tent she had become engrossed in the surface of the mirror so much so that his question, while innocent and spoken softly, was enough to make her jump. A tingle ran down her spine as she looked away from it.

Lady Katherine backed away cautiously. "I don't know, It's not reflecting the present. It's showing something else. Something..." she turned back towards it.

Jaw questioned, "Should we be messing with this thing?" Again his presence came as a surprise to the two of them. Neither had noticed him enter just as Lady Katherine had failed to notice Antonius before.

Micharas seemed intrigued. "We can't ignore it. If it's connected to the Alts or this forbidden magic, we need to understand it."

Jaw looked at it for a moment, he watched as Lady Katherine approached it, she seemed beside herself as though her movements were not her own. There was caution in her steps but evidently not in her mind as she reached out her hand. "Do not touch it." Jaw repeated breaking the silence and snapping everyone back to reality. His tone was harsh and commanding, like that which would be issued to a naughty dog.

"Of course." Lady Katherine said, returning to her senses and turning away from it. The group left the tent without searching it further. Jaw held open the leather flap until they had all left past him before he too left the tent closing it behind him.

"What was that?" Micharas asked, his curiosity still kept by the mirror, despite no longer being in its presence.

"I have never seen anything like it before," Lady Katherine answered, she still did not seem herself and purposefully seemed to be avoiding Jaws eye. "It could have been a communication device, or perhaps a portal device. A means to change appearance or form even. The possibilities are endless, yet," she paused looking back at the tent. "There was an unmistakable evil to it." Her words voiced the same truth that the rest of them had felt from looking at it.

"Should we destroy it?" Micharas asked, his question seemed to be directed exclusively at Jaw. As Lady Katherine did not seem in the right state of mind in his opinion to be charged with such a decision and Antonius had returned to gathering arrows.

"No." Jaw seemed very certain in his answer, though not even he knew why he felt that way. It was a feeling deep down inside of him that told him that their best bet was to simply leave it here.

"Antonius, how are you getting on?" Micharas shouted over to him. Antonius replied by giving a thumbs up, after a few more minutes of him searching the remains of the battle he returned to them. He had refilled his quiver with a selection of different arrows that he had found.

"Good, let's get out of here then. Perhaps we can find somewhere up the road that will work as a safe place to rest for the night." Micharas said to the rest of the party, who had been waiting around patiently.

The party, having distanced themselves from the camp, moved through the pitch-black countryside. The night air was cool, and the occasional rustle of leaves and distant hooting of an owl were the only sounds breaking the silence. The events of the long day lingered in their minds, the never ending swamp, the victory over the Alt war band and the encounter with the otherworldly mirror.

As they trod on the uneven terrain, Antonius dropped back to walk alongside Lady Katherine at the back of the group. He leaned in and broke the silence between them, "That mirror was strange, right? I mean, what kind of magic was that?" He whispered in a hushed tone, in an attempt to avoid being overheard by the other two up ahead.

Lady Katherine, her composure returning, nodded thoughtfully, "It's not any magic I'm familiar with. It felt... ancient, and not in a good way. Jaw was right we should be cautious about such artefacts. I feel like such a fool." She said covering her face with one of her gloved hands.

"Why?" Antonius asked, his voice, despite hushed, carried empathy.

Lady Katherine removed her hand, she looked upset with herself. Her brow curled down with the weight of the frustration on her mind. "I do not feel like Jaw trusts me." She whispered, "I don't know if it's something I have done or something I have said." She genuinely sounded distressed by the situation.

"I wouldn't worry too much about it." Antonius replied after a moment to consider Jaw and his mannerisms. "I think he is just like that with everyone." Antonius had to be honest with himself, since meeting Jaw he did not feel like there was much of a chance of the two of them being friends after all of this was over. He did not seem to have much trust in others, instead choosing to do everything himself. That said he did seem to have warmed towards Micharas so perhaps it was just a case of earning his trust. "Yes that's probably it." Antonius concluded to himself in his mind.

The countryside's darkness seemed to deepen as they moved further away from the battleground. Micharas, leading the way, turned to address the group.

"We should put some distance between us and the camp. We don't want anything following us," Micharas suggested, his gaze scanning the shadows.

Antonius nodded in agreement, still somewhat fixated on the mirror's unusual properties, he turned back toward Lady Katherine and asked, "Do you think it was connected to the Alts somehow? Like a communication device?"

Lady Katherine shook her head, "It's hard to say. The magic felt dark and forbidden. If the Alts were using it, they must be dabbling in forces they barely understand."

Jaw grumbled in agreement, a low rumble that seemed to echo the countryside's natural sounds. His words while not coherent demonstrated that he could at least hear them whispering behind him. The party continued through the dark fields, the crunch of gravel beneath their boots the only disruptions in the thick silence that surrounded them.

After what felt like hours, Micharas, signalled for a halt. The party gathered in a small clearing.

"This should be far enough for us to stop for the night," Micharas declared, his eyes scanning the perimeter. "We'll need to set up a watch. I will take the first shift. Antonius, you're next. Jaw, you'll have the last watch. Get some rest; we've got a long journey ahead of us."

With those words, the party began preparing for the night, setting up a makeshift camp in the heart of the pitch-black countryside. The shadows danced around them as they settled in.

The morning sun painted the Eastland Kingdom in a new light as the party prepared to resume their journey. Micharas carefully unfolded the map, its worn edges hinting at the countless paths it had guided them through. With a scrutinising gaze, he traced their route, comparing the landmarks to the drawn lines on the parchment.

"We're on the right track," he declared, a sense of uncertainty threading through his voice. "I think." He concluded, Antonius looked up from the spot that he had been laying.

"You think?" He questioned annoyingly. He watched as his brother rotated the map. Trying to get his bearings, he looked around the area that they had spent the night in, in the hopes of finding a landmark or some point of reference to confirm his claim.

"I am sure of it." Micharas stated, a lot more confidently this time, as to put everyone's mind at ease. He then rolled up the map and approached Jaw where he lay at the watch-point.

"Good morning," Jaw said, wearily looking up at him. The last few hours had been fairly dull, it had given Jaw a lot of time to think as he sat and watched the sun rise.

Micharas crouched down next to him and took out the map again, "We are completely lost." He explained to his seasoned adventurer friend. Jaw tilted his head back and looked up at the morning sky. It was a beautiful shade of blue, flecks of clouds painted against it, they hung gracefully in the air, setting the scene for the lovely days travel ahead of them.

"Okay, well east is that way." Jaw says in a hushed voice. He nods his head to indicate the direction. "We walk that way until you see either the path or something that you can find on the map." Jaw explained. To which Micharas seemed satisfied enough with this suggestion and rolled up the map, he held out a hand to help Jaw off the ground.

The group, now accustomed to the unpredictable nature of their quest, gathered their belongings and set off once again.

The days that followed unfolded across the Eastland Kingdom like chapters in an epic tale. The landscape transformed as they ventured deeper, transitioning from open fields to rolling hills and small woodlands. The sprawling beauty of the kingdom unfolded before them, a canvas of varying terrain under the vast, ever-changing sky.

As they walked, conversations flowed like the breeze through the fields around them. Magic became a focal point once more, with Lady Katherine often taking the lead in discussions. She spoke of the arcane forces they had encountered—the mirror's forbidden magic and the dark energy that lingered within the Alts. Her words wove a tapestry of mystery, leaving the others contemplating the unknown answers.

The Alts were not forgotten in their discussions. Tales of their skirmish with the war band were retold, each member recounting their role in the battle. Antonius shared stories of his precise archery, Lady Katherine recounted the spells that she had used and the years of study and practice to master them, and Jaw and Micharas detailed their strategic prowess in combat. The victory, hard-fought and earned, became a badge of honour in their shared narrative.

The journey, while physically demanding, allowed for moments of camaraderie and bonding. Laughter punctuated the air as they reminisced about the audacity of their plans and the unexpected twists they had overcome. As they traversed wide open fields, the conversations blended with the whispering winds, creating a symphony of shared experiences.

Through hills that rose and fell like the beats of a heart, and woodlands that cast dappled shadows upon the path, the party pressed on. The landscape, becoming an unsung companion in their travels, unfolded in a series of picturesque vignettes. Sunsets bathed the horizon in warm hues, and the nights brought a blanket of stars that watched over them along their journey.

Despite the unpredictability of their quest, a sense of purpose and determination fueled their steps. The capital loomed closer with each passing day. The Eastland Kingdom, expansive and diverse, rolled away beneath their feet.

Chapter 9

The small clearing nestled within the woods offered a brief respite from the dense vegetation that surrounded it. Tall trees, their branches interwoven to create a natural canopy, allowed rays of the setting sun to break through gaps, creating pillars of light. The air was infused with the soothing scent of dirt and vegetation, and the distant murmur of a stream added a melodic undertone to the symphony of the forest.

Antonius had set about gathering dry wood, creating a neat pile near the centre of the clearing. He meticulously outlined a circle of stones, each one carefully chosen and arranged to create a safe enclosure for the campfire. The sunlight, filtered through the foliage, painted a warm mosaic on the forest floor as he worked.

Micharas, the skilled hunter, emerged from the woods with a rabbit slung over his shoulder. Its fur, a mix of browns and greys, blended seamlessly with the earthy tones of the forest. With a flick of his knife, he expertly began to prepare the rabbit for their evening meal. The rustling leaves and the distant call of birds provided a natural backdrop to his task.

Lady Katherine, her eyes keen for foraging, had explored the underbrush and uncovered a variety of mushrooms. Delicate caps in shades of white and brown were carefully cradled in her hands. She moved with measured grace, her fingers deftly plucking only those mushrooms she deemed safe for consumption. Her findings promised to add a flavorful dimension to their meal.

Jaw had set about securing the campsite. He examined the perimeter, his keen eyes scanning for any signs of potential threats. His hands moved with practised efficiency as he reinforced their makeshift barrier with fallen branches and strategically placed rocks. The crackling of leaves underfoot and the occasional snap of a twig marked his silent but purposeful movements.

Antonius, proud of his stone-ringed fire pit, patted himself down in search of the flint that he had picked up while looking for rocks. He seemed to have misplaced it. Jaw, who was knelt by the barrier that he was securing, had been watching him as he worked. "Are you okay?" Jaw asked puzzled by Antonius's own confusion as he patted himself down frantically.

"I swear I picked up some flint," he proclaimed as he rummaged about in leaves and branches around his feet. Jaw looked around and, after confirming that everyone was busy doing their own things, he spoke.

"Move back," he instructed Antonius, who was in close proximity to the fire pit. Antonius, puzzled by the request, took a step back.

Jaw reached out his arm, still holding onto the barrier with his other hand, he outstretched his fingers and aimed the palm of his hand at the pile of wood before Antonius. Antonius's eyes widened in anticipation, lost for words at what he was witnessing, as Jaw muttered at a barely audible level, "Fireball." The flames burst from his hand with a tremendous amount of force as a single and small ball of flames propelled forth, striking the fire with a residual *thump*.

Antonius, awestruck by the display, came rushing over seemingly to assist Jaw in his duties as the fire crackled behind him. "You can do magic?" he whispered excitedly.

Jaw did not reply; instead, he simply nodded. His face held a stern and contemplative look as he continued tethering the branch screen upright using a vine of ivy.

Sitting on a fallen log, Micharas skewered the prepared rabbit on a makeshift spit, holding it over the fire. The scent of searing meat filled the air, awakening appetites dulled by a day of travel and exertion.

Lady Katherine, her hands filled with the vibrant colours of gathered mushrooms, began to prepare a savoury concoction. Her fingers moved with precision as she combined ingredients, infusing the air with the promise of a delicious meal.

Jaw, his watchful gaze now turned to the surroundings beyond the campsite, remained alert. The flickering firelight played on the edges of his features, casting shadows that seemed to dance with the secrets of the dawning night.

Antonius sat by, watching Jaw now with an intense stare. The sort of stare that you would expect given the sudden revelation that he and only he had just discovered. Jaw could see the statement boiling within him; he knew it was only a matter of time before the boy outed his secret.

As the sun dipped below the horizon the small camp took shape. The stones circled a crackling fire, the dancing flames casting a warm glow on the faces of the weary travellers. The aroma of roasting rabbit mingled with the earthy fragrance of the mushrooms, creating an enticing blend that permeated the air.

As darkness settled over the forest, the group gathered around the fire, their faces illuminated by its warm embrace. The clearing, once silent, now echoed with the sizzling sounds of their makeshift feast. The stream, its gentle flow and constant murmur in the background, added a soothing melody to the evening's symphony.

The small camp in the heart of the woods became a sanctuary, a temporary refuge where the trials of the day could be momentarily forgotten.

Antonius, unable to contain his excitement, suddenly blurted out, "Jaw can do magic!" The statement hung in the air, breaking the calm of the evening.

Micharas, caught off guard by this revelation, turned his gaze toward Jaw, his eyes reflecting surprise and a hint of curiosity.

"Magic?" Micharas questioned, his voice carrying a mix of disbelief and intrigue. "What kind of magic can you do, and how long have you been able to do it?" He leaned in, his eyes focused on Jaw as if searching for any sign of deception.

Jaw, who had been preparing himself for several days now to reveal this talent was not anticipating Antonius's revelation to come quite so soon. He looked up and met Micharas's gaze with a measured intensity. The flames danced in his eyes as he contemplated how much to reveal. "It's not something I advertise," he began, his voice carrying a hint of mystery. "I can manipulate fire. It's a talent I've had for quite some time."

Micharas raised an eyebrow, his curiosity piqued. "Fire manipulation? Why have you never used it before? We could have used that during the battles with the Alts."

Jaw's gaze remained steady, and he took a moment before responding. "It is true, I could have used it earlier. The thing is that I often forget that I can do it."

Antonius chimed in eagerly, "It was amazing! Jaw just pointed at the wood and said 'Fireball,' and then flames shot out from his hand and lit up the fire!"

Micharas nodded, still processing the information. "So, you've been hiding this talent from us all this time?"

Jaw's expression remained impassive. "It's not about hiding. It's about discretion. Magic is a powerful tool, but it can also be a dangerous one. There are consequences to its use."

Lady Katherine, who had been silent, observing the exchange, finally spoke. "Jaw, do you have other magical abilities?" Her voice, calm and measured, cut through the conversation.

Jaw hesitated for a moment before responding. "I have a few tricks up my sleeve, just like you do, but I only use them when necessary. I had been trying to decide when the best time would be to tell you but it just never came up. I am sorry if you feel betrayed by me keeping this from you."

Lady Katherine nodded, accepting his explanation for the time being.

Micharas, not easily dissuaded, pressed further, "How did you learn this? Have you always had this ability?"

Jaw's gaze shifted to the flames, memories flickering in his eyes. "I learned it a long time ago, in circumstances I'd rather not discuss. It's not the sort of thing you parade around announcing to the world."

As they talked, the fire crackled in the centre of the clearing, casting shadows that danced on the faces of the group. The mysterious revelation added a new layer to their understanding of Jaw, introducing an element of magic into their already complex journey.

The night wore on, and the small clearing fell into a hushed serenity. The crackling fire, now reduced to flickering embers, cast a dim glow over the sleeping forms of the adventurers. The rhythmic sounds of their steady breaths harmonised with the rustling leaves and the distant murmur of the stream.

Jaw sat alone, his back against a sturdy tree, staring into the vast expanse of the night sky. The stars above twinkled brightly, oblivious to the inner turmoil that brewed within him. Doubt gnawed at the edges of his resolve, whispering that revealing his magical abilities might have been a grave mistake.

In the silent theatre of his thoughts, Jaw argued with himself. He questioned the wisdom of laying bare a part of himself that he had kept hidden for so long. The dangers of trust, the vulnerability of openness, all echoed in his mind like a haunting melody.

His gaze fixated on the dying embers, the warmth now more of a fading memory. Jaw's internal debate intensified, the weight of his decisions bearing down on him. The night, usually a companion to his solitude, felt like an adversary, amplifying the cacophony of conflicting thoughts.

Just when the struggle within him reached its peak, a quiet rustle announced Lady Katherine's approach. She moved gracefully, her steps soft against the leaf-littered ground. Without a word, she settled beside Jaw, her presence a gentle balm to the tempest raging within him. The weight lifted, not through spoken reassurances but purely through her being there with him.

Lady Katherine hesitated for a moment, glancing at Jaw with a look of concern. "Is now a good time to talk?" she inquired gently, her voice carrying a sincerity that sought to bridge the gap between them.

Jaw, still staring into the night, nodded slightly, acknowledging her presence. "Yeah, what's up?" he replied, his tone gruff but not dismissive.

She took a deep breath before continuing. "I couldn't help but notice something was off. Have I said or done something to upset you?" Lady Katherine's concern etched across her face.

He remembered that she had tried to bring up this subject before. "No," He responded tersely, his gaze remaining fixed on the distant horizon. "I'm just wary."

"Wary of what?" she pressed, hoping there was more to his wariness than just her.

"People," Jaw admitted after a brief pause. "Especially people who can do magic."

This revelation surprised Lady Katherine, and she leaned back slightly, giving him space to elaborate. "Why magic?" she inquired, her curiosity evident.

"Your kind of magic," he clarified, his tone revealing a mixture of wariness and unease. "I've seen you cast spells without saying a word. Some of your spells seem to sustain themselves without your constant attention, and I've heard you cast in a language I don't understand."

Lady Katherine sighed, recognizing the source of his apprehension. "It's a matter of practice, Jaw. When a mage has had as much time to study and practice as I have, they can overcome the need to vocalise every spell. It becomes second nature."

Jaw, however, seemed unconvinced. "And the spells that sustain themselves?"

She nodded, understanding his scepticism. "I use a silent spell called 'Repeat.' It allows my spells to replicate themselves without needing my constant focus. It's a skill developed over years of study and mastery."

Jaw listened, but the mention of the language seemed to linger in the air. Lady Katherine noticed his focus on that particular aspect. "The language I sometimes use is ancient and powerful," she began, her voice carrying a weight of history. "It's a language tied to the roots of magic itself. It's not something I take lightly."

He remained silent, his gaze unmoving. Lady Katherine sensed the unspoken questions lingering in his eyes but chose to let the revelation settle.

"It's forgotten, isn't it?" Jaw spoke, cutting through the quiet with a question that held more power than any spell.

His words hung in the air like a revelation, and Lady Katherine's expression shifted from curiosity to stunned disbelief. Her eyes betrayed her shock, a flicker of vulnerability that did not escape Jaw's attention. In that silent moment, the weight of understanding settled between them.

Lady Katherine, still recovering from the surprise, remained silent. Jaw, watching her closely, continued. "You don't need to say anything. I understand."

She blinked, almost as if she needed a moment to comprehend that Jaw knew of a magic so deeply entrenched in secrecy. A magic that required not practice, but a profound understanding of ancient words, a power that transcended the norms of their world.

The revelation lingered, but Lady Katherine, with her practised composure, settled herself. Jaw, however, was not one to let mysteries linger. "You don't have to explain," he offered.

But she did. "How do you know about it?" she finally asked, her voice a mix of curiosity and caution.

Jaw's gaze, intense and resolute, met hers. "I've encountered it before."

She nodded, still processing the fact that her secret was discovered by a complete unknown individual in the middle of the woods. Jaw, seeing her silent struggle, decided to shift the focus of the conversation. "Enough about you. Let's talk about me."

She raised an eyebrow questioningly, it seemed very unlike him to invite her to pry. "Why don't you like magic?" she inquired gently.

Jaw took a deep breath, his eyes momentarily distant. "There was a fire many years ago," he began, the memories resurfacing like embers. "I took the blame for it. It destroyed my family home, and killed my parents. I didn't start the fire, but I ran from it." Lady Katherine listened, her eyes reflecting a mix of empathy and understanding. "The Village Elders held a trial. The choices were execution of a small boy or exile. Magic is powerful, granted it requires dedication to learn but I have seen it destroy lives, homes and kingdoms, I have seen wars waged over it. When all other weapons can be disarmed and removed from conflict a spell remains in the mind of the caster and no force can remove that, no matter how hard you try." He concluded, his wisdom and experience rang loudly in his words.

The weight of his past hung in the air, the echoes of a childhood marked by tragedy and misunderstanding. Thunder rumbled in the distance, mimicking the turmoil within Jaw.

Lady Katherine, sensing the depth of his pain, placed a comforting hand on his shoulder. "Thank you for sharing that with me," she said softly, her voice a balm to his wounded history. The rumble of thunder sounded again, a distant acknowledgment of the storms both past and present.

Lady Katherine let the weight of Jaw's revelation linger in the air for a moment, allowing the weight of his past to settle. Then, as if navigating a delicate dance, she continued her line of questioning with a mix of curiosity and genuine interest.

"How long did it take you to learn to cast Fireball? Can you cast other spells?" she inquired, her voice a gentle encouragement for him to share more about his magical abilities.

Before Jaw could respond, a low growl of thunder rolled through the sky, louder this time, as though the storm had drawn closer. The forest canopy above them rustled in response, and the faint pattering of raindrops began to tap against the leaves.

Lady Katherine, sensing the imminent rain, stood up, her focus shifting to the protective dome spell she was about to cast. However, before she could weave the incantation, Jaw placed his hand on top of hers, pinning it to his shoulder. She glanced at him where he sat on the floor still, puzzled by the sudden contact.

With a calm determination, Jaw lifted his other hand into the air. Lady Katherine watched in amazement and surprise as he spoke the word, "Repeat," followed by "Water Barrier."

As the last syllable left his lips, a translucent bubble materialised around their campsite. The rain, which had started to intensify, was now repelled by the magical shield. Drops of water slid off the invisible barrier, leaving them untouched beneath. The dome shimmered with a faint glow, creating an otherworldly ambiance within.

Lady Katherine's eyes widened in astonishment. "You can cast Water Barrier?" she exclaimed, the realisation of Jaw's magical prowess unfolding before her. The thunder grumbled above, seemingly acknowledging the magic that defied the natural order.

She settled back down beside him, the astonishment in her eyes fading into a contemplative gaze. The realisation dawned on her that Jaw had effortlessly cast "Repeat," a spell that took her considerable time and effort to master, a spell she hadn't mentioned, and he had not known about, until now.

A silent understanding passed between them as Lady Katherine nodded, acknowledging the unspoken exchange. "You are an enigma, Jaw. I don't think I have met someone with quite as many secrets as me before now," she remarked, a hint of admiration in her voice for the mysteries that surrounded him.

Jaw, now with his hand back on his leg and his head bowed, seemed to carry the weight of his own thoughts. "Sometimes secrets are the only companions worth keeping." he stated, his words lingering in the air like a profound truth.

As the night continued, the rain painted a soothing melody around them, a rhythm that blended seamlessly with the symphony of nature. The two of them eventually succumbed to the embrace of sleep, leaning against the sturdy tree. The forest, wrapped in the tranquillity of the night, cradled both of their secrets in its ancient arms.

As Lady Katherine opened her eyes to the new day, the first thing that greeted her was the absence of Jaw beside her. The morning light filtered through the canopy, casting a gentle glow on the clearing. She sat there for a moment, taking in the tranquil surroundings—the quiet rustle of leaves, the distant murmur of the stream, and the soft twittering of awakening birds.

The remnants of the rain lingered in the air, creating a fresh, crisp scent that spoke of renewal. The memory of the protective barrier Jaw had conjured hovered in her mind, a faint trace of wonder blending with the reality of the awakening day. She wondered, for a brief moment, if the magical shield had been a mere dream, a product of the night's imagination.

As she observed the woodland around their camp, she noticed Jaw at the edge of the clearing, engaged in gathering dry wood for them to put into a travel pack. The bubble was gone, leaving behind only the dew-kissed grass and the receding shadows. Lady Katherine questioned the reality of the magical feat, but the sense of serenity that enveloped the morning hinted at something more profound.

Micharas and Antonius were starting to stir, their movements synchronised with the gradual unveiling of the day. The sky above transformed into a canvas of radiant hues, the sunrise casting a warm crimson glow that painted the horizon. The branches above seemed to reach out to the emerging sun, creating a captivating dance of light and colour.

Lady Katherine couldn't help but feel a sense of relief, a gentle warmth spreading within her as the morning embraced the world with its vibrant palette.

The air, now free from the weight of the previous night's rain, held a clarity that mirrored the clarity in Lady Katherine's mind. The day ahead, promising and untarnished, whispered of new possibilities and the resilience that dawn brings after the darkest hours of the night.

The days that followed were a tapestry of diverse landscapes and changing scenery as the group pressed forward on their journey. The Eastland Kingdom unfolded its beauty before them once more, each step revealing a new facet of the land they traversed.

The initial days led them through sprawling fields, the grass beneath their boots giving way to the gentle undulations of the terrain. Sunlit meadows stretched out in vast expanses, quilted with wildflowers that swayed in the breeze. A herd of wild deer grazed contently on the edge, safely away from the reach of the hunters. The air carried the fragrance of blooming flora, a symphony of colours and scents that accompanied their every step.

As they progressed, the landscape shifted. Rolling hills emerged, their peaks and valleys offering panoramic views of the kingdom below. The sunlight played on the grassy slopes, creating patterns of light and dark that danced with the wind. Small woodlands punctuated the journey, providing a welcome shade and a brief respite from the open fields.

Days turned into nights, and the party's fellowship echoed through the countryside. Laughter and shared stories reverberated through the air as they reminisced about the challenges they had faced and the victories they had earned. The evenings, spent around campfires under starlit skies, became a ritual of bonding and shared experiences.

The journey led them through wide-open spaces, where the horizon seemed to stretch endlessly. A sense of anticipation filled the air as they neared their destination, the capital looming closer with each passing day.

Then, as they ascended a hill, laughter on their lips and camaraderie in their hearts, the joyous atmosphere abruptly shifted. The hill's summit unveiled a scene that silenced their mirth—a vast expanse of Alt forces sprawled out before them. The army, seemingly endless, expanded from horizon to horizon, a formidable display of military might.

The group halted, their expressions transforming from lightheartedness to stern determination. The Alt Army, a sea of warriors, archers, mages and banners, seemed to defy the very limits of the landscape. The reality of the impending confrontation hung in the air, and the once carefree journey now faced a formidable challenge that stretched far beyond the hills and meadows they had traversed, as they were slapped back to the reality of their mission.

The group, fear gripping their hearts, hastily retreated down the hill, their movements careful and swift in the hope that they had not been noticed. However, the ominous sound of a horn pierced the air from the edge of the Alt Army closest to their position, shattering any illusions of remaining unseen. Micharas, his face set in a mask of panic, shouted, "Run! Now!"

Antonius, almost instinctively, drew his bow and notched an arrow, ready to defend against the approaching threat. However, before he could release his shot, his brother seized him by the scruff of his back and forcefully pulled him away. "We can't fight an army of that size! We need to retreat!"

Antonius, still gripped by the fervour of battle, stared back at the hilltop, torn between the desire to stand and fight and the stark reality of their situation. Micharas, astounded that he had to convince his brother of the impossibility of their odds, led the retreat down the hill.

As they descended, a group of Alt scouts on horseback rose from the hill and began chasing the party. The urgency in Micharas's voice heightened as they realised escape was no longer a simple matter. "Keep moving! We can't let them catch us!" he shouted.

The scouts, skilled riders, closed the distance quickly, their mounts thundering over the terrain. Lady Katherine, spotted the approaching threat and alerted the others. The realisation that confrontation was inevitable settled upon them like a heavy cloak.

With no other choice, the party turned to face their pursuers. The Alt scouts, determined and relentless, closed in. The air crackled with tension as the two forces collided, the fate of the small group hanging in the balance.

The party, a well-coordinated unit in the face of danger, swiftly readied themselves for the oncoming threat. Antonius, his focus unwavering, lifted his bow and prepared to release an arrow. Micharas mirrored his brother's actions, grabbing an arrow from Antonius's quiver and drawing it, the string of his bow taut as he aimed with deadly accuracy. Jaw, the seasoned warrior, unsheathed his sword and raised his shield in a defensive stance. Meanwhile, Lady Katherine, the arcane force of the group, crackled with energy as lightning danced between her outstretched fingers.

The Alt riders, six in number, charged toward them, their weapons at the ready. Three brandished crossbows, and the other three wielded menacing spears. The clash seemed inevitable as their forces closed the distance rapidly.

The confrontation erupted with Antonius releasing his arrow with deadly precision, finding its mark in the opening of a helmet and knocking an Alt rider clean from their horse. Micharas swiftly followed suit, taking down another with calculated accuracy, his arrow whistled through the air, and crunched as it impacted the skull of his target. The air reverberated with the distinctive sound of a crossbow bolt being released, but Jaw, quick on his feet, lifted his shield, making a momentary judgement of the trajectory of the shot he dove through the air in front of Micharas and deftly blocked the projectile, catching it in the thick wooded shield. Antonius, displaying remarkable archery skill, released another arrow, eliminating the final archer as it embedded itself in the Alts chest, toppling him from his horse. The Alt corpse, already disintegrating, still attached to the saddle was carried off as the horse continued past them.

Lady Katherine, finally done gathering the energy she needed, unleashed a spell with a resounding incantation: "Tempest Wrath." The sky itself seemed to respond as lightning cascaded from her fingertips, engulfing the remaining three Alt riders and their horses in its devastating fury. In mere moments, the attacking pursuers were decimated, their forms left sprawled on the ground as they began to melt away.

The small party, having faced the immediate threat, took a moment to assess the aftermath, their breaths heavy with adrenaline. The field echoed with the sounds of battle raging towards them from the other side of the hill. The bellowing of horns marked the oncoming annihilation of them if they failed to make themselves scarce.

Micharas's voice cut through the chaos, his command clear and concise. The remaining horses, the only chance for a swift escape, were quickly claimed by the party. Micharas, agile and experienced, mounted his steed with practised ease and extended a hand to Antonius, who accepted the assistance.

Jaw and Lady Katherine mirrored the action, swiftly climbing onto the other horse. The Alt army, an ominous force, surged over the crest of the hill, their black metal and leather clad figures stark against the horizon.

Micharas urged their horse forward, flicking the reins and clicking at it with his mouth, a desperate attempt to outrun the impending onslaught. Antonius, gripping his brother tightly, could feel the adrenaline coursing through his veins.

As the horse galloped, the Alt archers began their deadly assault, filling the sky with a massive cloud of arrows. The world above them darkened as the lethal rain descended. Micharas, Antonius, Jaw, and Lady Katherine's eyes widened with dread as the storm of arrows loomed.

Lady Katherine gave Jaw a quick nod to follow suit as she climbed on and grabbed his waist with one hand, her mind quick and decisive, turned to face the approaching tempest of arrows. With a powerful incantation, she raised her hand and shouted, "Intercept."

A brilliant burst of dazzling blue light erupted from her fingertips, pulsing outwards towards the onslaught. The arrows, momentarily frozen in their descent, created a horrifying sight in the air. The party, their hearts pounding, raced ahead as the arrows one by one broke free from the magical restraint.

The arrows, like a relentless storm, continued their deadly descent, each one carrying the potential for destruction. Micharas skillfully guided the horse, a dance of life and death, as they weaved through the onslaught. The air was thick with tension, the rhythmic thuds of arrows striking the earth creating a dissonant melody of danger.

Lady Katherine, her eyes sharp and focused, could almost feel the deadly whistle of arrows passing perilously close. A sudden gust of wind accompanied the whooshing sound as an arrow, aimed directly at her, narrowly missed, grazing the edge of her cloak and missing both her and the horse. The party collectively held their breath, a momentary gasp within the chaos. It was a hair's breadth from disaster.

Jaw, positioned in front of Lady Katherine, felt the rush of air as the arrow sailed past her. Startled, he instinctively tightened his grip on the reins "Are you okay?" He asked out of concern, the resounding impact of the arrow striking the shield on his back sent vibrations through his body, a cold panic set in, knowing that she was between them and it.

"I am fine," She replied loudly, "It missed." A wave of relief ran over him at the sound of her voice. He flicked the reins again, and the horse, clearly also panicked, found extra energy to run.

Micharas, a steady hand on the reins, urged the horse to greater speed. The thundering hooves became a desperate rhythm of escape. The Alt army, now left behind, bellowed in frustration as their elusive prey slipped through their grasp. The sound of horns marked their annoyance. The distance between the party and the pursuing horde grew, but the echoes of battle lingered, a haunting reminder of the peril they narrowly avoided.

The party, hearts racing, pressed on, leaving the tumultuous scene behind. The need for escape painted every beat of the horses' hooves, each step carrying them farther from the immediate threat. As the adrenaline-fueled gallop continued, the distant sounds of battle faded, replaced by the rhythmic cadence of their own breaths, a symphony of relief playing in the air.

With the Alt army left behind, the party galloped on stolen horses, and faced the realisation that their journey to the capital had taken an even more urgent turn. The sprawling threat of the Alt army forced them to reconsider their route, opting for a longer but safer path to avoid detection.

The newly acquired horses became a boon to their mission, reducing travel time. The urgency to reach the capital heightened as they grasped the magnitude of the impending attack.

The party was newly fueled by a mixture of determination and uncertainty. The question lingered on Micharas's mind however, will the king heed their warning? The journey behind them had unfolded as a treacherous path, fraught with challenges, and yet they faced the weight of an impending conflict ahead of them.

Chapter 10

Another day rose in the Eastland Kingdom as the party stirred on the final day of their journey. The air carried a sense of anticipation, the distant sight of the Eastland Castle on the far horizon signalling the nearing end of their arduous journey.

As they packed their campsite, Lady Katherine couldn't help but comment on the looming silhouette in the distance. "There it is, the Eastland Castle," she said, her eyes fixed on the imposing structure. "A symbol of strength and history, overlooking the realm it guards."

Antonius, squinting against the morning sun, couldn't hide his excitement. "Finally, we're almost there! I can't wait to see the city up close."

Micharas, the appointed leader of the group, added, "Remember, we're not just here to see the sights. We have a crucial message for the king."

"Yeah yeah," Antonius replied, looking out at the horizon with anticipation. "I have been wondering something though." He paused, unsure as to whether the next thing he was about to ask would be considered a daft question or not."

"What's that then?" Micharas pressed him for his question as the group began to start walking.

"It's called the Eastland Castle, but it's a city with a castle inside of it. Does that mean that the castle is the Eastland Castle and the city is called Eastland or am I missing something?" Antonius asked his brother in a hushed tone, hoping that the other two would not be able to hear him just in case this was indeed a silly question. Though it was evidently no use as Lady Katherine was the one who answered him after Micharas considered the question himself for a few moments.

"The city is called the Eastland Castle. You see the castle itself is actually called The Throne of the Kingdom. It's an unusual citation I know, but the castle was built first and given the name The Eastland Castle. It was not until many years after that the city was built around it. At which point the king of the time decided that the entire city would mirror the name of the castle." She explained to them both.

"I see, thank you." Antonius replied, giving her a quick glance and a smile over his shoulder.

The journey had been a mix of challenges and revelations, and as they set off, the sight of the castle provided a renewed sense of purpose. The Eastland Castle, a formidable fortress with high walls, stood as a guardian of the capital. Its towers, visible even from a distance, hinted at the grandeur within.

As the party approached the city, the high walls became more defined, adorned with banners that bore the emblem of the Eastland Kingdom—a regal crown, resplendent against a backdrop of deep blue. The symbol, intricately embroidered in gold thread, fluttered in the gentle breeze, signalling their imminent entry into the heart of the realm.

Lady Katherine, her gaze fixed on the crown emblem, remarked with a sense of pride, "The crown, a symbol of our unity and strength. It's a fitting reminder of what we all fight for."

The castle, firmly situated atop the hill within the heart of the city, now revealed more details as they drew closer. Its towers, proudly displaying the same regal emblem, seemed to reach even higher, emphasising the authority and legacy it held over the land.

The party quickened their pace, the looming presence of the Eastland Castle urging them forward. The city gates, guarded by soldiers in gleaming armour, opened before them as they approached.

The mighty gatehouse stood as a bastion against attacks, a portcullis that could keep out the gods themselves dangled from it, poised and ready to drop into place at a moment's notice. The high walls of the city stretched upwards sixteen metres into the sky and stood a bold eight metres thick.

Upon entering the city, they found themselves on the bustling main market street, bathed in the warm glow of late morning sunlight. The lively atmosphere enveloped them as merchants hawked their wares, and the air was filled with the mingling scents of various goods. The aromatic blend of freshly baked bread, exotic spices, and the earthy undertones of leather goods wafted through the air.

Stalls lined the cobbled street, each vendor vying for attention with colourful displays of fruits, fabrics, and trinkets. The market was a symphony of sounds—the chatter of vendors haggling, the clinking of coins, the rhythmic clatter of hooves as caravans passed through.

The city seemed to pulse with life, and the party navigated the vibrant tapestry of its daily existence. Citizens of various occupations bustled about, creating a mosaic of diversity. A blacksmith, his hammer ringing against an anvil, crafted intricate pieces of armour. A street performer captivated a small crowd with acrobatic feats, adding a touch of entertainment to the busy scene around them.

As the party made their way through the market, they encountered curious glances from the locals. Some eyed them with mild interest, while others continued about their business with an air of indifference. Children played games in narrow alleyways, and stray cats weaved through the crowd in pursuit of unseen prey.

Lady Katherine, ever perceptive, noted the subtle shifts in the atmosphere. "We're not just strangers in a city," she remarked. "We're guests in a living, breathing entity. Each step we take here is a step into the beating heart of the capital."

The party, amidst the vibrant market street, found themselves standing before two distinctively different taverns, each exuding its unique charm.

On one side of the bustling thoroughfare was The Dirty Spoon, the high street's main tavern, inn and had its own stables adjacent to it. Despite its name, it stood as a presentable and much-loved establishment. The strains of live music spilled out into the street, inviting passersby to step inside. The building, with a certain timeless charm, boasted a stable nearby, a convenience for those arriving on horseback.

On the opposite side of the high street stood The Polished Turd. The promise of cheaper drinks beckoned, and the tantalising scent of baking pies wafted through its doors and windows, creating an irresistible allure. The tavern, obviously newer and less well-built than its competitor, lacked a stable but compensated with a wider layout. Despite its name and apparent simplicity, the sounds of merriment emanated from within, promising a jovial atmosphere.

Lady Katherine surveyed the options, a thoughtful expression on her face. "The Dirty Spoon seems more established, and the live music is a tempting offer. On the other hand, The Polished Turd might surprise us with its charm, and the smell of those pies is hard to resist."

Antonius eagerly added, "Perhaps we could split up and reconvene later? I've heard stories that the best tales are told in taverns, and I'd hate to miss out on any local gossip." Micharas looked at his brother with scepticism. He knew all too well what his younger sibling hoped to find inside.

Micharas, with a hint of caution, chimed in, "Whatever we decide, let's be mindful. We're here on a mission, and loose lips can sometimes sink more than ships."

As the group stood at the crossroads of the bustling market street, each member voiced their desires and considerations.

Antonius, his eyes gleaming with curiosity, gestured towards The Polished Turd. "I say we check out this tavern first. Cheaper drinks and the smell of those pies—it's too tempting to resist. Who knows what interesting characters we might find inside?"

Micharas, a pragmatic glint in his eye, had a different priority. "I need to get my sword sharpened. A dull blade is a liability, especially in unfamiliar territory. The blacksmith's should be nearby; I'll catch up with you all later."

Lady Katherine, wearied from the journey, expressed her inclination, "I would love nothing more than a proper bed after nights spent under the stars. Let's find an inn, perhaps inquire about the local rumours and news while we're at it. We can reconvene refreshed and ready."

Jaw, unwavering in his focus, stated, "I suggest we head straight to the king. Our mission is paramount, and the sooner we deliver our message, the better."

Antonius teased, "Come on, Jaw! A little diversion won't hurt. We can't just barge into the king's chambers unprepared. We need information and allies."

Lady Katherine, however, intervened, "We have a limited amount of coin, and I'm not sure we want to spend it all on drinks and diversions. How about we prioritise the audience with the king, and then we can plan our accommodations and other tasks accordingly?"

The group nodded in agreement, as Antonius conceded to his elders. All save from Micharas who had slipped away, leaving the main market street behind as he ventured into the underbelly of the city, in search of a blacksmith, but not just any blacksmith. He sought a specific one.

As Micharas slipped away from the bustling main market street, he found himself in a well-lit backstreet that ran parallel to the high street. The air here was filled with the scent of burning coal from nearby forges, and the rhythmic clinking of hammers on metal echoed through the alley.

The first shop he passed was named "Steelcraft Haven," its window displaying an array of finely crafted weapons and armour. The proprietor, a burly man with a grizzled beard, nodded in acknowledgment as Micharas walked by. Further down, "Enchanting Ember," a shop specialising in magical trinkets and enchanted accessories, caught his eye. Glowing amulets and shimmering rings were on display, enticing those seeking a touch of the arcane.

Next to it stood "Gemstone Glint," a jeweller's boutique that sparkled with the brilliance of finely cut gemstones. Rings, necklaces, and earrings of exquisite design were on display, capturing the attention of passersby with their allure.

Further down the backstreet, Micharas discovered "Arcane Alcove," a magical emporium specialising in potions and elixirs. Shelves lined with colourful vials contained potions for healing, invisibility, and even potions that enhanced one's physical abilities.

Adjacent to it was "Orbcraft Emporium," a shop dedicated to the art of crafting magical orbs. Glowing spheres of various sizes hovered within glass cases, each emanating a different aura of enchantment. These orbs were said to hold mystical properties, ranging from illumination to protection.

Continuing his exploration, Micharas came across "Scroll Symphony," a quaint shop dedicated to the creation of magical scrolls. Inscribed parchments filled the shelves, each containing a single-use spell making them accessible to non-mages. The shopkeeper, a wizened figure with ink-stained fingers, greeted him warmly.

As he walked further, Micharas noticed "Chronicle Crafts," a specialised establishment offering finely crafted spellbooks and tomes. The aroma of leather and parchment permeated the air, inviting magic enthusiasts to peruse the detailed volumes that lined the shelves.

Near the end of the backstreet, Micharas walked past the imposing "Money Makes Money Bank." The building was grand and covered with symbols of prosperity. A steady stream of people entered and exited, engaged in various financial transactions.

Finally he stood before a blacksmith's shop and forge, the name of the establishment was The Hunters Arms, nestled within the bustling backstreet, it presented itself as a haven for those seeking quality weapons and armour. The shop's exterior boasted a façade of dark, weathered wood, adorned with wrought iron detailing depicting scenes of hunting and forging. A finely crafted sign, depicting a crossed sword and hammer beneath a stag's head, swung gently in the breeze, announcing the establishment's name.

The large, open windows showcased a display of the shop's wares. Weapons of various types hung from sturdy wooden racks, catching the sunlight in a dazzling display. Swords with razor-sharp edges, gleaming axes, and unstrung bows were meticulously arranged, each piece a testament to the skill of the blacksmith who toiled within.

The forge, visible through a partially open door, emanated heat and the rhythmic clang of hammer on metal. Anvil and hammer rested at the heart of the workshop, surrounded by barrels of quenching oil and racks of unfinished weapons in various stages of completion. The air carried the distinct scent of hot metal, a sensory reminder of the craftsmanship in progress.

A low hum of activity filled the air as patrons and blacksmiths alike moved about, engrossed in discussions about weapon preferences and customizations. The sound of metal meeting metal, punctuated by occasional sparks, created a symphony that resonated with the heartbeat of the city's craftsmanship.

The atmosphere in the busy street was charged with a sense of purpose and anticipation. Micharas couldn't help but feel a connection to the age-old tradition of forging and the craftsmanship that defined the Eastland Kingdom. The Hunters Arms beckoned not just as a place to acquire weapons but as a demonstration of the city's dedication to the art of hunting.

As he stood before the shop, Micharas sensed the heartbeat of the city's craftsmanship, each strike of the hammer echoing the resilience and strength of the people. The bustling street, filled with the aroma of heated metal and the lively chatter of patrons, made it clear that in the capital, the art of blacksmithing was more than just a trade—it was a cultural cornerstone.

There was a loud clang as something was put down inside the forge, a figure emerged, shrouded in the residual heat and soot of his craft. The blacksmith, a formidable presence, stood tall and mighty before him. His muscular frame bespoke years of dedication to the craft, the sinews of his arms bulging with strength earned at the anvil.

Draped in a heavy leather apron, now bearing the marks of countless projects, the blacksmith revealed a physique sculpted by the demands of his trade. The flickering light from the forge played upon his features, casting shadows that accentuated the lines of determination etched onto his face.

Green eyes, sharp and discerning, reflected the weapons displayed in the shop's window, a silent testament of his creations. Long strands of brown hair, streaked with dirt and sweat, badges of his labour, were pulled back and tied into a practical knot, allowing him an unobstructed view of the workspace around him.

With deliberate motions, he wiped his face with a coarse cloth, revealing features weathered by both the flames of the forge and the passage of time. The lines etched into his forehead spoke of challenges overcome and victories won in the dance of steel and fire.

Setting aside his tongs, the blacksmith's gaze met Micharas's. A nod of acknowledgment passed between them, an unspoken understanding of the shared respect for the art of war. The blacksmith's hands, calloused and marked by a lifetime of shaping metal, now rested as he awaited the purpose behind Micharas' visit.

The air in The Hunters Arms grew tense as the blacksmith's eyes scrutinised Micharas, his gaze flickering with a discerning intensity. The weight of his gaze hinted at the anticipation of an impending storm, a gathering tempest on the horizon. The onlookers in the busy street felt the tension, their whispers hushed as they awaited the brewing conflict.

A subtle shift in the blacksmith's demeanour hinted at a looming revelation, an invisible force coiling like a serpent ready to strike. With a sudden and deliberate motion, he pushed aside the heavy oak desk before him, the scraping sounds echoed down the street as he rested his hammer atop of it, moving it with just one hand. The gesture was a harbinger, a portent of impending tumult.

For a fleeting moment, a palpable unease hung in the air, the silence amplifying the tension. He walked towards the adventurer, a grim scowl on his face like his wares had just been ridiculed by this man, this puny and frail looking man when compared to the might and size of the blacksmith himself. They stood for a moment, toe to toe staring at each other, Micharas needing to crane his head back to meet the man's eyes.

The mighty blacksmith enveloped Micharas in a bone-crushing hug, a display of genuine affection that shattered the preconceived notions of impending conflict. The unease that had gripped the street moments before now gave way to a shared sense of relief, the ominous atmosphere dispelled by the embrace.

Meanwhile, as the group continued their journey through the city, Antonius scanned the surroundings and noticed Micharas's absence. Lady Katherine, raising an eyebrow, inquired, "Where did Micharas run off to?"

Antonius shrugged. "He mentioned catching up with us later. Must have some business of his own to attend to."

With a collective nod, they decided not to dwell on Micharas' whereabouts and focused on their mission. The street they traversed led them away from the bustling market, gradually transitioning into residential areas. The architecture shifted from the commercial to the domestic, with houses lining the street, each bearing the unique marks of its occupants.

The atmosphere changed as well. The air was filled with the sounds of everyday life—children playing and the distant hum of day to day activity. The scent of home-cooked meals wafted through the air, mingling with the aroma of blooming flowers from well-tended gardens.

As they ascended the hill toward the castle, the social fabric of the city unfolded before them. The houses became more refined, the gardens more meticulously manicured. Residents in elegant attire passed by, acknowledging each other with nods of familiarity. The group found themselves walking through the heart of the city's social hierarchy.

Elite houses clustered the higher reaches of the hill, their facades reflecting wealth and status. Intricate wrought-iron gates guarded entrances, and well-tended lawns spread out before grand entrances. Lady Katherine couldn't help but admire the architecture and the evident prosperity that surrounded them.

Antonius remarked, "Seems like we're approaching the upper-class region of the city. The view must be spectacular from up there."

Lady Katherine, intrigued by Antonius's comment, suggested they pause for a moment to test his theory. The group turned around, their gaze tracing the winding road that led them through the city. The scene unfolded before them like a living tapestry.

The city sprawled beneath, its diverse districts interconnected by a labyrinth of streets and alleys. The gatehouse, a formidable structure, stood as a sentinel between the city and the rolling countryside beyond. The walls, sturdy and imposing, snaked their way through the urban landscape, an impressive display of the city's fortification.

The view extended beyond the city limits, capturing the seeming never ending hills and fields that stretched into the distance. The countryside, bathed in the warm glow of the afternoon sun, seemed to embrace the city in a tranquil embrace. The contrast between the bustling urban life and the serene expanse of nature painted a picture of harmony.

As the group absorbed the panoramic view, Antonius grinned, his theory confirmed. "See? Quite a sight, isn't it?"

Lady Katherine nodded in appreciation. "Indeed, Antonius. It's an incredible contrast between civilization and nature. Let's press on. The castle awaits."

The final stretch toward the castle proved to be a demanding ascent, the steep hill challenging the weary travellers after their long journey. Fatigue settled into their limbs, and each step became a confirmation of the endurance they had exhibited to reach this point. The architecture of the homes lining the incline were smaller than those of the social elites that fell back behind them, these seemed more like the homes of the more common folk, most likely inhabited by the castle's servants.

The steepness of the terrain necessitated unique architectural solutions, with some homes built into the hillside, their foundations anchored against the slope. Stone steps and winding pathways guided the way, and the evident lack of gardens between them. With many of the front doors opening straight onto the street itself.

As they approached the castle, its walls became increasingly visible, encircling the structure like an impenetrable fortress. The imposing fortifications were an empowering showcase towards the kingdom's commitment to security and protection. The group soon realised that approaching the front doors directly wasn't an option; instead, they were faced with the gatehouse of the castle walls.

Two guards, clad in gleaming armour, stood vigilant before the gatehouse, their eyes surveying those who sought entry. The high walls, crowned with battlements, loomed overhead, casting a shadow of authority. The gatehouse, a formidable structure in its own right, featured a sturdy portcullis that was lowered and locked in place.

As the travellers approached the gatehouse, the guards regarded them with a discerning eye. Lady Katherine, taking the lead, stepped forward with a confident demeanour. "We bear a message for the King," she announced, her tone carrying a blend of authority and respect.

The guards exchanged a brief glance before one of them, a seasoned warrior with a weathered expression, spoke. "State your business and present your credentials," he instructed, the weight of responsibility evident in his voice.

Lady Katherine, with a deft and subtle gesture, extended her hand behind her towards Jaw, the unspoken signal between them clear. Jaw, understanding the intent, approached her as if presenting something. In that moment, Lady Katherine, tapping into her magical prowess, summoned a neatly rolled parchment into her hand. With a quick and practised motion, she offered it to the guard.

The guard, curious but respectful, accepted the parchment and began to read its contents. The note, bearing an official-looking seal, declared:

"Lady Katherine Thorne, War Correspondent under the employ of Sir Shane," he concluded. Looking up at her with a scrutinising glare. He looked her up and down. Finally he seemed convinced based on her appearance and the paper. "And who are these?" He asked inquisitively.

"These are my bodyguards," she explained. "It was a very long and dangerous journey here and his eminence felt that I would require protection." she concluded. The two men behind her nodded.

The guard's stern countenance softened as Lady Katherine explained, a thoughtful expression replacing the initial curiosity. His gaze shifted to the two men flanking her, his eyes lingering for a moment on Jaw, who stood stoically, his presence emanating an air of quiet strength.

Satisfied with the explanation, the guard returned the parchment, acknowledging her entourage. "Very well," he said, his voice resonating with authority. With a forceful strike of his gauntlet against the metal, he commanded the opening of the portcullis.

The metallic clank echoed through the gatehouse as the heavy bars ascended, revealing the imposing gates leading into the Eastland Castle. The gates, complete with metal work depicting the kingdom's emblem—a regal crown—slowly swung open, revealing the inner sanctum of the castle.

As the group entered, the atmosphere changed from the bustling city streets to the more controlled and calculated environment within the castle walls. The air held a sense of formality, and the architecture spoke of centuries of history and power. Tall stone walls surrounded them, lined with banners displaying the crown emblem, fluttering proudly in the breeze.

The inner courtyard, a vast expanse with meticulously manicured gardens and cobblestone pathways, lay before them. Statues of past rulers and heroes adorned the grounds, capturing the essence of the kingdom's storied legacy. The castle itself, a sprawling structure of towers and battlements, loomed overhead, casting shadows on the path ahead.

A steward, dressed in fine livery, approached them, bowing respectfully. "And you are?" he asked courteously.

Lady Katherine leaned forward slightly, her gaze steady as she addressed the steward, "We come bearing urgent news, news that pertains not only to the safety of Celleos but to the very heart of Eastland Kingdom itself. Our journey has been one fraught with peril, and our message cannot wait. We implore you to take this information directly to the King."

She extended a hand, gesturing towards the parchment. "Those papers bear the seal of Sir Shane, and I, Lady Katherine Thorne, am a War Correspondent under his employ. We have witnessed the aftermath of the attack in Celleos and have crucial intelligence regarding a menacing force marching towards the capital."

Her voice carried the weight of urgency, the severity of the situation reflected in her eyes. "This is not merely a warning; it is a plea for action. Lives hang in the balance, and time is of the essence. Please, take us to the King so that we may convey the full extent of what we have discovered."

He took the parchment from her. Once he finished reading, the stewards gaze shifted from the parchment to Lady Katherine. "Wait here," he instructed, holding the document in his hand. "I will bring this to the attention of the King. Stay within the courtyard until summoned."

With that, the man turned and disappeared into the depths of the castle, leaving the group in the expansive courtyard. The surroundings were a blend of natural beauty and regal splendour. Vibrant roses filled the well-tended gardens, and statues of historical figures stood as silent sentinels, witnessing the passage of time within the castle walls.

The minutes passed in quiet contemplation as the group waited, taking in the magnificence of the Eastland Castle. Lady Katherine, Antonius, and Jaw exchanged glances, their thoughts lingering on the importance of their mission and the potential consequences that hung in the balance.

Eventually, the steward returned, an apologetic expression on his face. "My apologies for the delay. The King will see you now. Follow me to the audience chamber."

The group fell in step behind the steward, guided through the spectacular corridors of the castle. As they approached the audience chamber, the anticipation in the air grew palpable. The fate of the city rested on them.

The grand audience chamber awaited, its towering doors covered with intricate carvings swung open as Lady Katherine and her companions approached. Two guards, clad in the formal attire of the royal guard, stood at attention, swords at their hips, as they ceremoniously pulled the doors wide. The royal guard uniform featured deep blue tunics with golden trim, polished breastplates embossed with a regal crown and gleaming helmets tucked under their arms.

As the doors creaked open, the opulence of the room unfolded before them. The chamber was bathed in a warm, golden glow from ornate chandeliers that hung overhead. Elaborate tapestries hung from the walls, depicting scenes of the Eastland Kingdoms legendary history, previous rulers and many triumphs. Polished marble floors reflected the splendour of the room, and a richly carpeted pathway led towards the elevated throne at the far end.

The throne, an imposing structure of gilded wood and velvet, sat atop a dais engraved with symbols of the kingdom's might. Candles flickered in sconces along the walls, casting dancing shadows that added to the atmosphere.

As the group stepped into the chamber, a man, dressed in formal attire befitting a royal announcer, stood near the throne. He cleared his throat and announced, his voice echoing through the chamber, "Presenting Lady Katherine Thorne, War Correspondent under the employ of Sir Shane, bearing urgent tidings for His Majesty, King Fabian Aaron Hardcastle the First."

The room fell momentarily silent, the weight of the announcement hanging in the air as all eyes turned towards the throne, awaiting the arrival of the King.

King Fabian Aaron Hardcastle the First entered the grand audience chamber with measured steps, his regal bearing accentuated by the weight of the crown upon his head. A thick auburn beard covered his jawline complete with a full matching moustache, while clearly groomed, seemed wild and untamable in nature. Despite his innate ability to grow facial hair, his balding head spoke of the passage of time and the trials that he had faced. The crown, complete with beautifully crafted filigree and precious gems, sat upon his head with the quiet assurance of centuries-old authority.

A man in his late fifties, he had seen this kingdom grow and thrive over the last half a century. His arms, though hidden beneath his clothing, were clearly quite large in size, a result of the battle hardened training in his youth. His body now falling victim to the mockery of time had begun to become rotund from the luxuries that he now had access to in his position of King. A position which he had held for the last fifteen years.

Draped in robes of deep royal blue, embroidered with threads of gold that caught the light, King Fabian exuded an air of grace and power. The fabric cascaded in rich folds as he moved, each step resonating with the deliberate confidence of a monarch who had weathered many storms.

His face bore the lines of wisdom gained through years of rule, the kind eyes hinting at a benevolence tempered by the challenges of leadership. The regal demeanour, however, did not mask the approachability that radiated from him— an approachability that endeared him to both courtiers and commoners alike.

As King Fabian entered the grand audience chamber, flanked by the quiet magnificence of the royal guard, Antonius and Lady Katherine, guided by a profound sense of reverence, gracefully descended to one knee in unison. Their heads bowed, a gesture of respect and loyalty, they awaited the sovereign's acknowledgment.

Jaw, standing tall, chose a different yet equally respectful approach. His chin lowered in a sign of deference, and with a swift and controlled movement, he extended one arm forward, a brief yet meaningful bow that conveyed his acknowledgment of the King's authority.

The King's keen eyes observed this display of deference, a silent acknowledgment passing between ruler and subjects as the weight of the moment settled upon the hallowed halls of the audience chamber.

As he ascended the dais to his throne, the weight of the kingdom rested on his shoulders, yet he wore it with the poise of one born to rule. The chamber, bathed in the glow of candles and the golden hues of tapestries, seemed to bow in acknowledgment of his presence.

Upon reaching the throne, the King took his seat with a measured grace, throwing his cloak to one side as he sat. The crown, a symbol of his authority, caught the light and shimmered as if mimicking the majesty of the realm itself. The eyes that surveyed the audience held a blend of sagacity and warmth.

King Fabian looked upon the assembled group with a measured gaze, his eyes conveying both sagacity and warmth. Lady Katherine, standing tall yet respectfully, began to address the monarch.

"Your Majesty, we bring urgent tidings from Sir Shane," Lady Katherine began, her voice carrying a tone of authority and yet a hint of nervousness strained through her otherwise brilliant visage.

The King's expression remained composed, acknowledging her words with a nod. He decided to cut in and save her the hassle of telling him that which he already knew. "Indeed, Lady Katherine. Sir Erik's missive reached me, detailing the attack on Celleos and the impending threat on our capital. I am aware that three individuals played a pivotal role in turning the tide of battle." His voice a deep commanding boom, it left those that heard it with no doubt in their mind that he spoke for the kingdom.

Jaw couldn't help but smile at this revelation, a subtle nod of approval accompanying his expression. Antonius, too, shared a knowing glance with his companions.

King Fabian, however, maintained a calm demeanour, seemingly unswayed by the gravity of the situation. "Celleos, a modest town, managed to endure such an assault, and the tide was turned by a mere trio. If a small settlement can withstand such adversity, I am confident that the great city of The Eastland Castle with over thirty thousand men, can weather any storm that comes its way."

His words, though confident, left a lingering tension in the air. It was as if the King's optimism, while admirable, might be underestimating the true magnitude of the impending threat. Lady Katherine, recognizing the need to convey the urgency of their message, continued to address the monarch.

"Your Majesty, while Celleos indeed stood resilient, the threat we faced then pales in comparison to the formidable army that now marches here. The forces that approach us are vast indeed. We implore you to take swift and decisive action to fortify your defences and prepare for the battle that looms on the horizon."

The King listened attentively, his expression revealing a subtle hint of consideration. He regarded Lady Katherine with a contemplative gaze, "Have you, Lady Katherine, witnessed this formidable force with your own eyes?" he inquired, acknowledging the information he had received from his own sources but seeking firsthand accounts.

Lady Katherine nodded solemnly, her gaze firm. "Yes, Your Majesty. We encountered the army on our journey here. Their archers numbered so many that they blotted out the sun with a storm of arrows. The sheer magnitude of their forces was staggering, stretching from horizon to horizon, an ominous tide ready to engulf everything in its path."

Antonius, standing beside her, interjected, "Your Majesty, it was a sight unlike any other. We barely escaped their clutches, and the speed at which they march is relentless. The threat they pose is imminent, and we must prepare our defences accordingly." Lady Katherine shot him a cold look, as though to tell him not to interrupt her in this setting.

The King absorbed their accounts with a measured gravity. However, as Lady Katherine and Antonius conveyed the urgency of the situation, the King, confident in his city's abilities, responded with an air of assurance.

"I appreciate your concern, Lady Katherine, and your valiant efforts to bring this information to my attention," the King began, his tone unwavering. "However, I consider what you are saying to have a degree of exaggeration, no doubt to invoke fear, perhaps in the hope to incite a reaction out of me to spring into action, however, I have faith in the strength of this great city. We have survived many, many battles before, and this shall be no different. Our defences are formidable, and I am confident in our ability to repel or annihilate any threat that might choose to oppose us."

Jaw, with anger mounting inside him, like a volcano fit to burst, couldn't restrain himself. A brash and cold "Then you are a fool" cut through the air, a stark contrast to the measured tones that had preceded it. The guards in the room, dressed in formal attire, bristled at the bold statement, hands instinctively moving to the hilts of their swords.

The atmosphere shifted, tension weaving its invisible threads through the grand audience chamber. Jaw stood resolute, his fearless expression steadfast. The room seemed to hold its breath, a chilling stillness settling in as if time itself paused.

In the silence that followed, a dripping sound echoed in Jaw's ears, like water dripping into a bucket—a metronome of anticipation, each drop counting the moments until the resolution of this tense confrontation.

Chaos erupted as King Fabian, incensed by Jaw's bold statement, began to berate him loudly. The King pointed at Jaw, giving furious instructions to his guards to seize the offender. However, Jaw's attention was elsewhere, his focus consumed by the familiar dripping sound.

Completely oblivious to the conflict he had caused, Jaw looked at Antonius, who had turned towards him following his brash statement. The gravity of the situation was evident in Jaw's eyes as he firmly stated, "We are in danger." Drawing his sword with a swift motion, Jaw's actions triggered a synchronised response from all the guards in the room. Antonius, following in Jaw's foolish footsteps, drew his bow.

Amidst the escalating tension, Jaw's voice cut through the chaos. "Get the King out of here!" he shouted above the tumult, causing alarm and confusion among the guards. The audience chamber, once a scene of regal composure, now teetered on the edge of pandemonium as guards moved both to protect the King and apprehend Jaw.

The tense atmosphere in the room was abruptly shattered by a resounding crash just beyond the closed doors. The metallic clang sounded through the regal halls, akin to a suit of armour colliding with the cold stone floor. A subsequent rattle, as of something heavy bouncing towards the door, seized the attention of guards and courtiers alike. The initial fervour of the confrontation with Jaw subsided, replaced by a collective sense of anticipation and unease.

The guards, momentarily frozen in their tracks, shifted their focus to the closed doors as if awaiting the emergence of an unknown adversary. The air thickened with tension, and a hushed silence descended upon the chamber. Jaw, certain of the impending danger, turned his back on the guards with their weapons drawn for him, facing the closed door behind him instead. The sudden shift in attention heightened the suspense, leaving everyone but Jaw on edge, uncertain of the unseen threat lurking just beyond the imposing entrance.

Then came the distinctive sound, metal on stone, a haunting symphony that sent shivers down the spines of those gathered. It hinted at an approaching force, clad in armour, advancing toward the sealed doors. This sound was then followed by the tapping of many lighter footsteps. The guards closest to the entrance, their senses on high alert, rushed forward with determined steps. Their mission: to block the doors, to deny entry to whatever lurked on the other side.

As the guards formed a human barricade, a subtle murmur spread through the audience. Whispers of uncertainty mixed with the clinking of armour, creating a dissonant melody that underscored the unfolding drama.

In the midst of this tense ambiance, King Fabian, flanked by a few loyal guards, stood resolute. The situation etched lines on his regal countenance, yet his eyes gleamed with an unwavering determination. The guards, perhaps motivated by a sense of duty or driven by the King's example, attempted to escort him to safety.

"I wish to witness this for myself," the King declared, pulling his arms from their grasp. His regal authority demanded attention, and the guards, though concerned for his safety, respected his decision.

The metallic thump against the doors reverberated through the hall, a warning sign of the force pressing against them. The guards, standing like an unyielding wall, absorbed the impact, pushing back with determination. The door, struck again, moved forward but not as far this time. The unseen adversary was testing the strength of the barrier.

Then, in a sudden and violent burst, the doors were wrenched from their hinges with tremendous force. The guards that attempted to block the door and even several others within the immediate area, where decimated by the unexpected force of the assault, folded in half as the mighty oak doors first folded down, tearing from their upper hinge as the door struck the ground where the guards had stood, fortunately for the onlookers this happened so quickly that the gory scene would have been too fast for them to even catch a glimpse of.

The door bounced off the stone and bone beneath it and propelled by the force that struck it was sent spinning into the room, injuring many others and throwing dust across the scene. As the dust quickly settled, it revealed the breach in the once-imposing entrance. Through the shattered door frame, the audience hall glimpsed the source of the disturbance—a colossal Alt abomination. Its black steel-plated limbs protruded into spikes, and its immense stature filled the doorway. Muscles upon muscles rippled beneath its grotesque form, and a large sword, previously belonging to one of the guards, jutted out from between its ribs. However it seemed to stand alone.

King Fabian, unyielding in the face of this monstrous intrusion, met the creature's gaze with a steely resolve. The remaining guards, regaining their footing, readied their weapons for the impending clash.

The guard closest to the door measured the beast with a look of both fear and disgust combined. Though its eyes were locked on the King, it was not this Alt that the guard should have feared. Onlookers witnessed as the guard's throat was sliced by an unseen blade, which immediately invoked fear and panic throughout the room as others began to fall to this invisible threat. The large Alt then began charging towards the King. Unfortunately for it, countless guards, Lady Katherine, Antonius, and Jaw stood in its way.

Chaos erupted in the grand audience chamber as the invisible assailants continued their deadly assault. Guards, with terror etched on their faces, found themselves defenceless against an enemy they couldn't see. The room reverberated with the sounds of clashing swords, desperate shouts, and the anguished cries of those caught in the relentless onslaught.

The massive Alt, undeterred by the invisible attackers that fought alongside it, charged forward with a thunderous roar. Its black steel-plated limbs glinted menacingly as it closed the distance. The defenders, however, rallied against the approaching behemoth.

Lady Katherine, her eyes focused and determined, unleashed a burst of flames that engulfed the Alt's form. The creature roared in agony as the fire licked at its grotesque exterior. Antonius, with bow drawn and arrows at the ready, targeted the Alt's vulnerable spots, aiming for the joints between the black steel plates.

Jaw, ever the stalwart warrior, charged straight at the Alt, sword gleaming in the dim light of the chamber. He aimed for its legs, seeking to disrupt its charge and bring the towering monstrosity to the ground. The clash between Jaw's sword and the Alt's black steel-plated limbs echoed through the hall as it struck him with the back of its hand. He bounced off the stone floor as he was sent flying off to the side.

Despite the beast now being injured, it seemingly did not care. It stepped forward, rage burned in its black, soulless eyes as it approached the archer. Antonius was fast to react to its approach and took a step back, narrowly avoiding being hit by the behemoth himself. His heel connected with the door that now lay flat on the floor behind him. With a whistle and a point, he caught Lady Katherine's attention as he gestured down to it. The Alt swung at him a second time as the battle raged on around them.

Jaw picked himself up off the floor, sword still in hand. He pressed his spare hand against his temple, pulling it away to reveal blood in his palm. "That was some hit," he mumbled to himself, his head still spinning from the strike. He suddenly heard the dropping of water again, this time directly in front of him, and without pause, he dropped to one knee, twisting his torso on his planted foot to rotate to the left as he pulled his sword across his body and then in one slick fluid motion, he struck out in front of him.

His blade connected with something, and like a hot knife through butter, sliced it open. An Alt staggered backward and away from him, coated in its own blood it dropped to the floor. Jaw stood up and quickly surveyed the surroundings. From what he could tell, there were three more invisible Alt assassins in the room. He watched as Lady Katherine directed the door to lift from the floor with a spell. She gestured with her index and middle finger for it to rapidly rise from its place of rest and strike the chin of the monstrous foe.

Jaw smiled to himself, briefly catching the eye of the King as he rose from his knee and inverted his sword. He rushed across the room towards two guards as Antonius unleashed an arrow into the exposed throat of the giant Alt. Jaw dropped to his knees and slid on the floor as one of the guards in front of him was struck hard by an invisible blade across the chest. With a fluid punching and slashing motion, Jaw anticipated where the back of its legs should be and took them out from under it. The struck guard acted quickly and plunged his sword into the now visible creature's chest, ending it for good with a bone crunching twist.

Across the room, another guard had been backed into the corner by an invisible foe. Sensing that he would not get there on time, Jaw looked up at the injured man in front of him, weapon rescinding from the dissolving form of the Alt. "Give me your sword," Jaw instructed him. The guard looked taken aback from this request but handed it to him nonetheless. Jaw took it by the tip of the blade as he rose from his knees, back arched and weapon drawing back over his shoulder. He proceeded to launch the weapon across the room directly at the trapped guard.

The sword sailed through the air, spinning with deadly accuracy. It struck true, hitting the invisible assailant and freeing the trapped guard. The rescued warrior, grateful yet bewildered, picked up the weapon Jaw had thrown and joined the fight against the unseen enemies. The battle in the grand audience chamber raged on, a symphony of clashes, roars, and the occasional crashing of a weapon connecting with a solid surface.

As the guards' ranks began to wear thin, the remaining invisible Alts shifted their attention to the innocent and unarmed onlookers. The scene turned gruesome as the unseen assailants moved among the crowd, their invisible blades cutting through the air with deadly precision. The helpless nobles screamed and scattered, unable to defend themselves against the slaughter. The grand audience chamber, once a place of regal elegance, became a chaotic battleground stained with fear and blood.

Jaw seized the opportunity to strike the giant Alt from its blind spot. With a swift and calculated movement, he drove his sword into the creature's back, causing it to roar in pain and drop to one knee. Simultaneously, Antonius unleashed a barrage of arrows directly into the exposed areas of the massive Alt, seeking to exploit its vulnerabilities. However, instead of weakening, the creature seemed to grow angrier.

In a fit of rage, the Alt retaliated. It swung its massive arm, striking Jaw with incredible force, this time only disarming him. Jaw's sword spun through the air and landed somewhere in the room. The impact sent Jaw sprawling, but his warrior instincts kicked in. He quickly regained his footing and, with determination in his eyes, rushed towards Lady Katherine, who had her hand outstretched.

Meanwhile, the colossal Alt, unfazed by the arrows embedded in its body, broke into a full charge. It pushed past Antonius, knocking him to the floor, and set its sights on the King. The guards, overwhelmed and scattered, were unable to mount a coordinated defence. The Alt charged through the King's guard, its momentum carrying it dangerously close to the vulnerable monarch.

The grand audience chamber fell into a momentary silence as the giant Alt, its wicked intent evident, closed in on the King. In a swift and decisive move, Jaw reached Lady Katherine, urgency in his eyes as he grabbed her hand. With a simple yet commanding instruction, "The King," he communicated the need to protect the monarch. Lady Katherine nodded in understanding, and in the blink of an eye, Jaw vanished, in his place the King appeared, visibly shaken. His normally composed demeanour was replaced by a profound sense of fear, etched into his face. The recent brush with death had left its mark, and the gravity of the situation weighed heavily on him.

When the King looked up, his eyes met Lady Katherine's, a mixture of relief and gratitude evident in his gaze. Without uttering a word, he took her offered hand, a silent acknowledgment of the pivotal role she played in his survival. In that moment, a wave of gratitude washed over him, and the King, overwhelmed by the realisation of his narrow escape, pulled Lady Katherine into a brief but sincere embrace. It was an instinctive response to the intense emotions coursing through him, a silent expression of thanks and the recognition of the peril they had narrowly avoided.

In that moment, the colossal Alt, fueled by rage and malevolence, crashed against the throne with tremendous force. The once regal seat of power bore the brunt of the creature's assault, and the Alt slumped over it, its massive form gradually transforming into a repulsive pool of black slime. The room, earlier filled with chaos and violence, now witnessed the grotesque demise of the monstrous foe.

Amidst the melting remains of the Alt, Jaw lay, obscured beneath its bones and the revolting residue that was previously the flesh and armour of the creature. The sword that had protruded from the creature's ribs lay loosely clutched in his hand, the blade still lodged in the centre of the Alt's chest cavity. Jaw dropped the blade as his hand fell limply to his side. The once-threatening presence of the giant Alt now reduced to a nauseating pool of darkness.

As the last remnants of the invisible Alts were dispelled by Antonius and the remaining guards, a heavy silence settled over the audience chamber. The once-grand hall, witness to the fierce clash between defenders and monstrous invaders, now bore the scars of the violent confrontation. The air was thick with the lingering scent of burnt flesh, the echoes of roars, and the weight of lives lost.

Antonius, his bow still in hand, surveyed the aftermath with a solemn expression. The room, once filled with nobles, guards, and the King's presence, now held a sombre atmosphere. The casualties were evident, their sacrifices marking the price paid for the kingdom's survival. The guards, though victorious, stood among fallen comrades, their expressions a mix of exhaustion and sorrow.

The surviving nobles who had witnessed the horror from the sidelines emerged cautiously from hiding places, their eyes wide with shock and fear. The grandeur of the audience chamber had been shattered, replaced by a haunting reminder of the vulnerability that lurked beneath the façade of safety.

King Fabian, having regained his composure, approached Lady Katherine as the guards and Antonius rapidly attempted to free Jaw's body in the hope to prove that he had not been killed. The King took Lady Katherine by the hand, gratitude and concern etched on his face. "You have my deepest thanks," he said, addressing her with the utmost respect. "Without your intervention, the outcome could have been far grimmer."

As the guards successfully pulled Jaw free, a collective exhale could be heard through the chamber. The King's eyes shifted from Jaw's seemingly lifeless form to Lady Katherine, a mixture of realisation and acknowledgment colouring his expression.

"He's alive," one of the guards declared, his words cutting through the heavy air. The King's gaze lingered on Jaw for a moment longer, absorbing the weight of the situation. After a beat, he turned back to Lady Katherine, his tone more reflective.

"I see now that your associate here may have had merit to his earlier brash derision," King Fabian admitted, his voice carrying a touch of humility. "Perhaps I was being foolish. In light of recent evidence, I see how five of these creatures can easily get the best of almost thirty of my King's guard. I dread to consider what they could achieve when faced against our lesser-trained city guard."

Lady Katherine met the King's gaze with a solemn nod, understanding the implications of the situation. "Your Majesty, these creatures are unlike anything you may have faced before. I am not sure how they achieved invisibility, though I suspect one of their mages may have cast it on them. Their coordinated attacks suggest a level of intelligence that surpasses our expectations. You must be vigilant and prepare the city defences accordingly."

As the King nodded in agreement with Lady Katherine's assessment, Antonius joined the two of them. His expression revealed concern for Jaw's well-being as he provided an update. "He is in bad shape; they are taking him to the infirmary now," Antonius explained, the hum of worry evident in his words.

King Fabian acknowledged the gravity of the situation, turning toward Antonius with a reassuring touch on his shoulder. "I will make sure he gets the care he needs," the King declared, a sense of responsibility and commitment evident in his tone. His hand remained on Antonius's shoulder, a silent acknowledgment of the bravery and efforts displayed in the defence of the kingdom.

"Good work," King Fabian added, the words carrying both gratitude and respect. In the aftermath of the intense battle, the bonds between the defenders of the realm strengthened, and the King recognized the invaluable contribution of those who stood against the unprecedented threat.

Chapter 11

The heavy wooden door of the tavern creaked open, allowing a sliver of the evening light to spill into the dimly lit interior. The warm glow of flickering candles cast a comfortable ambiance across the room, revealing a space filled with laughter, clinking mugs, and the lively chatter of patrons.

Micharas and the Blacksmith sat at a sturdy oak table near the centre of the room, tankards in hand, engaged in jovial conversation. The walls, decorated with faded tapestries and mounted antlers, bore witness to countless tales spun within these cosy confines. The low hum of friendly banter intertwined with the distant notes of a bard strumming a lute in the corner.

As Antonius, Lady Katherine, and their companions entered, and approached the bar, the pair had become well acquainted with the surviving members of the Kings guard, following the events of the audience hall several days prior. The eclectic mix of patrons included locals who had made the tavern a second home and travellers passing through the city.

Antonius, breaking away from the group, navigated through the maze of occupied tables. The smell of hearty stews and roasting meats wafted from the kitchen, adding to the inviting ambiance. He finally reached the table where Micharas and the Blacksmith were seated.

"So," Antonius began with a teasing grin, "Where the hell have you been?" His eyes briefly flickered to the stranger sitting with them, a man of sturdy build and an air of familiarity. After a moment, recognition dawned on Antonius. "Andarius!" he exclaimed, grabbing his elder brother abruptly.

"You got big!" Antonius remarked, his eyes appraising the muscular frame of the blacksmith.

Andarius, his eyes fixed on Antonius, retorted with a chuckle, "And I see you are more or less the same." he joked in his deep voice as Antonius let go of him, releasing him from the embrace. Andarius clapped Antonius on the back with a hearty laugh, the sound merging seamlessly with the ambient merriment of the tavern. "Eight years gone, and you still look like you did when you all left here."

Antonius shot a mischievous grin, "Yeah about that..." He scratched the back of his ear, trying to decide where the best place was to start retelling his story.

Micharas, observing the reunion with a satisfied smile, interjected, "I have already brought him up to speed." He explained, the relief in Antonius's eyes was evident. "I heard the meeting with the King went well? I had heard rumours of an Alt attack in the castle." He did not seem all that concerned by the hearsay.

Lady Katherine walked over to their table with a confident stride. In her hand, she held a tankard of ale, a gesture of camaraderie in this convivial atmosphere. Her presence garnered a few curious glances from the patrons, but it was Andarius, the Blacksmith, who stood to greet her.

"Ah, Lady Katherine," Micharas said with a warm smile, "Allow me to introduce you to Andarius, our older brother." Andarius, ever the charmer, rose from his seat and executed a courteous bow. He took Lady Katherine's hand and planted a gentle kiss on it. "A pleasure to make your acquaintance, my lady, my brother here has spoken highly of you." he said with a twinkle in his eye, gesturing one of his large hands towards Micharas.

Lady Katherine, accustomed to various courtly gestures, offered a gracious smile. "The pleasure is mine, Andarius.." Her gaze then shifted to Micharas, who gave her a welcoming nod.

"I have been discussing our journey getting here and our recent adventures," Micharas explained, gesturing to the vacant seat at the table. "How did the meeting with the King go? I have heard rumours that there was an attack inside the castle?"

As Lady Katherine settled into her seat, she began recounting the events at the royal castle. "The meeting with the King was... eventful, to say the least. Alt assassins infiltrated the audience chamber, and chaos ensued. Jaw, unfortunately, got caught in the crossfire. He took a blow to the head but is recovering well in the castle infirmary. The healers assure us he'll be back on his feet soon."

Andarius, his expression shifting to concern, nodded understandingly. "Those Alt creatures, they are the ones you mentioned attacked Celleos right?" He looked to Micharas for confirmation. Micharas nodded.

Lady Katherine continued, her eyes reflecting the severity of the situation. "We managed to neutralise the threat, but it's clear that the kingdom is facing a growing danger. The King recognizes the need for stronger defences and has expressed gratitude for our intervention. However, he fears that the city guard might not be adequately prepared to face such threats."

Micharas leant back in his chair, thoughtfully rubbing his chin. "Any idea what he intends to do?"

Lady Katherine took a sip from her tankard before responding, "The King hasn't divulged the specifics of his plans yet. However, he intends to throw a banquet in our honour tomorrow night. During the banquet, he plans to reveal his strategy to strengthen the city's defences and address the growing threat of the Alt creatures."

Andarius rested his elbow on the table, his brow furrowed with curiosity. "A banquet, you say? That's quite the royal gesture. Do you think he has a solid plan in mind?"

Lady Katherine sighed, her expression betraying uncertainty. "I wish I could say for certain. The King is understandably cautious about discussing sensitive matters openly. We'll likely learn more tomorrow night, and until then, we should be prepared for anything."

As the group gathered at the table indulged in speculation about the King's intentions, the lively atmosphere of the tavern continued around them. The distant notes of the bard's lute, the clinking of drinks, and the hum of conversation provided a backdrop to their strategizing.

Antonius chuckled, taking a sip from his tankard. "Well, I hope the banquet is at least worth the wait."

Micharas nodded with a grin, "And I hope Jaw is back on his feet in time for it."

The party, after sharing stories, laughter, and strategizing for the challenges ahead, decided to call it a night. The warmth of the tavern, the merriment, and the events of the past month weighed heavily on their minds as they made their way upstairs to the rooms provided by the King.

Each room held a simple yet comfortable charm. The flickering light of candles danced on the wooden furniture, casting gentle shadows on the walls. The beds, adorned with neatly folded linens, promised a well-deserved rest. As they settled in their respective rooms, the weariness of the day began to lift.

Antonius, sitting on his bed, took a moment to inspect his bow and arrows. The familiar weight of the weapon in his hands brought a sense of reassurance. As he laid the bow by his bedside, he couldn't help but think about the upcoming banquet and the mysteries it might unfold.

Micharas, who had rented his own room using money that his older brother had given him, set about unpacking his belongings. His mind was a tapestry of plans and considerations. The kingdom faced an imminent threat, and the banquet would likely reveal the first threads of a solution. He took a deep breath, resolving to face whatever challenges lay ahead.

Andarius, having been filled in on recent events, sat by the hearth in thought. His brothers had experienced such danger and thrill, a sense of pride in his family as he rose from his chair and headed home.

Lady Katherine, her thoughts a whirlwind of spells and strategies, found a moment of solitude by the window. The moonlight spilled into the room, casting a gentle glow on the pages of the open book before her. Amidst the pages of history and lore, her mind drifted to Jaw.

As she looked out into the night, she couldn't help but reflect on Jaw's bravery in the face of danger. The memory of him standing firm against the invisible assailants, his sword slicing through the unseen foes, lingered in her mind. There was an undeniable strength in him, a resilience that had not wavered even when faced with the monstrous Alt, she could not shake the feeling though that in that last skirmish he showed his true colours and demonstrated what he was actually capable of in combat. The others had not seen the way he handled himself or the brutal force that wielded his weapon, but she had.

Her thoughts then turned to his recovery. The image of Jaw, resting now, his head cushioned on a soft bed in the care of the castle's healers, replaced the chaos of the audience chamber. She wished for his swift healing, his strong spirit mending alongside his physical wounds. The banter, the camaraderie, and the shared victories—they all felt incomplete without his presence.

As the night embraced the tranquil city, the party scattered across it, found a temporary refuge from the storm brewing outside its walls. In the quiet of their rooms, they rested, knowing that the dawn would bring new challenges and revelations.

The morning light illuminated The Eastland Castle as it rose, announcing the beginning of a day that held the promise of both mystery and celebration. In separate rooms, Micharas, Antonius, and Lady Katherine stirred from their slumber, the remnants of dreams fading as they prepared to face the challenges ahead.

As they descended the creaky wooden stairs of the tavern, a familiar face awaited them in the common area. The steward, a man of refined bearing and crisp attire, stood with an air of formality that hinted at the importance of the day's proceedings.

"Good morning," the steward greeted with a respectful nod as they approached. "I trust you had a restful night. The King has arranged for a tailor to outfit you with new attire for the banquet this evening. Please, follow me."

The trio exchanged glances, curiosity evident in their expressions as they trailed behind the steward through the bustling morning streets of the city. Its inhabitants were up and going about their daily routines, merchants opening their shops, and children playing in the cobblestone streets. The steward led them to a quaint tailor's shop nestled between a bakery and an apothecary. The sign above the door read "Filch and Thread."

Upon entering, the melodious jingle of a bell announced their presence. The interior was packed full with rolls of colourful fabrics, elegant mannequins displaying the latest fashion, and the subtle hum from the busy street outside. A distinguished-looking gnome tailor emerged from behind a curtain, a measuring tape draped around his little neck, wearing a stunning purple suit with a maroon shirt and bow tie underneath. He had a fantastic purple-dyed goatee, complete with a curled moustache.

"Ah, you must be the honoured guests," he said, his eyes scanning them appraisingly. "The King has instructed that I design outfits for each of you that complement your stature and grace. Please, come this way." His voice was delicate, dignified, and ever so slightly squeaky, as to be expected for his size.

They were ushered to a private fitting area where bolts of luxurious fabrics hung from the walls. The tailor, with practised precision, began taking measurements and discussing design preferences. He spoke of fabrics from distant lands, rich in texture and colour, and proposed styles that blended elegance with practicality.

As they contemplated the choices laid before them, Lady Katherine's eyes lingered on a deep sapphire fabric, Micharas found himself drawn to a regal shade of crimson, and Antonius considered a dark forest green. The tailor, attuned to their preferences, nodded approvingly.

Amidst the discussions about fabrics and designs, Lady Katherine couldn't hide her excitement. "I must say, being treated to new clothes is a delightful surprise. It's been a while since I indulged in such a luxury. I'm particularly drawn to this sapphire fabric; it reminds me of the evening sky just before the stars emerge."

The tailor, his eyes twinkling with appreciation for her expensive taste, replied, "Ah, a poetic choice indeed, my lady. The sapphire will undoubtedly enhance the regality of your presence."

As the fitting progressed, Micharas couldn't help but comment on the gnome tailor's impressive attire. "Your suit is quite remarkable, my friend. It complements your shop's aesthetic perfectly."

The gnome tailor beamed with pride, adjusting his maroon bow tie. "Thank you, kind sir. A touch of flair is essential, both in fashion and in life. Now, let us ensure that your outfits capture the essence of this momentous occasion."

As the final adjustments were made, the tailor stepped back, satisfaction evident in his expression. "You will be the epitome of elegance this evening, my friends. The garments have been tailored to perfection."

With the promise of their bespoke attire, the trio left the tailor's shop, the morning sun now higher in the sky. The steward, waiting outside, led them back to the tavern where they would don their new outfits later in the day in anticipation of the evening's banquet.

Before the wardrobe change, however, the steward suggested a visit to the market square, where preparations for the evening were already underway. The city's bakers, florists, and musicians were setting up stalls, creating a lively atmosphere in the heart of the city. The trio strolled through the market, absorbing the sights and sounds, and even indulging in a few treats from the local vendors.

As they explored the market, Antonius remarked, "It's incredible how the city comes together for these events. The air is filled with anticipation."

Lady Katherine, with a gleam in her eyes, added, "And the aroma of fresh flowers and baked goods is enchanting. This market truly captures the essence of a celebration."

Micharas, taking in the scene, nodded in agreement. "The market sets the stage for a memorable evening. It's an excellent tribute to the spirit of the city."

Their morning adventure through the market served as a prelude to the grand evening ahead. The prospect of the banquet, with new clothes in tow, added a layer of excitement to the day's unfolding events.

As the afternoon sun cast a warm glow upon the city of The Eastland Castle, Micharas, Antonius, and Lady Katherine prepared for the grand banquet in their respective rooms at the tavern. Each took their time, carefully donning the bespoke outfits crafted by the skilled gnome tailor. The air was charged with a sense of anticipation, and as they admired themselves in the mirrors, the new garments bestowed upon them a regal air.

Micharas, dressed in a deep crimson ensemble, wore a finely tailored doublet adorned with ornate gold embroidery along the edges. The fabric, a rich velvet, felt luxurious to the touch. The high collar was fastened with delicate golden buttons, and a subtle pattern of interwoven runes added an enchanting touch. A maroon undershirt peeked through the opening of the doublet, its fabric of the finest silk. He couldn't help but appreciate the fine craftsmanship. "These clothes do carry a certain gravitas, don't they?" he remarked to himself, adjusting the collar with a satisfied smile.

Antonius, sporting a dark forest green outfit, opted for a long tunic with a distinct V-neckline. The tunic boasted an intricate pattern of intertwined vines, embroidered with threads of gold, bronze and silver. The sleeves, slightly puffed at the shoulders, were secured with silver clasps in the shapes of leaves. The ensemble was completed with tailored trousers made of a durable yet comfortable fabric, with subtle leaf motifs along the seams. He grinned. "I never thought I'd wear something this fancy. It feels... different."

Lady Katherine's sapphire attire exuded grace and sophistication. Her gown, a masterpiece of craftsmanship, featured a fitted bodice that accentuated her slender figure. The neckline, a subtle scoop, revealed a glimpse of her collarbone. The gown flowed into a floor-length skirt, the fabric a shimmering blend of silk and satin. A delicate silver belt encrusted with sapphire gemstones cinched her waist, adding a touch of understated glamour. The gown's sleeves, sheer and flowing, cascaded elegantly down her arms. She took a moment to observe herself. "Indeed, it's a departure from the usual attire, but the elegance is undeniable." She spoke with a soft smile, her mesmerising eyes reflecting a hint of excitement.

Accessories played a crucial role in completing their looks. Micharas donned a pair of polished leather boots, their laces finished with tiny silver charms. A deep red cloak, fastened with a silver brooch shaped like a stylized phoenix, added a regal flair. Antonius wore knee-high leather boots, their clasps resembling a miniature bow and arrow. A dark green cloak, secured with a silver pin in the shape of a rampant stag, draped over his shoulders.

Lady Katherine, embracing the enchanting theme, wore silver-strapped sandals detailed with tiny sapphire embellishments. A delicate silver necklace, holding a single sapphire pendant, graced her neck. Earrings, simple yet elegant hoops, caught the light as she moved. A silver circlet, simple in its design, a plain band with engraved celtic knots sat comfortably on her brow, complementing the flowing cascade of her brown tresses.

The trio gathered downstairs in the common area, where the steward awaited them. His eyes widened in approval as he took in their transformed appearances. "You all look splendid. The King will surely be pleased," he complimented. "I must remind you however that you are obviously not permitted to bring your weapons this evening. Should they be necessary for whatever reason then they will obviously be provided at the time. We have taken the utmost care to make sure that it should not come to that, of course." He reassured them.

Micharas nodded appreciatively. "Not an issue." He said, his tone carried a certainty and trust. "And of course please give our thanks to the talented tailor, and the King for providing us with these fine clothes."

Lady Katherine, being the last to join them, descended the stairs with a grace that commanded attention. Her appearance, transcending the mundane, left Micharas and Antonius momentarily breathless. The pale complexion of her skin, ethereal eyes with their deep, mesmerising blue, and the cascade of long brown hair down her shoulders created a vision of otherworldly beauty.

Antonius, unable to conceal his admiration, quirked an eyebrow. "Lady Katherine, you look like you could outshine the stars themselves tonight."

She chuckled, a soft, melodic sound. "Flattery, Antonius, suits you well. I must say, you both clean up quite nicely as well."

With Lady Katherine now joining the ensemble, the steward led the group into the lively streets of the capital. Late afternoon had painted the city in rich tones of amber and gold as the festivities began in full swing. The market square was alive with energy, the air filled with laughter, music, and the enticing aroma of street food.

The street was lined with stalls offering an array of delights—sweet pastries, exotic fruits, and local crafts. The anticipation for the evening's banquet echoed in every cheerful exchange.

As they ascended the hill towards the castle, the scene unfolded like a painting of joyous celebration. Colourful banners fluttered in the breeze, and the castle gates stood open, welcoming guests. Musicians played lively tunes, and dancers twirled in colourful costumes, adding to the vibrant atmosphere.

Micharas, taking in the scene, remarked, "The city truly knows how to celebrate. This is more than just a banquet; it's a festival."

Antonius, enjoying the ambiance, added, "The King certainly knows how to throw a party. It's like the entire city came alive for this evening."

Lady Katherine, her eyes sparkling with delight, nodded in agreement. "It's heartening to see such unity and joy. Let's hope the evening is as enchanting as the festivities leading up to it."

With their spirits lifted by the exuberance around them, the group continued their ascent, the castle looming ahead like a majestic guardian overlooking the jubilant city below.

As they passed through the castle gates it revealed a spectacle of lavishness that unfolded within the courtyard. The air was alive with the rhythmic cadence of a minstrel's lute, harmonising with the laughter and chatter of nobles and commoners alike. The castle courtyard had been transformed into a eccentric celebration.

As Micharas, Antonius, and Lady Katherine stepped through the gates, the occasional glances and hushed whispers did not go unnoticed. Their bespoke attire, a stark departure from the familiar garb of adventurers, drew the attention of onlookers. Nobles in resplendent gowns and lords in finely tailored doublets regarded them with curiosity, their conversations pausing momentarily as the trio passed.

The courtyard, bathed in the warm glow of torches and lanterns, was a tapestry of colours and sounds. Tables covered with elaborate floral arrangements stretched across the space, while elven servants moved gracefully, ensuring goblets were filled and platters laden with delicacies were placed strategically.

The trio, led by the steward, navigated through the bustling crowd. The atmosphere was electric, filled with the clinking of goblets, the melodious notes of a minstrel's ballad, and the tantalising aroma of a feast fit for royalty. The celebration, a symphony of joy and revelry, seemed to envelop them as they made their way towards the main banquet hall.

For Micharas and Antonius, the grandeur of the castle and the opulence of the festivities felt alien. Despite the elegance of their attire, a lingering sense of being out of place rested heavy in their minds as they noticed the number of eyes regarding them as they moved. The tailored doublets and rich fabrics felt foreign compared to the comfort of leather and practicality of armour they were accustomed to. Their usual camaraderie, marked by shared glances and silent understanding, seemed to navigate a sea of unfamiliarity.

As they walked, the steward spoke in hushed tones, guiding them through the celebration. "This way, my friends. The banquet hall awaits." His voice, though soft, cut through the symphony of the celebration.

Lady Katherine, accustomed to the courtly setting, moved with grace, her ethereal gown catching the light as she stepped confidently through the courtyard. Her poise seemed to harmonise effortlessly with the regal surroundings, turning heads as she passed.

The trio approached the grand entrance of the banquet hall, its towering doors etched with spectacular carvings. The steward, with a nod, commanded the opening of the doors, revealing the opulence within. The hall, decorated fantastically with painting and chandeliers, echoed with the hum of conversation and the chiming of goblets.

As they entered, the eyes of the assembled guests turned towards them. The whispers, though hushed, were palpable. Micharas and Antonius exchanged a glance that spoke volumes. The magnificence of the Eastland Castle had opened its arms to them, but they couldn't shake the sense of being outsiders in this world of courtly splendour.

Yet, amidst the opulence, the excitement and festivity continued. The banquet hall welcomed them with the aroma of delicacies and the warmth of torchlight. The King, seated at the head of a long table, rose with a welcoming smile. The steward, having fulfilled his role, retreated with a nod of acknowledgment.

With a wave of his hand, the King signalled their arrival, the minstrel's lute softened, and the hall fell into a momentary hush. A single horn sounded, its clear notes cutting through conversations within the hall. The attention of the assembled guests shifted towards the trio as the herald stepped forward, holding a scroll of parchment.

"Announcing the esteemed guests, Heroes of Celleos, defenders of Eastland Castle, Micharas Ranger, Antonius Ranger, and Lady Katherine Thorne!" The herald's voice rang out with a ceremonial cadence, drawing the eyes of every guest towards the trio.

Micharas, Antonius, and Lady Katherine stood at the centre of attention, a moment of acknowledgement for their deeds. The King, with a smile, gestured for them to join the merriment. The courtly proceedings continued, and the trio found themselves surrounded by the elite of the capital, each guest offering nods of recognition and raising goblets in their honour.

The grand banquet hall buzzed with a symphony of laughter and the intoxicating aroma of a feast fit for royalty. The trio seamlessly navigated the lively crowd, engaging in a series of captivating conversations that unfolded amidst the opulence of the evening.

Lady Katherine, found herself in an animated discussion with Lady Marigold. The delicate fragrance of blooming flowers wafted through the air as they exchanged tales of enchanted gardens and whimsical flora. Between sips of exquisite wine and bites of tiny delicacies, they spoke of magic intertwined with nature, their conversation a celebration of the enchanting beauty that both the magical and natural realms held.

Meanwhile, Antonius, standing amidst a group of esteemed lords, clinked goblets with Lord Cedric. The rich, robust flavour of the wine complemented the hearty laughter that echoed through their discussion of battles and strategies. Antonius shared stories of their recent daring escapades, describing the rush of adrenaline on the battlefield. Lord Cedric, a seasoned tactician, nodded in understanding, emphasising the importance of swift decision-making to secure victory.

Micharas, his demeanour composed amidst the courtly ambiance, conversed with Lady Isolde. The tables covered with an array of culinary delights provided a backdrop to their discussion on inter-kingdom relations. As they sampled the exquisite fare, Micharas and Lady Isolde delved into the delicate nuances of diplomacy. The subtle interplay of flavours mirrored the intricacies of maintaining peace in a world where shadows lurked on the edges.

A collective conversation unfolded as the trio joined Sir Roysten, a knight of renowned honour and chivalry. Goblets were raised in toasts, the clinking sound blending with the jovial atmosphere. Sir Roysten commended the trio for their courage in the face of the recent Alt threat, their shared tales becoming a chorus of noble quests echoing through the hall.

As a hush fell over the grand banquet hall, a figure entered, drawing the attention of the assembled guests. Jaw, the brave warrior whose valour had become a beacon of hope in the past few days as his tale of bravery had been spread among the city, stepped into the spotlight. His attire, carefully chosen for the occasion, spoke not only of regality but also resilience.

Jaw wore a doublet of deep cobalt, richly embroidered with golden trim that glimmered in the torchlight. The fabric, a blend of fine silk and sturdy material, accentuated the strength that lay beneath. Trousers of a complementary shade completed the ensemble, tailored to allow ease of movement.

Upon his head sat a hat of royal blue adorned with a feather plume, a thoughtful touch to conceal the bandages that still cradled his healing wounds. The plume, a vivid burst of colour, added a touch of flair to his appearance. It swayed gently with his movements, a symbol of both his resilience and the celebratory spirit of the evening.

The ensemble was not just clothing; it was a statement. It whispered tales of bravery, of a man who faced the unknown with unyielding courage. As Jaw moved through the hall, the onlookers observed not just a warrior, but a hero dressed in the regalia befitting his triumph.

Jaw, the valiant defender, seemed to be the sole exception in the room who was carrying a weapon, besides from the royal guards. His sword, a symbol of both protection and defiance, hung confidently from his waist, a stark contrast to the more subdued design of the rest of his clothing. In the flickering torchlight, the polished pommel gleamed, catching the eye and drawing attention to the unyielding spirit it represented. Jaw's choice to carry his weapon in a room where others had left theirs behind spoke to a commitment that went beyond the boundaries of tradition—a pledge to safeguard, even in the midst of revelry.

King Fabian, his eyes reflecting genuine warmth and gratitude, rose from his seat at the head of the table. With a sweeping gesture, he beckoned Jaw forward. The herald remained silent, allowing the King to personally extend his welcome.

"Ladies and gentlemen," King Fabian's voice resonated through the hall, "allow me the honour of introducing a man of unparalleled bravery, a warrior whose valour knows no bounds. Jaw, the defender of our great kingdom and a true hero among us."

A round of applause rippled through the hall as the guests, noble and commoner alike, acknowledged Jaw's entrance with genuine admiration. The King, with a smile, offered a hand to Jaw.

"Step forward, my friend," the King continued, his tone warm and appreciative. "You risked your life to save mine, and for that, The Eastland Kingdom owes you a debt of gratitude. Tonight, we celebrate not only the strength of our kingdom but also the indomitable spirit of those who defend it."

Jaw, standing tall and resolute, approached the King, greeted not just by applause but by the collective recognition of a realm grateful for his bravery. The celebration had found its focal point, and in that moment, Jaw's presence illuminated the impressiveness of the castle.

Micharas, Antonius and Lady Katherine joined in the applause. Pleased to see their friend on his feet and well.

"And now that all of our guests are here." The King continued, his ever impressive booming voice cutting over the crowd, "Let the feast begin!" Plates and platters, laden with a decadent array of delicacies, emerged from the side doors at the end of the hall.

The savoury aroma of roasted meats, fragrant herbs, and freshly baked bread wafted through the air as the serving staff swiftly moved to distribute the feast among the tables. Guests eagerly took their seats, their eyes alight with anticipation for the culinary delights that awaited them.

Micharas, Antonius, Lady Katherine, and Jaw, distinguished among the guests, were prompted to approach the main table. As they made their way to the head of the hall, the murmurs of curiosity followed in their wake. The King and his Queen, seated at the centre of the grand table, welcomed them with warm smiles.

The main table, complete with an array of glistening goblets, polished silverware, and an assortment of fine wines, encouraged the guests of honour to take their seats. The plush cushions and intricately carved chairs spoke of a regal comfort that mirrored the opulence of the feast.

As they took their places among the royal hosts, the feast began in earnest. Servers moved with practised efficiency, placing platters of succulent meats, vibrant vegetables, and exquisitely crafted desserts before the guests. Goblets were filled with the finest wines, and the hall resonated with the sounds of laughter and the joyous spirit of celebration.

Micharas, Antonius, Lady Katherine, and Jaw found themselves in the midst of a gastronomic extravaganza. The flavours danced on their palates, a symphony of tastes that mirrored the richness of the kingdom they had come to protect.

As the feast continued in full swing, the atmosphere in the grand hall shifted from the indulgence of the banquet to the enchantment of dance. The energetic ballads of bards playing one after the other filled the air, enticing couples to the dance floor.

Lady Katherine, ever graceful, found herself drawn into the lively rhythm of the music. Antonius, with a twinkle in his eye, extended a hand, and they joined the swirl of dancers.

Micharas, initially hesitant, couldn't resist the infectious energy and soon found himself caught in the dance as well. His rugged charm and sturdy presence made him a sought-after dance partner, and he gracefully moved across the floor with various partners.

Jaw, despite the lingering soreness from his recent ordeal, embraced the celebration. He moved gracefully across the floor, blending into the joyful sea of dancers, becoming one with the lively cadence of the music.

Amidst the joyous revelry, the King and his Queen sat at the head of the table, observing the festivities. The Queen, with a mischievous glint in her eye, seized the opportunity to pull the King to his feet. "Come, my love, let the merriment encompass us," she urged, leading him towards the dance floor.

The King, though initially reserved, couldn't resist the joy around him. The Queen, with her playful enthusiasm, guided him through the dance, their laughter harmonising with the music.

As the dancing reached its zenith, the minstrel transitioned into a lively tune, the melody weaving a tale of hope and joy. The upbeat rhythm of a guitar accompanied a jubilant voice that sang of a beacon shining in the night, symbolising hope in times of celebration.

The minstrel, recognizing the perfect moment for a lively tune, began strumming a country-style melody on his lute. The infectious rhythm permeated the hall, and soon, the dance floor was alive with twirls and laughter.

As the dance partners changed and the lively tune enveloped the hall, Jaw found himself face to face with Lady Katherine. He took her hand in his, and with a graceful twirl, their bodies swayed to the rhythm of the minstrel's melody. The dance floor became a kaleidoscope of movement and laughter, each step a testament to the joy of the celebration.

Once the song concluded, and the lingering notes fading into the applause, the dance floor embraced a moment of stillness. Jaw and Lady Katherine, caught in the aftermath of the lively tune, found themselves pressed against each other in the soft glow of candlelight.

Amidst the shared laughter and jubilant atmosphere, Lady Katherine couldn't resist the opportunity for a cheeky remark. With a mischievous grin, she leaned in slightly and whispered, "Jaw, your sword is poking me."

Her playful jest drew a light chuckle from Jaw, he blushed as he glanced back at the main table where his sword was slung off the back of his chair. The shared moment of humour somehow put them both at ease as they pulled closer together and continued to dance to the music. Lady Katherine's head resting on his shoulder and his arm wrapped around her waist.

As the festivities of the night reached their crescendo, King Fabian, his expression turning more solemn, raised his goblet, signalling for attention and the music subsided. The ambient noise gradually came to a murmur, and a hush fell over the hall as the nobles and guests turned toward the monarch.

"Tonight, as we revel in the warmth of fellowship, let us also address the shadows that linger beyond our walls," King Fabian began, his voice resonating with a sense of duty. The music gradually subsided, and the ambient noise hushed as the nobles and guests turned their attention toward him.

The King's gaze shifted toward his men, who, with disciplined efficiency, wheeled a formidable ballista turret into the hall. The imposing weapon, a symbol of strength and defence, took centre stage, capturing the collective focus of the assembly.

"As the heart of the Eastland Castle beats strong, so too must our defences," the King declared, emphasising the importance of unity and resolve. The quartet —Micharas, Antonius, Lady Katherine, and Jaw—shared knowing glances, a smile flared across Micharas's face as he held out an open hand towards Antonius, who handed him a small pouch of coins. A look of upset and betrayal on his face.

"Andarius told me about them." Micharas whispered to Jaw. The festive atmosphere had transformed into a strategic discussion, the feast becoming a platform for addressing the kingdom's vulnerabilities.

The murmurs among the crowd betrayed a growing concern, a question that seemed to be held collectively through the hall: Why such a significant display of military might? King Fabian, attuned to the unspoken query, addressed the assembly with a solemn assurance.

"Scouts have reported to me that the Alt forces are not only vast in number but also equipped with siege towers and formidable beast units," the King revealed, his words penetrating the stillness that followed. A wave of realisation swept through the crowd, and the gravity of the situation became palpable.

"And so," King Fabian continued, "to protect our homes, our families, and our way of life, I have ordered one hundred and fifty of these ballista turrets to be mounted along our great cities' walls. Each one a guardian, standing watch against the encroaching darkness."

The murmurs in the crowd gained momentum, questions and concerns interweaving in a tapestry of shared unease. The word "wyverns" flitted through the assembly like wildfire, a whispered fear that threatened to overshadow the earlier festivities.

As the whispers grew, King Fabian, ever perceptive, acknowledged the concerns with a firm yet reassuring tone. "I understand the weight of this decision, my loyal subjects. But let it be known that our strength lies not only in the might of our warriors but in our bonds. Together, we shall stand against any threat that seeks to cast a shadow upon our beloved kingdom."

The weight of the King's announcement lingered in the air, but King Fabian, attuned to the needs of his people, seized the moment to rekindle the spirit of celebration. He raised his goblet high, a beacon of optimism in the dimly lit hall.

"Let this night be a testament to our resilience, our unity, and our unwavering spirit," the King proclaimed, his voice carrying the resonance of leadership. "In the face of challenges, we stand together, a beacon of light against the encroaching darkness. So, my friends, let the festivities continue! Dance, rejoice, and let the echoes of laughter drown out the shadows that seek to cast a pall over our land."

The nobles, stirred by the King's words, embraced the call to revelry once more. Shouts and cheers filled the room and then the music resumed, and the dance floor filled with couples twirling and weaving through the lively steps of celebration. The banquet hall, illuminated with flickering torchlight and the vibrant hues of noble attire, matched with the joyous energy of the night.

Amidst the renewed festivities, Lady Katherine, her expression a mix of mirth and contemplation, turned to Jaw. "I believe the wine has gone to my head," she confessed with a light laugh. "I need some fresh air, care to join me?"

Jaw, nodding in agreement, followed Lady Katherine as she gracefully made her way outside. Several noble couples got between them as he pursued her pale blue silhouette through the crowd. As he stepped into the courtyard, the cool night air embraced him, carrying the melodic strains of distant music from both within the castle and the streets of the city.

Lady Katherine had chosen a stone bench beneath a trellis, its vines bustled with beautiful blossoms. She settled onto the bench, her gaze directed upward at the canvas of stars that filled the night sky. Jaw, taking a seat beside her, felt the weight of the evening's revelations lifting, replaced by the serenity of the moment.

The nobles, glimpsing the scene from the banquet hall, exchanged knowing smiles. The courtyard, bathed in the soft glow of lanterns, bore witness to the quiet exchange between Lady Katherine and Jaw—a fleeting respite in the celebration.

Under the celestial tapestry of stars, Lady Katherine's distant smile held a trace of reflection as she nestled herself into Jaw's chest. The night air, tinged with the fragrant notes of oak and leather, enveloped them. She couldn't help but chuckle softly, a realisation dawning upon her.

"This has been nice," she sighed, her words carrying a hint of both contentment and joy.

Jaw, sensing the weight behind her words, held her a bit tighter. "It has," he replied, his deep voice resonating through the quiet courtyard.

As the night unfolded around them, Lady Katherine found herself compelled to delve into the enigma that was Jaw. With a gentle curiosity, she raised her head to meet his eyes.

"Why did you risk your life for the King?" she asked, her eyes searching his for the depths of his motivation.

Jaw's expression, stoic yet warm, remained unchanged. "It's just the way I am," he replied simply. "Can't stand by when someone's in trouble, my life has little worth when compared to that of a Kings."

She shook her head, the playful glint returning to her eyes. "You're silly, you know that?" she teased, her fingers tracing idle patterns on his chest. "Promise me, though, no more needlessly risking your life like that. Not for the King, not for anyone. Promise me."

Jaw, meeting her gaze with unfaltering sincerity, found himself captivated by her earnest plea. "I promise," he said, the words carrying the weight of a vow. And with that she lent in and kissed him on the lips, it was only brief but to them it felt like an eternity.

As the courtyard whispered with the night breeze, Lady Katherine nestled back into his chest, finding comfort in the quiet understanding that lingered between them. The stars above bore witness to the pact forged beneath their celestial watch.

The festivities within the castle continued to sound in the distance, the music and laughter becoming a distant serenade to the pair lost in conversation. Eventually, as the night reached its final verses, the couple rose from the stone bench.

With a shared glance and a silent understanding, they made their way back to The Dirty Spoon Tavern. The journey through the moonlit streets was accompanied by the lingering warmth of the night, the celebration gradually giving way to the peaceful embrace of a city beginning to go to sleep beneath the stars.

Jaw ensured Lady Katherine safely entered the tavern. Once certain of her well-being, he turned away from the lively city, ascending the hill toward the castle through the crepuscule of the night.

Amidst the dwindling festivities in the courtyard, where laughter and music lingered like echoes of joy, Jaw found himself approached by a steward. The dawning of the sun cast elongated shadows as the steward respectfully addressed him, "Sir, I have been requested to show you to a room."

Jaw, his senses still attuned to the medley of activity around him, arched an eyebrow in curiosity. "Here in the castle?" he questioned, a hint of surprise in his voice.

The steward nodded with a measured solemnity. "If you could follow me," he replied, gesturing for Jaw to accompany him. As they stepped away from the merriment, the steward began to lead Jaw through the heart of the castle itself.

Winding corridors unfolded before them, complete with opulent carpets that whispered tales of majesty and history. The stone walls, etched with the passage of time, bore witness to the countless events that had shaped the destiny of the Eastland Castle. Paintings hung from its many halls, capturing the gaze of noble ancestors in official portraits, while suits of armour stood sentinel, each piece a relic of the martial legacy of the kingdom.

Through the expansive hallways they walked, the steward offering glimpses into the castle's storied past as they made their way to a bedroom fit for a guest of honour. "The King insists that you remain within the castle walls as his guest until the ensuing battle," the steward explained with a quiet gravity, the weight of the impending conflict palpable in his words.

Finally, they arrived at the designated room, a haven of opulence within the fortress. The steward gestured courteously, inviting Jaw to enter. The regal canopy bed, the finely embroidered tapestries, and the warmth emanating from a grand fireplace welcomed him. The steward discreetly withdrew, leaving Jaw to the quietude of his temporary sanctuary, where the mysteries of The Eastland Castle whispered in every corner.

As Jaw hung his sword, he felt the weight of the night settle upon him. With a grateful sigh, Jaw allowed himself to succumb to the embrace of the monstrous bed. The soft linens cradled him, and as his eyes closed, the early morning sun outside the window painted a serene glow over the capital as it finally found rest.

Chapter 12

The dawn heralded a city awakening in a staggered cadence, with early risers navigating the cobblestone streets while others clung to the last remnants of slumber. In the quiet corners, dedicated souls emerged, their routines untouched by the revelry of the previous night. A diligent herbalist arranged potions in her modest stall, the delicate aroma of herbs wafting through the air. The fishmonger, having already returned from one of the many lakes that neighbored the capital, displayed the day's catch with a practised hand. These were the unsung protagonists of the city's bustling tapestry, the weavers of daily life whose threads intertwined seamlessly.

Yet, as the sun climbed higher, coaxing even the most reluctant from their beds, the hive-like nature of the city began to hum with increasing intensity. Shop doors clattered as they unlocked, and market squares came to life with the chatter of vendors. Merchants set up their wares.

The blacksmiths, their forges roaring to life, worked tirelessly to craft an arsenal befitting the defenders of the realm. Sparks danced like fleeting fireflies as weapons took shape beneath skilled hands. Armourers meticulously forged protective layers, each piece a testament to the dedication woven into the city's defence.

Amidst this unfolding spectacle, Micharas and Antonius, having forgone the solace of rest, ventured through the castle grounds and into the city's awakening pulse. Guards clad in gleaming armour conducted drills in the courtyard, their movements synchronised like a well-practised dance. The rhythmic clash of swords echoed through the air as they honed their skills in preparation for the impending conflict.

As the duo reached the edge of the courtyard, they were met by the imposing gates, once open in welcome, now stood resolute and closed. A guard granted them leave and the gates were closed once again in their wake. The portcullis, a formidable barrier, lowered with a thunderous clang, sealing the castle within its protective embrace as the two left its grounds. The transformation of the once-celebratory courtyard into a bastion of preparation spoke volumes of the impending storm that loomed on the horizon.

Along the city walls, the specially crafted ballistae, were carefully manoeuvred into strategic positions. The complex mechanisms of these colossal weapons were a marvel of engineering, their presence instilling a sense of reassurance through the community. By mid morning, the city, now fully awakened and mobilised, stood as a complete force against the battle to come.

"So what's on the cards for us today then?" Antonius asked his brother, looking to him for guidance for the activities of the day ahead.

Micharas let out a tired chuckle, his eyes showing a mix of exhaustion and determination. "Well, today's plan involves less partying and more of the clang of hammers and the thud of war drums. Looks like we're in for a day of preparation."

Antonius raised an eyebrow, a teasing grin on his face. "Ah, the sweet melody of war drums. Nothing like it to get the adrenaline flowing. But, gotta say, I kinda miss the dance floor vibe. Maybe we can convince the enemy to have a dance-off instead of a battle?"

Micharas laughed at the ridiculousness of the idea. "Yeah, imagine us facing off with swords and synchronised moves. Our foes would be scratching their heads, wondering if they stumbled into a war or a weird performance."

They shared a good laugh, the humour momentarily easing the weight of the upcoming fight. As they ambled through the streets, checking out the preparations, Micharas got a bit more serious.

"All jokes aside, Antonius, we should make sure everything is in order. The Guards are looking sharp, blacksmiths are deep in preparation already, the city's gearing up for war. We need to make sure that we are on top of our game as well."

Antonius nodded, his earlier playfulness giving way to a more thoughtful look. "You're right, as always, brother. Let's make our rounds, boost morale, and ensure that when the time comes, this city stands united and ready. And who knows, maybe we'll find a dance partner among the blacksmiths to liven things up a bit."

Micharas grinned at the idea. "A dance with a hammer and anvil, the truest form of artistry. I am sure it will be a real showstopper." They continued their banter as they weaved through the busy city.

Micharas and Antonius made their way through the bustling city streets, navigating the growing frenzy of preparations. As they approached their older brother's forge, the rhythmic clanging of metal against metal reached their ears, a symphony of craftsmanship echoing in the air.

The forge, nestled in a corner with billows of smoke rising from the chimney, was a testament to their older brother's dedication to his craft. The brothers entered the workshop, greeted by the heat of the roaring fire and the scent of molten metal.

In the dimly lit interior, Andarius looked up from his work. His eyes, sharp and discerning, assessed the newcomers.

"Well, well, if it isn't the dynamic duo," he greeted them, a hint of amusement in his voice. "What brings you to my humble abode today?"

Antonius grinned. "We're here to scrounge some of your finest gear, dear brother. You know, the kind that makes us look as impressive as you."

Their brother chuckled, setting aside his tools. "Impressive, you say? I suppose I could spare a moment to fashion you a couple of things. The looming battle has everyone scrambling for better gear."

Micharas nodded. "We want to be as prepared as possible. Anything you can provide will be greatly appreciated."

Their brother's stare softened, and he motioned for them to approach. "I'll see what I can do." He began picking up a collection of his wares as he shot measuring glances at the pair, after some time had passed he presented his selected items for them to try on.

Micharas, donned in his new armour, felt a blend of protection and flexibility that surpassed his previous gear. The leather armour, meticulously crafted, seamlessly integrated with a sturdy steel chestplate. The chestplate bore intricate engravings, a fantastic display of Andarius's skill and attention to detail. Despite the added weight of the steel, the design allowed for a surprising range of movement, vital for Micharas's agile combat style.

Andarius presented Micharas with a new bow, its skill in its making evident in the polished wood and expertly strung. However, when offered a new sword, Micharas declined, choosing to stick with the sabre that Jaw had given him. There was a sentimental value to the blade, a connection to a comrade and a reminder of their shared battles. He felt pride in carrying such a historical and meaningful artefact.

Antonius, on the other hand, found himself clad in full leather armour, a sleek and flexible ensemble that provided both protection and ease of movement. The supple leather, expertly stitched and padded, offered a balance between defence and agility—perfect for Antonius's nimble approach to combat.

Andarius then handed Antonius a unique bow of his own design. Crafted from oak, the unorthodox bow featured five strings, spaced two centimetres apart and slightly to the side of one another. "This bow is a bit of an experiment, my own creation. The design might look unusual, but I believe it can offer you something special."

Antonius examined the bow with a mix of curiosity and anticipation. "Five strings?" he remarked, one eyebrow raised.

Andarius nodded, a hint of excitement in his voice. "Indeed. Those strings are spaced just so, and slightly off-centre. It's all about balance and precision. The idea is to provide a more stable release, giving you better control over your shots. The spacing enhances power, and I've reinforced the structure to handle the additional strain."

Antonius ran his fingers over the polished wood. "It's unlike any bow I've seen."

"That's the goal," Andarius affirmed. "I wanted to create something unique, tailored to your style. You're a master archer, Antonius, and I believe this bow will complement your skills. It might take a bit of getting used to, but once you do, I'm confident you'll appreciate its nuances."

Antonius, a grin forming on his face, shouldered the bow. "Well, Andarius, if anyone can make the most of an experimental design, it's me, right?"

Andarius chuckled. "That's the spirit. Just remember, it's not about the bow alone—it's about the archer wielding it. And when people admire it, you can tell them where you got it from."

Both brothers were equipped with quivers filled with extra sharp arrows, each arrow meticulously crafted for maximum effectiveness on the battlefield. Andarius, with a twinkle in his eye, teased them about the impracticality of fitted armour during their finery, a playful jab at their appearance. "If you want these to fit perfectly, come back when you're not dressed like lords of the realm," Andarius laughed. "But, in all seriousness, take care of yourselves out there. These are dangerous times."

Micharas and Antonius, now armed with their new gear, thanked their older brother for his time, gifts and guidance. As they left the forge and made their way back towards The Dirty Spoon.

They sat on a wall outside the tavern and watched the town going about its business in the afternoon sun. After some time had passed it was Antonius who yet again broke the silence. "So, brother," he began with a sly grin, "any thoughts on our dear Lady Katherine and Jaw? I heard they left the party together last night, hand in hand. Seems like love is in the air."

Micharas raised an eyebrow, a smirk playing on his lips. "Love, you say? Well, I wouldn't jump to conclusions. It could be that they simply decided to take a moonlit stroll and discuss the finer points of battle strategy."

Antonius chuckled, nudging Micharas playfully. "Ah, yes, the romantic allure of siege tactics and military manoeuvres. Nothing says 'Kiss Me' like a well-executed pincer movement."

Micharas joined in the laughter, but his gaze became distant for a moment. "That said, it's good to see them finding solace in each other's company. In times like these, bonds form in the most unexpected places. If there's one thing I've learned, it's that love and friendship can be powerful motivators on the battlefield."

Antonius nodded, the mirth in his eyes replaced by a more contemplative expression. "True. We fight not just for ourselves, but for those we hold dear. If Lady Katherine and Jaw have found something special in each other, it might just be the strength they need in the days to come. In all seriousness though, where are they? Surely they don't intend to spend the entire day in bed."

"I hope you two are not talking about me," a voice chimed in, drawing the attention of Micharas and Antonius. Lady Katherine walked towards them along the bustling high street, her vibrant presence contrasting with the subdued activity around her. In her arms, she cradled a small collection of books, pressed to her chest.

Micharas grinned, shooting a playful glance at Antonius. "Guilty as charged. We were just discussing the romantic escapades of our dear Lady Katherine and the valiant Jaw. Rumour has it you two left the party hand in hand."

Antonius added with a teasing smile, "We were wondering if love had officially conquered the battlefield."

Lady Katherine rolled her eyes, but a playful smirk danced on her lips. "Oh, spare me your jests, gentlemen. Jaw and I merely took a stroll to discuss strategy, not to pen sonnets under the moonlight."

Micharas feigned innocence, "Strategy, you say? Nothing like a moonlit tactical discussion to set the mood."

"I can just imagine it now. 'Darling, let's flank left and surprise the enemy. Oh, and by the way, your eyes are as deep as a well-defended moat.'" Antonius joked, holding back tears of laughter.

Lady Katherine shook her head, laughter in her eyes. "You two are incorrigible. But, as much as I'd love to entertain your whimsical notions, I have some important reading to do. Knowledge is power, after all."

She gracefully joined them on the wall, placing the books beside her. Antonius leaned in with exaggerated seriousness. "Ah, yes, the mighty pen, mightier than the sword, they say. Although, I have my doubts when facing a charging cavalry."

Micharas chuckled, "Let her have her books, Antonius. Knowledge might not block a sword, but it can certainly guide it."

Lady Katherine, not one to be outdone, retorted, "And a well-timed sonnet can disarm even the most hardened foe." The trio laughed amongst themselves as the smell of lavender wafted over them.

Jaw lay on the ornate bed, the festivities of the night still replaying in his mind. His thoughts were a tumultuous mix of elation and uncertainty, and he couldn't shake the weight of the kiss that lingered on his lips. He touched them lightly, as if to capture the sensation once more.

Questions danced in his mind. Was it merely the result of Lady Katherine having indulged in too much drink, or did she genuinely harbour feelings for him? The uncertainty of the situation left him feeling both wonderful and foolish, caught in a whirlwind of emotions. He berated himself for simply leaving her at the tavern, wondering if he had missed a golden opportunity.

As he pondered these thoughts, time seemed to stretch, minutes feeling like hours in the solitude of the bedroom. The echoes of the night's revelry played in his mind like a haunting melody, and the flickering candlelight cast dancing shadows on the chamber walls.

The air in the room held a hint of the festivities, a mix of ale, laughter, and the faint fragrance of Lady Katherine's perfume. Jaw's mind replayed the moments leading up to the kiss—the shared laughter, the stolen glances, the smell of her hair, and the warmth of her presence. The memory was a tapestry of emotions, woven with threads of joy and uncertainty.

He couldn't escape the feeling of missed chances, a nagging thought that tugged at the edges of his consciousness. Jaw's internal struggle played out in the quiet of the room, the ornate bed serving as a witness to the silent turmoil within.

With a determined sigh, Jaw pushed aside the lingering uncertainties, realising that the rising day demanded his focus.

Dwelling on what-ifs wouldn't serve him well in the impending challenges. Rising from the four-poster bed, he felt a surge of resolution, eager to wash away the inescapable feelings of regret that clung to him. Grabbing his sword from the end of the bed, he affixed it to his belt, ready to face the day ahead.

As he strode down the castle hallway, a concerned servant approached, a furrowed brow betraying her worry. "Sir, are you alright?" she asked, her gaze flickering over him.

Jaw offered a small, reassuring smile. "I'm Jaw, a guest here. Just had a bit of a late night. I need to clean up. Could you point me to a bathroom or a washing basin?"

The servant's expression softened, and she nodded. "Of course, sir. Follow me, I'll show you to a bathroom." She led him through the labyrinthine corridors of the castle, her footsteps tapping in the quiet passages.

Eventually they reached a large set of double doors, the servant opened them and led him inside.

Jaw found himself in a lavishly appointed bathroom that spoke of both functionality and luxury. The room was expansive, adorned with beautiful tilework that covered the walls, depicting scenes of majestic landscapes and mythical creatures. The floor was laid with large, polished stones.

In the centre of the room, a grand bath took prominence. The tub, carved from marble with ornate patterns etched into its surface, stood on clawed feet, exuding an air of regality. The sides were gilded with gold and silver accents, enhancing the allure of the bathing vessel.

Adjacent to the bath, a small table held an array of plush towels, neatly folded and ready for use. The towels themselves were of the finest quality, soft to the touch and inviting. A small, intricately carved stool stood nearby, complete with a cushion for added comfort.

On one wall, a shelf housed an assortment of oils and perfumes, each vial meticulously arranged. The scents ranged from delicate florals to rich spices, offering a myriad of choices to enhance the bathing experience. A silver tray held a collection of finely crafted soap bars, their fragrances mingling with the warm, humid air of the room.

Large, arched windows complete with delicate curtains allowed natural light to filter into the space, casting a soft glow over the opulent surroundings. The curtains themselves, made of sheer fabric, swayed gently in the breeze, creating a dance of light and shadow on the floor.

The servant gestured towards the magical faucet, a device Jaw was unfamiliar with. "This faucet produces hot water. Simply turn it like so," she demonstrated, as crystal-clear water cascaded from a golden spout, filling the tub with a gentle, melodic flow. Steam rising from it in a plume. "and you'll have a warm bath ready in no time. Will you require assistance in bathing?"

Jaw could not help but notice that even through her professional composure and expression that there was a faint hint of hope as she eyed the mighty warrior before her. "No, I am sure that I can manage." He replied with a friendly smile.

She lowered her head in understanding a smile played on her lips as she did so. Seemingly thinking that it was unnoticed by Jaw who was marvelling at the splendour of the room. "If you need anything else, just ring the bell for assistance." She said, pointing to a small golden bell by one of the legs of the stool.

"Thank you," Jaw said appreciatively, and as the servant left, he turned his attention to drawing the bath. Stripping off his clothing, he felt the weight of the night's festivities lift with each piece removed. There was a therapeutic quality to shedding the layers, as if the water he was about to immerse himself in would wash away not only the dirt and grime but also the negative emotions that lingered from the night before.

He walked across the stone floor, which he found cool to the touch beneath his bare feet. As he approached the shelf of oils he selected a few, lifting them, uncorking them to smell before replacing them.

Jaw perused the array of soap bars on the shelf, each one emanating a distinct fragrance. His senses were immediately captivated by the sweet and refreshing aroma of lavender and mint. The soap bar, covered with mesmerising patterns, promised a revitalising experience. He carefully picked it up, appreciating the smoothness of the soap against his palm.

All the while the bathtub filled behind him. Once it was satisfactorily full he turned off the tap and clambered inside.

As Jaw immersed himself in the warm water, he couldn't help but appreciate the decadence of the surroundings. The bathroom was a sanctuary of relaxation, a testament to the grandeur of the castle itself. The soothing ambiance, coupled with the exquisite details, turned the act of cleansing into a ritual of rejuvenation, preparing him both physically and mentally for the challenges that awaited beyond the ornate door.

The soap lathered effortlessly, its rich foam carrying the invigorating scent. He began with his arms, the soap gliding smoothly over his skin, cleansing away the dust of the road and the weight of uncertainties. The warm water embraced him, easing the tension in his muscles.

As he moved on to his hair covered chest, sculpted and scarred by battles and training. It felt nice under the caress of the soap as his hands glided effortlessly across the toned muscles and along his tense shoulders and biceps.

Next, he focused on his legs, the soap working its magic as he washed away the remnants of travel. The water, now carrying the earthy tones of the soap and dirt, cascaded in rivulets down his body. He revelled in the decadence of the moment, the spectacularness of the bathroom elevating a simple act into a ritual of indulgence.

Jaw then turned his attention to his coarse, brown, unkempt hair, fingers massaging the soap into his scalp. The fragrance intensified as he worked up a luxurious lather, the suds clinging to his hair like a fragrant veil. The warm water, now infused with the essence of lavender and mint, rinsed away the soap, leaving his hair feeling refreshed and revitalised.

Emerging from the bath, Jaw felt a renewed sense of vigour. The soothing warmth of the water, and the invigorating aroma had transformed a mundane task into a moment of indulgence. The bubbles and water cascaded down his body as he rose, it swept back and forth in the tub beneath him as he ventured forth. The heat of the sun coming through the window shimmered off of his bare, wet body as he reached for the towels on the nearby table.

After he was dry he approached the shelf with the oils and perfumes on it that he had explored before his long soak in the bath. Reaching out he took one of the bottles that he had smelt earlier and dabbed a small amount of the oil on his hand. He then proceeded to rub it into his hair, across his chin and into his chest. He replaced the cork and began to get dressed.

Jaw, now dressed and scented with a subtle aroma of the chosen oil, felt a renewed sense of vitality. The fragrance clung to him like a whisper, a subtle reminder of the indulgent moments spent in the glorious bathroom. With each step, the scent of lavender and wildflowers accompanied him, an invisible cloak of aromatic luxury.

Deciding to explore the city, he made his way through the castle grounds, passing the once-celebratory courtyard now transformed into a bastion of preparation. The guards, getting ready for their morning drill, nodded at him in acknowledgment as he traversed the familiar path towards the gate.

As the gates opened and released him into the heart of the city, Jaw took in the sights and sounds that had eluded him during his stay thus far. The cobblestone streets stretched before him, lined with bustling stalls, merchants preparing their stalls, and citizens starting to go about their daily lives.

The still rising sun cast a warm glow over the city, casting long shadows that danced along the edges of buildings. Jaw meandered through the streets, curious to discover the nooks and crannies that hid tales untold. The slow and quiet morning hush of its people preparing for the impending conflict.

In the midst of this urban symphony, Jaw's attention was drawn to a peculiar shop nestled within the small back alley that he was walking down. Its windows, though smudged with the residue of time, offered a tantalising glimpse into a world of eclectic treasures. Stacks of mysterious objects, each with its own tale, filled the dimly lit interior.

Intrigued, Jaw approached the shop, the worn wooden sign above the entrance swinging slightly in the morning breeze read "Carters Curios". The bell above the door chimed as he stepped inside, announcing his arrival to the elderly shopkeeper who was diligently buffing a pair of weathered boots behind the counter.

"Good morning," came the raspy yet welcoming voice of the shopkeeper, the wrinkles on his face unfolding into a warm smile.

"You are open early," Jaw remarked, taking in the assortment of curiosities that cluttered the crowded shelves.

The shop, though small, was a treasury of odds and ends. Dust danced in the rays of sunlight filtering through the grimy windows, giving the space an air of forgotten enchantment. Shelves bowed under the weight of ancient tomes, peculiar artefacts, and trinkets from lands unseen. The scent of old leather mingled with the mustiness of ancient parchment, creating a distinctive aroma that bespoke the shop's rich history.

The counter, where the shopkeeper diligently worked, was a mosaic of tools, parchments, and intriguing objects waiting for attention. Jars filled with curious liquids lined the edges, each holding the promise of forgotten alchemy.

Jaw meandered through the narrow aisles, his eyes dancing from one item to another. A collection of masks filled one of the corners, each one whispering of distant cultures and mysterious rituals. Antique maps, yellowed with age, beckoned him to explore uncharted territories.

The shopkeeper, having paused his work on the boots, observed Jaw's wanderings with a knowing glint in his eyes. "Early bird catches the worm, they say," he remarked, his voice carrying the weight of countless tales. "What brings you to my humble emporium on this fine morning?"

Jaw, his curiosity piqued, turned to face the shopkeeper with a friendly smile. "I was on my way to a blacksmith to get some armour, but I couldn't resist the mysterious allure of your shop. It called to me, and I had to explore."

The elderly shopkeeper chuckled, a sound that seemed to carry echoes of bygone eras. "Ah, the call of curiosity. It's a melody that lingers in the air here. Many adventurers have found themselves drawn into the tapestry of wonders within these walls." He gestured to the objects that surrounded them.

As he spoke, the old man shuffled over, his steps measured and deliberate. His gnarled fingers gestured towards a shelf that held an array of peculiar artefacts. Among them, one item stood out—a shoulder pad crafted from gleaming steel, with intricate engravings that told a tale of dwarven craftsmanship. What truly captured the eye, however, was the sizable stone-bound book chained securely to the steel, its pages weathered and seemingly untouched by time.

The old man happened to catch Jaw staring at it. "That, my friend, is a relic with a story as old as the mountains," the shopkeeper said, his eyes twinkling with the joy of sharing a hidden narrative. "It's a shoulder pad worn by the scribes of a forgotten order. The book, you see, holds the secrets of their arcane knowledge. Bound to steel, it served as both protection and a conduit to the mystic arts."

"It looks heavy." Jaw joked with a chuckle as he continued looking around the shelves.

The old man chuckled in agreement. "Yes, the dwarves are not known for making light artefacts, it is true." He nodded as he spoke.

The old man drew closer, his senses keen despite the passage of time. A subtle sniff revealed the lingering scent of Jaw's recent bath, a fragrance that spoke of cleanliness and a momentary escape from the rigours of the world. Weary but perceptive eyes examined the man standing before him, taking note of the richness in Jaw's attire—an indication of wealth and power that piqued the shopkeeper's interest.

"You mentioned that you are seeking armour?" the old man inquired, his voice carrying both curiosity and a shrewdness born of years of experience.

Jaw, feeling the weight of the old man's scrutiny, nodded in response. "Indeed. I'm on a quest for better protection, something sturdy for the battles that lie ahead."

A knowing smile crept across the shopkeeper's face, as if he could read the unspoken tales etched into Jaw's features. "Armour is more than just a shield for the body, my friend. It tells a story, reflects one's journey and purpose. In this humble emporium, you may find more than steel and leather. You may find a piece of history that resonates with your own."

With that, the old man gestured towards a dimly lit corner, where suits of armour stood like silent sentinels, each with its unique design and character. The glint of metal beckoned, promising not just physical protection but a connection to a legacy that transcended the battlefield.

"Feel free to explore, try them on, and let the spirits of the past guide your choice," the shopkeeper offered, his eyes twinkling with a blend of wisdom and mischief. "For every piece here has a tale to tell, waiting to be continued in the chapters of your own adventure."

Jaw wandered over to the suits of armour standing in the corner of the shop, each piece with its unique allure. The glint of metal and the faint echoes of untold stories surrounded him, creating an atmosphere charged with mystery. The shopkeeper observed with a knowing expression, allowing the armour to weave its silent tale in the canvas of Jaw's imagination.

Among the suits, there was a set of intricately crafted plate armour, its surface engraved with etchings that told of battles long past. Next to it, a sleek leather ensemble whispered of stealth and agility, designed for a nimble and cunning assassin. Further down, a set of chainmail glimmered, its links tightly woven together.

The shopkeeper, sensing Jaw's fascination, approached again with a warm smile. "Found something that catches your eye, I see. These sets have seen the rise and fall of kingdoms, witnessed the turning tides of battles long forgotten. Each one has a tale to tell, waiting for a new chapter in your hands." As Jaw contemplated the choices before him, the man finally asked, "Do you need any help trying them on?"

Jaw nodded appreciatively, accepting the offer. "That would be appreciated, thank you."

The shopkeeper guided Jaw through the process, helping him don each piece with a practised ease. The weight of the armour settled on Jaw's shoulders, the metal and leather holding him in a protective embrace. The pieces melded seamlessly, offering not just physical protection but function.

As he secured the strap of a formidable breastplate, Jaw couldn't help but be curious about the origins of these artefacts. "Where did you get these sets? They seem to come from a myriad of realms."

The shopkeeper's eyes sparkled with memories as he began to share his story. "Ah, my friend, these treasures are the fruits of a lifetime spent adventuring and discovering the secrets of the planes. I've traversed distant lands, delved into forgotten dungeons, and crossed paths with warriors whose stories deserved to be preserved. Each set here is a relic of those journeys, a testament to the diversity and resilience of those who once wore them."

He paused for a moment, a glimmer of excitement in his eyes. "If you're interested, I have another set in the back—a piece that holds a different story. Would you care to take a look?"

The shopkeeper, with a nod of approval, guided Jaw through the process of removing the armour, each piece returned to its designated stand with a careful reverence. As the suits settled back into their silent vigil, the shopkeeper motioned for Jaw to follow him into the concealed depths of the shop.

Ascending a creaky flight of stairs, the air around them changed, and Jaw found himself stepping into the personal domain of the elderly proprietor. The space above the shop bore the mark of a life rich in experiences and eclectic curiosities.

The old man opened a door on the landing, it led into a small cosy room complete with a fireplace, leather armchair and bookcase. The warm aroma of aged wood and the soft glow of ambient light greeted Jaw as they entered. The door was closed behind them, creating a sense of privacy as the old man gestured toward the set of armour displayed proudly on a stand.

The armour before Jaw was a true masterpiece, a harmonious fusion of steel and leather that whispered tales of both protection and agility. The steel components were meticulously crafted, providing formidable defence without sacrificing mobility. The leather, adorned with knot-like patterns, seamlessly integrated into the armour, adding a touch of elegance to its functionality.

The embroidered patterns on the leather were a spectacular example of the creator's skill, each knot carefully woven into the material, creating an intricate design. As the light danced on the surface, the patterns seemed to come alive, telling a silent story that only those who donned the armour could truly understand.

The steel chestplate, which bore a central emblem reminiscent of the ethereal blue halo of an angel, drew the eye with its simplistic beauty. The balance between steel and leather was evident in every detail. The cuirass, protecting the torso, seamlessly transitioned into the faulds and tassets, offering flexibility without compromising protection. The leather components, treated with care and expertise, retained their supple quality, providing comfort to the wearer.

As Jaw traced his fingers along the armour, he could feel the smoothness of the steel, the texture of the embossed leather, and the cool embrace of the entire ensemble. It was a work of art that transcended mere protection; it was a symbol of the ancient craft of armour-making, a bridge between the past and the present.

The old man, watching Jaws' reaction, spoke with a sense of pride. "This set has a unique history, my friend. Crafted by a master armour-smith in a forgotten corner of existence, its enchanting design provides unparalleled protection."

Jaw couldn't help but be captivated by the allure of the armour, the stories it held, and the craftsmanship that spoke volumes about the dedication of its creator. The old man, with a knowing smile, waited for Jaw's decision, understanding that sometimes the true value of armour lay beyond its physical and even magical attributes.

Jaw regarded the old man with a mix of gratitude and respect, recognizing the sentimental value woven into the fabric of the armour before him. "Are you sure you can part with this?" he asked, a note of consideration in his voice.

The old man, his eyes reflecting a lifetime of memories, nodded solemnly. "It's time for this armour to find a new purpose. And you, my friend, seem destined to carry on its legacy."

"Then I shall wear it with pride," Jaw declared, a genuine smile lighting up his face. From his pocket, he produced the Platinum Coin, its gleaming surface catching the sunlight streaming through the window. Holding it up for inspection, Jaw inquired, a cheeky grin on his face as he offered the valuable coin. "I assume this will be enough?"

Chapter 13

The afternoon sun cast a warm glow over the cobbled streets of the town, and a gentle breeze carried the fragrance of lavender over the party. Micharas and Antonius were seated on the wall outside The Dirty Spoon, enjoying the pleasant weather. Lady Katherine stood nearby, books clutched in her arms, the trio seemed engrossed in a light-hearted conversation, which hummed with laughter.

As they joked among themselves, a figure emerged in the distance, striding purposefully along the busy street. The glint of metal and sweet aroma caught their attention, and they turned to see Jaw approaching, his new armour reflecting the soft light of the sun.

Micharas squinted, a playful smirk forming on his lips. "Well, well, who's this shiny newcomer gracing our presence?" He nudged Antonius with his elbow, mischief gleaming in his eyes.

Lady Katherine, joined in the banter. "My, my, Jaw, you clean up rather nicely. I almost mistook you for a knight on a quest. Have you come to rescue us from the perils of mundane conversation?"

Jaw, having seen his fair share of banter over the years, chuckled and gave a dramatic bow. "Fear not, fair Lady Katherine, for I am here to add a touch of excitement to your day. As for you two, I did not realise they permitted goblins inside the Eastland Castle."

Micharas feigned a gasp. "How dare you, sir knight! I will have you know that we, too, have acquired new armour." He gestured proudly to his and his brother's attire.

Lady Katherine rolled her eyes with a smile. "Yes, it seems the blacksmiths are now crafting armour for all kinds of beast-folk. But truly, Jaw, that armour suits you. Where did you find it?"

Jaw, standing tall with a sense of pride beneath the equipment, began to respond when a horn sounded from high up on the walls. Bells chimed throughout the city, their resonant tones interrupting the banter and bringing a sudden hush to the lively streets. The party exchanged eerie glances, their attention drawn to the source of the unexpected sound.

The sound of horns and bells resonated through the town, injecting an air of urgency into the previously relaxed atmosphere. Without a moment's hesitation, the group exchanged glances and, as if guided by an unspoken agreement, sprang into action. Micharas led the charge as they moved with a newfound agility, fueled by adrenaline.

They navigated the cobbled streets with a sense of purpose, weaving through the crowd of townsfolk who had also been stirred by the unusual disturbance. As they reached the base of the stairs leading up to the towering walls, Antonius couldn't help but voice his concern, his voice barely audible over the commotion.

"Surely the Alts are not here already?" he mused, a furrow forming on his brow. The notion of the Alts, known for their unpredictable raids and swift attacks, added a layer of tension to the situation.

Micharas, bounding up the stairs beside his brother, shot him a reassuring grin. "Let's not jump to conclusions, Antonius. It could be a false alarm or a warm up."

Lady Katherine, keeping pace with the brothers, added a touch of wisdom to the conversation. "We won't know until we reach the walls. Whatever it is, we'll face it together."

The ascent was swift, fueled by a mix of curiosity and a shared sense of duty. They emerged onto the towering walls, where guards were already assembling, their expressions a blend of concern and readiness. The battlement they entered was abuzz with activity. Guards hurriedly organised, securing bolts for the ballistae, the massive crossbows poised to defend the city.

Jaw, his keen eyes scanning the horizon, joined the guards at the battlement, his presence commanding attention. "What's happening?" he inquired, his voice steady despite the unfolding uncertainty.

A veteran guard, a weathered expression etched on his face, turned to address the group. "Scouts have reported movement in the distance. We're not sure who or what it is yet, but we're not taking any chances."

As the party gazed beyond the walls, the landscape revealed little, shrouded in the mystery of approaching dusk. The guards continued their preparations, adjusting the aim of the ballistae and ensuring a ready supply of bolts.

Antonius, his eyes narrowing as he scanned the horizon, couldn't shake the feeling of unease. "It could just be a scout party moving ahead of the main army."

As the group peered into the horizon, a sudden movement caught their attention. Emerging from a distant tree line, the unmistakable visage of the Alts spilled forth, their presence shattering any hopes of a false alarm.

Lady Katherine, standing at the forefront of the wall, reacted with swift determination. She held her hands out before her, palms facing each other, and uttered the words, "Eagle Eye Hole." A subtle energy emanated from her fingertips as she expanded the gap between her hands, causing the air itself to warp and bend as it to convex before their eyes.

The magical feat she performed created an area of magnification, like a window into the distance. The previously distant Alt forces now came into sharp focus, revealing the extent of their numbers and the ominous purpose with which they approached the city.

Antonius squinted, observing the enhanced image. "Well, that's not as many as I expected. Are they trying to pull some kind of trick?" He exchanged glances with the others, a hint of scepticism in his tone.

Micharas, with a smirk, commented, "Looks like the big, fearsome Alts decided to bring a picnic instead of an army. Those are hardly the numbers we anticipated." He gestured toward the distant Alt forces with a casual wave.

One of the guards on the wall chuckled, overhearing Micharas's remark. "Hah! Is that all they've got? I've seen more people waiting in line for the bakery on market day. Siege towers and all, they must be trying to compensate for something."

As the party took in the sight, it became evident that the Alt forces, though equipped with siege towers, were indeed fewer than anticipated. The guards on the wall exchanged bemused glances, and the tension that had gripped the air began to dissipate.

Lady Katherine, maintaining her focus on the magically created aperture, spoke with a mixture of relief and amusement. "It appears they brought a modest entourage. Either they're underestimating us or they've got something up their sleeves. Regardless, it might be to our advantage."

The enemy, despite their smaller numbers, marched resolutely towards the city, their siege towers looming ominously. As they entered the effective range of the ballistae mounted on the wall, the guards, though not yet fully proficient with the massive crossbows, unleashed a barrage of bolts.

Surprisingly, the guards displayed an unexpected level of accuracy, with each bolt finding its mark on the Alt siege towers. The massive wooden structures, perhaps hastily assembled or poorly reinforced, crumbled under the impact of the bolts. It took only a few well-aimed shots to bring down each tower, much to the surprise of the onlookers.

Amidst the cheers of the guards celebrating their success, Lady Katherine, standing near the ballistae, cast a wary glance back at the horizon. A chill ran down her spine as realisation dawned upon her. "Stop!" she howled, her voice cutting through the cheers.

The guards, caught up in their triumph, hesitated for a moment before continuing to fire upon the approaching forces. However, Lady Katherine's sharp eyes had caught something that eluded the others. As the last siege tower fell, she turned her attention to the distant enemy ranks.

Without wasting a moment, Lady Katherine climbed onto the wall in front of the nearest ballista, determined to halt the barrage. "Ceasefire! Hold your bolts!" she commanded, waving her hands to convey the urgency of her order.

A grizzled guard, accustomed to command, stepped forward with a frown. "Get out of the way, you foolish girl. We can't let them advance."

Ignoring his protests, and with a wave of her hand and a disapproving scowl, she enacted a spell that caused the guard's mouth to vanish from his face. Panic flashed across his eyes as he clutched at his face, unable to speak.

The sudden and unsettling silence that befell the guard drew the attention of others in the vicinity. They watched in shock as Lady Katherine demonstrated the consequence of disobedience. The sudden display of the magic she wielded spread the message that she was not to be trifled with among the guards, leading to a tense standstill on the wall.

Lady Katherine, with another wave of her hand, restored the guard's ability to speak. Before he could utter a word, she swiftly explained her observation. "They're luring our fire. This small display of their army, these crudely built siege towers—it's all a front. They're trying to disarm the city before the main force arrives."

"Shit," the guard muttered, a look of concern settling over his features. He turned to address the rest of the guards, his voice urgent. "We need an ammo count! How many bolts have we fired?"

A mumble spread through the crowd as guards along the city wall began counting the remaining bolts. The whisper of information reached the leading figure, and he exclaimed in outrage, "Half?!" Realising the dire situation created by their mistake, he swiftly issued orders to his men. "Get to the blacksmiths immediately! Instruct them to make more bolts. Now, go!" He directed several of his men to carry out the urgent task.

The guards, spurred into action, scattered along the wall to relay the message and ensure a swift response from the blacksmiths. The urgency in their movements mirrored the gravity of the situation—the need to replenish the dwindling ammunition before the main Alt force arrived.

Lady Katherine, having conveyed the critical information, maintained her vigil on the wall. Her eyes focused on the retreating Alt forces, now regrouping beyond the range of the ballistae. The deceptive tactics employed by the Alts showcased a level of cunning that demanded a strategic response.

As the guards hurried to secure additional bolts, Jaw, Micharas, and

Antonius gathered near Lady Katherine. Jaw spoke with a sense of determination. "We need to fortify our defences. If this is just a prelude, we can't afford to be caught off guard."

Micharas, his brows furrowed in contemplation, nodded in agreement. "Lady Katherine, any insights on their strategy? We need to anticipate their next move."

Lady Katherine, her eyes never leaving the battlefield, spoke with a measured tone. "They've shown their hand, but the true threat lies in what they're concealing. We must prepare for a larger assault. Reinforce the gates, gather the townsfolk to safety, and make sure the blacksmiths expedite the production of those bolts." She instructed not just her team but the guard captain.

Antonius, scanning the horizon with a wary gaze, added, "It might be a little late for that."

The forces on the wall turned their attention to the horizon, where a formidable sight met their gaze—more than ten thousand Alts creeping forth from the tree line. Among them were additional siege towers, ladders, and a vast number of archers. Lady Katherine, recognizing the imminent threat, took control of her spell from earlier, redirecting its focus to the middle of the approaching army.

As the magical aperture expanded, tracking a figure within the crowd, a hush fell over the defenders on the wall. This Alt was unlike the others, heavily armoured from head to toe in black metal. His helmet seemed devoid of a visor, concealing his face in an air of mystery. A large bow adorned his back, crafted from metal with an unusual spike protruding from the grip. The spike, when drawn, would point back towards the wielder, a design suggesting a unique and potentially perilous method of use. As though it demanded the sacrifice of its wielder.

The figure moved with a purpose through the ranks, his presence commanding the Alt Army's full attention. Despite the lack of visible arrows or traditional weapons, the aura of menace he exuded suggested that he was a force to be reckoned with. The layered plates of his armour left no gaps at the joints, creating an impenetrable barrier that spoke of expert craftsmanship.

Lady Katherine, her eyes fixed on the armoured figure, noted the absence of traditional weaponry. The lack of arrows or a visible melee weapon raised unsettling questions about the capabilities of this formidable Alt warrior. The atmosphere on the wall grew tense as the mysterious figure continued to advance, leading the ever growing Alt army with an air of confidence that sent shivers down the spines of those who beheld him.

As the defenders on the wall prepared for the impending assault, they observed the Alt Commander waving his arms in the air, seemingly delivering a speech to his forces. "I did not realise they were this civilised," Micharas whispered to Jaw as they watched the spectacle unfold. The Alt Commander's actions hinted at a level of organisation and communication that diverged from the brutish stereotype they had come to know.

The sudden cry of a creature pierced the sky, its eerie echo resonating through the city and instilling fear and distress in the hearts of all who heard it. "Wyvern!" one of the guards screamed, his eyes widening as he spotted the winged creature flying toward the Alt forces on the distant horizon. "It's not just one!" another shouted in fear.

As the defenders strained their eyes, the sky in the distance filled with the unmistakable visage of winged nightmares. Lady Katherine, reacting swiftly, directed her spell in their direction, attempting to discern the nature of the approaching threat. However, her actions only fueled more fear among the crowd as they realised that the Alts were not merely boasting wyverns in their numbers—they were riding them.

The sight of Alts mounted on wyverns added a harrowing dimension to the unfolding conflict. The winged creatures, with their sharp talons and fearsome presence, struck terror into the hearts of both defenders and townsfolk alike. The realisation that the Alt forces had not only a formidable ground army but also aerial support elevated the level of anxiety on the city walls.

Jaw, Micharas, and Antonius exchanged troubled glances, the gravity of the situation sinking in. Lady Katherine, maintaining her composure, sought to rally the defenders. "Prepare for an aerial assault! Direct those ballistas skyward captain!" she called out, her voice cutting through the rising panic.

As the defenders on the wall adjusted their ballistae to face the impending aerial threat, the Alts revealed that they still held cards in their hand. From the depths of the woods behind the twenty-thousand-strong and still-growing army, monstrous beasts began to emerge, adding a new layer of complexity to the unfolding siege.

Jaw, with a mix of recognition and concern, pointed out the first creature to his companions. "Armadents," he muttered, his eyes narrowing as he observed the massive armadillo-like creatures lumbering forward. Each Armadent boasted a naturally armoured body, capable of withstanding generic arrows and blade attacks. However, the Alts had taken it a step further, equipping these formidable creatures with additional black metal armour, enhancing their defensive capabilities. These armoured Armadents were not just formidable in their own right; they were being ridden by Alt warriors, turning them into mobile platforms of destruction. Not only defensive in nature however the Armadents also have long natural claws on each of their feet.

Micharas, scanning the growing array of beasts, identified another threat.

"Feral Pouncers," he declared, his tone revealing an escalating touch of concern, it even quivered a moment in terror. The large feline creatures, lacking eyes, possessed a keen sense of smell, hearing, and taste. Their sleek black fur indicated their nocturnal nature, adapted for hunting in the darkness of the night. With a combination of heightened senses and predatory instincts, the Feral Pouncers posed a stealthy and deadly threat.

The guards on the wall observed with growing alarm as the Alt Commander, having drawn his weapon, reached over his shoulder for an arrow. Lady Katherine swiftly refocused her spell on him, sensing that his actions held a sinister significance. A compartment on the Commander's back opened at his touch, revealing hidden ammunition within his armour. With a sadistic calmness, he drew forth a remarkably long arrow with a thick black metal head.

As the Alt Commander readied the arrow in his bow, the defenders on the wall exchanged puzzled glances. "Surely he doesn't think he can hit us at this range?" Antonius questioned, his disbelief evident. The Alt archer was positioned outside the effective range of their ballistae, and the terrain was downhill. It seemed an impossible shot.

Before anyone could respond to Antonius' question, the Alt Commander unleashed his arrow. The projectile struck the wall almost immediately, defying any traditional arc trajectory. There was no graceful arc to its travel; in fact, there was no travel at all. The moment it left the bow, it impacted the wall. And it did not merely bounce off the formidable stone blockade either, it exploded on impact.

The explosion was both sudden and catastrophic. Chunks of rubble scattered across the wall and the city behind it. In an instant, the city's defences had been breached. The section of the wall that bore the brunt of the attack was obliterated, and the guards who had manned that portion were now nothing but bloody, gory remains. The remnants of their bodies, mixed with stones and dust, rained down upon the onlookers below.

The ringing in the ears of the witnesses was deafening as they stood on the wall, mouths agape, wide-eyed in shock at the sheer destructive power displayed by the Alt Commander's arrow. The once secure barrier that protected the city had been shattered, leaving the defenders in a state of disbelief and vulnerability. The Alt forces, seizing the advantage, began their advance with renewed ferocity, exploiting the breach in the city's defences.

"Don't just stand there!" The captain shouted, regaining his composure faster than most. The captain's urgent command jolted the defenders back to reality, and they scrambled to regain their composure. With a swift wave, he signalled for the archers to ready themselves as the Alt forces pressed forward, exploiting the breach in the city's defences. The defenders, though shaken by the sudden loss of a section of the wall, swiftly moved into action.

The archers, their faces determined, notched arrows onto their bows, drawing the strings taut. The air was filled with the resonant hum of bowstrings as the defenders unleashed a volley of arrows towards the approaching Alt forces. The projectiles arced through the air, seeking their targets amidst the sea of enemy soldiers.

Lady Katherine, still positioned on the wall, extended her hands in a sweeping motion. A radiant energy emanated from her fingertips, enveloping the arrows mid-flight. With a focused concentration, she redirected the trajectory of the arrows, aiming to maximise their impact on the advancing enemy ranks.

The defenders on the wall, bolstered by the magical assistance, continued their onslaught. The rhythmic twang of bowstrings and the whistle of arrows filled the air as they sought to thin the approaching forces. The archers aimed for the siege towers, the armoured Armadents, and the Feral Pouncers, targeting key elements of the Alt army in an attempt to disrupt their advance.

Despite their efforts, the sheer number of Alt forces presented a daunting challenge. The enemy, undeterred by the rain of arrows, pressed forward with determination. The Armadents, now closer, shrugged off the arrows with their natural and enhanced armour, their massive claws tearing through the air.

The Feral Pouncers, lacking eyes but guided by their heightened senses, weaved through the barrage of arrows with an uncanny agility. The Alt riders atop them skillfully avoided the projectiles, as they began pressing closer to the city walls.

As the Alt forces closed the distance, the defenders on the wall faced the harsh reality of the situation. The loss of the breached section left them with a vulnerable flank, and the Alt Commander, still a formidable presence in the distance, continued to direct his forces with calculated precision.

The captain of the guard, a stern expression etched on his face, directed his men to cover the breached section of the wall. As they hastily moved into position, weapons drawn and ready for the impending clash, Jaw intervened.

"Wait!" Jaw's voice cut through the chaos, and he approached the captain with a determined look. "Don't station them there. Follow my lead; I've got an idea."

The captain, momentarily taken aback, nodded in reluctant agreement. Jaw quickly moved to the edge of the breach, staring down into the gap in the wall. His eyes gleamed with a spark of inspiration. Without hesitation, he shouted, "Ascent Repartus!"

The words echoed over the din of battle, reaching Lady Katherine's ears. She turned to Jaw with a look of utter confusion, in disbelief of the incantation he had just uttered. The ground beneath them rumbled, and the entire wall shook as if responding to Jaw's command.

To the amazement of the onlooking defenders, the earth itself began to rise, filling the breach in the wall. Large chunks of rock and soil surged upward, forming a makeshift barricade that sealed the gap. The captain and his men, initially puzzled, quickly grasped the brilliance of Jaw's unconventional strategy.

The rising earth solidified, creating a sturdy barrier that effectively closed off the breach. The defenders stared in awe at the transformed landscape, their temporary fortification standing as a demonstration of Jaw's ingenuity in the midst of chaos.

Lady Katherine, still processing the unexpected turn of events, couldn't help but acknowledge Jaw's resourcefulness. "Well, I suppose that's one way to close a breach," she remarked with a mix of amusement and admiration.

The captain, realising the tactical advantage provided by Jaw's impromptu solution, rallied his men to fortify the newly created barrier. The defenders shifted their focus, reinforcing the elevated ground and preparing to repel the Alt forces attempting to breach the wall.

The city echoed with the terrifying screech of wyverns as the winged beasts high in the sky, rapidly closing in on the front line. The guards, alerted to the impending threat, quickly manned the ballistas, aiming at the approaching wyverns. With swift precision, they launched the massive bolts into the air, hoping to intercept the flying menace.

The first wyvern, caught off guard by the unexpected counterattack, succumbed to the powerful impact of the ballista bolt. The bolt struck it directly in the chest and it plummeted to the ground, a trail of dark smoke marking its descent. The guards, momentarily relieved by their success, prepared to take down the remaining wyverns.

However, the surviving winged creatures, now wary of the deadly projectiles, displayed a heightened agility. They skillfully dodged the oncoming bolts, their movements unpredictable and evasive. The guards, realising the difficulty in hitting the agile targets, adjusted their tactics, attempting to predict the wyverns' flight patterns.

The once-confident defenders found themselves facing a new challenge as the wyverns weaved through the air, avoiding the deadly bolts with unnatural grace. The screeching of the winged creatures intensified, adding an additional layer of chaos to the already tumultuous battlefield. The guards, determined to protect their city, continued their relentless efforts to bring down the elusive wyverns, knowing that the airborne threat posed a significant danger to both the defenders on the wall and the city below.

Micharas and Antonius stood side by side on the city wall, bows in hand, their arrows notched and ready. Antonius, his eyes scanning the approaching enemy, spoke to his brother. "Micharas, focus on the ones carrying the ladders. We can't let them get to the walls."

Micharas nodded in agreement, his grip tightening on his bow. "Got it. Ladders are our priority." With that, they unleashed a string of arrows, aiming for the Alt soldiers carrying the ladders with swift and precise shots. As they began to do this so too did the other archers.

As the first arrows found their marks, felling several Alts that rapidly approached the walls, Antonius kept a watchful eye on the ladder carriers. "Incoming on the left," he called out, directing Micharas's attention to a new threat.

Micharas swiftly adjusted his aim, sending arrows toward the ladder carriers approaching from the left flank. "Thanks for the heads up, brother," he acknowledged, his focus unwavering as he continued to pick off the advancing Alts.

The rhythmic sound of bowstrings releasing played like the score of battle along the wall as the brothers worked in tandem, their arrows finding their targets with deadly accuracy. The Alts, undeterred by the rain of arrows, pressed on with determination. Micharas, Antonius and the bulk of the archer forces however, remained steadfast in their defence, communicating seamlessly to keep the ladder-borne threat at bay and the enemy as far from the wall as they could.

The brothers' coordinated defence held back the initial wave of Alts attempting to breach the walls, but the unexpected climb of the enemy onto the walls added a new layer of complexity to the battle. As Micharas and Antonius continued to fend off the immediate threat, a sudden realisation struck them — the enemy had found a gap in the city's defence. Further along the wall they had not been making the same priority decision.

Antonius, still firing arrows with focused determination, called out to Micharas. "We need to hold them off here. The others will need to regroup."

Micharas, nodding in agreement, drew his sabre with a swift motion. The clash of metal against metal resounded as the first Alt warriors made it onto the wall. The brothers fought side by side, their movements fluid and coordinated. Micharas parried a blow aimed at Antonius, his blade flashing in the chaos of battle. With a rapid and decisive reversion of his sword he slashed the throat of the attacker.

Antonius, acknowledging the dire situation, shifted his focus between firing arrows and parrying the incoming Alts with his bow. "We can't let them break through. Hold the line!"

The narrow wall became a battleground, with the brothers defending against the relentless onslaught. The clang of steel, the twang of bowstrings, and the shouts of both defenders and attackers filled the air. Micharas, with a swift and calculated strike, incapacitated an Alt warrior attempting to breach their defence. He kicked it hard in the side of the knee bringing it to the ground and then removed its head with his blade.

Antonius, glancing at the chaos around them, shouted, "We need reinforcements!"

As the Alts pressed forward, more defenders rushed to the aid of the brothers and the struggling guards. The battle on the wall intensified, with the defenders desperately trying to regain control.

With the reinforcements arriving, the tide of the battle on the wall began to shift. Micharas and Antonius seamlessly integrated into the ongoing skirmish, showcasing their combat prowess. Each swift movement was a dance, a choreography of skill and agility.

As they engaged Alt warriors on the contested portion of the wall, Micharas swung his sabre with precision, deflecting an incoming strike, he ducked under the arm of the attacker as Antonius released one of his three drawn arrows catching it in the eye, it punctured deep into the back of the fiends brain and dropped it to the floor.

Antonius then turned and in close range to friend and foes alike he released his two remaining drawn arrows at the same time. Both arrows curled through the air as they felled two more Alts who were engaged in combat with the guards.

Their coordination was a spectacle, a symphony of combat where each movement complemented the other. Micharas and the melee guards would create openings with his sabre, allowing Antonius to exploit them with his precise archery. The defenders around them were inspired by the display of skill, fighting with renewed vigour.

Amidst the clash of steel and the twang of bowstrings, the Alts struggled to contend with the dynamic assault. They pressed forward, inching the invaders back toward the ladders. As they fought, Micharas dropped to one knee as he sliced down the middle of one of the Alts, his sharp blade cutting through its leather armour and flesh alike. As the creature started to melt away Antonius loosed an arrow through its chest striking down a second Alt behind it who staggered backwards into a third and sent it toppling off the side of the wall.

The guards, witnessing the brothers' prowess, rallied around them. Together, they formed an impenetrable front, repelling the invaders with each calculated strike. The severed ladders lay discarded on the ground below, a testament to the defenders' resilience.

As the immediate threat was quelled, Micharas caught his breath and exchanged a nod of gratitude with Antonius. "Good work, brother. It wasn't our line to hold but we held it nonetheless."

Antonius, wiping sweat from his brow, smiled in return. "We should regroup with the others." Micharas nodded at him and the pair left this portion of the wall in the capable hands of the guards.

Meanwhile, Jaw, a sense of urgency in his eyes, grabbed Lady Katherine's arm and led her towards one of the ballistae stationed on the wall. The two approached a group of guards who were struggling to manage the heavy machinery. It took two guards to load a bolt, while another manned the ballista, a task that proved demanding under the pressure of the ongoing battle.

Jaw, with a decisive tone, instructed the guards, "Hold on, lads. We'll take it from here. Do us a favour though and drag over a second ballista." He gestured for the guards to step aside as he addressed Lady Katherine. "I've got an idea, but I'll need your magical touch to make it work."

As the guards hastily brought a second ballista and additional bolts, Jaw turned to Lady Katherine. "Remember that trick you did with the door in the audience chamber? Can you use Lesser Telekinesis to direct these ballistae? We need precision and speed if we're going to make a difference."

Lady Katherine, understanding the gravity of the situation, nodded in agreement. "I can do that. Just tell me where you need them aimed, and I'll take care of the rest."

With the guards providing the necessary equipment, Jaw and Lady Katherine positioned themselves at the ballistae. Lady Katherine focused her energy, her hands poised over the machinery, ready to weave her magic. Jaw, a determined look on his face, surveyed the battlefield.

"Alright," Jaw shouted over the chaos, "we need to target those siege towers first. Take out their means of getting over our walls. Lady Katherine, be ready to adjust aim as needed."

As the guards loaded the bolts into the ballistae, Lady Katherine extended her magical influence, embracing the heavy machinery with the finesse of her telekinetic abilities. The ballistae responded to her command, their aim adjusted with uncanny precision.

Jaw, observing the unfolding coordination, shouted out strategic targets. "Left tower! Higher! No, wait, focus on the archers behind it!" Lady Katherine, attuned to his instructions, guided the ballistae accordingly.

The bolts soared through the air with newfound accuracy, finding their targets with devastating impact. Siege towers crumbled, and groups of archers were scattered, their advance halted by the unexpected barrage. The guards, relieved of the heavy burden of aiming, worked diligently to reload the ballistae under the efficient guidance of Lady Katherine's telekinesis.

Jaw, a sense of satisfaction in his eyes, acknowledged Lady Katherine. "Fantastic work! Now, let's keep this up. We need to give our archers on the wall a fighting chance."

Jaws satisfaction quickly turned to frustration, as he observed the slow and cumbersome reloading process of the ballistae. His eyes shifted upward, locking onto the approaching wyverns with a glint of inspiration. Without hesitation, he turned to Lady Katherine, a determined expression replacing his momentary frustration.

"Switch with me," he instructed, positioning himself between the two ballistae.

Lady Katherine, momentarily puzzled by the request, complied, moving to the side as Jaw took her place. It became apparent that Jaw intended to attempt something beyond the ordinary. His eyes fixated on the ballistae, and with a resolute determination, he extended his hands towards them.

In his first attempt to channel the magic required for Lesser Telekinesis, the weapons seemed reluctant to respond. The heavy ballistae resisted his command, as if the very notion of someone untrained attempting such a feat was preposterous. Lady Katherine watched with a furrowed brow, an innate understanding that such magic demanded years of practice.

Unperturbed by the initial struggle, Jaw shook his body about, as if physically loosening up. A second attempt followed, and this time, something changed. The ballistae responded to his command, albeit with a slight wobble. Jaw, a triumphant grin spreading across his face, directed the ballistae to aim at the approaching wyverns.

Lady Katherine, her confusion now mixed with a hint of disbelief, witnessed the improbable. The ballistae, under Jaw's newfound control, shifted their aim towards the sky. The magical manipulation, typically mastered through years of disciplined practice, seemed to bend to Jaws will.

Jaw, now in command of the enchanted weaponry, shouted over the noise of battle, "Remember the spell you used to enchant Antonius's arrow before," His words hung in the air for only a moment before Lady Katherine, with a resounding nod, already understood his plan. She positioned herself between the bolts, hands raised as she worked her magic to enchant the projectiles.

Jaw, eyes fixed on the vast number of remaining wyverns in the sky, released the shots upwards towards his first target. The enchanted bolts, initially losing momentum, suddenly found a renewed force and launched themselves forward. They tore through the air, devastating the wyvern's attempts to evade, puncturing both its wings and sending it plummeting to the ground.

The guards, witnessing the success of the enchanted bolts, rapidly sprang into action to reload the ballistae. As they reached for the heavy bolts, a surprising revelation unfolded – the projectiles seemed to lift themselves. Lady Katherine, utilising her magic, had taken charge of the reloading process, seamlessly synchronising with Jaw's strategy.

The well-oiled machine of their plan began to play out with precision. Jaw, now freed from the burden of manual reloading, maintained his focus on the remaining wyverns, directing Lady Katherine to enchant the next set of bolts. As the bolts levitated into position, ready to be fired, the guards marvelled at the magical synergy between the pair.

The enchanted ballistae became a formidable force against the aerial threat, the bolts striking true and sending wyverns tumbling from the sky. However, amid the success of the efforts so far, they had all neglected three very important, very deadly foes.

As Micharas and Antonius rejoined the other two, there was a sudden and ominous crash below them. An Armadent, its massive, armoured form akin to a living battering ram, had reached the gate. The air filled with screams along one end of the wall as the Feral Pouncers, with deadly grace, clambered onto the defences. A panicked silence gripped the defenders as the Alt Commander loosed another arrow at the wall, his deadly precision unquestionable.

The defenders, momentarily caught off guard by the multiple threats, quickly regrouped. The guards scrambled to reinforce the gate, preparing to engage the Armadent with a mix of desperation and determination. Micharas and Antonius, drawing their weapons with swift proficiency, prepared to face the Feral Pouncers threatening the wall.

Jaw, having temporarily halted the wyvern threat with the enchanted ballistae, turned his attention to the immediate danger of the commander and his destructive arrows. Lady Katherine, still coordinating with him, shifted her focus to providing support where it was most needed.

As the chaos unfolded on multiple fronts, the defenders braced themselves for the next wave of the Alt assault, each member of the party ready to confront the unique challenges posed by the Armadent, Feral Pouncers, and the relentless Alt Commander. The battle for the city had escalated into a multi-faceted struggle, and then amid the turmoil they shot a glance at the horizon as the realisation set in that the Alt forces had never stopped emerging from the forest beyond.

Micharas, his eyes narrowing with determination, voiced his concern amidst the battle. "We need to fall back and reinforce the front gate. The Armadent and those Feral Pouncers have compromised the wall's defence. We can't stop the Alt Commander, so the wall won't stand a chance anyway."

Antonius, equally aware of the dire situation, nodded in agreement. "He's right. We can't hold the wall against these odds. We need to regroup and defend where the city is most vulnerable."

Jaw, voiced his reluctance to abandon their position, "We can't just retreat. Lady Katherine and I can still hold our ground here. We can buy time. Every moment counts."

Lady Katherine, her eyes scanning the battlefield, spoke with a calm determination. "Jaw is right. We can't let them breach this point. If they do, the city is exposed from within. Micharas, Antonius, go. We'll hold the line as long as we can."

Micharas, torn between the urgency of the front gate and the loyalty to his companions on the wall, hesitated for a moment. The weight of the decision hung heavy in the air.

Antonius placed a hand on his brother's shoulder. "We'll be back. Trust them, and trust in our ability to make a difference at the front gate."

The party, now divided by necessity, prepared to face the distinct challenges that awaited them. Micharas and Antonius, with a final glance back at Jaw and Lady Katherine, sprinted down the stairs towards the front gate where the Armadent threatened to breach the city's defences.

Jaw, turning his attention back to the immediate threat, prepared for the relentless assault alongside Lady Katherine. "I will deal with the Commander. You keep them off me as long as you can." He said to her with a smile as he once again took control of the ballistae. This time, Lady Katherine noted, he did it all too easy as they swung into life at his command.

She turned her attention to the Feral Pouncers, sleek predators with black fur that glistened like the void. Their eyeless faces heightened the eeriness of their approach. As they gracefully advanced, the guards along the wall became easy prey, helpless against foes that relied on senses far keener than sight. The impending danger loomed, a silent and deadly threat that intensified the urgency of their defence. The fate of the city now hinged on the ability to withstand the relentless assault of these nightmarish creatures.

Chapter 14

Micharas and Antonius stood vigilant, weapons at the ready, stationed at the front gate. The mighty Armadent relentlessly crashed against it from the far side, each impact shaking the sturdy structure. Guards in the gatehouse desperately dropped rocks and poured hot oil in an attempt to deter the armoured beast, but their efforts seemed futile against its unyielding assault.

Inside the city, a tense atmosphere washed through the guards as they prepared for the worst. Positioned strategically, spearmen stood with their weapons poised to strike, ready to engage the formidable foe when the gate inevitably gave way.

The Armadent, its natural armour reinforced by the black metal plates affixed to its massive form, continued its onslaught, undeterred by the defensive measures taken by the city's defenders. The clash between the armoured behemoth and the determined guards intensified. With a resounding crash, a claw broke through the gate. In its struggle to release itself from this bind, the creature inadvertently pulled at the portcullis, bending and breaking the metal as it withdrew. Then, with one final charge, it crashed through the gate, decimating the wall around it and the gatehouse above. Dust and debris cascaded down, engulfing them all as the creature exploded through the formidable defence.

The Armadent gave no pause for delay, and as the dust and debris settled, it emerged with terrifying swiftness. Its colossal form, a nightmarish fusion of natural bulk and dark metal, loomed over the stunned guards. The creature's eyes, devoid of mercy, glowed an eerie red in the dim light that filtered through the settling dust.

With a horrifying slashing, the Armadent's massive claws lashed out, swift as the strike of a deadly predator. The screams of the guards, caught in the grip of this monstrous assailant, sliced through the air like a chorus of terror. Antonius and Micharas, could only bear witness to the horror through the agonised cries that echoed through the once defiant defences.

The Armadent's movements were anything but silent, like a war drum to the gruesome symphony of suffering it orchestrated. Each strike, each execution was nothing but a gory, ferocious mess, as it left a trail of destruction and despair. The remaining guards, paralyzed by fear and the ghastly spectacle before them, attempted futilely to defend against the relentless onslaught.

They pushed forward, desperately thrusting their spears into the creature, but the sharp blades found no purchase on its formidable armour. The courageous attempts only intensified the gruesome scene, as the Armadent continued its merciless rampage through the ranks of defenders.

As the dust settled, revealing the horrific aftermath, Micharas and Antonius locked eyes on the rider atop the nightmarish beast, and their stomachs turned. It was unmistakably him—the Mighty Alt Warrior known as Ethor. Despite the party's previous confrontation with him in the streets of Celleos, here he stood once again, atop the Armadent, his open-faced helmet revealing a visage of menace. His towering, muscular figure loomed over the chaos, and strapped to his back was the unique spade-like maul, a weapon that had brought terror before and now promised to do so again.

The revelation of Ethor's return sent a chilling wave of realisation through the defenders. The formidable foe they thought vanquished had emerged once more, leading the charge on the monstrous Armadent. The air filled with a mixture of dread and disbelief as the Alt Commander, presumed dead, now stood as the harbinger of destruction upon the gates of The Eastland Castle.

Questions began to churn in the minds of the two heroes. Was the overwhelming assault a result of facing the same Alts repeatedly? The unsettling thought lingered, threatening to distract them from the immediate danger. Antonius snapped back to reality as Micharas threw himself at his brother, knocking him out of the path of the Armadent's blood-soaked claws.

"Snap out of it!" Micharas shouted, urgency in his voice. "We have a job to do. Let's put this beast down." Micharas rolled away as he landed on his brother, pushing off and springing back into action, sabre drawn and at the ready.

"Right!" Antonius agreed, swiftly rising from the ground. He drew an arrow and knocked it into his bow as he rose, shouting to Micharas above the cacophony of combat, "Do you have a plan?"

Micharas, scanning the monstrous Armadent, quickly formulated a plan. "Focus on the beast first," he yelled back. "Worry about the rider later. Right now, he can't harm us or the people of the city. Let's bring down the creature!"

As the two brothers coordinated their efforts, Micharas elaborated on the plan. "We need to target its vulnerable spots. Aim for the joints where the armour plates meet. The neck and the underbelly are our best bets. I'll draw its attention, and you go for those weak points. Once it's dead, we can deal with the rider."

With a shared nod, the brothers engaged the Armadent, Micharas boldly confronting the creature while Antonius took aim at the suggested weak points.

The battleground rumbled with the Armadent's relentless attacks, its armoured form an imposing force against the city's defenders. Micharas danced around the massive creature, his movements agile and precise. With each strike of his sword, he aimed for the joints between the black metal plates and the natural armour of the beast, drawing its attention away from the vulnerable guards and towards himself.

Antonius, positioned strategically, showcased patience and precision with every arrow he released. He focused on the suggested weak points—aiming for the neck and underbelly. Each shot was a calculated move, a testament to his archery skills. The air was filled with the whistle of arrows and the clash of steel against armoured scales.

The guards, intermingled with the two heroes, fought valiantly against the Armadent. They thrust spears into the gaps between plates, attempting to find purchase against the creature's scales and reinforced body. Some guards risked close-quarter combat with swords and axes, attempting to distract the beast and create openings for Micharas and Antonius. They watched as one unfortunate guard thrust his sword between the armour of the creature's rear leg. The beast then inadvertently turned, following Micharas's movements and toppled the guard who was struggling to free his sword from the bind that it had ended up in.

He found himself on the flat of his back staring up as one of the large feet of the creature came down on his head and chest. The crunch of his skull and the squelch that it made as the Armadent removed its foot was enough to cause the remaining guards that pursued close-quarter combat to move away from the creature, out of fear of meeting the same fate.

The Armadent was a relentless adversary. It swung its colossal claws and tail, creating chaos and scattering guards in its wake. Micharas, with a dancer's grace, weaved through the creature's attacks, delivering swift strikes before evading its retaliations. As he slashed at its throat for the umpteenth time he was forced to release his weapon as he ducked backwards and away from an oncoming claw.

Antonius, having spotted this momentary falter in his brother's form, released an arrow towards the creature's face; the Armadent had no choice but to take the hit. Despite the arrow doing no damage to the mighty beast it caused it to close its eyes for a split second, giving way from Micharas to reclaim his blade from under it.

The battle stretched on, the city's defenders and the two heroes facing an uphill struggle against the monstrous creature. The air filled with the clash of metal, the roars of the siege-beast, and the desperate shouts of guards rallying against the overwhelming force. Micharas continued his antics, keeping the creature's attention on him, while Antonius maintained a steady rhythm of arrow after arrow.

As the fight wore on, the Armadent showed signs of weariness. Its movements became sluggish, and the once-impenetrable scale armour displayed fractures. The guards, encouraged by the sight, intensified their efforts, coordinating with the heroes to exploit the weaknesses exposed by them.

One of the guards embedded his spear into the flank of the creature, amazed to have found a gap in the defences. As he withdrew his weapon the blade glistened crimson in the late afternoon sun. Micharas and Antonius seized the opportunity to deliver the final blows. Micharas, his agile movements now more akin to a predator closing in on its prey, slid under the creature's belly. With a swift and precise strike, he targeted a gap between the armoured plates, sinking his sword deep into the creature's gut.

The Armadent rose up on its hind legs as it let out a roar in pain, its rider tightly gripping the reins to hold onto it. As it did so, Antonius, positioned strategically to the side, fired a final arrow with unwavering accuracy. The projectile found its mark and embedded itself into the creature's throat, the shot clearly punctured its wind pipe as its roar became a gurgle.

The Armadent, brought itself back down to the ground as Micharas pencil rolled out from under it just in the nick of time, unfortunately however, he was not the only one to have been under the creature when it came down. Two guards, spears in hand, had seized their chance to stab the underside of the creature when it rose up. The onlookers could only admire their bravery as the beast smashed its clawed hands down on top of them, killing them both instantly.

Their sacrifice had not been in vain however as despite it leading to their undoing it had also marked the end of the Armadent. Their spears which had failed to find any purchase on its stomach were thrust deep inside its body as it slammed down upon them. Its strength finally depleted, letting out a final, sad, gargled moan before collapsing to the ground in a cascade of dust and debris. Blood pooled beneath it as it twitched, the remaining life-force ebbing from its remains.

As the Armadent fell, the surrounding guards paused in a mixture of exhaustion and relief. Micharas, covered in the creature's ichor, pulled himself to his feet, his expression a blend of triumph and weariness. Antonius, bow still in hand, joined his brother, and the two shared a moment of silent acknowledgment.

Yet, amidst the victory, the attention turned to the rider atop the defeated behemoth. Ethor, the Mighty Alt Warrior, showcased an uncanny grace despite his massive size. As the Armadent's lifeless form crumpled, Ethor seemed to anticipate the motion. With surprising agility, he rolled from the creature's back, landing on his feet with a controlled and graceful movement that defied his immense stature.

The realisation settled in—defeating the Armadent was only the first step. Ethor, untouched by the battle so far, stood ready to continue the assault. Guards, recovering from the intense fight, readied themselves for the next phase of the battle, their focus now squarely on the formidable Alt Commander who drew his weapon, ready to wreak havoc upon The Eastland Castle.

Meanwhile, the arrow, unleashed by the Alt Commander, streaked through the air with near-instant speed. It struck the wall further along the city, detonating upon impact. The resulting explosion blasted a substantial opening in the once-impenetrable barrier. Debris and dust billowed into the air, marking yet another breach that allowed the Alt army to surge forth.

Jaw, witnessing the destructive power of the Alt Commander's arrow, felt a surge of urgency. "We need to act swiftly!" he exclaimed, his eyes narrowing as he observed the unfolding mayhem.

Lady Katherine, her focus decided, nodded in agreement. "I'll divert the Feral Pouncers. Keep your eyes on the Commander. We can't let him cause more havoc."

As Lady Katherine channelled her magical abilities to create a defensive barrier against the approaching Feral Pouncers, Jaw's attention honed in on the Alt Commander. He adjusted his grip on the magical ballistae, controlling it with precise hand gestures through Lesser Telekinesis. Positioned strategically, he aimed the enchanted weaponry at the Alt Commander, determined to disrupt his plans.

Jaw's hands moved with practised precision as he manipulated the ballistae, redirecting its aim towards the Alt Commander. The mystical energy coursing through the projectiles added an element of unpredictability to their trajectory. The Alt Commander, caught off guard by the unexpected shift, dodged the first shot narrowly.

Undeterred, Jaw continued his assault. The next shot from the ballistae soared through the air, a combined effort of magical finesse and mechanical force. The Alt Commander, now aware of this threat, attempted to dodge again, but Jaw noticed something that he had not seen before in his tactics. The Commander placed his hand on the shaft of the bolt as it reached him, not dodging outright but pushing the projectiles away from him as he moved away from it in turn, this way as it struck the ground and transferred all of its kinetic energy into the dirt it was far away from him.

Meanwhile, Lady Katherine's magical barrier held against the relentless onslaught of the Feral Pouncers. Her efforts bought precious moments for the guards to regroup and reinforce the breached section of the wall. However, the barrier could only protect them from the felines attacking directly. Some of the cunning creatures had started to scale the sides of the city wall to bypass the barrier.

Jaw, recognizing the need for a momentary break, relinquished his grasp on the ballistae and used his powers to reload them. As he released the enchanted weapons, the Alt Commander, now well aware of the threat the pair posed, readied an arrow in his bow and took aim at their location. In a frantic hurry to intercept the arrow, Jaw released one of the bolts.

An explosion erupted just off the side of the city wall, catching Lady Katherine off guard. The close proximity of the blast caused her to jump in surprise, and in that moment, her magical barrier faltered. The explosion also drew the attention of one of the remaining wyverns, which swiftly descended upon their location from above. Simultaneously, the Feral Pouncers attacked from the side, and the Commander unleashed another arrow from the battlefield.

In the face of the converging threats, Lady Katherine stamped her foot on the cold stone of the city wall, unleashing a burst of energy. A nova of freezing ice radiated from her, creating a sudden flash freeze that enveloped the immediate vicinity. The Feral Pouncers, caught in the magical frost, found their agile movements were no match for the burst of magic, their feline forms ensnared in ice.

Simultaneously, Jaw, realising the impending danger of the Alt

Commander's arrow, unleashed his remaining bolt with determination. The enchanted projectile streaked through the air, intercepting the Commander's arrow mid-flight. The clash of magical forces erupted in a burst of light and a tumultuous explosion, temporarily blinding those in close proximity.

Amid the flash, Jaw's keen senses detected the ominous approach of the wyvern. The winged beast, its fiery breath poised to unleash destruction, charged towards their position. Having now spotted the imminent threat, Jaw swiftly relinquished control of the enchanted ballistae and propelled himself towards Lady Katherine who's back was turned towards him. The pair, entwined in a desperate embrace, plummeted from the sixteen-metre high walls.

The flames from the wyvern's hellfire licked across the top of the city wall, leaving behind a trail of devastation. In the chaotic descent, Jaw swiftly positioned himself beneath Lady Katherine, attempting to shield her as they rotated through the air. The collision with a rooftop was jarring, sending them bouncing from one structure to another before finally landing on the hard ground in a heap.

As Lady Katherine scrambled to her feet, confusion etched across her features, she noticed Jaw lying unconscious beside her. Panic seized her as she knelt beside him, shaking him frantically in an attempt to rouse him. The sounds of the ongoing battle and the city's desperate cries for help became distant echoes, drowned out by the deafening pulse of her own fear.

Time seemed to elongate, each second stretching into an agonising eternity. The chaos around them faded, replaced by a surreal silence that mirrored the dread building within her. In that moment, the world became a blur, and the possibility of losing Jaw overwhelmed her senses.

She continued to shake him, desperation evident in her actions. Her hands trembled as they clutched his shoulders, and her voice, a quiver of vulnerability, called out his name amidst the tumult. The reality of the city under siege faded into the background, eclipsed by the visceral fear that she had lost him.

Then, as if emerging from a trance, Lady Katherine's surroundings snapped back into focus. Jaw, still unconscious, lay before her. The sounds of battle returned, the screams of the city resuming their relentless cadence. She shook him once more, a desperate plea for him to awaken.

And, as if responding to her call, Jaw's eyes fluttered open. The relief that flooded Lady Katherine was palpable, a mix of gratitude and the lingering shock of the sudden fall. She clung to him, the realisation of his presence grounding her in the midst of chaos.

Lady Katherine, her breath catching in her throat, helped Jaw to his feet amidst the chaos of the fallen city. The abrupt fall had taken its toll on him—his usually steady movements marred by a pronounced stagger. The weight on his injured leg revealed the extent of the damage, a vulnerability she hadn't seen in him before. Blood, an unsettling contrast against his usually composed demeanour, seeped from beneath his hairline.

As she gingerly supported him, guiding him to a more stable position, a deep concern etched across her face. The realisation that Jaw was hurt, and hurt badly, tightened a knot in her stomach. Just moments ago, she had thought she had lost him. The overwhelming relief of seeing him open his eyes after their harrowing fall now blended with the stark reality of his injuries.

Her trembling hands, marked by a mixture of fear and determination, cradled Jaw's face as she assessed the wound on his forehead. The exposed flap of skin was a visceral reminder of the peril they had just faced. With a steadying breath, Lady Katherine placed her hands over the gaping wound and uttered a spell, the soft glow of "Lesser Heal" weaving through her fingertips. The arcane energy worked its subtle magic, and the wound responded, stitching itself together, leaving only a faint trace of its former severity.

Yet, as her fingers traced the contours of his face, the gravity of the situation sank in. The injured leg, a hindrance to his mobility, remained beyond the reach of her magical mending. Lady Katherine's eyes reflected a mixture of frustration and helplessness as she admitted, "I can do nothing for your leg."

Jaw, ever resilient, brushed off the concern with a smile that couldn't quite mask the discomfort. "Don't worry about it," he quipped, "I've had worse." His attempt at humour, though valiant, couldn't fully mask the strain and pain he felt. Yet, even in his weakened state, Jaw remained resolute, unwilling to let the injuries deter him.

The backdrop of the city in turmoil served as a harsh reminder of the ongoing siege. The distant sounds of combat, the distant wails of the distressed city, all faded into the background as Lady Katherine focused on the injured man before her. The emotional rollercoaster of thinking she had lost him and then realising he was still here, battered but alive, created an unmistakable tension in the air.

She held onto Jaw, supporting him not just physically but emotionally, too. Her voice, a gentle murmur in the chaos, broke the silence. "Jaw, I thought..." Her words caught in her throat, the unspoken fear lingering in the air. The weight of the moment hung between them, the unspoken acknowledgment that in the turmoil of war, each moment could be precious and fleeting.

Jaw, meeting her gaze, offered a reassuring nod. "I'm here, Lady Katherine." His words carried a quiet strength, a testament to the resilience that had defined their journey so far. "We should try to find the others." He encouraged, as he hobbled towards a nearby street with her clinging to his side, supporting him along the way.

The once bustling Main High Street now stood as a grim battleground, the remnants of the breached gates serving as a haunting backdrop to the unfolding chaos. Micharas and Antonius, having successfully vanquished the Armadent, turned their attention to the ominous figure approaching them — Ethor, the Mighty Alt Commander.

As Ethor advanced, his open-faced helmet revealed a visage of menace, and the unique spade-like maul in his hand promised devastation. The brothers exchanged a resolute glance, their determination undeterred by the challenges that lay ahead.

The street reverberated with the clashing of weapons and the guttural roars of the Alt forces surging through the gap where the gates once stood. Guards, valiant in their defence of the city, engaged the enemy with a fervour that mirrored the desperation of the situation. However, the relentless tide of Alts threatened to overwhelm the outnumbered defenders.

As Ethor closed the distance, the brothers assumed their battle stances. Micharas, his sabre gleaming with the remnants of Armadent's blood, stepped forward to meet the Alt Commander, while Antonius, bow in hand, prepared to provide ranged support, though he now only had a few arrows remaining. The city guards were gradually thinning in number, leaving the burden of defeating Ethor on the shoulders of the two heroes.

Ethor, the mighty Alt Commander, swung his massive maul with unbridled force, aiming for Micharas. The sabre-wielding warrior, a blur of agility, deftly parried the initial blow, the clash of metal echoing through the air.

Meanwhile, Antonius seamlessly transitioned between targets. His arrows sought out Alt archers and warriors with deadly accuracy, disrupting their attempts to coordinate an intervention with Ethor and Micharas's fight.

Micharas, showcasing his prowess, countered with a rapid series of precision strikes. His sabre danced in the air, each move calculated to exploit the chinks in Ethor's formidable armor.

Ethor, undeterred, simply let the blade slash into his flesh, he then responded with a charging assault. Micharas, like a shadow, evaded with acrobatic finesse, leaving the Alt Commander to collide with the stone-paved ground.

Antonius continued his ranged onslaught, dynamic in his targeting. Arrows whistled through the chaos, finding their marks among the Alt forces attempting to flank his brother.

Seeing an opening, Micharas executed a masterful feint, deceiving Ethor and delivering a precise strike to the Alt Commander's side. Ethor, momentarily off balance, grunted in response as the blade sunk into his side.

Ethor adapted, employing his maul as a shield to absorb Micharas's subsequent strikes. With a powerful shove, he created distance, his eyes fixed on the brothers with a glint of menace.

Antonius, assessing the evolving dynamics, adjusted his aim. The Alt archers attempting to exploit Ethor's shield bash found themselves at the mercy of Antonius's unerring arrows, with a rushed and yet dedicated movement Antonius clung to the shadows of the street and moved around to the spot where the archers now melted into a pool.

He reached into the slime and recovered his arrows, to his joy he found that one of their quivers had clearly been scavenged from a guard and had not melted away. He shouldered the grim trophy and readied himself for the next wave of Alts as they pushed through the breach.

Meanwhile, Ethor unleashed a spinning attack, aiming to catch Micharas off guard. Micharas, ever nimble, executed a backward flip, avoiding the whirling maul with breathtaking precision.

As Ethor attempted to regain control, Micharas and Antonius coordinated their efforts. Micharas engaged Ethor with yet another flurry of strikes, forcing the Alt Commander to defend against the relentless assault.

Antonius, recognizing the need for covering fire, unleashed arrows with renewed intensity. He grabbed a handful of them and with skill unlike he had shown before he knocked all five of them onto a separate string each, drawing them back at the same time and releasing a relentless barrage of projectiles. Each one killed an Alt, stopping them dead in their tracks as they barreled over from the blow.

In a sudden shift of the deadly conflict, Ethor, recognizing an opening in Micharas's defence, following his flurry. He swung his maul in a rising cleave, delivered a powerful strike. The impact reverberated through the air as the sabre-wielding warrior was struck hard in the chest, the force of the blow sending him flying backward.

Micharas, momentarily disoriented by the unexpected hit, struggled to regain his footing. The flow of combat shifted dramatically as Antonius, witnessing his brother's injury, adjusted his focus to provide support.

Sensing the urgency, he quickly assessed the situation. His arrows continued to rain down on the encroaching Alt forces, but his attention was divided between the ongoing assault and the need to support his injured brother.

Micharas, recovering from the powerful blow, steadied himself. Blood trickled from a wound on his chest, a demonstration of the insurmountable force behind Ethor's maul. Yet, with unyielding determination, he raised his sabre, ready to rejoin the fray.

He pushed forwards, leaping from one foot to the other as he darted to his foe. Micharas stabbed at Ethors exposed neck but it was no use, the Alt strategist had already predicted this move and raised the pole of his weapon up, knocking Micharas's blade above his head. He kicked Micharas's legs out from under him and then with his maul already on the rise from the block, he slid his hands to the end of its grip, rotating the weapon in the air high above his head, he prepared to bring the maul crashing down on top of Micharas where he lay.

An arrow struck Ethor hard in the head, it collided so hard that it forced his helmet off him. He turned his furious gaze upwards, halting in his attack as he found Antonius. "You!" He growled.

Antonius smiled at the brute, arrow already drawn and at the ready. "Me." Antonius replied as he released from mere metres away. It struck the Alts head hard as it bore itself through his eye and straight out the back of his skull.

Blood, brain and skull fragments pattered the floor behind Ethor as he dropped his weapon and collapsed to his knees. Micharas rolled out of his way as he crumpled to the ground where he was just laying. "Good work." He said with a blood filled cough, pulling himself to his feet.

Realising that further resistance was futile, Antonius cast a desperate glance at Micharas. Their unspoken communication conveyed the severity of the situation. With a solemn nod, they made a swift, albeit painful decision – retreat.

As the brothers hastily retreated through the war-torn city, destruction unfolded around them like a nightmarish tapestry. Buildings, once standing proud, now crumbled in the wake of the Alt onslaught. The cries of the wounded and the clash of steel filled the air as they navigated through the chaos.

Alt forces surged forward, filling the void left by their fallen leader. Fire engulfed structures, casting an ominous glow on the devastated streets. The once vibrant cityscape now lay in ruins, a stark contrast to the hopeful landscape it had been mere hours ago.

Micharas, wounded but determined, led the way as they weaved through the debris-strewn alleys. The destruction chased them like a relentless spectre, a reminder of the dire consequences of their failed defence.

The Castle, perched atop the hill, loomed as their last bastion of hope. The brothers raced uphill, fatigue and desperation driving them forward. The Alt forces, sensing victory, pursued them with relentless determination.

As they reached the Castle gates, the King's guards recognized the severity of the situation. A commanding figure among them signalled for the gates to open, sparing no time for hesitation.

The massive gates creaked open just in time, allowing the brothers to stumble into the safety of its courtyard. Behind them, the destruction of the city continued to unfold, from their newfound perspective atop the hill, Micharas and Antonius looked out over the city they had fought so desperately to defend. The once lively streets now lay in ruins, smoke billowing into the early evening sky. The distant sounds of battle echoed as a haunting reminder of this relentless siege.

Their breaths heavy, the brothers exchanged a sombre glance. The city, a testament to their resilience and sacrifice, now bore the weight of war. The Castle gates closed with a heavy thud, shutting out the desolation beyond.

As they stood within the safety of the Castle walls, the reality of their situation sank in. The battle was lost, and the city faced a certain fate. The brothers, battered and bruised, braced themselves for the challenges that lay ahead, their gaze shifting from the desolation outside to the fortress they now defended.

As Micharas and Antonius caught their breath within the shelter of the Castle walls, their eyes surveyed the courtyard—a temporary refuge from the chaos outside. The air hung heavy with the scent of burning debris, a reminder of the battle that raged beyond the protective gates.

Amidst the hustle and bustle of guards securing the Castle perimeter, one figure approached the brothers. A seasoned guard, armour adorned with the sigil of the city, stepped forward with a nod of acknowledgment. His eyes, weathered by years of service, held both weariness and resilience.

The guard greeted them with a sombre salute. "You've fought valiantly today, not much more could have been done." He said, his words suggested that the conflict had been witnessed from the walls of the castle.

Micharas, his breath still ragged from the tumultuous retreat, nodded in acknowledgment. "But what of our companions? Jaw and Lady Katherine. Did they make it within the safety of the Castle?"

A flicker of sadness passed through the guard's eyes, and he chose his words carefully. "I'm afraid not, brave warriors. The last we saw of them they were thrown from the city walls by a wyvern."

The news hit Micharas and Antonius with a weight they hadn't expected. Jaw, the resilient warrior, and Lady Katherine, the skilled mage, had been stalwart allies. The reality of their absence left an ache in the hearts of the brothers.

Antonius, breaking the momentary silence, spoke with a trace of urgency. "The citizens, at least. Were they able to find refuge within the keep?"

The guard nodded, a glimmer of relief in his eyes. "Yes, many were able to retreat into the keep. It's packed, but they're safe for now. The city has endured much, but its heart still beats within these walls."

As the guard spoke, Micharas and Antonius took in the reality of their situation. The Castle, now a haven for the remaining defenders and citizens, stood as the last bastion against the encroaching chaos.

"We must gather our strength," Micharas said with a determined look. "The fight is not over. The Castle must hold. What of the gates? Are they secure?"

The guard reassured them, "The gates are reinforced and guarded. The Alt forces won't break through as easily. We'll make our stand here, for the city and its people."

As the guard moved to attend to his duties, the brothers exchanged a knowing glance. The weight of responsibility pressed upon them—the defence of the Castle, the safeguarding of the citizens, and the memory of fallen comrades. In the face of adversity, Micharas and Antonius steeled themselves for the challenges that lay ahead, their resolve unbroken despite the losses suffered on the battlefield.

Chapter 15

Jaw and Lady Katherine moved with the utmost caution through the now crowded streets, reaching the breach that had once been the city's formidable front gate. The once-imposing structure now lay in ruins, it had proven to be little more than a mere inconvenience in the face of the Alts. Their covert journey was abruptly halted as the ominous figure of the Alt witch emerged, her presence shrouded in black robes, wielding a staff crafted from the arm of a demon, its bony fingers clutching an eerie eyeball.

She halted ominously beside the skeletal remains of Ethor, the Alt commander whose mortal trappings had once again given way to his skeletal frame. With an air of dark authority, the witch extended her free hand towards the remains and began to command, "Rise, Ethor. We have work to do." Her cold voice left a chill on the early evening air.

As the bones began to glow with an otherworldly green radiance, Jaw and Lady Katherine exchanged hushed dialogue, keenly aware of the need to remain undetected amidst the vast number of Alts surrounding them, oblivious to their presence. Lady Katherine leaned in, her voice barely audible over the ambient sounds of the city.

"This is far beyond anything I have encountered before. That staff, those incantations—this is like no necromancy I have studied," she whispered to Jaw.

He nodded in agreement, his eyes fixed on the unfolding spectacle. "There's a dark energy at play here, something twisted and ancient. We need to tread carefully."

A vial on the witch's hip began to glow in tandem with the escalating brightness of Ethor's bones. Lady Katherine's eyes widened with concern as she whispered, "It's not a spell! He is a wraith!" Her voice grew louder as the realisation of what she was witnessing struck her.

The tension in the air thickened as the resurrected Ethor materialised before them, a spectral puppet animated by forces beyond the mortal realm. The scene flowed seamlessly, capturing the eerie atmosphere and escalating sense of dread as Jaw and Lady Katherine grappled with the unfolding supernatural events.

Jaw and Lady Katherine observed in stunned silence, as the Alt Commander with the bow stepped through the breach, his imposing figure clad in gapless armour. His voice echoed from within the metallic confines as he joined the pair, a dark and drawn-out tone infusing his words, "What happened this time, Ethor?"

Ethor, now returned to life, responded with a gravelly undertone, "The prisoner again. He is proving to be a persistent thorn in my side." His words carried the weight of the battles fought and the toll exacted on him.

"You are lucky that Zelly owns your soul. Otherwise, this would be thrice that you would have fallen in battle," the Commander retorted, his voice dripping with a mixture of authority and disdain. He nodded approvingly at the Alt witch, acknowledging her role in Ethor's resurrection. "Good work."

A wicked smile crept across the witch's face, sending shivers down Jaw's spine. Her expression could only be likened to that of a murderer staring down at a victim without remorse, without empathy. The smile of someone who is truly unhinged. "Thank you, Kazus," she replied, the words laced with an unsettling satisfaction. It left a feeling of sickness in the pit of his stomach.

"We have a castle to collapse," Ethor interjected, redirecting the focus to their ominous mission. The urgency in his deep gravelly voice added a sense of impending doom to the already charged atmosphere.

Kazus, the Alt Commander, surveyed the surroundings with a calculating gaze. "Indeed, let us not waste time on pleasantries. We have a task at hand." His words resonated with a dark determination as the trio, now reunited, moved with purpose towards the heart of the city.

"We have to stop them." Jaw said as he began to try and hobble after the three commanders.

Lady Katherine's voice, tinged with concern, reached Jaw's ears, "Jaw, in your current state, I'd be surprised if you could take on the regular Alts, let alone their leaders. We can't confront them head-on." She whispered as she pulled at his arm drawing him back.

Jaw nodded solemnly, acknowledging the obvious limitations imposed by his weakened condition. "I know, Lady Katherine, but we can't just stand by and watch the castle be destroyed. We need a plan, a way to hinder them without direct confrontation."

Lady Katherine pondered for a moment, her eyes scanning the surroundings for any potential advantage. "We can't stop the leaders, but perhaps we can disrupt their minions. Create chaos among the ranks to slow them down."

Jaw considered her suggestion, realising the strategic value in targeting the foot soldiers rather than the formidable leaders. "You're right. If we can sow confusion, it might buy us enough time to figure out a more permanent solution. But we have to act quickly."

Lady Katherine nodded in agreement. "Let's find a vantage point, somewhere we can observe their movements and strike at the opportune moment. We need to be strategic about this, Jaw." She said, knowing full well that he was prone to acting first and worrying about the consequences after.

Jaw and Lady Katherine stealthily ascended a dilapidated bell tower that had been attacked by wyverns, its crumbling structure offering a strategic vantage point overlooking the vast expanse where the Alt forces gathered. From this elevated position, they could see the Alt leaders orchestrating their dark plan, surrounded by a legion of obedient minions.

As the setting sun cast an eerie red glow upon the burning, ruined city, Lady Katherine began to weave her incantations. Her hands moved gracefully through the air, drawing upon the energies that surrounded her. Jaw watched with a sense of awe as she summoned the power to cause mass confusion among the Alt forces.

With a whispered invocation, Lady Katherine unleashed the spell "Obey" she said, as a brilliant pulse of purple energy cascading down from the tower, it spread through the streets and Jaw watched as it seeped into the eyes and open mouths of several of the Alts. The enchantment took hold of those that it infected as they turned simultaneously to look up in their direction, "Go forth and cleanse this city of your kind." Lady Katherine commanded, waving her arm out as she spoke. Confused shouts and clashes of weapons echoed through the early night as the once-unified force descended into internal strife.

Jaw, said nothing and simply watched on silently. His feelings towards this sort of magic were already known to Lady Katherine and she took no pleasure in using it in front of him. She turned her attention towards him as he stared out over the city in ruin. "It won't last long, Jaw. We need to get to the castle." She touched his arm expecting him to withdraw it from her, but he didn't, he just nodded in agreement with her statement.

The two of them moved with cautious determination, slipping past the Alts who were preoccupied with the chaos ensuing among their own ranks. Lady Katherine led the way, her steps deliberate and calculated, as she guided Jaw through the shadows.

The damaged leg slowed Jaw down, making each step a calculated effort. Lady Katherine glanced back at him, concern etching her features. "Can you manage, Jaw? We need to reach the castle swiftly."

Jaw gritted his teeth, determined to overcome the pain. "I'll manage. Just keep leading the way."

As they neared the castle, the sounds of battle reverberated around them. The confusion spell had created a temporary reprieve, but time was of the essence. Lady Katherine, with her keen senses, detected a momentary gap in the Alt forces as they made their way through the backstreets up the hill.

Meanwhile in the castle, Micharas and Antonius stood for a moment in the midst of the courtyard, the clash of steel and the shouts of battle echoing through the air, beyond the walls. The confusion spell was clearly causing quite the spectacle outside.

As they paused for a moment, deciding what to do next, a steward, clad in the castle's livery, approached with an air of haste. He bowed respectfully before addressing them, "Sirs, the King requests your immediate presence. He awaits you in the east wing library."

Micharas exchanged a glance with Antonius, and without uttering a word, they followed the steward through the bustling courtyard and into the heart of the castle. The stone walls seemed to absorb the tension in the air, and the flickering torches cast dancing shadows on the tapestries that hung along the walls of the corridors.

They soon arrived at the grand doors of the library. The steward pushed the heavy doors open, revealing a scene of urgency and concern. King Fabian, was standing by a large window, looking out over the scene below, he looked over as they entered, his expression a mix of weariness and defeat.

"Thank you for coming," the King expressed, dismissing the steward with a nod. As the doors closed behind him, King Fabian removed his crown and placed it on the head of a stone bust, a symbol of the weight of responsibility he bore. He ran his hands across his face and turned to them, his voice bereft of its usual commanding tone.

"Be honest with me," he implored, his voice now a defeated and sombre husk, it bore no comparison to his usual commanding dignified self. A man who had been forced to watch as he lost everything. "We have lost this battle, haven't we?" His gaze sought theirs, searching for the truth in their expressions.

Micharas met the King's gaze with a resolute expression, "Your Majesty, as long as there are still people to protect, we have not yet lost. The battle may be fierce, but the war is not over."

The King listened, his eyes searching for reassurance in Micharas's words. However, a heavy silence lingered in the air as the truth of reality weighed on them all.

King Fabian, with a heavy heart, spoke with a mixture of regret and sorrow, "You don't understand, Micharas. This city, this kingdom, it's not just a matter of winning or losing a battle. What has taken six hundred years to build, generations of labour under numerous Kings, has crumbled in a single afternoon under my rule. I've failed, not just as a ruler, but as a protector, as a leader."

His voice carried the burden of responsibility. As he turned away from them, facing the window once more, his words became a lament for a kingdom slipping through his fingers.

"I thought I could uphold the legacy of my forefathers, ensure the safety and prosperity of our people. But now, look at it," he gestured towards the window, the once vibrant city now a canvas of destruction and chaos. The Alt army marched triumphantly through the streets, their presence an ominous spectre of doom.

"Everything we've built, all the sacrifices made by those who came before us, gone in the blink of an eye. The city, our legacy, is in ruins. And it happened under my watch," he continued, his voice laden with remorse. "Now they march toward the heart of our kingdom, and there's near to nothing standing in their way."

The King's words echoed through the library, a mournful dirge for a kingdom on the brink of collapse.

Antonius, though young, spoke with a sincerity that belied his age, "Your Majesty, we may have lost battles, but as long as we stand, we can regroup, strategize, and fight back. It's not over until the last man falls. And once we have retaken the city we can rebuild. "

The King nodded, appreciating the young man's resolve. However, his own self-reflection continued unabated. "Antonius, my boy, you speak with the vigour of youth, and it's admirable. I thought our city was impregnable, a bastion of strength. Pride blinded me to the signs, and now they pay the price for my shortcomings."

His voice trembled with a mix of regret and self-reproach. "I could have done more to prepare, to anticipate this threat. The illusion created from our past victories clouded my judgement. I failed to see the changing tides, the shadows creeping toward our gates. And despite warning!" He said angrily at himself as he turned and gestured towards the adventurers from Celleos, who came to him with first hand accounts of the destructive power of their foe.

As he paced the room, his gaze fell on the busts of his predecessors, each carried the weight of responsibility borne by those who ruled before him. "Six hundred years of history, of triumphs and challenges overcome, and it all crumbles because of my arrogance. I should have been more vigilant, more cautious." All the King could see now was his own failings, all he could do was wallow in his own self pity.

Micharas spoke up. "I have not slapped a King before, but if you don't bring yourself out of this, I will," he said in jest. "Your majesty," he added, as though realising what he had just said could have been taken as an attack on the King, and adding this small token of formality would be enough to save his insolence. The King stopped pacing and looked at him. He looked at them both, and then he began to laugh.

The King's sombre demeanour cracked, and a surprised chuckle escaped his lips at Micharas's unexpected comment. The tension in the room eased as a hint of mirth replaced the heavy atmosphere.

"Well, Micharas, if ever there was a time for a royal slap, I suppose this would be it," the King replied, a wry smile playing on his lips. "Your candour is a welcome respite in these dire moments."

Antonius couldn't help but join in the laughter, the sound a brief reprieve from the weighty matters at hand. The King, now facing them with a newfound lightness, seemed momentarily freed from the burden of his earlier despair.

"I appreciate your honesty, Micharas," the King said, his tone softer. "Perhaps a dose of reality is what I needed. Now, let's not dwell solely on the shadows. What do you propose, my friends?"

Antonius, his youthful determination shining through, spoke up, "Your

Majesty, I think it's time you joined the front line. Your presence among the men might be the inspiration they need to turn the tide!"

Micharas, ever the pragmatic strategist, shook his head. "Your Majesty, the men on the wall have that covered. They'll be driven by their duty. We should head to the keep, secure it. In the event that the royal guards falter, we'll be the final line of defence for the citizens."

The King, considering the options, turned to the window once more. The Alts were now at the gates of the castle, a horde of twisted figures and dark magic. Their siege engines stood as ominous silhouettes against the burning sky.

With a heavy sigh, the King made his decision. "I will go to the wall. Micharas, Antonius, head to the keep. Protect my people." He gripped both of their hands, a mixture of determination and vulnerability in his eyes. "I wish you the best of luck. May the Gods watch over us all."

As the trio separated to face their respective challenges, the fate of the kingdom hung in the balance, with the castle gates now trembling under the assault of the relentless Alt forces.

The King, his decision made, moved with a solemn determination. He reclaimed his crown from the bust, the weight of it on his brow a symbolic burden that spoke of centuries of rule. The steward, a figure of loyalty and duty, assisted him in donning his armour, each piece clicking into place like the low notes in a dirge.

A sword, a relic of battles past, was placed in his hands, the blade shined in the candlelight, its polished surface perfect and without flaw, having never seen a battle. The echoes of history rattled like chains in the castle corridors as the King walked toward the courtyard.

The torches lining the hallway flickered, casting dancing shadows on the stone walls. The air felt heavy with the weight of impending doom. The King's footsteps, usually booming with authority, now seemed to reverberate with a quiet acceptance.

As he descended the spiralling staircase, the beauty of the castle contrasted sharply with the sombre reality it now faced. The intricate tapestries depicted tales of triumphs and victories, but today they hung like silent witnesses to an imminent tragedy.

The courtyard awaited him, a serene expanse that had witnessed ceremonies, celebrations, and now stood as a threshold to a battle that could redefine the kingdom's fate. The moon hung in the early night sky, its silver glow lending an ethereal quality to the scene.

The King's gaze swept over the courtyard, the banners hanging limply, the stone statues standing sentinel in the stillness of the night. He knew he walked towards almost certain death, yet there was a serene tranquillity in his demeanour. The burden of leadership, the weight of the crown, and the inevitability of sacrifice converged in this quiet moment.

He stepped into the courtyard, the heavy gates looming ahead, with fires burning beyond them, setting the night sky ablaze. The sound of the Alts' relentless assault echoed through the stone walls. With each step, the King embraced the inevitability of his fleeting life, a monarch marching toward destiny with the weight of a kingdom on his shoulders.

Meanwhile down below, in the concealed darkness near the castle wall, Jaw and Lady Katherine took a moment to assess their situation. The towering structure loomed before them, its stone facade a daunting barrier. As they emerged from one of the back alleyways they could see the entrance to the castle up ahead.

Though far from a sight of refuge, the gates were already swarming with Alts. Archers fired down upon them from the gatehouse but regardless of how many they killed it did not seem to thin the unending tide of attackers. One thing was certain, the pair were not about to get in that way.

Lady Katherine, her eyes glinting with determination, turned to Jaw. "We need a way in, and quickly. The longer we stay out here, the more chances we have of being discovered," she said, her voice hushed to avoid drawing attention.

Jaw scanned the wall, his gaze narrowing in thought. "I can't climb in my current state, and even if I could, we need a quieter way in. The chaos outside won't cover the noise of us scaling the wall."

Lady Katherine nodded in agreement. "We must find an entrance, perhaps a door left unguarded?" It seemed like a long shot but she felt it was worth suggesting nevertheless

As they circled around the castle in a desperate attempt to gain entry they observed the Alt Commander, now identified as Kazus, as he moved skillfully around the back of the castle. His armour, though formidable, seemed to contain yet more secrets. With a tap on his thigh plate, a concealed hatch opened, revealing an orb made of crystal with a swirling purple ink-like substance inside.

As Kazus squeezed the orb, he vanished from sight, leaving only the lingering of the dripping sound that Jaw had come to associate with invisibility magic. Lady Katherine, seemingly unable to hear this sound, tried to get Jaw's attention, pointed out, "It's an invisibility device. The fluid inside sustains the spell, but it will dissolve over time. We need to be cautious, he could be anywhere."

Jaw, however, was focused on tracking the faint echoes of the dripping sound. He was able to follow the invisible commander's ascent of the castle wall. Lady Katherine sighed, realising that her words had fallen on deaf ears. She watched Jaw with a sense of curiosity and irritation as he seemingly just started staring at the castle wall.

Jaw listened carefully as the sound dissipated over the wall and out of range, he then abruptly shifted the conversation. "So, how do we get up there?" He asked calmly. His words shattered any hope Lady Katherine harboured that he had been attentive to the previous topic.

Staring at him in disbelief, Lady Katherine tried to mask her frustration. Jaw, oblivious to her emotional state, attempted to get the discussion moving as he assumed that she was stumped for ideas. "How about the spell that raises the ground upwards?" he suggested.

"That would be too loud, and I'm not sure I could raise a pillar high enough for us to get onto the wall," Lady Katherine dismissed the idea.

Undeterred, Jaw pressed on, drawing from their shared experiences. "What about that teleport spell you used in the audience chamber to swap me and the King's location?"

With a sigh, Lady Katherine clarified, "The spell is called 'Substitute.'" Jaw's hopeful expression waned as it became evident that this idea wouldn't suffice, based on her tone of voice and the name of the spell.

"Maybe some kind of bubble that we can ride on?" Jaw grasped at straws. Lady Katherine, shaking her head, conveyed the impracticality of the suggestion. Another sigh, this time escaping from Jaw's lips as the reality of their predicament settled in.

Lady Katherine's eyes sparked with an idea. "I do know one spell," she declared, her voice holding a hint of excitement. "But I haven't actually used it properly before, and we would need to misuse it to make it work. It also gives me a chance to test a theory."

Jaw, relieved that she was taking the lead, responded eagerly, "Well, I am willing to try it if you are." His eyes reflected gratitude, glad to follow someone else's lead for a change.

"I was hoping you would say that," Lady Katherine admitted with a daunting grin, causing a sinking feeling in Jaw's chest. It seemed he had agreed to something more adventurous than his own plans.

"The spell is called "Blink,"" she began to explain, "named so because it can move you in the blink of an eye, but only to another location that you can see. It's a very powerful spell and requires years upon years of studying Animus magic to master it." Lady Katherine tried to simplify her explanation for Jaw, who nodded in understanding. "So, how does it work?" he inquired.

Shaking her head with a playful smile, she remarked, "It really is a complex spell, and I neither have the time nor the wax pencils to explain it to you right now." She glanced at him, hoping he'd catch her cheeky joke. Jaw, however, nodded seriously, taking her words to heart. "So obviously, the flaw here is that we cannot see the top of the wall from here," she continued. "So instead, we are going to go straight up into the air and then down onto the top of the wall." As she laid out her plan, Jaw's face paled.

"Not sure I like the idea of falling from wall height a second time today," he joked, a touch of uncertainty in his laughter.

"It will be fine," she reassured him, a comforting smile on her face. "Just close your eyes."

Jaw took a deep breath, trying to calm the nerves that fluttered in his stomach. Choosing not to close his eyes as instructed, he tightened his grip on Lady Katherine, mentally preparing for the unexpected journey they were about to embark on.

Lady Katherine, her focus unwavering, began to recall how to cast the spell. A soft hum resonated, and Jaw could feel a subtle shift in the air. She locked her eyes on a single particle of the pure magical essence that coursed through their world otherwise known as Animus. Doing so required a huge amount of her brain power and concentration to accomplish, as a particle of Animus is no bigger than a particle of any other element.

Suddenly, a sensation akin to weightlessness enveloped them. Jaw's stomach churned momentarily as they seemed to be falling all of a sudden.

After what felt like a mere heartbeat, the disorienting sensation ceased. Lady Katherine whispered, "See, easy." Jaw let go of her and stumbled to the side, his feet tapping against hard stone as she grabbed a hold of him again to stop him falling. She put his arm around him to help him keep upright and chuckled sweetly. "This is nice, you should hurt your leg more often. I can't remember the last time I received this many cuddles."

Jaw blushed as he looked around, a feeling of disorientation, on top of that the blood had all rushed to his head, increasing the pressure in his ears. To his surprise, they were now perched on top of the castle wall, the night breeze brushing against their faces. The distant sounds of battle echoed from below, a constant reminder of the chaos that unfolded beyond the fortress.

Jaw couldn't help but marvel at Lady Katherine's mastery of the spell. "That was... something else," he admitted, still processing the abrupt change in their surroundings.

Lady Katherine grinned, a glint of triumph in her eyes. "Now, let's find a way to help inside," she urged, scanning the castle's interior for signs of their next move.

As they navigated the unfamiliar territory, the fate of the kingdom rested on the choices they were about to make within the looming castle walls.

Chapter 16

Micharas and Antonius descended the stone staircase, the air thick with tension and the metallic scent of blood. Their footsteps rattled loudly with each step they took as though the very air itself understood the urgency in their task. As they reached the bottom, they approached two royal guards stationed at the entrance to the keep. The guards, wearied and silent, leaned against the stone walls, their eyes fixed on the unseen turmoil beyond the castle gates.

"The King sent us to reinforce the defences," Micharas stated, seeking acknowledgement from the guards. However, there was no response, only an eerie silence that hung in the air like a shroud.

Antonius, growing uneasy, noticed blood dripping from one of the guard's gauntlets, slowly tracing its path down the handle of his halberd. The young warrior's eyes widened with concern as he shared a quick, worried glance with Micharas.

"We'll do what we can to help," Antonius declared, though his words felt like echoes in the stillness of the corridor. The guards remained stoic, their silence revealing more than any words could convey.

Micharas, with a sense of urgency, patted one of the guards on the shoulder, attempting to draw his attention. However, the guard slumped sideways, unresponsive and lifeless. The unsettling sight triggered something in their minds and like a struck match to gas, they acted.

Micharas and Antonius surged into the keep, surprised to find the heavy doors unlocked, as they burst through them. Micharas unsheathed his sabre, ready for combat, while Antonius swiftly knocked an arrow to his bowstring.

The scene that greeted them within the keep was one of horror and despair. Lifeless bodies lay scattered across the cold stone floor, the grim fate that had befallen the citizens of the once-great capital. Micharas, taking in the gruesome tableau, pointed his sword toward the lone survivor in the centre of the room.

His initial words caught in his throat as shock and fear gripped him momentarily. The survivor, however, began to rise from the dead, and Micharas could do nothing but stare.

Kazus stood before them, a figure both fearsome and otherworldly. His armour, a melding of dark metal and ethereal shadows, clung to his form like a second skin, now that they could see him up close it was evident that there were no signs of gaps in the protective layer. His helmet concealed all of his face, there was no visor slit, no eye-holes of any kind in fact, and no opening to allow air inside. His bow hung from his back; it was not attached to him via a sling, but seemed to be clipped onto the spine of his back somehow. Kazus's presence exuded an air of malevolence and power that sent shivers down Micharas's spine.

The Alt Commander slowly raised his hand, revealing a small pink stone nestled in his palm. With deliberate movements, he brought the stone towards his helmet. A strange metallic resonance filled the air as his cold voice echoed within the confines of the armoured shell.

"It is not here; I shall return to the group momentarily." The Commander lowered his hand and turned toward Micharas and Antonius. As his gaze fell upon them, as he spoke again, his voice devoid of human warmth.

"Hmm, the prisoner that keeps causing issues for Ethor," the helmet turned as if his attention shifted from Antonius to Micharas. "And a brave fool with the sword of Rufus." The duo readied themselves for the imminent confrontation, fully aware that they were facing their most formidable opponent yet.

"Stand aside," the Commander instructed, his tone devoid of empathy or emotion. "This is not your tomb." His words carried a chilling certainty, a stark warning that engaging him now would lead to their demise. The message held no arrogance or pride; instead, it conveyed an absolute truth. If they chose to fight, this would indeed become their final resting place.

Antonius unleashed his arrow, a swift projectile aimed at the Alt Commander who had orchestrated the massacre within the keep. The arrow sliced through the air with deadly precision, hurtling towards Kazus, the architect of the unfolding battle. Despite the proximity between them, Kazus exhibited an uncanny level of agility, gracefully evading the oncoming projectile with a subtle lean to the side.

"Very well," the metallic voice resonated, acknowledging the unspoken challenge. The duo observed as Kazus shifted his stance, lowering himself to the ground, his hands gliding to his lower back. A distinctive metallic click echoed as he drew two wakizashi from their concealed sheaths. The elven-like blades gleamed in the dim candlelight, reflecting the grisly aftermath of the surrounding carnage. Each weapon whispered tales of countless atrocities, a grim instrument, a silent witness to the blood they had spilt.

Antonius swiftly knocked another arrow, determined to keep the pressure on Kazus. He released the string, and the arrow sailed through the air with lethal intent. However, Kazus intercepted the projectile with a swift slash of his wakizashi. The arrow shattered into splinters, its trajectory disrupted by the Alt Commander's precise blade.

Seizing the opportunity, Micharas charged forward, sabre in hand, seeking to engage Kazus in direct combat. However, the Alt Commander, also pushed forwards and with deft movements, seemingly positioned himself in Micharas's shadow, using the seasoned warrior as a shield against Antonius's ranged attacks.

As Micharas swung his sabre at Kazus, the Alt Commander effortlessly parried the blow, the clash of steel ringing through the air as he directed Micharas's sword upwards. Kazus dropped to one knee and with an instinctive slash cut into Micharas's right thigh. Antonius, recognizing the challenge, attempted to find an angle for a clear shot. Yet, Kazus remained elusive, skillfully manoeuvring to keep Micharas between them. It seemed like a game to the Alt, with Kazus maintaining a strategic advantage that seemed insurmountable.

The Alt Commander's metallic voice settled with a chilling calmness, "You cannot escape your fate. Stand down, and perhaps your end will be swift." But the brothers, fueled by determination and defiance, pressed on, even as the odds stacked against them.

Micharas, grimacing in pain, rolled to one side, creating a momentary opening for Antonius to loose an arrow. The projectile, however, merely glanced off the Alt Commander's helmet, leaving him unfazed. The relentless pursuit continued, and without needing a command, Antonius prepared another arrow.

As Kazus closed in on Micharas, the seasoned warrior regained his footing, but the Alt Commander was relentless. With a swift slash, Kazus targeted the back of Micharas's knees, sending him back to the ground. Antonius seized the opportunity to fire another arrow, but it met the same fate as the previous ones, deflecting harmlessly off Kazus's impenetrable helmet.

Now turning his attention to Antonius, the Alt Commander closed the distance rapidly. Antonius, realising the imminent danger, swiftly fired another arrow, but Kazus skillfully deflected it once more with the edge of his weapon as he moved. As the Alt Commander reached Antonius, he executed a precise slash at the young archer's throat. In a desperate move for survival, Antonius used his bow as a makeshift barrier, but Kazus's blade sliced through all five strings with cold efficiency.

They twanged loudly in the lifeless room, "The battle is over," Kazus declared in his metallic monotone. "Submit." The Alt Commander's words hung in the air, a reminder of the overwhelming force they faced.

With no other recourse, Antonius, fueled by defiance, unleashed a sudden punch at the space where Kazus's face should be. The blow echoed inside his armour, but the Alt Commander remained unfazed. "Very well," Kazus responded, almost amused by the futile attempt to harm him.

In an unexpected turn, the Alt Commander handed one of his weapons to the young archer. The move was perplexing, a departure from the expected brutality. The blade gleamed ominously as it changed hands, leaving the brothers to contemplate the unspoken implications of this unanticipated gesture.

"If you truly wish to die a warrior, who am I to stand in your way," Kazus remarked, his attempt at humour lost in the emotionless cadence of his voice. Antonius accepted the offered wakizashi, feeling the weight of the alien weapon in his hands. Unlike his brother Micharas, he had never trained with a sword, making the blade an unfamiliar companion.

With a determined resolve, Antonius readied himself, holding the wakizashi by the hilt in both hands. Kazus waited for the young archer to make the first move and Antonius had no intention of keeping him waiting. He lunged forward, attempting to thrust the blade into the unseen gap between the Alt Commander's helmet and chestplate.

However, his weapon would never discover such a weakness. As Kazus effortlessly deflected Antonius's attack and countered with a swift diagonal sweep of his own blade across the boys chest. The movement was calculated, fluid, and ultimately devastating. Antonius, brought to his knees by the merciless strike, stared up at the Alt Commander, the wakizashi clattering to the floor at his side.

The tense atmosphere in the room was abruptly interrupted by a voice that pierced the silence, echoing through the chamber. Micharas, unable to move, could only watch as his brother knelt at the feet of the Alt Commander, the blade poised for a final strike. The voice, unmistakably that of the witch Zelly, carried an air of urgency.

"Kazus, we need your assistance in the throne room. We may have found it," Zelly's words reached the Alt Commander, causing him to pause in his impending action. The gravity of the situation seemed to shift, as if the very fate of their dark mission hung in the balance of the information Zelly held.

Kazus, reclaimed and sheathed both of his blades, and turned away from Antonius, leaving the young archer alive but defeated on the cold stone floor. As he turned his voice echoed forth once more with the same unforgiving, inhuman metal resonance. "Until next time, prisoner." They watched as the Commander moved with purpose, his metallic footsteps reverberating through the room as he exited and climbed the stone stairs beyond, leaving Micharas and Antonius in the aftermath of their seemingly insurmountable encounter with the Alt forces.

While this was going on however, at the top of the castle walls, Jaw and Lady Katherine observed the unfolding chaos below. The King, flanked by his loyal guards, was swiftly guided away from the besieged gates, recognizing the imminent threat. The royal guards took decisive action, moving the King to a more secure location within the castle.

The Alt forces, under the command of Ethor and the ominous Alt witch Zelly, gathered at the gates with a palpable sense of purpose. The clang of armour and the murmur of dark incantations filled the air, creating an ominous symphony of impending doom.

"We should follow them," Lady Katherine suggested, her voice filled with urgency. "You are in no state to fight, and I have a feeling that the gate is about to..." Her words were abruptly cut off as the gates disintegrated, melting away under the influence of the witch's powerful spell. The once imposing gates were reduced to nothing more than a black residual slime, sizzling from an unseen heat.

"You don't say," Jaw commented dryly, his eyes fixed on the Alt forces storming through the breach into the unprepared courtyard.

"Come on," Lady Katherine instructed, gesturing toward a door atop the wall that led inside the castle itself. The urgency in her voice matched the dire situation unfolding around them. The pair hurriedly made their way through the door, seeking refuge within the castle's walls as the chaos of battle raged on below.

Jaw and Lady Katherine hurried through the castle's corridors, their footsteps echoing against the cold stone walls. The flickering light of the burning city on the horizon cast an eerie glow through the windows, creating dancing shadows that seemed to mock the chaos outside.

As they navigated the dimly lit hallways, the distant sounds of battle in the courtyard reached their ears. Clashes of metal and guttural roars reverberated through the castle. The once-grand tapestries that adorned the corridors now hung like forgotten lore, bearing witness to the crumbling of a once-mighty kingdom.

The journey to the throne room was fraught with tension. Lady Katherine led the way, her senses keenly attuned to the surroundings. Jaw, with his damaged leg, moved with a noticeable limp, yet determination fueled his every step.

The corridor eventually opened up into a grand hallway decorated with portraits of past rulers, their eyes seemingly judging the current state of affairs. The flickering light from the burning city outside played upon the ornate rugs underfoot, creating an illusion of movement that added to the surreal atmosphere.

As they neared the audience chamber, the sounds of the ongoing battle grew louder. The clash of weapons and the cries of both Alts and castle defenders echoed through the stone halls, underscoring the urgency of their mission. Lady Katherine pressed on, her hand tightly gripping Jaws, as they scanned the halls for any signs of danger.

Finally, they arrived at the massive doors leading to the chamber itself. The once imposing entrance now seemed to quiver under the weight of the calamity. With a shared glance, Jaw and Lady Katherine steeled themselves for what lay beyond and attempted to open the newly fitted doors. Yet unsurprisingly the doors would not budge.

The pair pounded on the imposing doors, their urgent pleas for entry muffled by the cacophony of battle outside. After what felt like an eternity, the sounds of clanking chains and the shifting of heavy wooden beams reached their ears. The doors creaked open slowly, revealing a group of royal guards hastily unbarring the entrance.

As the doors swung open, Jaw and Lady Katherine hurried inside, greeted by the flickering chandelier light of the audience chamber. The air inside carried a tense mixture of relief and apprehension. The King, surrounded by his remaining royal guards, stood near the throne, his eyes widened with a mixture of surprise and joy at the unexpected arrival.

"Jaw! Lady Katherine! By the gods, it's good to see you alive!" King Fabian exclaimed, his voice carrying both relief and gratitude. The royal guards, though wearied by the ongoing battle, maintained a vigilant stance, ready to defend their sovereign at a moment's notice.

The guards behind them hurried to reseal the room, though for what good it would do, Jaw thought to himself having just witnessed the gates to the castle melt before them.

Lady Katherine, though composed, couldn't hide the concern etched on her face. "Your Majesty, we came as soon as we saw the breach. The Alts are inside the castle. They will be upon us at any moment."

King Fabian's expression shifted from joy to grim acceptance of this fate. "We must prepare for their onslaught. Gather what you can, fortify the chamber. We shall make our stand here."

The King's orders had barely left his mouth, as the remaining guards sprang into action. They rearranged furniture, stacked barrels, and formed makeshift barricades to slow down the advance of the Alt forces. Torches flickered on the walls, casting dancing shadows that seemed to mimic the turmoil outside.

As the preparations continued, Jaw took a moment to survey the room. The once regal audience chamber now bore the scars of the kingdom's desperate struggle. The royal tapestries hung askew, and the polished marble floor was scuffed and stained with the residue of hastily made decisions.

Lady Katherine's sharp eyes assessed the room, and with a frown, she turned to the King. "Your Majesty, we need a plan. Is there any other way into or out of this room?"

King Fabian, weariness etched on his face, considered the question. "No, this castle was designed with defence in mind, but not against a threat from within. There are no secret passages or hidden exits. We must hold this ground."

As the King spoke, a sudden iridescent glow enveloped one of the walls. The air seemed to shimmer, and from within the radiant light, figures emerged. Zelly, the Alt witch, and Ethor, her loyal commander, permeated through the magical barrier as if passing through a veil.

"Your majesty," Zelly's voice echoed with a cold satisfaction, "Your fortress is no longer impenetrable. The walls that once protected you now serve as your coffin."

King Fabian, a mix of anger and despair in his eyes, raised his sword. "You will not triumph here, witch! My people will not bow to the likes of you!"

As King Fabian raised his sword in defiance, Zelly's smirk deepened. "You have no people to speak of," she retorted, her voice carrying a chilling truth that hung heavy in the air, a truth the King refused to acknowledge.

In an instant, the royal guards, loyal defenders of the realm, rushed forward to protect their sovereign. However, Zelly's hand was swift, they watched as dark magic enveloped the room like a suffocating shroud. The guards gasped for breath as an unseen force constricted around their throats, rendering them powerless. Their struggles were futile as their life-force was drained away, leaving only lifeless husks in their wake, their bodies collapsed to the ground.

Ethor, the Alt commander, moved with brutal efficiency. His spade-like maul cleaved through any guard who managed to get even remotely close. He struck one guard so hard with his weapon that his blow split the helmet of the suffocating guard, crushing him to the ground with a resounding crunch, blood-soaked shards of metal from his desolated helmet scattered the floor.

"Ethor, deal with them." Zelly instructed coldly.

Jaw took a pained step forward, resting his weight on his injured leg. With one arm extended to the side, he signalled his protective stance over the King and Lady Katherine. Despite the throbbing pain in his leg, he held his ground, determination etched on his face.

Lady Katherine, ever attuned to the ebb and flow of magic, felt a dark energy emanating from Zelly as she retrieved a small pink stone from her pouch. The absence of a finger on Zelly's hand, a reminder of a past encounter with Antonius, did not go unnoticed by Jaw.

Ethor, the towering Alt commander, hefted his spade-like maul, ready to fulfil Zelly's command. The atmosphere in the room grew heavier, the air charged with anticipation as the inevitable clash loomed.

Jaw, sword in hand, awaited the giant's approach, as he watched the witch behind him seemingly speaking into the stone.

The giant charged forwards towards them and in an instant, no, in the blink of an eye Jaw was at him. Ethor's massive form, meant to strike fear into the hearts of his enemies, now found itself ensnared by Jaw's relentless assault. Grasping at his throat, the giant collapsed. His blood spilling from the open wound created by Jaws' unseen strike, the fallen beast's blood dripping from his sword.

As Jaw reached down to the floor, his hand closed around a small metal shard. Holding the pink stone retrieved from her pouch close to her face, Jaw listened as the witch crowed into it, "Kazus, we need your assistance in the throne room. We may have found it." A sinister smile crept across Zelly's face as she returned the stone to its pouch.

Behind Jaw, the remains of Ethor once again melted to nothing more than bones. Zelly raised her hand toward the corpse and began to talk to it "Ethor..." She began. Seizing the opportunity, Jaw discarded the shard of metal toward Zelly. The sharp projectile twisted through the air with unexpected grace as it curled toward its target.

Time seemed to slow around them as they all watched the shock in Zelly's eyes. Instead of reaching for the fallen Alt's remains, she shifted her hand to protect the vial on her hip. The metal shard whizzed towards it, finding the gap where a finger should have been. The fragile container shattered into pieces, and its contents spilled across the cold stone floor.

A malevolent aura filled the room as the remnants of the vial spread, forming an iridescent pool. Zelly's eyes widened in disbelief, and a sense of dread crept over her face. The loss of whatever essence the vial had contained, now gone. She glared at him in fits of rage as the fluid beneath her feet marked her shoes and nothing more.

Jaw, seizing the momentary advantage, stood defiantly, his sword at the ready. The King and Lady Katherine, witnessing the turn of events, exchanged glances that spoke of both hope and uncertainty.

"Enough of this!" She howled. "Just give us the girl!" Zelly's desperate cry echoed in the chamber, a plea laced with frustration and urgency. The room seemed to hold its breath as she demanded the girl's surrender.

Jaw, caught in the tumult of conflicting emotions, turned to Katherine with a look of confusion and betrayal. His guard dropped for just a moment, and in that vulnerable instant, Zelly seized the opportunity. With a wave of her staff, she unleashed a potent spell, a surge of darkness, like black lightning, that struck Jaw with a force, he staggered backwards, no longer caring about the pain in his leg. Katherine screamed, though her voice did nothing for him.

Jaw looked down at his chest. There was a hole where everything should have been, the tattered remains of his chestplate hung from him like a broken shield. The last few moments of life rushed through his veins as his life-force left his body. There was no walking this injury off, he thought to himself. Katherine rushed to his side, tears streaming silently from her face. She screamed something but the words fell only on Jaws deaf ears as she thrust her hand at the witch. A spell emitted from her and sent the smiling hag slamming backwards against the wall.

She looked down at Jaw, his blood pooling around them, as his head lay in her lap. Staring up at her, his eyes transfixed on her form. She sobbed soundless tears as reality took a hold of her heart, he was gone, and there was nothing she could do to change that.

Amidst the magical turmoil, the banging on the door intensified. Someone outside the chamber was desperately trying to breach the barriers, a relentless determination audible even through the chaos within the room. King Fabian readied himself for the attack, as the door finally gave in.

Micharas and Antonius burst into the hall, their eyes wide as they took in the scene that had unfolded before them. The brothers swiftly assessed the situation, taking in the sight of the fallen Jaw and the looming threat of Zelly.

Micharas, despite his injured legs, pushed himself forward with sheer determination. Antonius readied an arrow against the bow borrowed from his brother, his focus fixed on Zelly. The room crackled with tension as the witch raised her staff.

Just as Zelly began to weave her dark magic, aiming for Jaw and Katherine, King Fabian, in a selfless act of protection, stepped into the line of fire. The spell intended for the duo now collided with the King, its malevolent energy coursing through him.

The King, already weary from the ongoing battle, staggered from the spell, his last thought was confirmation that he had at least earned redemption in this conflict. "Even if it was just a shred," he reassured himself as he collapsed to the ground.

Antonius's arrow stuck true as Zelly's head recoiled backwards, it stared lifelessly up at the ceiling above them as her body began to rot away into the disgusting black tar like substance, leaving only her scarred naked skeletal remains in its place.

A sudden silence that enveloped the courtyard and the distant city streets was a stark contrast to the cacophony of battle that had raged just moments before. The absence of the Alt forces left an eerie stillness in its wake, and Micharas, with a mixture of confusion and sorrow, looked out into the aftermath.

The once bustling city now lay in ruins, a sombre reminder of the destructive power that had swept through its streets. The remnants of the Alt army, which had posed an imminent threat, were nowhere to be seen. The absence of their presence, though a relief, cast a shadow over the victory, as the cost had been steep.

In the throne room, Lady Katherine continued to cradle Jaw's lifeless body, her tears now mirrored by the shimmering light from the chandeliers above. The King's body lay testament to the fate of the entire city.

The profound emptiness that settled in the room mirrored the void left by the fallen, and as the survivors grappled with the aftermath, the kingdom stood at a crossroads, forever changed by the events that unfolded within its walls.

Under the moonlit sky, Lady Katherine, Micharas, and Antonius emerged from the castle, the silvery glow casting a poignant atmosphere upon the aftermath of the recent battles. The air hung heavy with a stillness that echoed the hollowness left by their losses, each step weighed down by the burden of grief.

The trio made their way to the outskirts of the castle, a covered cart rolled on before them, pushed by Antonius. They made their way into the woods, which stood as solemn witnesses to the city's tragic downfall. The scent of earth and pine enveloped them as they entered the shadowy embrace of the trees.

In a moonlit clearing within the woods, they prepared a final resting place for the fallen. The soft whispers of leaves underfoot seemed to offer a melancholic symphony as they carefully dug graves with borrowed tools. Antonius, accustomed to the precision of his arrows, now used those same hands to delve into the damp soil, a stark reminder of life's fragile nature.

First into the earth went King Fabian, his regal presence reduced to a lifeless form. Lady Katherine, tears glistening in her eyes, murmured words of gratitude and sorrow, acknowledging the void left in a kingdom without its monarch.

Beside him lay the queen, her life claimed, like so many others, within the keep by the hand of the Alt Commander Kazus. The body of their eldest brother, Andarius, could not rest in the same way; the ruins of his forge surrounded by the remains of the Alt forces suggested a valiant fight until his last breath. A true Ranger to the end.

Jaw followed, his imposing frame now stilled in eternal repose. Micharas, his shallow wounds tended to by Lady Katherine's magic, stood solemnly over the grave. As the loyal friend and companion, he bid his silent goodbyes in the embrace of the quiet woods. The air seemed to hold its breath, and even the moon cast a softer light upon the scene, paying homage to the fallen.

The clearing, bathed in moonlight, became a sacred resting place for those who had bravely faced the chaos. A profound silence enveloped the trio as they stood together, their grief shared beneath the celestial glow, honouring the memory of those who had fought and died.

Finally Micharas broke the silence as he began to speak.

"The balance between good and evil has always remained fairly even. Without one side, the other would have full and total power over all that was, all that is and all that is yet to be. Perhaps this is why it happened, no-one can say for sure."

"All that we can be certain of is the side which we stand on and the sacrifices that we must face along the way. Homes, once filled with laughter and warmth, now lie in ashes. Our loved ones, the echoes of their voices still linger in the air, have been ripped from our embrace. We stand amidst the ruins, the remnants of our shattered lives scattered at our feet. But you know what they say about a man who fights with nothing left to lose. We will just take a moment's silence now to remember those who gave their lives today, so that we can stand and fight tomorrow."

Micharas's voice, though heavy with sorrow, carried a steely resolve as he continued, "As we stand on this precipice of despair, let us remember that it is precisely in these moments that the strength of our character is tested. The path ahead is obscured, and the weight of our grief threatens to pull us into the abyss. But, my friends, we are not defined by the darkness that surrounds us; we are defined by how we rise from it."

"Every sacrifice made, every life taken, was not in vain. Their memory becomes a beacon, guiding us through the shadows, and while we still do not know what motivates the campaigns of our enemies, we will continue to fight them at every turn. The legacy of those that we lose will be etched not only in the annals of history but in the very fabric of our beings."

"Our fight does not end with their passing; it is a torch passed from hand to hand, illuminating the path for the next generation. We carry their hopes, dreams, and aspirations in our hearts as we march forward into an uncertain future. The embers of our determination must not be extinguished by the winds of despair."

"And so we stand, shoulder to shoulder, united by our shared grief and unwavering resolve, let us take this moment of silence to honour those who have given everything. Let their spirits infuse us with the strength to face the challenges that lie ahead. For in the hallowed silence, we find the echoes of their courage, a reminder that even in the darkest hour, we can emerge into the light."

"May their memories be a guiding star in the night sky, leading us towards a dawn where justice triumphs, and the sacrifices of today pave the way for a brighter tomorrow." The words lingered in the quiet night, a solemn tribute to the fallen. After a few minutes of reflective silence, Antonius turned to the others.

"So what now?" His voice carried the weariness of a soul burdened by loss, the weight of that hung around the shoulders of four now resting on just three.

"What's the next place on the list?" Katherine and Micharas asked in unison, their voices echoing a shared determination to carry on the fight and see this quest through to the bitter end.